THE CHOSEN

Also by David Ireland

Novels

The Chantic Bird
The Unknown Industrial Prisoner
The Flesheaters
Burn
The Glass Canoe
A Woman of the Future
City of Women
Archimedes and the Seagle
Bloodfather

Plays

The Virgin of Treadmill Street
Image in the Clay

THE CHOSEN

DAVID IRELAND

BY THE TRIPLE MILES FRANKLIN AWARD-WINNER

VINTAGE

A Vintage Book
published by
Random House Australia Pty Ltd
20 Alfred Street, Milsons Point, NSW 2061
http://www.randomhouse.com.au

Sydney New York Toronto
London Auckland Johannesburg
and agencies throughout the world

First published by Random House Australia in 1997
This edition published in 1998

National Library of Australia
Cataloguing-in-Publication Data:

Ireland, David, 1927– .
The chosen.

ISBN 0 09183 722 7.
I. Title.
A823.3

Cover design by Gayna Murphy
Typeset in ITC Caslon 224 by J&M Typesetting
Printed by Griffin Press Pty Ltd, Netley, South Australia
10 9 8 7 6 5 4 3 2 1

To my parents

Acknowledgements

John Carroll, of La Trobe, for his work on dispositional guilt.

Margaret Connolly, my agent.

Helen Daniel, critic, for reading an earlier draft of the manuscript, and for her directness in telling me it wouldn't do. Her much-needed rocket gave me the momentum to cut it and make something better of what remained.

Alison E. Gosbell for information on medical student dissections in the summer holidays at Sydney.

Jamie Grant, my editor, for suggestions, corrections, understanding.

C. J. Hayhoe for thoughts on the desirability of Prime Ministers hiring court jesters to advise when boots and hats grow too small; for anecdotes; and observations such as the contemporary lack of initiation rites for young males and the absence of widely accepted examples of manliness.

Luisa Laino for the text design.

Meredith Rose, publisher's commissioning editor, for her enthusiasm at the galley stage.

Hannah Rother, of the Victorian Tapestry Workshop.

Julie Rovis for the cover design.

E. M. Sommer for phrases such as 'people are incompatible'; and 'some things are slightly possible'.

Contents

1	*Monday, September 1*	1
2	*Tuesday, September 2*	5
3	*Amaza Aprahamian*	13
4	*Chokeback Jones*	27
5	*Adora Weller*	41
6	*Howie Gleet*	54
7	*The Baby Face Gang*	66
8	*Basildon Bond*	77
9	*Dando Rocavera*	88
10	*Doctor Kidd & Miss Dodwell*	99
11	*Shoey Mortomore*	110
12	*Lord Henry Ball*	118
13	*Lumpy Van Tran*	131
14	*The Old Couple*	143
15	*Boobiak's Waterfall*	152
16	*Pursey & Etrog*	160
17	*Leanne Fusby*	166
18	*Nurse Pain*	174
19	*Doctor Clitterhouse*	179
20	*Angel Zuccalo*	190
21	*Carmen Mummo*	198
22	*Macaterick Black*	207
23	*Merle Bird*	218
24	*Knudsen Boult*	227
25	*Leon Undermilk*	237
26	*Alastair Pryde*	247
27	*Helen Welland-Smith*	255
28	*Sonya Ergot*	265

29	*Fatstuff*	273
30	*Juniper Grey*	281
31	*Chainsaw*	291
32	*Zorella*	299
33	*Duke Jensen*	310
34	*Big Betty Vroecop*	322
35	*Bubba Ylisaka*	330
36	*Pat Hooligan*	340
37	*Twitch Mitchell*	346
38	*Miles Blandish of Lilly Pilly*	357
39	*Saint Salivarius*	365
40	*Borrowdale Blow*	377
41	*Crasher Coy*	383
42	*Daniel Dogstone*	391
43	*Peewee Prewitt*	402
44	*Edwold & Day*	410
45	*Hollywood Hossan*	421
46	*King Khan*	430
47	*Treesha Khalal*	439
48	*Wayne Door*	451
49	*Zuzz*	457
50	*Old Clampett*	464
51	*Edward Cuttlebone*	474
52	*Uncle Carbuncle*	480
53	*Gungible Gumes*	489
54	*Cornelia Dogwood*	501
55	*The Blaze*	510
56	*Wednesday, September 3*	518

one

Monday, September 1

'Therefore her exile from so much of herself had to end. She was determined it would. There was a kind of home towards which she was turning, a home of the spirit ...'

My book was nearly done. I had the next sentences in my head. I had paused to reflect that all who have once interacted are connected, however tenuously, while memory lasts, and that perhaps when memory hides, events, bloodstreams, and interactions carry their own remembrances.

We had been connected, my main character and I. She sometimes seemed to have no idea how unusual she was. She felt she was quite ordinary, used to the self she felt she inhabited—or did it inhabit her? Nevertheless, simply by being herself she was of an elite. Tastes, education, the choices she made, the ideas that attracted her, the theories guiding her. These things separated her life ineluctably from the lives of most of those around her. Not that she was above or they below, she was simply grouped separately. She was off to one side, or they were. What she was had separated her out, had chosen for her.

At that moment, someone tired in my chest and obviously unsuitable for the job was carrying a last armful of heavy books up laborious steps. Near the top, straining and dizzy, he dropped the lot with a clattering chaos of impacts and collisions. It was more than a warning. I began to key in the final sentence of my book: '... a home of the spirit where she would free herself of life and live outside the cage of blood, where she would extend the field of her experience to poetry stripped of words, music without sound, feelings minus flesh, and begin the inward thinking that comes before thought.'

The book was done.

I saved the work, printed the final pages, shut down the computer and sat back to bathe myself in the afterglow, which is my name for everything the words leave unsaid.

Never mind the blow. It would come. If not now, then later. I had reached an age where it had less reality. After all, death was said to release us from all bonds, wasn't it?

When the pain gripped into me, then shook me like a fist collapsing an empty beer can, it took my breath away. Its intention was unmistakable, but I had finished the work that had engaged me for so long and laughed with desperate relief. With what breath I had I shouted at the pain, 'It's finished! I win!'

I'd expected that special clamping spasm for years. On the first day of spring it had come.

I saw Yarrow's face turned sideways as I remembered her before she left, her thick hair cutting me off, hiding her eyes. She worked at her keyboard, her hands like quick birds playing the keys with movements that to me were visual melodies. The things those hands controlled. Yet she was difficult to hold, like water. She wore her impatient black. I never interrupted at such moments, imagining her silences full of happenings, though when she spoke I tasted the words as they came from between her lips. I loved her strength, her ambition, her staying power, her velocity. Her energy in action was beautiful, her vitality and quick brain intoxicated me. Perhaps everything about me was a reason we could never be together, but I had been trying to find myself in her, a new self, hoping it would be better than the one I knew.

I had won indeed. Having a lifelong horror of leaving work unfinished and at the mercy of others' incomprehension, the almost diabolic happiness of completing that final page and leaving no loose ends was like winning a race.

You have to get to the end before you understand the beginning, my father Jackson Blood used to say. I understand neither beginning nor end. My life seems to have consisted of not understanding much at all. I accept, go along with, reconsider, then sometimes back off and start again. But then, I'm not as good a man as he was. I seem to remember him saying the same thing about his father, Jameson Blood.

In the end I managed without too much fuss. The pain held me, but gradually hurt less until it seemed to be holding me together, supporting me. It became a shining steel track carrying me forward. I couldn't get off it, but at least I was moving.

Then it was no pain at all and I was able to think clearly and breathe more easily. I got up from my chair and left the desk. The episode was behind me. I didn't want to make too big a mouthful of it.

Standing, in a sense, outside myself, looking on, my head felt a lightness peculiar at first, then a wonderful airiness and exhilaration buoyed me, like sudden flight among coloured winds. Since Yarrow left I had enjoyed nothing unreservedly, but I enjoyed this. The rest of my body—was it reaction?—felt such strength and vigour I wanted to leap in the air and shout in a voice to encircle the planet.

I was restless. After constant application to one task it was time for a change of direction.

I looked into the part of me which contained a lifetime's interwoven desires, experiences and delayed decisions, and picked over a jumble of unacted desires and odd souvenirs. One was a postcard of the Reception Hall tapestry in Parliament House. Another was a baby's white sock, one of a pair my mother Lillian kept when my twin brother Jonathan was born dead. All those years ago. Any sadness should long since have been washed out of the white cotton. A third was a sentence, physicist Richard Feynman's: 'If you could pass on only one sentence to the future, let it be this: all things are made of atoms, little particles moving around in perpetual motion, attracting each other when they're a little distance apart, but repelling upon being squeezed into one another.'

A fourth memento was an irregular prism of transparent perspex I'd kept on my desk for decades. When I first held it horizontally and looked into it, a piece of theatre concerning certain flesheaters was being performed, a spectacle that renewed itself in a different form, with a new title and fresh cast each time I picked it up. I thought of it as a special window on the roomy world I carried with me, populated by a lifetime's throng of happenings and people of whose origins I often had no immediate memory.

I looked into it and saw myself. I was uncaged, and with a bird's freedom.

I danced a few steps for happiness at this beginning of a new phase of my life, and made a spring as energetic as any I'd made before, even when I competed in the school sports, or used a pole to vault over a friend's high fence in Bellbird Corner, and felt the thrill of being high in the air for a time, and looking down. And when I landed, the feeling of being a visitor.

two

Tuesday, September 2

That feeling returned when I stepped out of my white pickup onto the shaly ground on the flattened top of steep Wiradhuri Hill and looked south on the little town of Lost River, a town poured into a bowl-shaped valley, one of many among the tree-covered ridges and hills of the Southern Tablelands.

I looked around in all directions. I saw, surrounding the soft little town, a stern land, silent, masculine, unforgiving, over which farmers sweated to feminise it and force it to produce. An intermittent breeze on the hill was busy sorting fallen leaves and whispering to itself as it worked.

My appointment with the town council was half an hour distant. The white of day seemed a rather washed-out kind of light, the day infirm, the sun an inflammation of the sky, though a number of arm-in-arm clouds were happily walking on air.

The stone walls of the retired Church of the Good Shepherd, which I had rented, reflected the warm rust colours of local hilltop shales and red foxes.

One moment I was on steep Wiradhuri, the next my white pickup translated me to a meeting of suits in Lost River Council Chambers. No one is typical, but I was the odd one out, as always. We stood in an arc before the altar of their dove-grey computer, while a speaker, in tones of weird jokiness, uttered words, or bottletops.

An affirmative finger materialised in front of us, jabbed the print key, the printer began its controlled stutter and put out a wide white tongue coated with about fifty names. One suit-sleeve extruded a wrist, with hand, which took the paper and handed it to me.

It was headed 'Lost River Tapestry Project, Davis Blood, Weaver'.

Then followed the names of those whose lives, as told by them, were to figure in the tapestry, along with addresses in Lost River and round about. All had accepted this local honour, their letters of acceptance on file.

Suits containing council members, lawyers for the council and for benefactor Miles Blandish, extended congratulatory hands of all genders and clasped each other's bare skin in primitive ritual gestures of unaccountable and—to me—annoying solemnity.

Blandish had decided to give the town a tapestry to decorate the walls of the chamber in the new civic centre. He'd donated Rugby Park and other real estate, and was the largest landowner in Kippilaw County, with eight thousand hectares of prime grazing land south of the town and into the southern ranges. His gift would support a weaver for a year. It was my understanding they'd used a randomising program—for impartiality—to extract the names of a percentage of the ratepayers from their records. By politically sensitive chance Blandish's name was on the list.

My stomach felt hollow, as if I hadn't eaten for a week. They expected words. I think of speech as resembling mathematical formulae applied to physical processes: what can't be measured or described is left out. I gave them some words, trimmed before being uttered, folded the paper, shoved it under my sweater. With my general shagginess and combative look I must have seemed as out of place as a drunk in church.

The suits closed ranks, separating into what could have been chance groupings, and began to speak together with a kind of exhausted cordiality about a proposed new jail and a high-temperature incinerator for the town. An agenda of civic progress. There would be a vote taken the following August, and plans, or a campaign even, to deal with the inevitable protests.

I cleared out. I was to weave the listed names into a tapestry and have it done in a year. A sample of the lives of Lost River's present-day people, a kind of what-it-was-to-be-them, to go into the history of the town for as long as the wool and linen yarn, and the town, held together.

Outside, in Budawang Street, there was traffic noise, there was the sight of citizens with heads craning towards windows, legs scissoring in walking mode, fingers diving for shelter in handbags, eyes sparrowing this way and that, feet ducking flatly in splayed patterns on the bitumen footpaths, and all populating the floor of an ocean of spongelike air holding up soft woollen clouds by the tonne.

I had a new job of work, a new life, another new home. I would be absorbed, each day full. I tasted a momentary contentment.

My white pickup, in exploratory mode, took me through the town's suburbs—Dalgety Park, Elderslee, Nerrigunyah, The Hill, then lifted me smoothly to the top of Wiradhuri Hill to my reconditioned church. Its innards had been removed, and partitions had chopped it into habitable rooms, leaving a wide workroom open to the rafters. One attempt at domesticating God had been abandoned. Awe and solemnity had gone from Wiradhuri Hill. Though perhaps the breath from past hymns still clung to the roof timbers.

Since I left Bellbird Corner, life, to me, had been a wandering without a home in either place or people. It was years before I realised I was hopeless at living close to others. I don't understand it, but there's some way in which I don't treat people properly. I'm that kind of outcast. Perhaps the problem was parallel to one of my mental pictures, in which the world was fiddlesticks, the game in which a bunch of coloured rods is held upright, then allowed to fall in a tangle. Life consisted in picking up the rods separately without disturbing the others. I wasn't good at it, I disturbed too many others.

And yet. To have someone to put an arm around. Or reach out and touch a hand. Yarrow? But I couldn't expect that.

Inside the front door the smell of fire. I ran around but there was nothing burning. A baby's little white cotton sock lay on the floor. I hung it on a picture hook and began to organise the kitchen and something to eat until I realised that the empty feeling in my stomach was a churning of excitement. But why? With me, a meeting with stomach-churnings was as rare as meeting relatives who really liked you. I put it out of my head.

My loom stood undressed in the work space. That smell of burning. A premonition? A memory? Was there a way things had to be? The smell, I decided, was a stray memory that had fizzed, crackled, sparked, or bubbled into view. No more significance than muted seastorms in a seashell. I got busy dressing the loom.

When the job was done, the shadows had gathered and stuck together, the sky darkened and colour drained from the world. Outside in the cool September air the night was moonless, the darkness blacker than I was used to. On the tablelands the stars' cold fire and unblinking brightness were clear and vivid down to the horizon.

Under the brilliant slash of the Milky Way—a myriad bright dots on a cosmic graph—the black countryside below Wiradhuri Hill was an ocean of night. Two or three distant farm lights suggested ships making for diverse destinations. On the south side of the hill, down in Lost River, electric blue and orange lights laughed at night. Above the town, high into the sky, a glow as if Lost River was on fire.

With one speck of light darkness was defeated. The situation was not symmetrical: in sunlight there were no specks of darkness. Well, not that I'd seen.

My loom was dressed with warps stretched vertically from knee level to high above my head. The warps were firm and right, the design for the border had been transferred from the cartoon I drew to the warp strings, along with 'db', my weaver's mark; the colours decided, yarn chosen, bobbins wound.

Tomorrow I would consider my first subject, a woman who had died some months earlier but whose name was still on the ratepayers' roll. In common with most small towns Lost River had no complete list of residents and didn't bother with a town electoral roll, as some did. Rentpayers were out of it, regarded as being transients or not committed to the town.

Have you ever felt life was a digression? And that death would open your cell door and give you the chance to travel? Well, I felt as light-headed as that. I lay down to rest my eyes, perhaps to sleep, thinking of petrol caps and how it would be to have a passenger lift down the centre of Wiradhuri Hill to its base. Would it be hot down there?

I woke in deep blackness with a dream bright in my head. Unusually, its details were sharp, and stayed. My salvage crew had hauled up a conquistador's statue from ten fathoms off an island near Shark Bay, and while they celebrated I began the work of chipping away barnacles and encrustations from the gleaming metal until the face of Freud stared, sightless and uncomprehending, back at me. Sharp pains in my stomach forced me to stop work. I pressed my middle impatiently, resenting the interruption, and wasn't surprised when, after a brief choking, I brought up a large child. I resumed work. The child examined me carefully. I looked at him and noticed my own features spread like a mask on his face. Two of me?

'Well?' I demanded, with some irritation.

He shook his head, ran off, and with his hands held out sideways fingertipped a long aisle of white pickets one after the other so that the noise made was continuous, though intermittent. Each picket became a representation of me—or perhaps him—at different ages and sizes, and stretched into the distance. He disappeared into a large rounded boulder.

I turned over and looked for sleep again, and more dreams, vaguely troubled by memories of Yarrow giving me looks like direct love letters. Memories? That had to be a mistake.

A moment, and it was morning, the hill bombarded by photons.

I woke to magpies' conversations. By the time I'd had breakfast, the bird noise was deafening, mostly noisy miners and harsh-voiced honeyeaters, but with crimson rosellas not far behind, and three magpies doing aerial battle with a gang of choughs over territory. Bees were in the grevilleas; quiet, hovering native bees and noisy-winged bumble bees. Hours later they would be slow bees, heavy transports, legs thickly socked with pollen.

The air tasted white. Below me in the distance the town looked like a theory. I couldn't be sure if the buildings were solid or drawn on the air, flimsy enough to be erased, or knocked over by some great whacking reality.

You know how it is when you wake feeling happy? Maybe the night's latest and most easily forgotten dreams have set your day-starting mood just right. Whatever it was, I felt something really good had passed into me, getting into every corner, illuminating every vein, so the glow started deep, near the bone. Days like this prompt me to tuck more of life inside me, partly as a kind of buffer against those other days when I feel I'm too much with myself and the world recedes, bits break off and blow away.

The smell of burning was gone. I felt at home on my hill, comfortable as a politician sitting on a large majority.

I worked in broad swathes of light, doors open, but wished for more doors. The light wasn't as bright as it ought to be.

Someone had stolen the big brass doorknob from the church's front door. I replaced it with a brushed steel affair, all I could get in the town. If you can imagine a tungsten breast, that's how it looked. Unpainted, but that's not unusual with such things.

Behind me, outside in the sun, the black cat was ensconced in the green canvas chair by the white-enamelled iron table at which I will eat breakfast in fine weather. The red dog had dug a shallow depression in the grass just off the moss-edged flagstones and was curled in that, ready for anything except effort.

I've noticed that at any waking moment not occupied in eating, live creatures look round considering, working out what they can and can't do—and get away with—and what they might do if they had the energy and thought the effort worthwhile, for all the world as if they're aware that, providing they can cope with the consequences, they're free to do whatever they like.

Just like that stout magpie in the black and white regalia, hunting in the grass within a metre of the watchdog's back.

Such broad freedom might seem like hot air at first, or

reserved for the very daring, like those who soon will thrust themselves out into space in the search for new and compatible planets outside our neighbourhood, but at the level of everyday life, living by this kind of freedom, each day, each minute, is a choice, as individuals make decisions about what they do with the amount of freedom they're capable of.

I do it too. I begin work. But why do I do what I do? And how does everything else decide what to do?

The Lost River tapestry would be a focus of pride for the town, a magnet for tourists, a restatement of the importance of local government, a triumph envied by cities and towns throughout Australia, an historical asset increasing in value every year. It would feature real people, not an empty forest of silent trees as does the specimen in Canburrow, as I call the place, in that monument to the forever tame and tentative spirit and compulsive ordinariness of Middle Australia: a disturbed rabbit burrow half in and half out of the ground. A seat of government which can be walked over. Or is it a disguised bunker?

three

amaza aprahamian

Aphra 'Amaza' Aprahamian was my first tapestry subject. Her niece, named Aphra in her honour, who had written the acceptance letter, appeared from Sydney for the interview. The early September day was still. Afternoon seemed to begin before noon and went on like a long calm out-breath. I didn't quite finish the border I'd begun.

I was still burdened by a fragment of my latest remembered dream, which left me feeling withered as an old sheep, body mostly water, useful only for the skin. Or fertiliser.

My mouth was dry. I was conscious of the effort I made to swidgel my tongue left and right over my lips to moisten them. The niece, a medical student, watched me. Probably judging where to make the first post-mortem incision, or wondering whether my brain would display all the arcane convolutions of a pile of spaghetti.

So poised she seemed, so calmly confident of the superiority of youth. I was conscious of the contrast she made with the monster sitting opposite her in the Aprahamian house on Kioloa Avenue, whose features the years had chewed and spat out. I wondered if she had secret tastes to widen the eyes and slacken the jaw. Aphra would fill in the picture of her dead aunt, with details I and the town's webs of gossip couldn't know.

Confidence, for many public performers, comes when a delicate golden contempt is achieved and the audience, out there, is gently despised. Red-cheeked Amaza intuited this at an early age, helped by the ready-made audience inside her head to whom she spoke and sang, for whom she performed for years before she faced a public beyond her control. Like the rest of us she early felt that compulsion to come out well, or within the range experience had taught her to be comfortable with, in that constant activity of humans—and perhaps of many other organisms—which is the making of comparisons between themselves and everyone they meet, see, hear of or imagine, in order to answer the eternal question: how do I compare?

She discovered she had something of her very own, great manual dexterity and a marvellous ability to deceive. In addition, she was quite short, and felt added assertiveness was necessary to survive in the forests of the tall. On that foundation she built her distinctive personality and created her own environment. It didn't occur to her to be like other girls and not stand out from the crowd, nor to want what they wanted.

Around Lost River the environment she created was an affirmation of Aphra. No wet patch of concrete was safe from her 'AA', scratched into footpaths, engraved deeply in dish drains, new kerbs and gutters, anywhere temporarily plastic. Often she was accompanied by the family pet, a mixed dog with long, meaty, fallen ears, a resigned expression and sufficient saliva for all the dogs in the street. He was baptised Sirhan, but known as Slobberguts.

Aphra intuited also that among six billion others, egalitarianism was a sick joke, and the drive for equality en masse a drive for the equal subordination of the powerless. She wanted to be famous, for being Aphra, and was convinced she would be. Ambition, greed, desire to win, superiority: she had all the virtues.

'You can't hide a cough or a talent. You'll see,' she learned from Grandma Aprahamian, who kept remembering aloud the killing times in the old country, and lamenting her long-dead husband who always bought her more jewellery when what she wanted was more love. His was exhausted.

Magic was to be Aphra's life. She christened herself Amaza; it turned out to be a roadworthy image. She fended off other kids who wanted to know what she was practising, saying, 'Champions don't need company.' She wanted to say modesty belongs with the devious, but didn't. They were as jealous of her as Cleopatra's sisters were of their future queen.

Her own audience was all she needed, it gave her criticism unsoftened by the attempted friendship of girls who might bribe her with easy praise just to get a morsel of information to retail. She freed herself from them, just cut off and kept apart like a tower.

In that tower, so tall above the town, she traversed horizons no one else knew. She saw and graciously accepted fame and sweet success and the tower got taller every year until Lost River was a long way beneath her.

The house in Kioloa Avenue, apricot brick with white trim, just across Monash Road from the red-brick convent, had its share of 'AA' engravings and also a growing library on conjuring, sleight of hand, illusions, magic acts.

Lost River High, along oak-treed Parkes Street a few blocks away, benefited from her growing expertise at concert time. She developed her own costume by year ten and performed at the RSL, the Workers', the bowling club and at parties. Since she was bright, her teachers and parents thought she ought to go on and become a postulant for legal or medical orders, but magic claimed her. It was the disappointment of her mother's life that her daughter didn't go to university. It would have made no difference if you were one of those who claimed that the possession and exercise of talent was violence against the untalented.

She developed her own patter, which grew into a format of telling stories while she got her act under way; it began when she played clubs in neighbouring towns where the audience wasn't so much wood as chilled steel. Her first story was the old one of the woman and the snake, with the apple as a present; she worked it in with comments on the town. She had tricks to make the audience wait, so that they called for the magic impatiently. Abrakazam! There it was, under the scarlet cape. Applause. The stories themselves, however, were another thing.

Amaza hated Lost River. In her little tales she held up to gentle laughter quite recognisable people, mentioning habits, peculiarities, odd ways that distinguished them and gave them the indefinable thing called personality.

The pride people felt in their differences, when those differences were held up in public, turned over and examined, collided head-on with the mirth they provoked. Like the story of the clatter of a certain retailer's false teeth in the porcelain hard on the heels of her stomach's distress call of 'Barf!'

Amaza was dying to get out of Lost River. It didn't matter to her if she abused and slandered it. Perhaps, like many who hate their home towns, she would have hated whatever place she was familiar with.

Gradually, as she developed her talent, she began to dump on the town indiscriminately. Failings, mistakes, adulteries, sheep stealing, cattle duffing, the mice plagues, the dog and rat wars of an earlier century. All got a serve. Gossip, busybodies, Australians too dry to dream. Her subject matter helped blast her out of Lost River on to a bigger, state-wide stage, and once at a distance she really attacked. Well, she knew Lost River.

The Mitchells, the family with the most businesses in town, were an easy target. And old Emma Mitchell, the matriarch with so much clout, figured in many little vignettes of influence, political trickery, corruption, nosiness.

'Country people have such good eyes, they always know where you are and what you've been up to,' Amaza said, among her unsociable truths.

In the early days one of the Hooligan family had helped hang a Jensen, the one who fought on the scaffold when he got his hands untied until they sedated him with a rifle-butt.

One of Lumpy Van Tran's relatives had been a lay preacher until he turned bushranger in 1865.

One of the Door family had been the notorious Admiral Moonlight. Most of his robberies fell apart, from poor timing or incompetence. He was christened Admiral because he was completely at sea in his chosen profession. His hanging, however, proceeded without a hitch.

Saint Salivarius, also a tapestry figure, had an early relative, a Gleet, who rode with the Jensen gang of bushrangers and was hanged with him. They were the last men executed in the regional jail in a town not far distant.

Cancer-eye cattle, crook sheep, scabby mouth, dirty wool—the sins of the locals were broadcast by an ambitious young woman who referred to her place of origin as 'a village in a valley' that its lazy young were reluctant to leave. She was as confronting as a policeman with his breathalyser held out. And always an extra serve for sharp-eyed, sharp-tongued Emma Mitchell. What did Amaza care that her targets were impaled by her hostile words, which stuck in their flesh, and hurt, and wouldn't come out? What did she understand of the idea that the roles of oppressed and oppressor, attacker and defender, were reversible in daily life?

When the flicker of television arrived in the mid-fifties she was happy as an oyster at full moon. For big tricks like the two girls sawing each other in half and the dribbles of blood from the cut boxes, she had longer stories. She used the same characters, the string of bit-players she developed in Lost River, with only the names changed. She was too busy to marry; a husband would have been an impediment. Close up she showed a bright-eyed and red-cheeked interest in people which resembled affection, but no one was dear to her.

One of her funny ideas was that death is a coloured ball rolling over and over but not on a surface, rolling in empty space. She used it in her disappearing acts.

She had a follower on the Lost River *Bugle* who professed in letters and wan postcards to love her insanely, but she destroyed all such communications except a photograph captioned 'A newsman of yours forever'. It displayed a face you might see on a whimsical limb-fitter or reclusive night-shelter designer. She never referred to the journalist responsible.

When she was over fifty, her brother Benjamin's daughter Aphra was born. Amaza made a fuss of the child and always had time for her between tours. The child's mother was an attractive but serious and withdrawn woman who worked at the X-ray centre, positioning patients for ultrasound, mammography and radiology, getting the barium down the patients or up, as the case may be, and keeping it there. Often, walking in Budawang Street, people whose faces she didn't recognise averted their eyes slightly from hers. She had medical ambitions for her daughter.

When little Aphra was available, Amaza told her stories and

gave her scraps of her own wisdom. Love little and long, Aphra, lots of love is soon stale. Don't wait till you're happy to laugh, laugh now. In her pleasantly down-to-earth voice she would rummage among her routines, tell of when she was a child and went into the room full of horrible laughter, her adventures with the Murrumbidgee mugging fish, of the cow with the bloodshot eyes that glared and chased people, the frog jumping out of a split rock, the blood test which showed she had the sap of a tree. There was the tale of the apprehensive pied quail, with crust, of how the universe is an excretion of God, a story that made nonsense of a common phrase about which end of the universe Australia inhabits. And one of how cooking is the gift of the god of chance, for long ago a baby fell into a campfire and the smell of roasting realigned the minds of all around the fire and roast dinner was discovered. She told of the Cobar conical duck and its serial adventures and long life.

As the girl got older the stories kept pace. Amaza's young audience was rapt at the story of derelict houses where echoes of bygone dances were detectable, ancient words, shouts from the past, or a quiet gnawing. It seemed to the girl that Aunt Amaza had experienced every shade of feeling possible. Even the anarchic changes of mood of the Coleambally coffee cat, which has to be restrained after too many saucers of cappuccino and looks absurd with its milk moustache.

By the time the girl was fifteen, Amaza had abandoned stories and talked of everyday things, such as that you can be told in words how to use a violin bow, but words can't tell you how to produce a sound, then a fair sound, then a beautiful sound: you have to do it. And that if you want to perform in public, you have to prepare in private. She said it was easy to be free: just do it.

And there was the virtue of having a secret head. She had imagined a second head for herself, loaded all her magic acts and stage knowledge into it, then transferred the new head into the original one, which, unburdened, she used for the details of ordinary life.

She was seventy, the years had eaten into her skin, a disease with the bite of acid. Back in Lost River, the town she had renounced like a mistaken belief, she had changed. Her whole life had been taken up with the assertion of Amaza; now when you spoke to her it was like talking to someone busy with something else, or someone talking to God. She seemed deaf, but wasn't; astray, but she was sharp as an auctioneer when it suited her. When she was prepared to talk it was like talking to some mothers when they're old: what you say doesn't engage them, they're dying to pour out everything on their minds no matter how many times you've heard it, because it's important to them and they might not get another chance to keep their lives alive in words. You try hard to get behind the waterfall of words to the cooler cave of sense behind it.

All about the years of performing, being hanged in public, put in a locked bag in a tank of water and getting out before she drowned, with the keys in her rectum or on thread attached to her bridgework. And the small town east of Perth where she was caught in the act by a wife sensitive to adultery when it came too close to her. And still you worked hard to keep up with all she said. It was a stew of adventure, gossip, risks, disappointments, backbiting, loss, display, success, applause, yet at the end you felt there was another story untold you could only guess at. Not quite parallel to the spoken narrative. Did she have new histories to weave into future performances?

There was a vague smell about her, industrial chemistry's idea of rose perfume. It didn't suit. Was she serious when she talked of doing another series of shows? She looked more mysterious and menacing than ever, thanks to age, and was constantly being assured her public was dying to see her again.

On the morning of the second day of Lost River's annual Show, Amaza was found lying on the red cedar couch in the garden gazebo on the lawns of the house in Kioloa Avenue, her hands folded at the wrists for sleep. She was cold. The head of the couch was down flat, as she liked it, her head stretched back, no pillow, her nose white, nostrils pointing to the sky. She'd been dead between twelve and eighteen hours. A tray, with empty coffee cup and cake crumbs, sat on the gazebo bench.

Amaza Aprahamian would dump no more on living or dead. Death was not a role for her now, death was Amaza.

It was some months after Aunt Amaza had died. At Sydney in the Blackburn building doing an optional dissection of head and neck in the December holidays at the end of her second year, was medical student Aphra, who had recognised her Aunt Amaza's head, now detached from the body she had willed in a phase of generosity. She'd reached in and pulled it out of the vat, in its plastic, and put it in front of herself on the bench. Most heads that have been in formalin for a while get to look much the same, just faces without thoughts, but this was a head Aphra had looked at and listened to for many years. She would do the superficial muscles, then get on to the nerves after lunch if there was time.

The yellowish head was actually half a head, left side, sawn down the middle while frozen to show brain, oral and nasal cavities, teeth, mouth, tongue, trachea and spinal column. It was enough. It was almost too dead, like something the university ought to send back.

There was the mole with the strong shiny black hair coming out of it, still shiny, and there was the hockey scar just under her eyebrow that she covered with liquid make-up when she thought of it. The remaining cheek still had a slight coral-pink colour, but broken capillaries contributed to the colour. And yes, the brown eyes—eye—with the touch of green in the iris, and the fleshy translucent growth like a steep-sided blister at the base of the nose. That mouth, which had talked so much, was silent as a microphone. The eye expressed a vagueness, a dopiness never evident in life, but also a gentle innocence. And the funny ear, thick and pale, with the top edge folded over tightly. Aphra wondered if anyone had told Aunt Amaza as a child to be sure to clean properly under that fold. There was no sign of half a secret head within what she was holding. Was death a form of expression irrespective of what was expressed?

Great crested surgeons! Here she was, scalpel in hand, and there was a segment of Aunt Amaza on the bench. She knew she had acquired no doctrinaire compassion; did she have any at all? Wonder who's got the rest of her? Silly. How would I know the other bits? She was always dressed when I saw her. The death of her aunt had changed her, she felt, as a cold sea alters the shape of land.

Sorry, Amaza, she said under her breath as she inserted the tip of the scalpel. This is one situation that's hopeless. No further deception, no illusions. She began to giggle. No one noticed. Death was in the air and on the nose, in a place filled with bright young persons dedicated to serving as many patient people per day as they could manage and looking forward to the rewards. Sorry, she apologised again as the surgical steel bit deep into the dead flesh; to perform in public I need to practise in private, Aunt. To be a surgeon you have to do more than read books, you have to do the knife bit.

(In my head I drafted a yarn for the surgical steel. Oyster grey?)

She remembered Amaza's roomy nouns, the Cobar conical duck and the head within a head, and laughed aloud into the near silence. Impatience, and something else, gripped her. She went for it. Went right to the bone. It seemed at that moment that the room was filled with horrible laughter. A familiar voice asserted itself from the half-mouth on the bench: 'The banks of the Murrumbidgee were very steep there, we slipped going down. I went right in, feet first. Cold! You wouldn't believe how cold. The mugging fish batted me in the face, goosed me enthusiastically, and when I defended myself attacked my tits, which were growing strongly then. I was very conscious of them, even imagining they unbalanced me when I walked. It was in the town that they were received with most approval. The men—and ladies—who found excuses to touch them, starting with the oldest ones first, were …'

Long after the dissection of the nerves, long after Aphra had put the head away in the bin and washed and left Blackburn, Amaza's voice went on. Into the rest of her life. That small puncture mark at the back of the nose up into the base of the skull looked like nothing more than the sort of spot under a crust of dried blood that people pick from their noses in cases of atrophic rhinitis, or when the weather has been very dry. Aphra dismissed it as of no significance. She certainly wasn't going to follow whatever it was into the brain. Probably just an artefact of the dissection, or someone messing about at the time the head was originally frozen and sawn.

As I worked on the last of the border I thought of Amaza as a new kind of lock with a barcode attached. You open the lock by passing a light-pen over the barcode. There's so much magic these days. As I finished I was aware that I was working with my mouth slightly open, tongue out. I was a boy again, doing my drawings in the old house in Bellbird Corner, and my mother saying, 'Just look at that tongue.'

The border finished, I stretched my legs outside in the sun, looking down at the town from the church, marking where the highway approached from the north, Explorer's Hill with its lookout to the east, Big Hill on the west of town, the rim where the big houses snugly looked down on Lost River, and the ranges to the south.

It took eleven trials to come up with the cartoon I wanted for Amaza. Before the light was gone I decided on colours and began to number them on the cartoon. Sorrel, peacock blue, topaz.

A cow bell sounded hollowly in the cooling air from down near North Arm Road. A celebratory bell. What a beautiful day it had been. I smiled at the hills to the east, north, and round to the sunlit west. The eastern hills had grown a film of pink light over their green covering of trees.

What an evening. Good enough to eat.

The next days passed pleasantly in work, then it was time for another portrait. I was settling in well, I thought. The people I met had entered Lost River by birth or migration. As I got about the town I began to see how much of Lost River had entered them. Perhaps the town thought itself in them.

I had a recurring image of the town fitting itself round them, moving with the speed of sand round beached boats, rocks or dead bodies, without planning, without supervision.

To me Yarrow would always be young. But I would have seen youth in a wrinkle, if it was hers. Her face floated often before my eyes. Her voice sounded in my head, her clear syllables strung together in her own special voice-tunes. Her speaking voice had a singing quality so that in full flight I heard the tunes she spoke leaving her mouth, rising up, then cascading, and splashing down over her so she bathed in her own music.

Those were the sounds, the words were something else. She didn't want to be credited with fortuitous features of her appearance. The words pretty and beautiful had much the same status to her as mouthwash or truth. Theories and knowledge were heaped in her head like new worlds. Sometimes I thought she'd been brutalised by books.

How many times I'd wished I could be in love again so I wouldn't be in torment to her. Suddenly she had gone. Left no word. The stone face of solitude was my companion. Each memory since I first saw her led back to her and welcomed the miracle of how all her shapes fitted into a place in me that was ready for her.

How many times had I wanted to watch her sleep, to wonder where her dreams took her. Too late now to wish her as my home. Too late to experience her waking, then to assault the day with the joyful clatter-clang of breakfast, tinkled rims of cups, chimed and dropped spoons. I must stop myself or I'll begin to think of her as a breathing idol, and that's a no-no. Or develop the smooth relaxed features of an omnivore with a meal in prospect.

She had been caught up once in domestic entanglements, and tied too tight. 'I flew too low,' her verdict was. Four times I saw her. Only four, though we spoke many times. Had she written her book on the book written on an earlier theorist of the psyche? She had cut off completely. Residues of either the Christian or Marxist confessions clung to her, it was sometimes hard to tell which, but she saw her golden age ahead rather than behind. Often I found it difficult to say to her what was on my mind, since for her the only respectable thought was oppositional, as the only significant life was struggle. Most of my concerns were private, individual, and pointed to her. Her mind was on higher things, which I thought of as party games. I mean, how does a dry materialist dressed as a rationalist think comfortably in symbols? With such difficulties, why didn't I have the sense to turn away and head in another direction? Instead, she turned away. I remained pointing towards her as my north.

Had I thought of her as a toy, to look at, touch, and play with?

I still don't know how to think about it. It's hard to persuade old words to fit new feelings, they never quite cope.

four

chokeback jones

Club Babel was Lost River's nightclub. I spoke, while I waited for Jones, to the blank, hammered-back face of a veteran of two wars. The face told me that the building, on a corner over Budawang Street, had been a furniture showroom leased by a company that went under. We were on the first floor, the club opened at five, to start the night early and catch what pennies were around. Half the town was printed on the glass of the big window near me. Some of the town moved, scattered shoppers wombatting casually across the road, heads down.

The mouth in the face worked easily on good jaw-grease, like the hucksters, politicians, persuaders and urgers continually talking to anyone silly enough to listen. After twenty minutes the voice was getting to me, its tone a dead ringer for that of the quarrelsome mahogany wasp, all flashes of movement and stings. I almost got a glow up from having him breathe at me.

Chokeback would be delayed. Supervising a cross-country race, his wife Yeti told me. Next week the soccer carnival, then the new maze project on school land, and once a fortnight at the jail in the next town teaching English comprehension. God knows how he finds time to come home to his family, she said. I had a sudden memory, decades old, a smell of after-school feet.

The veteran pointed out the spot where Morrie the Magsman's father died laughing, and for some reason I remembered the morning's large magpie child crying *meep meep* and being fed by a mother no bigger than her infant. The mouth suggested a time in the far past when all things spoke the same language, and also our present, when words are no longer enough yet silence is ineffectual and absurd.

The shape of the man which organised itself in the doorway looked so unplaceable, so undifferentiated, so difficult to stereotype, it might have been a teacher. I got up, away from the mouth at last, went over and negotiated drinks, and sat with Jones by another window with its slightly different picture of the street, ready with start-off questions.

Not necessary. He knew what I wanted, and like the Huskisson dogfish that thinks it's a shark and attacks anything, got stuck straight into his story.

His broad fingers came with small, almost triangular nails; his eyes were penetrating, pale oyster-knives; his voice a grappling-iron. When he spoke, his bottom teeth showed. His ears curved outwards at the top, came in near his head, then the lobes pushed outwards again. Each lobe had a sharp horizontal crease in the fleshy part. Reminded me of a Gilroy I once met, but that was in another context.

There's more, and less, to this town than there appears to be. I'm a teacher, live in Gold Street two blocks west of the Workers' Club where the other teachers drink. Oh yes, they see themselves as workers. It's a working-class occupation. There are so few lanes open for promotion: principal, deputy, head teacher, head of department, that's about it. The mass of us keep the same relative position for forty years and retire with the status of the old-style clerk. No wonder so many teachers vote Labor; they're all on one level, a proletariat on middle-class salaries.

How we get here is not an explanation of what we are; however, I came here from Sorrydale on the western slopes of the Divide. A wanderer, like so many teachers, until I die, but what's death? A habit sculpted and modelled deeply into the flesh of body and brain?

The nickname? I was never a scrawny dissident, but, older, if I saw something stupid, or the department brought out a more than usually crazy idea—and some of their ideas were as much help as a tin of baked beans to a starving snake—I used to pipe up. Like abolishing big set exams because of strain on the weaker ones, and instituting constant assessment so there are exams throughout the year and perpetual strain on all. Tough on the bright ones who enjoyed school and swotted up in the last six weeks and came top: now they couldn't relax. Constant assessment is mostly used as a discipline aid, since the old, and teachers, have largely thrown away their authority. Anyway, I got into so much hot water and time-wasting kerfuffle that I trained myself to choke back my reactions. Like I choke back my anger when I hear two teachers, man and wife, talking poor mouth on two good salaries.

I have a natural sympathy for the kids who get the wind in their tails and don't want to do what they're told, but I'm supposed to be preparing them for a world where they'll only get a job if they do what they're told. Some of my colleagues protest at life being a race, but they've won their race and now they're coasting.

Teachers. What idiots we are. Put up with conditions a factory worker wouldn't tolerate. Millions a year go in fees to the union, usually a vocal minority hostile to the traditions of their own society and for whom education is the continuation of politics by other means, who stir us with extreme left-wing stuff when most of us aren't left wing at all, and pay no attention to job conditions. No hot water to wash your hands, no decent soap, no lockers to hang a coat, stow a bag; so there are raincoats over chairs, wet umbrellas on the floor or making pools in the corner. No couches in the staff room, no dignified toilets, el Raspo toilet paper. And some of the men getting around in old sneakers and jeans like something the cat brought in, as if it were their day off. No wonder the kids look down on us. Our new informalities don't sit well with respect.

A teacher. A Judas bullock that leads the other animals up to the drench, the dip, the semitrailer, the stunner. Generations come and go, trusting the Judas as they advance towards the knife. Am I leading the kids to a life of nothing? What am I not telling them that they need to know? I work ultimately for a government beyond our state government, one that sees education as fitting people for its purposes. Get these exact words, mate: Part of the purpose of higher education is to help government achieve its social objectives. What a paltry aim. We're headed for a party state.

When I was a kid my favourite character in Tamworth was a guy a thousand years old with a blue shirt and bushy white beard down his chest, who pushed a fruit barrow round the streets. Spoke little, just pushed and sold.

I joined here as a temporary, been here eighteen years in five different rooms. I have two schools. One's on paper in the regional office, neat and tidy, with a mission statement of currently approved aims, carefully written annual report, low discipline problem, feel-good policies: the imaginary school constructed for stability and promotion, to show visitors or the public. I work in the real school, at the chalkface, in front of kids alert and attentive as tortoises, some of whom are known to the police, some come in half drunk or stoned or with the effects still apparent of what they put into themselves last night at their rave parties, and some of whom lose regularly, here in Club Babel, more than I'd care to lose in a year. Most lives are mimicry; whom do they mimic?

I should be like the teacher who thinks he's crash-hot, no discipline problems at all. He comes in and says, 'All got your books? Your paper? Right. Shut up and read and don't bother me.' All of which is like a red rag to a pterodactyl and his class relaxes like a dead horse. In the staff room he's called Fig Jam—Fuck I'm Good, Just Ask Me.

A centre of apathy. I'm Anti-father, substitute for their parents, teaching them so they can read ads and write behind the wash-sheds: Things go better with coke.

You think I'm grunchy, don't you? Well, it depresses me.

School's supposed to teach them how to look after themselves in the world, speak the truth, tell right from wrong, sense from nonsense, tolerance, wait your turn, a fair go, honesty. A lot of them never hear those things at home, or not till they play some sport and find they have to play by rules. Even then they argue with the referee as if they're all equal, players and referees, and rules can be negotiated. They can talk, I'll give them that. Articulately illiterate, poor little bastards. I know that I shouldn't transmit values, but I'm their only conduit apart from television and its sisters.

So many bright eyes, strong voices, vigorous bodies ready to spring expertly into a failure larger than pimples before they start. Circuits are there, but the current is switched on only for short bursts each day and the education system cuts them off at the pass mark, repulsive outcomes of the system. Yet they could all pass, with distinction, tests for eating, breathing, getting out of the way of a bus, or picking up other girls or boys. Primary school taught them to write, but some hold a pen the way a chimpanzee holds a stick, digging in an ants' nest for a snack.

I have some good classes, wonderful kids. Even the bad classes have only a few really bad kids, even the year twelve class with the town's drug dealer in it. I know the drongoes might straighten up later, maybe even fluke a job with an uncle. But in class they go berserk. Brains with enlarged ventricles, real air-heads.

The ones who'll succeed sit quietly, concentrated at the back of the room. Ignore the vegetables, succeeders! Work! Stay together, it's easier to do the right thing when everyone you know does it. Forget the bright faces and young available bodies after school, and the social chit-chat: they're merely sparks struck that live a second or two, then nothing. I'm sorry for the noise, the disruption, as discipline reports get written, the delay as some kid is ejected who doesn't want to go, a natural for the house of correction.

'You can't do that to me! I'll sue you!' he squeals. I try to avoid their breath, they infect the alphabet. If only the parents understood that the more you know, the more you can learn, they might help, but they prefer the contentment born of ignorance. Singly, or in the street, the kids can be spoken to. In a mob, insanity prevails. Marx knew nothing of the class struggle.

And when you come back after lunch to 7E5, say, the bottom English class, the room's full of domestic gas. Or in class one kid lets go with a fart full-throated and blaring, or some evil toad contributes one that's furtive, spreading like an indecent ground-mist. All hands to the windows. Thank God there's no air-conditioning or it'd be all over the school. Or you see it creeping down a corridor. Land of the wide brown fart.

What thick-skinned rhinoceros fly, what witchcraft, does it take to revive these zombies, these yawning young with their transient pustules? Oxygen thieves, a lot of them. Life runs off them. The future is one of those rubber castles where all falls are cushioned. No bruises.

I had one kid who was sure light was a liquid squirted over a dark world, it lasted twelve hours till the sun evaporated it. Another wouldn't go out at night in case he got black air on his face. I've got boys who, asked what they'd need alone on a desert island, always mention hair conditioner, and they're not kidding.

Class discipline is officially adjusted to the sensitive. The tougher ones, who could stand a little discomfort without turning a hair, aren't compelled to shut up or get on with their work. Some do none, bring no assessable tasks for marking, then complain bitterly when they get no marks. They have no books, no pens, no paper; on the phone their parents swear they were given their equipment. Honesty is rare as black tigers with white spots. You phone in your own time, of course.

When the assertive girls don't do their work, their excuse is that Stephen and Andrew didn't do theirs, either. Yes they did, you say, here it is. Did they crawl up your bum or something? one asks. More paperwork, more letters home, less teaching time. Or further complications if all the rest say, 'You only thought she said that,' and the deputy head asks you, the teacher, to produce a witness from a crowd of peers whose interest it is to stick together.

You want to listen, I'll keep talking. We're so isolated from the community I've got no one to tell it to. To the public we're very distant objects.

Behaviour? Once the saying was: You wouldn't do that at home. Now it's: You're not at home now. Feet on seats, farting, playing with themselves; never been taught at home not to.

The boy called Slug with the huge donger that's a school joke. Kids saying 'Suck my sausage' to women teachers. And if you ask them to do something, the expressions on their faces! Alarmed as Jesus with thorns on his head, then some bastard getting stuck into him with a whip. What the hell next? the face says.

There was the boy from Lebanon who said he'd killed eighteen men. One who beat his chest and wailed. One who wet himself when his pants were on backwards and he couldn't get it out. One tried to bribe the boss with two Lifesavers: not two packets, two naked lollies in the palm. The ones sent out of class who run away, jobs for the police. The one the other teachers say not to suspend, or he'll go out robbing shops all day. The constant refrain: What do we have to do this for? The complaint: We never have to take our feet off the seats for Mister Gold. And the excuses, thin and weak and wingless as an anorexic tit. Yet maybe they'll cause little trouble later, apart from having children.

Oh, and the violent girls garrisoning the toilet block. One poor girl never ever, in six years, went to the toilet at school; the big girls had guards on it. They'd duck the heads of those they didn't like in the toilet bowls. In year seven the chief bully told this girl, 'You looked at my boyfriend.' Some cultures have rules about who you can look at; trouble is the rest don't know those rules.

This is a big whinge, but I have to speak up for teachers. And sometimes you need a whip and chair to get attention. As for teaching!

How can I stand in front of that rabble and begin to discuss with them whether humans are vile worms, helpless puppets or free agents? Or whether there's a universal grammar of action? Or discuss the danger of the government constantly pressing to privilege the collective at the expense of the individual? How many would understand the words? The concepts? Some would, yes, the precious few I feel so sorry for. Or how to show them that political parties are merely private organisations with their own agendas, decided privately, whose aim is to take over government?

How will I get through to them that increasing centralism means a lame republic? That the centre must not hold. That the executive must be severed from the legislature. Or discuss whether a republic, when Crown land's gone, will give us better freehold with rights above and below ground, as is the case in other republics such as the US? Or whether the new internationalism is a cover for a new imperialism? And if patriotism's a no-no, what of self-determination? Or, if we have a clear national identity, what becomes of multiculturalism? Or is multiculturalism a word meaning fragmentation? How can I set them on fire for a bill of rights to defeat the onslaught against freedom of religion, of the press, of opinion, speech and expression? And they don't understand when I give them the phrase 'a publicity-shy politician' as an example of oxymoron.

I'd like to tell them of the task I see for humans, of preserving the fragile decencies and civilities, not throwing out customs, manners and traditions that still support us and make our lives possible. That trying to justify morals, customs and manners with reasons is like trying to explain the origins of words before using them.

Eden's gone, the tribe's gone, with its common aims. What we have is ourselves, the distilled experience that is tradition, the evolving law, language, culture we inherited, and the rules embodied in our institutions, plus the always resurgent desire for freedom, which is impossible in the tribe or collective but essential, to leave room for the unpredictable.

I go on a bit, don't I? But I care about the rotten little sods and what they do with this brief flash of light between the two darknesses.

(Words blew out of his mouth like dry leaves in a breeze. I could imagine him as a soldier, going into battle cursing.

He went on.)

How can I explain to them, with their ten-second attention span, that human knowledge is at best a wobbly edifice, that there's corruption at the base? No logical or experiential foundations tie it rationally to the world it purports to describe. How can I do that without them stupidly throwing out the whole thing and saying there is no truth? As it is, they'd rather gather new facts and new habits than think.

To survive I must have an unquenchable hope that not all children will succumb to the rubbish and the conflicting messages they're soaked in; like the harm of glancing at a cigarette ad compared with the lack of harm in watching a ninety-minute X-rated porno video; like why it's wrong to kill a convicted murderer and right to kill an unborn baby or an old man who's sick and crabby and no use to anyone else. And if we're constructed by our environment, where does censorship stand? Or are there elements within our environment that aren't obvious? And if no is to mean no, why does it mean yes to the psychoanalyst? And if there's no truth, who's to say anyone is correct or incorrect?

And how to get across to them that a federal system limits the sovereign power by dividing it and giving government only certain definite rights? That the constitution's job is to limit government power? And there're feet on seats, missiles flying round the room, and some kids are away looking after the baby while Mum's at work, some representing the school at regional sports, and another away because his bird is very sick and his friend is helping him because he's so upset.

How can I prepare them to resist those rationalists who say

they must be able to state the reasons for their actions and beliefs, and relinquish those for which they can't produce evidence? Remember your Hayek? 'For we not only know more than we can express but also more than we can be aware of or test, and much that we do well depends on assumptions outside the range of what we can either say or think about.' Remember Gödel? 'Among the determinants of rational processes there must always be some rules which cannot be stated or even be obvious.' On a more mundane level we talk of and use every day electricity, mass, gravity, light and so on, but can't state what they are.

Yet each year when I do exam duty and the packed assembly hall is quiet as a prison waiting for an execution, I have such sympathy for the lot of them. Time, for them, is dividing into innumerable futures. I look round at the hundreds of backs hunched over their exam questions and those I feel most for are the great lumps of kids, the hefty louts who are going to write nothing but bumf and bumfodder and score about fifteen percent, proficient in noncommunicative language, experts in intuitional geometry, which they use to scan the girls' talents, boys who ought to be out of school already, working among men in physical jobs that don't exist anymore.

At that moment there's no spieler trying to be plausible about the bambam thundersnake, no demented adolescent careering about the classroom making a racket like the roaring dolby. It's just one year's eighteen-year-olds feeling the truth breaking out on their skins like sweat or pimples; the full impact of their subordinate position in the world as they try to please their elders and get a foot on the ladder and climb the rung to liberty, which is a little money, a tiny bit of power over your life, a house and family, a profession, maybe a business, at all events a job, and goodbye to complete dependence. I know I shouldn't grumble that even if they crap on the exam paper they get four marks out of twenty.

And maybe, just maybe, there's another kid in that hall who'll pass, and go on to do something useful for the world, and one day many years later will remember that some little thing I said, not even aware I said it, some casual, accidental comment, made the difference between a life of deeply unsatisfying comfort, that's so easy for most to attain these days, and a strenuous life turned outwards to others, with all the personal rewards it brings.

Plenty of times I think I should get that cart, stock it with fruit and veg, and start pushing, but in that exam room I cancel the thought. I wouldn't leave teaching, not for all the tea in china. I'll do what I can, even for the oxygen thieves.

Right now it's internal exams, so I've got marking tonight, unpaid overtime, and the rest of the week. If I finish on Sunday I'll veg out. Tomorrow it's back to a staff room full of words like slags, dags, shits, sluts, scumbags and pusbuckets, and they're not talking about politicians. And to a classroom where I'll give a passable imitation of the Deniliquin drover-fish rounding up tiddlers and guppies.

I asked him about the town's name, and he was a teacher immediately.

'As with many regions of New South Wales in the early days, settlers spread to the Southern Tablelands to begin their laborious symbiosis with sheep before government officials in Sydney were aware of it. The first few had vague ideas of Scottish names, since the highlands and tablelands reminded them of their birthplace.

'When they came over the hills with their sheep around 1820 there had been good rains and the river was a real river.

In the following years it shrank back to normal: small pools and longer stretches of water, like a Morse message. In drought, more dots than dashes. By the time Sydney heard of the settlement the place was known as Lost River.'

'Pretty much like other small towns?' I asked.

'All different, all much the same.'

'Unusual things happen?'

'Everywhere. You find out when you give a Year Seven class a little exercise on family history. It's one thing they all love. There was a woman died here at Show time. You wouldn't believe the things the kids wrote about it. Rumour, slander, silly things their parents said. Sometimes I think there's an organised whispering campaign.'

'Was that the Aprahamian woman?'

'Yep. Rumour is it was murder. A woman who came to the town a few years back is cast as the villain.'

'Anyone go to the police?'

'No fear of that. The police want facts. People would have to push themselves forward for everyone to see. Nothing in their lives requires them to be hard, accurate or uncomfortable. It's all done for them now. No village Hampdens here.'

'Why pick on that woman?'

'They took her up at first. She loved the place, did a lot for the town. Loads of energy. Got elected to council. Then they turned. Too many bright ideas, suggestions. Made the rest look stupid. Nice talking to you.' He was gone.

Chokeback was a living marathon. He was at the sixteen-kilometre stage, where the first severe pain strikes, well under halfway. The Jones marathon was being run in a bowl with five scallops round its rim, with a road out at the lowest point of each scallop. The highway bypass skirted the town on its western side, concealed under Big Hill from Lost River, protecting and hiding the town.

Babel was starting to fill. The sheer mindlessness of smoothly clicking poker machine wheels pushed me out into Budawang Street. The soft comforting swish of relaxing traffic soothed me.

I thought of marathon colours as I sat in the Holly Tree, pouring coffee into me. Ideas were shaping for the cartoon, and colours, mainly the muted brightness of saxe-blue. I watched people passing in the Eureka Mall, then leaving the mall, ready to head towards Wiradhuri Hill; the afternoon light hit me like a wall, the collision making me gasp. I inhaled enough light to float me, and the pickup, to the hilltop.

I searched the lighted air of the valleys round about for any flecks of darkness. Nothing but light.

Yarrow was a circle drawn in beach sand. I stood within her circle, feeling its warmth until a different tide came in. Was she alone now? I hoped not. I accept that she was never understandable. I liked her madness, that desire to be boundless. And when I say she was beautiful, I mean first of all her strength. She had a triumph about her, yet was insular, self-contained. Like a traffic roundabout thickly planted with natives all in bloom.

five

adora weller

Her voice faded in carefully, armoured yet attractive, pleasant as petals on flowers that eat unwary insects. Or perhaps fingers. She suggested a meeting at the Wool Expo and Wine Festival. She spoke out of a deliberation that contained no casualness, the sort of intentness capable of planning a golden hour. A screen of some sort surrounded her. Somewhere a saxophone saddened the silence.

On the way down Wiradhuri Hill I recalled a cautious undercurrent of warmth in her voice and had a body image of a first clash lip to lip, but no face to put behind the adversary lips.

As I was crossing the north arm of the river, driving beneath the highway overpass and along Grimmett Street past the racecourse and stable complex, a light shower of rain smelled fresh and sweet on the bitumen, a warm wetness, steam rising from the road. What would she be like? Should I photograph my subjects? I'd heard she posed on the grass at the Olympic pool every summer, and after an hour, if she was alone, made one elegant dive and went home.

Left along Hereford Street to the showground entrance. The local 2LR news had spread the story of a burglar permitted to make love to a spinster—that was the word—of twenty-nine. Why was I thinking of that? Did Lost River have a sexual crisis? Or only me?

Veins fascinated me when I was a child; they do still. One at her temple blue, another near the angle of her jaw. Then there was her white neck, where veins ran green so close to the surface. Everything about her suggested she thought she'd be good to eat. She was elegant as a carrick bend laid out in new rope on an expensive deck, before being drawn tight.

The red and white noise and apparent confusion of the wine hall I pushed into the background as Adora spoke of the daffodil festival, the handicrafts market at St Kevin's, tennis, and of the film society which used the Bijou Theatre for its screenings. She barely sipped the local red in its plastic wine-glass, and asked me what colours I saw in her share of the tapestry, while I was imagining the nine-tenths of her flesh she deliberately concealed. And its weight. She smiled with uncertain warmth. I found myself looking at her as if I had two pieces of toast to put her between.

She was still in card-contact with her favourite English teacher; she noticed how some young men removed their jackets and shoulders at the same time; she seemed to feel women's eyes were sharper than men's since their wrist-watches were smaller, and because women could see dust and marks where no man could. She spoke of town rumours, scandals, and asserted, in confidence, that Leanne Fusby had been a mudwrestler. Very powerful. At the Show on that day six months ago she noticed Leanne had a button missing from her blue dress. Lost in a struggle? And someone saw her going back to the Show at two o'clock on the Saturday. Someone else saw her buying petrol in a tin the day before the Show, and her with that lovely tangerine Chevrolet that she kept so shiny. Why a tin? Did she have a secret car in that double garage?

Okay, so who was Leanne Fusby?

The one everyone thinks was responsible for the Aprahamian woman's death. Not that I believe it. People need their gossip. Without stories the world is a complete mystery. I need to tell myself stories constantly about how my mother could leave Lost River, and me, and go to the Gold Coast with my father.

Adora spoke also of freeing herself from what would prevent her from being herself. I nodded as convincingly as I could. I don't have that problem, I'd like to be free of myself.

The transition was so subtle I didn't notice at first. She was talking of the mother she'd lost, not to illness but to the sun. Her parents retired after her father's accident. A persistent note in her voice said: Mother, come home. Then, before I knew it, I was not only in the wine hall but also in her bedroom tasting her usual Sunday nights. The screen round her sculpted tranquillity felt like a sheet of plate glass between us.

'There's something very funny about this town,' she said, then began her story, her right hand tortoising over her left arm.

My wallaby thoughts, brown and stationary for long periods, become suddenly animated and hop off, leaving me to follow. They turn and look back. A huntsman spider clings to the ceiling, I can't tell if she sees me. My thoughts fall into an empty pit, I jump in after them.

Everything is more than it seems, more than can be said, but here I am, twenty-six, and all I have to show is a pink-collar job in a pie shop, where you get nothing for nothing and very little for a dollar, a new cadet-blue Bellara, nice flat in Grimmett Street—a pretty street lined with claret ash—more clothes and shoes than I know what to do with, and another Sunday night alone, together with the feeling that tomorrow will alter today as today blurred yesterday, and the days will go riding over me for a lifetime.

I remember to say, night and morning: I am. Which I've done ever since my mother left. God, I wish I was still sixteen and could come home from school to her every day. And we'd talk. Talk. Why do mothers leave daughters? I turn off the raucous television, with its screech of public secrets, go to bed with the cat on her blanket at my feet, and shut my eyes against the streetlight to hold the loving darkness in, feeling happily held and cocooned.

Tonight I'm being a sandy shore. I slope gently down to a pacific sea on which at any moment passionate pirates may appear, parched invaders, with an eagerness, yet an attractive reluctance, to be civilised. Life is often lonely, but filling it with imaginings, it never lacks interest.

In my bed I walk in the fierce sunshine of childhood with heraldic animals for company: lions, emus, lyrebirds, the phoenix, echidna and the hymn-singing duck. And gryphons immobile as nylon nasturtiums in the twin windows of Simple Simon's Pies and Cakes. I speak to the animals in tongues of my retractable and copper-coloured theories on men as underdone Australians, and of my recumbent policy: wait and see. They answer perceptively. I know humans are no more rational than other animals, though men less than women. And why do men retain so much child in them? Females grow away from play early, into rules and seriousness. Boys never outgrow toys.

When I was nine I knew I would be lonely. At eleven I was sure of it. Even with other kids, on the margin of their games, the spectre of loneliness would tug at my sleeve to remind me.

Now I'm an empty house and only a phone joining me to my mother. I have to remember and imagine her eyes.

I don't want to be humble: let me have, have. To experience, to feel copiously. The men I've known, the Knudsens, the Joneses, the ones I'd rather not mention, were able to lift only a corner of the mystery. I don't care that my body is described as earth-moving equipment. It ends with a shrug, as usual. Who cares? Soon I'll sleep, ready for another Monday, though the part that dreams is awake whether I sleep or not.

Monday. Other women seem to find work romantic, as if what men have always done must be interesting. Is it a con-trick? To get us all to be ants with a dry-as-dust life of work and customers? Will I get like men, satisfied with discomfort and subordination all my life? Deep down I'd rather be apart from all their silly pressures and priorities. Anyway, how can I be equal to men? And which men? They're not equal themselves.

I still have my girl-vision. Someone whose dream I fit comes through the shop door, takes me away. The lucky dip. Still my preferred vision.

With eye-windows shut, in the darkness of my head I see moon-washed rocks, dim roads, houses and faces, blanched sheep and cows. I see roan horses across the street in the stables, trees wet with moonlight, and a fox in an old coat hurrying away, rear end lowered. The future is a darkness, lightened moment by moment.

Will corsairs ever land here on this shore that I am, draw up their craft on me so their keels drive deep furrows into the tanned, receptive sand? Furrows that curve over and outward under the weight of the driving hull. They say love is too difficult, but I don't mind just the physical, if it's a man I can want. I'm attracted to so few. Perhaps I give the impression I don't need them. I should never have tried with coarse comics like Coy and Jensen. Am I too masculine, do I allow my male self too much say? If only I had my mother to speak these things to. Perhaps there's a sort of intention in the way things are and how they got that way, as poets say.

'There's no fate, Adora,' says the streetlight. 'Nothing's predetermined, there are no allotted parts.' Then is it a case of improvising all life long? Even improvising death, so that it's situated somewhere between thinking, touching and feeling?

'Look at it as freedom, Adora.' Streetlights talking. I've got more freedom than I can handle. I could have continued at school after Year Ten, gone to university, but with Dad's accident another earner was needed. And I once longed to do great things. Just once to rise above my daily self and do or say something so unusual that it would open people's eyes to things they'd never considered. Just once. I lost my chance. Perhaps Dad was right when he used to catch me picking my nose. 'Picking winners? Bit of pick and flick? Get in there, Digger, watch the chips. Never knew a nose-picker any good yet.' Thanks, Dad.

Then he had his fall in the foundry onto a fresh casting. Left an imprint, lost a foot. Such is life, he said. Mum and he went to live in the sun. Goodbye, Adora. Named after a biscuit. The past leans against me like a wall I must hold up. I refused to leave Lost River. All my friends are here, I said, whom I knew years ago, whose memories I'd recognise and who'd recognise some of mine. What friends? Gone, like blowaway grass. Gaps in a diary. And the ones who remain seem to hate me now. I wish they'd said so then, I needn't have kept their memories all this time for nothing. Funny place, Lost River. How do all the people exist? Where does the money come from? Add up all the industries, all the jobs—there're a lot of people over. Who supports them all?

I don't suppose I'll ever know myself fully, but desire, venereal desire, that's all I seem to be. Is there a universal grammar of desire? I have my joys, but just beneath the surface of joy there's a drowning woman. Where's ecstasy? Where's deep annihilating love? Where are all the men? How many frogs and toads will I have to kiss before I get a prince? I know in my heart I'm free to go, to do, to be: is that why I can't move? Yet our life these days looks as if it's more and more freedom, but it's not real: it's freedom to do and say and be and look at and taste and aim at silly trivial things.

When I shut my eyes and burrow into the darkness in my head I feel I could have done anything. Could have. My motto. I push out the thought of nylon nasturtiums and managing a pink pie shop, trying to keep it cheap and cheerful, and Monday's delivery of two packets of doughnut mixture and one tub of fondant. Plus extra bread. I eliminate the insistent stab of failure that I lacked the energy to study at night to make up for my shortened education. I so miss that tertiary training in writing essays. Though it's not too late. I could do external, or open learning, but will I? If I could unpick the past, where would I insert myself and do differently? So many places.

Let it be more than words. All words and no play makes me a dull biscuit. Let me not become cold inside, not be a woman closed. All the joinings I've had so far were unsatisfactory. Meant nothing. Sometimes I wish I hadn't said no so often. Though it was hilarious with that unreconstructed Freudian who insisted my disagreement with his suggestions proved I secretly agreed, that my no meant yes. And even more so when I got loud about it.

I take holidays, I meet yobs and slobs who hang round those places. Parasites. I come home gladly to the streets and landscapes and countryside that are part of the way I think, how I see the world.

Wally Welland-Smith says when he's too long away he gets randy for the smell of cowpats and long grass. He loves our landmarks: the light on Explorer's Hill, the bridge, the old wool store, trees in Anzac Park. The homeless men coming out of the hostel in Merino Street, rumpots and winos, all showered and smelling of the same soap, are part of the town. Young schoolgirls talking of Sadie and Maisie are part of home now. God! Slaves and masters at thirteen, and me craving romance and some gentle intelligent strength who will listen to me, look at me admiringly, think about me in absence, and bring plans and suggestions for our future for me to approve. I must be old.

Even the polibabble of Carlotta and her friends in the Labor Party, who think they know how the rest of us should live, it, and they, are part of home. And the poor things in Butterdale with only one oar in the water. And unemployed kids with clap-sticks and a songstick stuck with bottletops busking outside Eureka Mall: all part of home. Even if it is a welfare town.

When I think of that piece of metal with the naked footprint in it that my father requested from the foundry as a souvenir I know that God is not a good person and is nothing like being in love, but more like the Paligomar glass fish that shatters when you touch it but still sticks its poison into you, and which you are forbidden to vilify or harm.

The streetlight asserts: 'Act out your desires, Adora. Let loose your whims. Vilify! Harm!'

Where there's buying and selling there's mostly good manners, traditional ways, ancient civilised customs of courtesy, and so there is in a pie shop, with sandwiches, cakes, doughnuts and the mystic meringue to exchange for money to buy more ingredients and pay wages.

If the years crumble and no one comes, what will I do? What do I need to get me moving? A terrible fright? Catastrophe? Is there something in this Australian air that sneers at seriousness and looks at determined effort with a monumental shrug? It's not the air, it's me. Why is there no real meaning? Is it because God's not watching anymore and we're not enough by ourselves? If the Darwin stuff is correct, why aren't men more suited to women? Why don't they want what I want? I want a man strong and independent as they traditionally were—I don't want someone I might have to support—but flexible and ready to go my way. And I want to keep my own independence and exercise my own strength. Choosing is fine, but having everything to choose from is having nothing. What I most want is to be loved and cherished and safe. Or the other thing.

I'll think of the secret moss-green wilderness in me, behind the shore, my personal wilderness untrodden by beasts or people, insects or coloured birds, where no strangers are allowed. I'll walk there, feel the contours with my feet, touch leaves and rust-streaked rocks with my hands, smell the exhaling plants, moist earth, pallid creekwater. Then I'll sleep, and rise again tomorrow and say: I am. Giving thanks that I have nothing inside nibbling me slowly to make itself bigger.

I've been a sandy shore today, tomorrow I'll be the wilderness itself: mysterious, unexplored. With secret plants, herbs, flowers, and creatures unfamiliar, uncatalogued. A place where people will want to be, to stroll and look. To inhale the clean breath of living trees. To widen their feelings of what life can be. A wilderness will direct the fortunes of Simple Simon's. And the day after that I'll be a sneaky rhizome travelling unseen under the groundskin.

Inside me has no name, but no matter what sallow mornings I wake to, I am stronger than loneliness or nylon nasturtiums.

Will I always be left behind? Always walk alone, an unsolicited woman? Will I ever be innerly and outwardly, thoroughly enloved?

The other thing? Oh, that.

Once I'd reminded her, a whole town of feelings flowed out in talk. Had she meant to conceal them? How many levels were there? What other trigger-phrases had I missed? With the right questions, what else might have come out?

It was Knudsen. He told me lots of things. Gave me books to read. About sex. He pointed out that I do have power over my life. With that power has come a great rush of sexual desire. I don't mean for a man, it's separate, I mean for everything about sex: the body, nakedness, touching and feeling, sexual display, sexual celebration among people like myself. I've got the power, now I want the sex. As if power turned on a tap and it all came flowing. But it's pure sex, sex without semen. I don't really want all the bother of one particular man. Eventually, yes. But for day-to-day, no.

Knudsen went on about cybersex, lipstick feminists, cyborgs, goddesses, computer orgasms and the messy kind, about easy interfacing, unlocking sexual energy and the fires that burn in me. He made me dizzy with his binaristic, metaphorological, technophobic, machinic. All those spiky words. Now I want to be free with sex, but not among men, among women. I get magazines. I find I have a taste for seeing others being sexy, and for being free myself. So far only in my room. I send away to a woman in Sydney for things to help me realise myself.

I'm working towards total body orgasm. But the main thing for the future is that, if I know myself, I can save that eventual man in the future the clumsiness of not knowing me and what I want. And the myself I mean is not one label, it's the range of things, female and male, that go to make up the me inside, in the proportions that make me what I am.

If ever there was a motive to move, sex is it. To the city, I mean. Where it's all so easy. But I can't seem to prise myself loose from Lost River, my home. And I'm not one of the New Amazons. I don't hate men.

She had a way of rubbing her right forefinger back and forth across her bare lips when she was thinking, that disturbed me. She was, to me, someone else's erotic poem. You smile and show appreciation, but it's never quite your taste.

I don't have daydreams based on recollections and representations, but on further possibilities previously reined in. Weaving is a way, for me, to forget what I lack. Mostly I feel I'm not enough. What I weave becomes part of me, filling me out to a more satisfying size.

The erotic poem that was Adora was shaped like a beautifully formed female foot. It carried within it memories of the wide range of situations it had traversed, and sensitivities to the rough places, to the hot and the cold. It wanted to be in places it couldn't yet imagine clearly, but had to rely on direction from elsewhere before it took one step. It was dying to go, to travel, to be somewhere else, to find, to be active. But the power to move was not in its possession.

Her parting smile, automatic and designed to shed herself of unnecessary company, put me in mind of a word. Millivolts, that was it.

I hurried back to the church full of her brazil-nut brown hair, which kept falling over her right eye, her veins, her flower-like voice, to catch their colours in yarn while they were fresh, and to rough out her cartoon, which when finished would be copied onto the warp strings.

With Adora's cartoon done, I began to lay down a pick of weft between alternate rows of warps. The chrome colour of the streetlight occupied me for a while, then slubs in the yarn distracted me before I got a move on. Even then I had to stop and get away from the loom. What was the matter with me?

I went outside and did my usual exercises for when I feel restless, a few bends and stretches; then faced the hills and breathed them into me until I had trees growing in me and white-faced cattle mooching in my fenced paddocks on bottom land, even a hawk on a fence.

I felt a little fresher, but not quite right. Then a feeling washed over me, of utter wretchedness. I worked as best I could till it was time for bed.

I had an alarming dream around dawn. Yarrow's voice asked, 'What's important?' I'd been obsessed by her all the more since she turned away from me, playing a tape of her voice, looking at bits of her handwriting, trying to recover fragments of her, but her questions always hit me amidships and I felt as intelligent as a dead wombat by the side of a country road.

When I didn't answer right away she came through the phone. My eyes felt like fingers. I found I could see through her skin to the organs beneath. She mounted a rostrum I hadn't noticed and carefully peeled the transparent flesh from the nakedness of her ribs and muscles. Why deny me the sight of her skin, and its delicate smell? She threw it, still flexible, into a corner while children's voices sang outside the window. Or were they crying? Her voice said, 'There'll be more than time for you to begin the strict labour of classifying and annotating your lifelong collection of mixed feelings.' A small patch of white skin remained round her navel. She hung her arm bones round my neck, her skinless eyes looked at me in a superior manner. Her voice had a laugh in it, like a display of fresh vegetables and coloured fruits as she said, 'We love in a different way now.'

The children's voices cried thinly in the distance, died away, and I woke, loathing myself. I felt completely discouraged. The zip had gone out of me, like a Dobermann with distemper. As I wrestled with breakfast I felt something inside me, a lump of aversion, a knot of misery-muscles turning me away from my work and from my new life with a strength greater than desire, turning me right back round in a circle to face what I did and felt when I was young.

I walked through the patch of grevilleas planted by the potter, an earlier owner of the disenchanted church. Something from the past was attacking me. This wasn't just a case of weaver's dread.

Whatever the name, I couldn't let it beat me. I returned to begin a new day at my loom, as to a friend who would keep me occupied, and wove till I could no longer see clearly. It was late at night. Even so, I threw myself on my bed as if I were in retreat and full of the shame of it.

six

howie gleet

Opposite the saleyards and not far from the council depot, the Shearers Arms in Corriedale Road was the pub furthest from the business end of Lost River. It was a two-storey corner building with a history dating back to 1889 and a clientele eager to continue its history; being the furthest pub from the town centre was part of its pride. The licensee, Agnes McRorty, recently painted the pub mission brown, and enlarged the Shearers Arms sign in white.

Howie Gleet drank there, his father at the Mountjoy. Howie hated hearing his father's talk of politicians going to earth in Canberra, pronouncing the words 'federal government' as 'feral gov'ment' and likening the country's self-styled leaders to an introduced pest with continuous jaw movements.

Howie never showed his dad any violence, so perhaps an Oedipus tag was inappropriate. An analyst hoping for a short burst of fame might perhaps have allotted him a Titan complex, for, like the Titans, he rebelled against his dad: he would not drink in the same pub, something that might indicate far deeper disturbances to suggestible professionals hungry for new theories to ride on.

Howie was born outwardly deformed, his neck twisted to the left; he had to turn his body to look to the right. His spine developed an extra bend, enough to push his ribcage out to the right. Sometimes, when he stood, he seemed to be still in a sitting position. He had little eyes, black as passionfruit pips, and ears like outriggers.

His father, short and surly and one-time Dutch oven champion, ate prodigiously, slept interminably and loved the dark. Other residents of Aztec Flats called him the Termite. A new breed of psychic analysts might hang a Thanatos syndrome on him. His employer had sent him fishing twenty years early. Howie called him Mister Gleet on his father's instructions. Gleet was also an unemployed spitter: he spat and was unemployed wherever he was, and his spitting habit earned the family a dishonourable discharge from Aztec Flats. Which is how the boy came to be brought up in the little old rented fibro cottage in Ypres Street, Elderslee, with the antique hydrangeas on both sides of a set of six damp front steps. The house was painted in heritage colours—Mum's idea, someone in the family with humour.

Mister Gleet had always been poor; it was easy, no effort at all. His comment on his son's deformity was 'Hard stools, son.' With his drinking mates in the darkest corner of the Mountjoy he lived in a past as distant as the Sturmer Pippin, and had only a sneer for the present and its people, and that included his children.

'Times are bad,' he would say, 'but there's still meat to be had while the poor live.' Bald as a side of bacon, he had two political ideas. One was that in spite of utopian conditions of work, government servants had never agitated or struck to help bring the rest of the workforce up to their level, miserable bastards. The other was unstated, a background to his life. It was that government was first a referee, then a refuge, then a weapon of the poor against the rich. Perhaps that was why so many Australians seemed to trust government and to want to give it more power.

Grandmother Sarah Gleet, who decades before had been on the battle, lived in the house too, and was regularly told she was useless by her termite son. In drink he would explain reasonably why she should die; and she closed the blinds every chance she got, to get used to the dark, perhaps. Her life had been one of slavish household work, drinking tea, digesting food in poor circumstances, and looking round tiredly for a chair. The prints were worn from her old fingertips.

'I look and remember,' she cackled. 'I'm no use? What use do you want? Want to eat me? Make soup? Do it after I'm dead, but bury the bones and give me a plaque so people will know I was here.'

'Tough old thing,' Howie's mother approved, cutting up Gran's meat into lozenges no bigger than Minties. She wouldn't wear those teeth.

Granny Gleet was transformed, full of life and movement, in her classic role as an elderly moll at her granddaughters' and grandsons' christenings; busy and fussing, clucking and smiling, among the stiff and slow older Gleets and their rigid and tongue-tied young. But only then. She expected all her life to die in sight of a larger world where good things were, which were not hers. Only to look at.

Like any other poor family, the Gleets wanted money, entertainment and consumer goods, though not enough to go after them with any great energy.

Sentimental people blather about mankind's solitude; Howie knew it at firsthand. He played with other kids sometimes, but mostly by himself, and always his apartness, his isolation, instructed him in how special he was. It also bolstered a certain toughness of mind, which, for someone different, was handy to have. He coped well with Doc, their dog, whose food had to be thrown, never given by hand, on account of its bad eyes.

If you can imagine a boy playing cricket in Ypres Street between the sporadic traffic, which has hardly increased to the present day, and all the time hugging to himself the knowledge that he was of a different tribe to the other kids, and a pretty special tribe, well, it was like that. He never got into the habit of hoping. Most things were an expected surprise. Like the time he found in an abandoned shed the resting skeleton of a cat, and visited the cat after school for conversations about the past, and to keep it up with what was going on in the world, like new cat food and stuff.

He came to glory in his difference and wouldn't be put down by anyone. Cheeky as a Jack Russell terrier intimidating a puzzled Rhodesian ridgeback, he stood up to the biggest boys knowing he could only be knocked down, and aware that the one who did it would wear the brand on his forehead to his dying day in Lost River. Cripple-kicker. Kick any cripples today? Not a catchy tune. Big brutal girls were a different matter. He kept out of their way, they had no traditions of restraint. No matter how big they were and how hopeless the fight, among the boys the joke would be on him.

In primary, Howie scared the other kids with stories of his birth. 'Born in a blacksmith's shed in Gulargambone. Couldn't get me out, so they put a chain round my neck and dragged with a tractor. The shed came too. The whole town pulled, that's how I got crooked. And this is how I scare people. I'm a monster!' He would rear up with arms spread and head to one side and kids would run, yelling. Some didn't run, but gave him a whack to see how he handled that. When he whacked back, they were satisfied he was okay.

Others went to the teacher to tell on him, and Howie learned how, under the guise of compulsory kindness and legally enforced good manners, even a joke in the playground was part of a wider culture, and that culture was repressive, with government power following citizens and children into the most private and innocuous corners of life. In the name of caring for us, authority would dictate matters of acceptable words, prohibit free expression of opinion for any number of respectable reasons, and lean heavily on people until they changed their patterns of living. And no one said a word.

Mr Moir impressed on his class that your future was something you had to make for yourself. Howie got the message. Everything was in his hands. He looked at Mr Gleet and at Mum, who accepted Gleet's ridicule in public as if it were a natural thing, and the message was reinforced: there was no help there. Was he adopted? Even Mum and Dad weren't of his tribe.

The teacher might have put his message into different words. He might have said, you are gods, you are buddhas. Imitate no one, neither Buddha, nor Christ. Follow your own road to wholeness, create a new world in yourself and around you. He didn't.

Howie's aim was to show a crooked person can be as good as a straight one. He would never have the education to do big things in the world. For one thing, he didn't have the ability. He could see that by looking at the other kids and their schoolwork. His world would be Lost River. He would make himself fit his world, he would make himself a success, and would do it by being necessary.

Just the same, he loved school, loved being singled out as a 'trier' and loved being special. He needed his differences from others, they were satisfying, they identified him. It was great to be described as being as persistent as a fire in a stack of tyres.

Then it was time to leave school. Okay, so he wasn't as bright as some, yet he could work as well as anyone and was tough and tenacious as the whaleback cockroach. He'd get a local job where people knew him. It was harder than he thought, he had to reach inside himself for more toughness.

After months of knockbacks he turned up at the newly opened plastics factory on the industrial estate, a twin to one at Newcastle. They produced injection mouldings, making kitchenware items and diversifying into automotive and engineering products. Some of the new plastics were so good they did the work of metals.

Howie asked Marv Mitchell in personnel for a list of job descriptions, and, finding one he thought he could do, went along to John Coy, the employment officer, and offered to do it for ten dollars less than the list wage, just to get a start. Desperate to make an impression, like an actor with one line to say, he went down bit by bit to fifty dollars less; it was still more than the dole.

John Coy, brother of the footballer Crasher Coy, was a big fan of his brother's style of taking the ball up the middle. He recognised a kindred spirit of his brother's, though packaged differently. He was so taken with Howie's persistence that he made up a job on the spot. Howie would be an extra pair of hands to assist anyone who needed something fetched, carried, watched, packed, unpacked, posted, called for, listed, labelled or put away.

'There's your job,' he pointed. 'Out there. Go for your life.'

Howie got a broom and swept the forecourt, noticing how the broom, scraping the concrete, pushed the bigger bits of dirt further, leaving little bits safe in the cracks. He was a little bit. He'd found his niche as a completely unknown industrial prisoner who welcomed his imprisonment, with its new status.

Howie's attitude and energy made him an ideal employee. He went round the works constantly to see if he was needed. He got so he knew where he'd be wanted before the credit manager, machine operator, purchasing officer, cost clerk, despatch manager, storeman, accountant or truckdriver knew. In eighteen months he knew more than any other person about the daily details of the place, and John Coy was congratulated by the general manager on his judgment.

He could work without supervision and loved being among people who did their work properly. He never felt accountable to other employees for his opinions or zeal. He'd begun paying off the old Ypres Street house after the landlady got rid of her rental properties and offered them for sale to the tenants. He was proud of being a ratepayer. Mum would always have a roof over her head; maybe not in the serene savannahs of the well-off, but at least in Ypres Street.

'Money is the most important thing for people,' he assured me. 'It means freedom. And the second thing is being cheerful. Gives you courage to get things started, and energy to get things done.'

I admired his spirit and his doggedness, also the fact that he was one of those ready to see that whatever grievances he had might be unjustified, and didn't mean that they gave him a claim on others.

'A few laughs never flattened me,' he said, referring to his shape. 'I regard myself as one of God's chosen people: I got born. In these lying times they give us names that gloss over our condition, people like me, but which draw more attention as others translate the new soft words into older, truer words like cripple and deformed. Why not say things straight out? Why keep changing the words, as if that makes it better? Or hides it? I don't need that. When I look out from inside my head I'm no different from the good-looking people of the world.'

He'd been elected secretary of the Model Plane Association, and even invited me along to their next flying day. His favourite band, The Was, a group of four desiccated young men, played music to him of how things used to be in a world they had discovered in newspaper files and magazine journalism, so that Howie daily lived in at least two worlds.

Apart from his resilience and steely persistence, there was more to Howie Gleet. Two secrets, one of which he told me. This was May Seventh, his special day: 'It was wonderful. I call it The Day. A kind of vision, a window on another world. I saw the air suddenly stop still, just like the glass top of Gubba Dam at dawn. Houses, trees, traffic, quiet as rocks. When I looked close I saw every stone, every pebble, every gibber had a face I knew from the town. I knew then I'd remember that day as long as I lived. The magpies stopped crooling and got all quiet in their nests, the swallows on the wires beginning to do their maintenance and smarten themselves up, they stood still. Cats asleep, dog with her head down. The trees with not a single leaf impatient and irritable. The sky with more and more blue crowding into it.

'The Day told me life was wonderful. And the tranquillity when liquid time ran down the trees, houses, light poles, the ridge to the east, the high hills of the Divide to the west, and settled and hardened into a protective coating that held the world still and silent as if it were all inside a crystal that would preserve it as long as I live, is all in me. The years tell me I'm twenty-nine but the vision I had that day hasn't aged. I see it now, I just look inside its crystal coating: my Day, my Eden, and it's alive in me like it's my soul. I can see it without looking, I feel it without touching. Look around, day or night, land and sea, sky and stars and life itself: how did it all get here? What is it? You don't know, neither do I, but it's alive in here.' He patted his chest.

The second secret was something his mother showed me as I sat waiting to see Howie again. He'd rung saying there was a rush to get an order away and he was busy as a Pialligo pocket platypus. In the lounge room, afternoon sunbeams swirled with little dusts.

His mother brought out a file box full of sports pictures showing moments of extreme effort. Sprinters, jumpers, marathon runners, wrestlers, pole vaulters, javelin throwers, footballers caught in the air, cricketers in mid-shot, Jersey Joe Walcott's face knocked sideways, a judo *uchimata* throw, the classic picture of the Sudanese wrestlers with the victor riding in triumph on the loser's shoulders, a racing driver spinning out a second before his death: every sport imaginable.

'He's kept these since he was a boy. They're part of what he is. Boxes and boxes of them. Don't tell him I showed you. I thought you should know.'

When Howie came back I asked him about the talk I'd heard that he didn't mind dobbing in his workmates, a behaviour that left him friendless as a referee. His answer was, roughly, that he believed the health of the company and the contribution that health made to Lost River was worth more than the passing embarrassment of a few sickie-takers and petty bloody thieves.

He didn't mind saying that the woman boxer, Fusby, threatened to pickle the Aprahamian woman for things she'd said, and spread her on bread. He was proud of the Gleet connection with Admiral's Hill. Old McDonald, the first settler, had exclaimed when he stood up there and surveyed the blue and rounded hilltops stretching into the distance, 'Like the waves of the sea! I feel like an admiral!' And a Gleet, one of the shepherds, heard him say it.

'All dead now. And why not? Death is second nature,' he said. Something about his eyes and the way he went about things put me in mind of a pair of fine and finicky tweezers made of stainless steel.

Whatever it was that was eating at me made me feel ill. Not disabled, but so off balance that I found myself doing strange things. I'd made a kind of refuge of Club Babel. The Whispers bar, actually. Maybe a combative weaver should guard against self-destructive behaviour. Everyone says so. Maybe some outside person or thing or force was acting through me. Maybe a lot of things. Anyway, what's a few head-butts? A bit of noise? A dance or two on a table or four? I didn't mean it with the chair, merely lifting it, no intention of throwing it. Australians are shy of unauthorised singing, they're easily embarrassed. People became reluctant to talk to me. I started to imagine they knew things about me that I didn't remember telling anyone. That money. The knife that night. The carpark mêlée. That kicking. The time an unlucky punch pushed the nose bones back into that guy's brain. So they said. I felt my past was like a soapstone sculpture nail-marked, scratched and hacked about by a series of hostile strangers' reckless actions. Strangers with my name.

The world and your past life don't come at you in any logical order that I can see. It's difficult to deal with such concerns when you're troubled with a kind of deadness inside, as if your own body, your own blood aren't real to you, aren't solid. As if your whole self means nothing and what you do has no significance.

I woke today still green about the gills, with the word Abontil in my mouth. In the dream I was leaving it meant wonderful, mind-expanding things, a key to many parts of the human universe. But as I realised I'd been asleep and was waking, the hefty, important meanings slid off the word like skin off a two-week corpse, till only the letters were left. I tried to grab after the disappearing wonders, which faded as they receded, and I was left with only the skeleton, the word, then seven unconnected letters like angular, clumsy beads. Worthless. The full moon grinned down like a lottery winner on a world of losers.

Howie was a cairn of stones such as you see on hill properties where favourite animals are buried. His cairn concealed things I could only guess at. There was something strange about Lost River, each person I met seemed split off from the rest. Bordered by a stockade of—what? Dislike? Self-regard? Or was it merely the way the town protected its privacy from an intruder?

How could a face contain all I saw in it? And to watch her walk, and wonder how weightless she seemed on the rigid ground. To follow where she walked and wonder if, out of sight, she disappeared into another world outside of and containing this one, corners and tracts of which can sometimes be glimpsed in this world.

When she had gone, her absence told me of all the things I would perhaps never do. The street from which she disappeared opened up and was no mystery at all, but only because she no longer dominated it.

I see her face when I wake. For a little comfort I get out the two photographs of her that I have, and search her face. My small tide of pleasure points, I think, to an ecstatic state that is vast and pervades a boundless place that is the natural home of wonders. My time of knowing her was a dream, it didn't last. My debt to those brief times runs on. I try to forget how long the days became when she was gone.

Did she feel I was weak because I wanted her more than she wanted anyone?

Last night I drank too much and woke in the minor hours. She was a baby, a rather large one, and I had her on my chest so I could feel her quick heartbeat.

'How's your metaphysics?' she asked. I told her that since the day I saw her go nothing has satisfied me. I wanted no assembly of elected common folk to rule me, no reckless republicans, just one flamboyant monarch: her. Fitted by a lifetime for the position.

I wonder if she ever thought she might contain tiny capsules in which waited beautiful children.

seven

the baby face gang

For days I felt cold on odd patches of my skin: the backs of my hands, a cheek and eyebrow, a chill up my right arm. It was my own special dog's disease. I did some warp mending.

The wretchedness hadn't left me. At the same time there was another me, one that stood alongside, watching but uninvolved, asking whether my struggles were due to a fault-line in me that reached back to my twin brother. Perhaps, with Jonathan born dead, I had never been properly born myself. Or had I done something to him in the darkness, and part of me remembered?

What was it from the past that had ambushed me?

The Khouris organised themselves into a group on their front verandah and talked only of their dead son, Mikey. They had short eyes, as the saying is: couldn't see higher than their kids. Not that such people are as rare as the spangled drongo is in Lost River, or the spotted clownbird.

Many things must be known already before we can learn anything new, Mr Khouri feared. He had the stance of the tremulous president bird. Someone who knows nothing can't be taught, so at what stage of their lives did Matthew Shugg, Mark Zilinska, Luke Perrier and little Mikey Khouri learn to be what they were and do what they did? There may be a hundred schools of psychology, but there are a million schools of behaviour, he said, so there's plenty of room for more theories and therapists. Not all the family scares, the reported crimes of children, the warnings to steer clear of the young and never get their breath, seem to stop humans from increasing the sum of global misery by making children, and there is no child so terrible, so evil, so foul, but someone can be found to be its mother. Deadly complications are born every minute: murderers, judges, terrorists, accountants, legislators, parents.

Shugg, leader of the gang, had been an angelic baby, with clear blue eyes and the gentle expression of a stereotype Jesus, though for all anyone knows the real baby Jesus was a ratty opportunist with little piggy eyes, a con-man's candid eyelashes, and a nose-picker extraordinaire. Another reality underlay Shugg's mild babyhood expression, a reality that showed later in an unsmiling deadpan face, a fixed glassy stare like a blue-eyed snake, as arresting as a richly snotty nose. Only other kids saw it; for adults he threw the switch to mildness as smoothly as any politician.

Mrs Shugg's dearest wish, her heart's desire, was to be left alone. For this reason she even gave in to her husband's promptings in the clothes she wore, though she felt they made her look like his mother. She put ginseng on her baby's boy-blue dummy and prayed for calm and quiet and not to be bothered. When Shugg was alienated from high chair, nappies and the clutches of elderly relatives, she warned him about everything she feared and reminded him that Mother's eyes were on him. He couldn't care less whose eyes were on him, he loved an audience and feared nothing. His father, Ron, was an Australian by immersion; he took to the water as soon as he arrived from Halifax, England, and never lost his lust for it. They had the biggest pool in the street.

A normal child, Shugg soon began to gobble his food aggressively and eliminate its waste joyously. Anal retention, if explained to his mother, would have been met with disbelief. He was as annoying as the sharp-edged ankle-dog or the python-jawed bedbug, depending where he was. Nothing moderated his tantrums; he did as he felt, he was self-contained. His neck was thick, his legs short: he could bend from the hips and touch the ground with the palms of his hands, feet together and legs straight. He thought all pigeons were called Isobel because the Shuggs' pet pigeon was, that darkness began at sea deep down, and that each day the sun disinfected the germy air of night.

Dirt loves boys, and lives in their neighbourhood. Before his gang was in existence Shugg played with other boys, all filthy dirty, grinning like dogs and running about continually. They tossed rubbish in abandon, others picked it up in bags. He developed a fascination with stones. Adults might imagine lumps of dolerite were for road base and art works, but boys were wedded to their primitive uses. Perhaps the first scientists to observe gravity's effects were boys with stones, old women with large shrivelled breasts, and old men with long slack scrotums, but none of these groups bothered to make a mouthful of their findings with equations, measurements and theories aiming to subdue the future.

In class, doing stories in paint, Shugg was asked why his figures always seemed to be cutting heads off and killing each other. 'Because I feel good. Real energetic,' he explained generously. In sixth grade he produced a writing effort called 'The Grandmaster', about a person who reached this elevation by walking with a sword along a line of twenty-four malefactors and cleanly severing each head with a single blow.

He was at the age when, if you see something first, it's yours. In common with most, he learned freedom but not restraint. Things talked back to him, so it was in order to thump them. He learned a lot about adults from watching *Ren and Stimpy*, an animated cartoon, ignoring domestic models as lacking punch and pungency.

Zilinska, Perrier and soft little Mikey gathered round Shugg, drawn by some attractant they recognised, as suited to each other as bums to seats, swearing to be always ready to rob their mothers or break up their families. They were The Culvert Gang, then The Slaughteryards Four. Shugg was the air they breathed. Males in company often try to outdo each other in craziness and daring. No one could outdo Shugg, so he was leader. Compared to him the others seemed weaker, half-hearted, less brave. Maybe civilisations grew from small groups, as a cell mass does, with no supervision, no outside organising, with its ability to grow and transform itself hidden inside it.

The gang loved End of the Universe, New Massacres, Cut and Kill, and the hundreds of video games that with star blips in red signalled the obliteration of objects, people, cities, without the blood, mangled limbs, hospitals; surgeons with saws and sharp knives, needle and thread and traction frames; without the police and court proceedings of real life. It was all easy, impersonal, with no rotting bodies. Zap! And that was it.

All four were from the town, and only occasionally said writ for wrote, drug for dragged, brung or brang for brought, driv or druv for drove. But all four knew exactly the spot on a thigh to cork it, on the upper arm to paralyse it, the back of the hand to make a kid yell out, under the nose to bring tears to the eyes, on the inner elbow to disable the funny-bone. Never mind the rabbit-killer, kidney punch, wind-snapper, ball-banger, the heel down the front of the shin or even the humble foot crunch. This cheerful native armoury was expanded by karate and its brothers, as well as kick-boxing, and the many subtle tricks hidden within the various traditional sports. And why not? The cells of their bodies were of unimaginable age and at home among those of other predators with no set mealtimes.

On a lesser level, Shugg kept a Mosquito Flats hippopotamus bug in a matchbox to make squeal those girls who would squeal.

It had been a spring of merry grass, a summer of silver showers and heavy growth, and by March 23 the browned-off pastures of autumn, and the dry native grasses, were ripe for drying westerlies. Umber cowcakes warmed in the sun, quiet sounds rippled through the thin heat haze. Bird sounds fell out of trees.

Out past Gubba Dam, Lost River's reservoir and fishing spot, weeping willows and basket willows along the creeks flicked their leaves in the hot westerly; magpies in stringybarks sang their liquid notes with passion. A few paddocks from where a farmer was baling hay, his tractor engine humming confidently, four children crouched in the landscape. Against the long line of dark pines shepherding the road to the farmhouse, sudden smoke rose in shapes never seen before, a king brown snake hurried majestically through the grass, called away urgently, numberless small insects hopped and scurried blindly from the place of smoke and flame. Four boys in cotton T-shirts ran for the road away from the fire and were on their bikes on the Western Road as the bushfire enveloped the little shallow valley and raced east up over the hills to get to the town.

Good-looking well-dressed people get better service anywhere, and baby-faced calm-eyed kids don't get questioned, though other kids suspect them. The four watched from Big Hill as the bypass stopped the fire.

Mr and Mrs Khouri didn't know, but it seemed the four loved

cruelty and violence, as if thinking and feeling were nothing and only being mattered; as if they lived outside a moral world, where actions had no significance but were just a source of satisfaction or sorrow. What was easiest was right. And it was all made easier because the adult world had lost confidence and courage and worshipped youth.

From getting their enemies in the Christmas hold, or dropping their pants to brown-eye impressionable women, they graduated to a little fringe Satanism, reciting the Lord's Prayer backwards so Satan would come, but he never did, so they gave that idea the big A. Shugg kept a tight hold on the three: they would aim at victims now. Just thinking about it at home gave them a warm glow; they had aims, ambitions, they were a team, they were solid. Shugg would tell them the names of the victims later. Their leader had the zest and energy of a meteor.

Who can explain them? Were they oppressed by the ozone hole? The greenhouse effect and the coming doom? Did land degradation weigh on their minds? The special needs of animals? Was it advertising? Television? Violent videos? High lead levels? Fear of female authority figures? Was attendance at school an intolerable burden? Was it violence against them, or some kind of abuse, to ask them to tidy their rooms or be home in time for tea? Had they already reached life's uncomfortable limits? The Khouris didn't know.

'We give religion, then morality, the shove, now there's no one to warn the young,' Mr Khouri puzzled helplessly. 'And I remember my wife proudly holding our boy up when he was a baby to see him pee. Look, he works, she said. I can see it now.'

At least they weren't nasty to their parents, like some. If the Oedipal metaphor was applicable universally, you'd expect millions more father-murders than there are, and a raft of mother-matings. Perhaps the metaphor applied only to its originator.

The gang practised tying the hangman's knot, hoping for the return of the death penalty, and weighed the benefits of rope, guillotine, needle, gas and firing squad: they saw themselves as the executioners and sniggered at nappies for the condemned. They were as charming as a full frontal of peanut butter being expressed from acne spouts.

Mr Khouri implied that Shugg was on the right track in his pursuit of liberty for himself. Government was continually gaining ground, its powers becoming as all-enveloping as in the days of the despots. These were dark times, he said. Enlightened people lectured us to love government more and laws were being churned out like sausages for things better left to decency, consideration, good manners and choice. Not that he condoned Shugg's ideas: no one has worked out a way of keeping society together without traditional ethical principles.

Whether you happen to be a splinter beetle making your way along an acacia branch, an Oodnadatta barking duck looking for water in Neale's Creek, or a cylindrical pipe-dog rolling joyously downhill, the same doom of all life falls, even on baby-faced boys of thirteen using their powers to the full, extending each day their freedom of action. If you are on the highway in a car you've hot-wired and your head is filled with arcade games, the oncoming cars in a section of two-way traffic tend to resemble blips on a screen, no more. In the arcade, the player survives every crash.

They hadn't reached acne stage. They would never shave or reach wrinkles. A month's road deaths in one hit. Six bodies suddenly relaxed and floppy as dead rabbits. The meteor burned out. The game stopped.

Police followed the dark grey carpet runner of bitumen where the north-east end of town tilted up into the surrounding hills, using the map found in Mikey Khouri's bedroom. The four garottes of nylon curtain cord were in plastic in a police station cupboard. On to a dirt road, out of sight of the town, then on foot among granite boulders on the ridge, looking for disturbed earth. Wind in casuarina patches chanted, 'Shush, shush,' but no one spoke anyway. Long stalks of rain made acute angles with trees that sought and sensed the vertical. Forked lightning, a map of rivers in the sky. When the public minders and tidiers found diggings, they too dug.

Black fungus on bone announced a find, bits of leg, a partly cooked thigh. A blackened campfire sat just above where the scree started below the hilltop. Hucklebones, knucklebones, guts with chopped white vermicelli working in the cavities, but no heads, hands or feet. The Lost River *Bugle* carried heavy headlines, serious articles, many letters explaining the world of childhood. It says something for humans that no matter how many tragedies, murders and massacres, they can be surprised at the next one. No satisfactory explanations for Shugg and his gang came to light, merely guesses expressed in the jargon of the day, and despite the fact that all four lived with families that seemed decent and orderly, the very opposite was implied in news reports and public prints.

The Anglican priest on Shugg insisted that no generation learns from the past, only experiences afresh. The Pyramid Church pastor over Zilinska, and Father Cavanagh over Perrier's remains were more hopeful. Soft little Mikey's family had no religious outlet yet in the town, and were spared words, but the family and its honour were sacred as the Caaba to them. They were profoundly ashamed.

Half a kilometre along the ridge from where the burned body parts were found, there is a low heap of rocks. In the centre, at the base of the pile, under some copies of the *Bugle* and in a plastic bag bearing the advertising of the drive-in bottle-o at the Royal, was a collection of scrotum bags, little shrivelled purses still with their contents. On a necklace of the curtain cord used for the garottes were threaded a matching number of little penises. The same number of families had received calls allegedly from missing offspring to say they were sick of home life and being told what to do and were clearing out to Sydney. Where it was easy to live for years undiscovered and unknown. Only Shugg and his boys knew where the rest of the victims was hidden.

'Why?' agonised the Khouris as I was leaving. 'He was a good boy at home. Was it bad company? What makes boys do things like that? How can bad things, crimes, be eliminated?'

It was no use asking me. It was a sunny day, a band of high pressure was over the continent controlling the weather, but where did the high pressure come from? I think looking for the roots of actions is like looking for the place where the weather starts on a spherical planet. Crime can't be eliminated, only constrained.

Mr Khouri stood there in tears on their front verandah, with his arm round his wife's shoulders. Mrs Khouri was dry-eyed. She remembered her little Mikey calling out in the street that she'd swallowed a watermelon seed when she was heavily pregnant with the third, just to look good to his mates. It wiped the smile from her face. For them he'd give up his own kind.

What could I say? Ours wasn't really a violent society. It was tame and orderly, docile and law-abiding. The decree to metricate was instantly obeyed; the failed entrepreneurs of the eighties, who ruined so many in the greed years, walked the streets unmurdered.

'Once I thought there was progress and the world getting better. Not now. We're headed for worse evil. Once I thought death was the consummate liar, now I think it may be the only truth. Goodbye. May your eyes open for many years yet.'

Mrs Khouri took him inside, prepared for the long wait for his old mind to come back, and shut the door as if sealing something inside the house.

Ron Shugg, silver hairs among the blond, worked at the Pig, as they called the bacon factory. I spoke to him the day Pickpocket won the Lost River Cup by a short half-head. Ron was a blocky, cheerful guy, his Halifax vowels not yet flattened by Lost River ones. Joyce and his daughter sat in the stand, eating and drinking from plastic, his remaining son Alec hanging round him like a lost soul.

'Run along, Acker,' Dad said kindly, when he saw I wanted to talk about his gang-leader son.

'Run along what?' the youth asked, and received a friendly clip over the left ear. He made his way reluctantly to the stand as if he knew he'd be one-out and unnecessary among the females of the family.

'Kids. Who can understand them?' Ron Shugg said. He drank well, but hadn't reached dropgut stage. Everything he said boiled down to that first helpless statement. Even the story of his dead son speculating that Mrs Fusby killed Amaza secretly by pushing her eyeball aside with a spoon and injecting brandy into her eyesocket so no one would see the puncture. Poor Mrs F was a blank page on which people scribbled their bad dreams.

I returned to what was wrestling inside me. Were they matters that ought to be vomited right out of me? A self-disgust powered by memory? Maybe there was a spring in me that had broken, or come loose at one end.

Yarrow, at this distance, seemed such a contrast, firm and self-reliant as a headland. Mind you, she'd take short cuts, moral ones, and was merciless to fools. How did I escape? Perhaps I didn't. Some of her words were hot to the touch, too hot to pick up. But compared to her, other times, other people, seemed like so much smoke.

My last sight of the Shuggs, seated in the bottle-green stand, eating continually, was of a family for whom getting over a death was now a way of life.

I sometimes buy two of everything and set out two glasses. Whether or not I'm still capable of love, I still have the feelings. I didn't know she was the home I was looking for until that moment I saw her.

She says the core is desire, but where are her desires? Wrapped in paperwork? Along with her paper theories?

eight
basildon bond

The cautious cattlebird avoids wet feet, and worse, by steering clear of emergent occasions. I made a temporary resolve not to put a foot wrong in Lost River, to give whatever was inside me a chance to settle down. At least for a day or two I was demure as a visiting supporter surrounded by a home crowd. I wasn't sick, yet unsettled was too mild a word. I woke a lot at night even after a good twelve hours' work. Several times I imagined something was with me as I slept. Part of a dream? The red dog woke once or twice with a bark, and since there seemed to be nothing to bark about, I put it down to a sudden waking from a disturbing dream. He didn't deny it.

Once the something seemed to be very close. Near my face. My right fist lashed out—it sometimes works independently—and connected. A crash, a tinkle, and I had decked the bedside lamp. What was I doing?

The action calmed me down. Then Yarrow's voice. Three-eighteen by the radio clock. With that voice could her parents have predicted her astringency?

'What's important?'

'Who's this?' I asked stupidly.

'You know very well who it is,' she said in a huff, and was gone. Was it love? But love's too big a word. She lives in my head, where I live, that's all I know. It seemed not to matter that she was often hasty, quick to condemn, and appeared to regret nothing. My mind had entered her so many times, had been killed in her, yet did it again and again. I went back to sleep, feeling there must be something I'd done, but didn't remember. In addition to all the things I hadn't done, but did remember.

I caught up with Bond at the Historic Engines display, part of the Steam Rally. He was in favour of both the new jail and the high-temperature incinerator, but guessed they'd both be defeated at the August vote. The council thought more of attracting tourists and would go for charm. Already Budawang Street was getting out the paint, the flats and facades above the shopfronts beginning to look decent. They called them heritage colours: paspalum-green, sorrel-brown, rust-yellow.

I hadn't expected gossip from Bond. Perhaps he was searching for something to say. He'd heard that an abandoned car in Forest Road had disappeared near Show time, reappeared after the event, and that Mrs Fusby had a winch. There was even a tale going around that once in an East Sydney brawl she had plucked someone's eyes out and played swingles with them. He had no taste for such stories. His manner was benign as a chimp's picking lice off Uncle Charley's back, but under that husky voice, low and controlled, I had the weird feeling that he was inwardly bellowing.

I couldn't bring myself to tackle him about personal gossip supplied by Morrie the Magsman. This was that, womanless, he was into Dunlop sex, with a pump-up anal plug, ejaculating type, the sort of thing some like because it feels good whatever their formal orientation. He was said to have received the special reinforced cardboard package containing a 'virtual vagina' with four powerful motors, as it says in the ads. He drove a late model car that put me in mind of a futuristic jogging shoe.

We got down to tapestry business.

Since he'd pieced himself together as a child, he'd always been diligent, delighting in work. Work was an obedience, he felt secure in its laws, though he worked better for himself than he would have for others. He loved the sound of engines, the kiss of chisel on stone, knock of hammer on nail, the music of saws, and later of lathes, the beauty of the finished product. His chief joy was to be busy as three people putting out a grass fire with wet bags.

'Some believe in God, money or the future. I believe in work and duty. To me, work is another kind of holiday. My business is my religion.' He was thirty-five then, and the young woman he spoke to drifted away. They all did. Bas was the death of any party. Marriage wasn't an option for a man serious about a career, the personal robs you of too much time, he was about to say. He had no clear idea he was talking to other humans with lives of their own.

As a boy in Euroa he helped carry tools from here to there to help Dad in the panel-beating business. Les Bond Crash Repairs, Spray Painting. It was from Dad he learned that government was too visible, always talking, always in your face. Said it could do everything, but couldn't.

Bas was inventive. Mum did the accounts and typed invoices, statements and purchase orders on a heavy Olympia typewriter, an utterly reliable machine. Bas invented a platform for it so Mum, when she wanted the machine out of the way to clear the desk for checking invoices against work dockets and delivery receipts or writing up the cash deposit book, simply pressed a lever to raise the machine on four small wheels, then released the lever when the machine was moved to its new position. He learned that his labour was not the source of value, his idea was. Labour was just a resource.

If you invent, and your employer, Les told him, has rights over your invention, you are a serf. Bas decided he'd let others be serfs, he wanted to count for something; he'd be an employer. From the time of that decision he had a floodlit picture in his head of his own engineering works: buildings, machines, offices, powerlines in, trucks moving out, parking for reps wanting to sell him what he wanted to buy, a gate-keeper checking loads, even the cyclone wire fence round the lot. He went away to school in Melbourne as one of Euroa's bright boys, did a science degree, and eventually started his own materials testing business in Lost River on the new industrial estate in Dalgety Park, doing contract work for oil companies and engineering and mining concerns.

He was reasonable with his staff, almost indulgent; big enough to understand that some he helped when at their lowest would avoid him later, sensible enough never just to throw staff—or labour—at a problem, hoping it would go away. He believed work should include an element of play, which enlivens the day. This could have been a commercial disadvantage for Bond Testing and Research, except that its services were in great demand. Usually no business can survive which doesn't use the most severe and stringent methods favoured at the time by the most successful enterprises, but this business was sound because it answered a need that continued to grow. Just as Mum showed him old safety pins which were sturdy affairs, and which she treasured for that reason, but each bracket of years brought a thinning of the wire used to make them, so manufacturers were constantly trying to make their products using less raw material, and accurate testing was their constant need. This need bothered him. His prices were proportional to need, so he felt the market was a kind of extortion racket. He tried not to think of it. His secretary helped: that individual constantly went on about how he found accountancy exciting.

The power corridors of his ears weren't open to malice and tale-bearing; he was usually as unflappable as the Coober Pedy spherical plant, which never loses it equilibrium. He could laugh at himself, with good reason, and didn't lost his temper with the supple policies of blundering government, even though its hunger for unlimited power made business a war. He always remembered how Dad told him of being a Labor supporter until the Whitlam years, when he discovered, or realised, that business was a citizen too, not just a foreign body, parasitical and malign, on the rest of the country, but a creator of wealth and a provider.

Bas had a simplicity of manner that often disconcerted clients as well as staff; it was like the simplicity of the great in days when such beings were to be encountered. Perhaps it had to do with his way of standing perfectly still while you spoke to him, motionless as the Stockinbingal staring lizard and with the same calculating intelligence gleaming in his shiny grey eyes. But for that sense of power and concentration he could have been an item of furniture. In fact, he was bumped once or twice by visitors who hadn't noticed him.

He was convinced his vocation was to produce wealth—he had proved it, after all—and that such a vocation was a sacred thing. It was a great responsibility, as he looked at his office workers and factory staff, to know they were all engaged on work thought out and made possible by him, and that families, children and futures depended on him keeping his head above water.

His work fascinated him. 'The world stands on the shoulders of the engineer and uses the tools of the technologist; its imagination is fed by the scientist.' It sounded like answers to a catechism, but was announced brightly, like someone admitting to having an unfashionable disease and hoping no one believed it. He was a hard man to be clear about. He wanted his workforce to be themselves, he said, to be independently minded, to value and develop their differences as individuals. 'Slaves follow orders, individuals cooperate. Your value to others lies in your difference from them.' It was his way of being an enlightened employer; it seemed simple enough to him. When he looked more closely at them he found two main groups: passengers and operators. Operators were risk-takers, those who wanted power and didn't care how they got it. They lived lives of effort and intrigue. Bond was the insurmountable pumpkin blocking their way to supremacy. How they must have hated him, he thought. At the other extreme were those for whom a life of strenuous effort was a forbidding prospect. They did little with their freedom, took no risks. They took life easy, appearing to want nothing more than day-long comfort. They were born employees rather than potential employers. The worst were the cheetahs and lynxes who spied work far off and ran like the wind. Passengers.

The moment the reality matched the picture he'd formed of his engineering works, a shadow began to darken it. He was forty-seven. It was as if something visited the various sections of the works and covered one thing at a time with a curtaining web of dark specks, which gradually coalesced into a heavy shadow.

Gradually he began to know what the shadow was. It was that knowledge leads to more knowledge, theory to more theory. New knowledge opens the door a little wider to an awareness of more ignorance. The process of which he was a part was circular, though not returning to the same place. A spiral. More ignorance, effort and knowledge forever spiralling on into the darkness of the future. There was no end, just as there was no end to collecting stamps. And once he thought happiness was to know. He couldn't explain why this constituted a shadow over his life; perhaps he needed to feel there was a reachable goal, a final purpose, but if so, the problem was in him. It was all endless, and empty. Information without meaning.

He worried that science and knowledge generally resulted in a stripping down of humanity to the bare animal and to social compulsions. Copernicus, Darwin, Pavlov all reduced humans, and this reduction empowered government.

'Knowledge has bound us, not freed us. It's a treadmill.' He seemed to be saying science was a traitor, a tool of government.

After fifty, he used to wake some mornings convinced he was married. Over his breakfast egg, always with a rather resigned yolk, a shop egg, he'd look round guiltily for a partner who wasn't there, who had never been there, but who even in absence was capable of disciplining him for unspecified male disorders, mental misconduct, and general uncouthness, such as smelling of codpieces, or the specific uncouthness of being male, but whose presence would have meant company, an end to aloneness, and someone to touch and sense, or even cling to, if it came to that. Being alone had produced its own trauma in him. Perhaps his psychology had been affected by his mum's attitude to a long list of horrible things he couldn't change in himself and his habits, and being male was possibly one of those; but his mother had been there for him and now no one was.

Nothing to look forward to. He began to feel old and past it, like Adam's Uncle Ron. He couldn't sell up and go live in the sun, he didn't have guts enough to live with the shame of being useless. He went round visiting ex-employees in difficult circumstances, people at whose farewells he had tried to knit together his notes into warm speeches. He knew it was prospecting for grief, but he took his sagging responses and did the visiting, where it was welcome, until the shadow covered that. By that time it was the subject of scribbled slurs on walls. More and more bits dropped out of his picture, like a computer screen going under to a virus. What thieving fingers had been in his brain? Had mind-hoppers got in and chewed away?

There was no love in his life, no children, not even a close friend to pass the business on to. He began to be resentful, then angry when he had to deal with official bodies that operate on the principle that society is a creation of government, rather than the other way round. He'd never been consciously angry before. He'd never had to push himself to work. Each day he drove to an empty site and performed mechanical actions in darkness. In one week of desperation he got rid of all his books and journals, repositories of such a lot of him. Gave them away, just like that. It was as close to suicide as he would come.

Fifty-two, when the eyebrows begin to grow and you crop them sharply or look like Menzies. My mind has become a stranger to me. Losing the first few dead leaves of memory. I feel like a tail-in-the-mouth fox, unmotivated and foolish. Next thing is to die. Death's in all of us; a seed, a ripening fruit. Go from a tub of live guts to a tub of dead ones. So many people on the planet now, no time to miss the dead, but who'd miss me?

Young, I worshipped Einstein, whose lab was paper and pencil. I believed in science. Perhaps our view of it is at fault. We look for big laws that obtain everywhere all the time, statements unrestrictedly general, trying to lasso the future. Maybe there are no such things. Grand unified theory? Dreadful moment if it comes: all have to lower their sights to details, to practical problems. I wish I could have made a clearing in the forest of ideas and erected some modest dwelling there, but I feel I've somehow burned a love of physical science into cinders of guilt and despair.

I was so full of hope at university. Everything seemed possible. Leibniz told me there were more explanations of observations possible than observations themselves; Cantor, that there were more classes of numbers than numbers. So there are more solutions than problems, more diseases then symptoms. The world of invention and theory was wide open. What happened? I found science is like art or poetry, there's so much imagination, inspiration and daring required, and I'm more like a mechanic, a drudge. I found I couldn't do more than one thing. I've done that. But the knowledge I have is no comfort, it's cold knowledge, no life in it. Not everything is worth knowing. Knowledge itself is endless, and futile because there is no end. Often it's worse than futile, since it can generate evil.

Sometimes I get an insistent feeling that there's something beyond truth, more important. I call it the Unknown, or the Beyond; it communicates with us by putting ideas in our heads. Stuff like justice, playing by the rules, the evils of cruelty and greed, that sort of thing. Words like sorry, and ought and do not.

Often people have something hidden in their lives which they try to locate and live in. I don't have it or feel it. I'm a sort of undersoul. Maybe our meaning, people like me, is in each other, like ants, so that each individual effort is an ineffectual gesture and only the whole effort counts. I've never been certain I was meant to exist. Not much of a note to go out on, is it?

He was an edge bordering an area of practical achievement and useful products. Beyond him was weedy wasteland where the future was forming. Some yearn for deeper meaning in their lives, but he hadn't thought yet of yearning. On his face was a look of conscious stupidity such as I've seen on the faces of fathers whose young daughters are teaching them to knit and they know they're never going to get the hang of it. I had it once myself.

Bond finished by squaring off in advance about the strike question I hadn't asked. 'It was an idea to give the unemployed a chance. Let them sit an exam and if they do well they could challenge a job-holder, who would have to do as well in the same exam.' This brilliant idea was an addendum to a shake-up talk he'd given in which he proclaimed that Australia still had a frontier, a West, and it was in every town. It was a task which Australians turned from too easily to the junior comfort of paddling in the shallow sea of play, but he admitted that trying to inculcate seriousness and duty in some Australians was like trying to develop moral fibre in cats that came from broken homes.

His idea reminded me of a truth-moment in which a woman said to me, 'You want the whole world to love you but you don't give a stuff for any of them.' Was this why Yarrow said I was egocentric. How do you stop being egocentric? Aren't we all?

I haven't always been a bastard. I mean I've done other things ... Though when you are a bastard you're constantly surprised how many love you for that reason. Since I was a child I've wondered at those who talked of meaning in human life. Being started by and born to others, without my knowledge or permission, seemed to be a guarantee the whole business wasn't entirely serious, and certainly not symmetrical. Once born, why should I, apart from the needs of survival, feel obligation to anyone or anything? What if I didn't like this world? What if I didn't like the rules, thought the rewards absurd, the people fools? What if there was nothing I wanted to do? What if I lived my life thinking, Stuff the world? I know plenty who do. On the other hand, even with no meaning to life, there was no reason to be miserable.

Late that night, work finished for the day, my head seemed very light, held in my hands. It's a funny thing to think you were once a big part of another person's life, as I was of my mother's. What did I know of what was important? I wish I'd been a big part of Yarrow's life. Which was impossible; she wanted me to be not too close. What kind of damned social evolution was it when females demanded apartness?

I'd been a big disappointment to my mother in her last years. When she breathed out for the last time in that nursing home a dryness came into my world. What does it mean to love your mother? I've never known. A mother's a mother, a door who opens and lets you in from a long past you have no idea of.

A nurse, dressed in patient blue, came in to check she was gone. I felt my face separating out into components, like a dashboard. Gone. To a place where every structure crumbles, deconstructs and subsides. Or so they say. We need more metaphysics, Yarrow said. I say deny no gods, admit them all.

nine

dando rocavera

He appeared suddenly at the Country Weekend. You know the sort of thing: shearing, spinning, a bush dance, local food, a parade and country music everywhere. He was watching the woodchop, half of the axemen locals, the rest from the south coast, and a big Tasmanian. He wasn't forthcoming, obviously hating questions. He mentioned an old teacher, his family, people he knew. He didn't mind being in the tapestry but was content to let others tell the story.

From others I heard how, as a boy of seven, he saw a vision in the flames of their wood fire one winter's night. He saw a person not human who said, Follow the flame. Whatever that meant. Another said he saw someone who kissed him and said, Wait for me. A guy called Radionoff, who drove a concrete truck for Kimberly Konkrete, said he was clever at school. A teacher found him reading a book of blank pages; he pointed to the invisible words of the story he was reading.

Dando was a quiet, withheld man, in whose bearing there

was such strength and repose that, facing him, I felt silly and excited as the Delungra running duck. I went to see his mother.

He was born fearless, impregnable, apart. However upset or hurt there was no cry, no appeal for help or mercy. He never had a nightmare, never a wet dream at puberty. As a child he noticed that their dog could speak without words, without making a sound. His family wondered where he came from, there was no one like him in the Rocaveras or Mitchells as far back as anyone could remember. He was born just on sunrise at the beginning of winter, one of those calm tableland days that seem to be all afternoon, in the year of the volcanic eruption near the equator that yielded such marvellous sunsets and killed large numbers of people.

Marie Rocavera said he was a wonderful child from the moment he was born; a sweet baby, such a sunny, calm disposition, who never once cried. This last phrase was loaded with what, to me, seemed like regret, as if she'd like to have comforted the child in distress or calmed him in a roaring rage, and her motherly desires had not been given scope. He was never in a rage, never frightened of the dark. He said he knew the grass would be green again when night had lifted. He wasn't bad-tempered, always good-natured from the time he cleaned his tongue in the morning and put his spoon away in its special rack.

'He listened to everything, watched all that went on,' she attested. 'He said once, "Why don't people fly apart?", when he heard his uncle in a bad temper. And at sixteen his young brother Leon asked what was a good thing to be, and he said to try to go beyond yourself, choose the most difficult thing and you wouldn't be wasting your life, and people who knew you would say, 'That's a hell of a man.'

Darnelle, his older sister, once bought her mother for Christmas a little book, *How to Break Even With a Dominant*

Child, but Mum wasn't sufficiently amused. She thought he had a picture in him of the person he wanted to be, that in him was something he revered. She felt he held himself in, always trying to build up the part of himself that he valued.

People handy with theories tell us the brain generates its own model of the world through experiencing the senses that serve it; it's unlikely to fit comfortably into a preformed image of the world laid down by someone else, whether parent or government. Dando's world apparently formed early.

He first came to local notice in primary school. He would fight anyone. In grade four he could subdue kids in all six grades. Even Zorella, two years older, wouldn't take him on. The other kids loved him, he was never vicious or cowardly and so brave that he was game as Ned Kelly and had a heart like Phar Lap's. Phar Lap's heart, on display, is actually the heart of a draughthorse: truth comes second to myth.

In year seven at Lost River High, a new English teacher, who didn't understand Dando's effect on his peers, was having trouble with a usually beautifully behaved class: kids up the walls, standing on desks, fighting, throwing things from windows, destroying the books and pens of less violent kids. The hullabaloo was frightening. The new teacher behaved like an aggravated magpie: noisy, fierce, threatening, but finally ineffectual. The class took no notice. Then Dando was at the door, he'd been to the dentist. Cool as a gun barrel, he whistled sharply and walked to his desk. The room was still before he got there. The silence had that busy echo of suddenly extinguished hullabaloo. The other teachers told him to be grateful he'd won the jackpot. They'd fought over Dando, every classroom he was in was quiet. It got so bad that when the new term timetable was worked out, Dando was given to the new teacher to avoid favouritism.

On playground duty, and lunchless, the teacher took a child aside and asked why they behaved when Dando was there.

'He'll crunjle you,' was the answer.

'How do you spell it?' as if it mattered.

'Crunjle or crungell. Sort of crush, crunch and mangle. If you muck up. He can fight anyone.'

Yet outside school he didn't pursue the surreal, in the form of the usual delinquency of destruction and rearrangement of physical objects in public. He was authoritative, and much admired. He did things, actually took the jump. He was violent where others hesitated to be rude. Where they were passive he had faith in himself. The admiration of the other boys ran off him like water off a duck's back.

The English teacher of the day of pandemonium—excellent word—taught in Lost River for ten years, took a promotion out west for twenty, then came back as deputy principal six years back. He remembered Dando well, had followed his career.

'He seemed to be a person who didn't suffer. At harmony in himself. Never seemed to feel disappointment, never puzzled. He either knew what to do or would know and wasn't fussed by present ignorance. In a way he accepted everyone and detested nothing. Except disorder. He loved order. We discussed evil one day and he said, "Any evil people do is caused by no one else than themselves, they choose and decide to do bad things knowing they're bad." As if our theories of environmental effect didn't exist.

'He was cavalier in his attitude to science. It had all been wrong in the past, he said, and honours, position and reputation had been picked up for their lifetimes by people and theories you'd laugh at today. And when we spoke of punishment and its link to revenge he said some bad deeds call for more than tears and forgiveness, like when you owe money, you pay back money, or another country attacks you with guns, you attack them, just call it defence.

'There was a fight after school, Dando and a year twelve boy from another town. The fight stopped when the stranger deliberately picked his nose and wiped it on Dando's school shirt. Dando walked away; he wouldn't fight angry. A fight deserves respect; with anger there's no respect, he said.

'Some proficiency is necessary to recognise the virtuoso, and most of us could see he was marvellous at football, but he refused to play team games regularly, only when he felt like it. I saw him skim in on the ball once, like a Candelo drinking hawk, picking it up one-handed. One touch and he was gone. He had no taste for the applause. When the crowd clapped he stared and turned away. Didn't need it.

'When he was seventeen I had the good fortune to persuade him to put in an essay to a competition sponsored by Meesner Construction, in the new industrial park. The title: "What I Believe". He didn't bother with the essay form, preferring to list his beliefs and leave it at that. It was a feather in my cap to get him to do anything. In those days, before the reforms, kids couldn't be expelled for anything short of very bad behaviour, and provided he was left alone his behaviour was excellent. This is his essay. I made copies.'

What I Believe

The world is full of death, killing and disease, and that's natural as sunrise. We have a short time, we're free to cram it with living or veg out and let it pass like a dream.

Wars and murders skim off surplus population. Peace is the lull between fights. There's more to life than love and kindness.

People aren't worth much, they're rotten and corrupt and like children. Lots are born fragile, born to be small, born to suffer. Each is a potential enemy to the rest, whether in war or competition. I do my thing, others are free to do their thing. If they get in my way I go over the top of them, but if they do the right thing I won't hurt them.

No one's got the right to feel safe or have a quiet life.

People see things differently, so they can't ever agree unless some outside force makes them.

People need a chain of authority bottom to top, and obedience, with suffering if they don't keep the rules, then they'll be happy. A few unpleasant actions early often averts worse things later.

Some people are smart at school. I'm smart in myself.

I never surrender to the power of the majority. The free and the fearless have no place on committees or where there's voting.

It's fairer for everyone to start in a line and finish the race according to speed, rather than handicap the best.

People strong enough are tempted to take everything, temptation is harder on them.

Anyone can do anything as long as they can handle the fuss that comes later. Laws operate afterwards. Nothing can stop them, only incompetence, lack of means, lack of ability, someone else exercising a similar right, or fear.

Jesus Christ was right in one thing: enter life at the narrow gate. The wide gate leads to misery and waste. Narrow and austere, and getting on top of yourself—ignoring yourself—is the way to life and success.

JC's other secret was becoming a little kid again: do what occurs to the you in you, it's a different brand of selfishness. The world owes me a living. When school's over I'm off to collect. And that's it.

'In class discussions he once said, after talking about Hitler, Stalin and Mao, that the next great lunatic dictator may be a woman. He said Orwell was wrong: Big Sister is the danger, she has an implacable urge to increase her power from considerable to total. I asked him about this later, and he opened up about his family: "Dad's gentle, he sits back. Mum's the powerhouse in our family, she gets the ideas that shake the house. Most of the ideas are crap ideas, but no one has the energy to oppose her. She loves planning, but has no idea of unintended consequences. She's the centre, all power radiates from her. My dad's Dagwood and Homer Simpson, he pulls the levers of power and talks in a loud voice, but the levers are disconnected, it's all electronic now and Mum has the remote control.

"'I take my family as a warning of the coming womanisation of the world. Females are already in effective control of males. They stand back, blank-faced and eternally unhappy, but in silent command, while mannikins and puppets called men perform silly actions to please and impress them. With them in control I see the most terrible wars the world has ever seen. Why? Because a woman's world is out of whack. Gentleness and tenderness bring on their opposite. What people are, underneath, will surface with all the more violence for its temporary subjugation under the suffocating blanket of niceness, kindness and forgiveness for everything, no matter how frightful, in our female voters' world of no failures, no pain, and where it's no disgrace not to be courageous. Men have a warrior component. Gentling and womanisation is counter to our survival in the coming warrior societies. The animal savagery and evil in us is our defence in dangerous times. Women are a trap. Under the shape and the cosmetics they are matriarchs waiting to subjugate. Men must learn never to look into their blank eyes. That look stiffens the sword, but turns it to stone. Overthrow the mother, I say."

'So what do you say to that?' asked the English teacher.

'Only phew!' I replied.

'In class when I quoted Mill, he pricked up his ears. He was hungry for ideas. Mill said: "The first liberty is when limits are set to the power of government, and the second is freedom from the tyranny of the majority." He loved that. People immobilise you, tie you to their minds, he said. The individual is king, cooperate only if it's necessary.

'When one of the girls said you ought to be clear why you do things, he replied that if you stopped doing all the things for which you didn't know the reason or that you didn't control, you'd be dead in minutes. We had a good discussion that day. I even got in my favourite point about walking along a busy street and not being able to count the traditions that are being observed while you do it, there are so many.

'He left to work with MacMurdo, the current Mister Big. He has that big house on the hill in Durras Circuit. Never made it to control after all, which has its pathos.

'Where did he come from? Was he a bunyip god rising from the unruffled billabong called Lost River? Are there others like him? What if they got together? He seems not to need other people. His human relations seem to be his paymaster, associates, victims. And his family, of which he is intensely protective. No friends, no woman, not the Greek alternative, no companion. What sort of man is that?'

Some of Dando's old teacher's speculations were blown out of the water a few weeks later, for Dando had married and now lives in his mansion surrounded by fruit trees and early spring flowers in full and vivid bloom. He commutes to Sydney for business affairs when necessary. He and Siri are expecting their first child. He has a house on the coast, apartments in Sydney and the Gold Coast, owns motels and refuses to add much to his old teacher's reminiscences, apart from a gloss on the subject of revenge and an about-turn.

'If I said it now it would be like this. Insults penetrate; even when avenged the barbs may never come out. And a revision. Rescue the mother. She leads us downward and makes us fight her, but we must be brought down in order to go forward, and fighting her makes us strong. Upward leads to separation from the real world.'

He refused to be drawn on the subject of that gorilla, Zorella, who also worked, at a lower level, for MacMurdo. Nor would he talk about individuals. He did say death was the manufactory of human history, but I didn't understand and had no time to ask.

I had difficulty with both the colour and the design of Dando's pathos in rising only to second in command in his chosen profession, and in his back-down on the subject of women. From my experience I'd say he lacked one gift: that of constantly, perhaps mindlessly, craving more. He got to a point where he had sufficient power and money to quieten his conscience, and began to want human warmth.

A kind of failure, I suppose. Or had he experienced for the first time something mysterious, like love, rising in himself, which in some way gave him a flash of insight into the immense seriousness of the reality that lies behind the appearances of the world?

He is co-operating on a book project with a writer researching desire and criminality.

I felt again the unease, the dismay that attacked me weeks before. A constant feeling of being out of order and miserable. What could make me unhappy? Certainly not the ordinary ups and downs, the routine disappointments. Some kind of darkness inside? Some emotions that needed to see the light of action? I'm not the right person to feel revulsion at myself. I felt like an intruder in the world.

At two in the morning I woke with a childhood smell of lead pencils in my nose, and had a picture of myself leaving for school in Bellbird Corner, a kiss for my mother, schoolbag over my shoulder. I felt her eyes on me to the corner. Once I doubled back, and there she was, still looking at the place where I'd disappeared. Such love. You were never in any doubt about your mother in our family.

Why did I sometimes feel I didn't fit the world? That I was a polluted environment? In Lost River I'd begun to feel uneasy talking to people, as if I owed money, or had done them a bad turn. In the street I barked at several dogs, but they pointedly ignored me.

I'd filled my time with work stretching into the distance so that I'd made myself incapable of doing nothing. Many times I'd felt the impossibility of being by myself, and looked for company, but then behaved so badly, got so disgusted with myself, that I tried to squeeze this slavish need out of my tissues. It didn't work.

Thread your heddles, weaver! As I worked on Dando I saw myself making a weaver's poem, verses that contained the accidents that happen, like duplicating warp ends or finding I'd given them uneven tension. Or broken a warp end. Or beaten down the weft unevenly and got streaks in it. Selvedge problems. How about counting the picks per centimetre and applying the figure to a different yarn? I've done that. A poem of frustration and mistakes. Colours? Jaundice yellow, uneasy grey, sick verdigris. Should suit me. Heddle-horrors.

Dando was a new algebra, with strange symbols, different rules. The rules were in long skinny lists like the program for an extra-terrestrial computer with eyes on stalks.

Another restless night, another dream. I met Yarrow in a narrow polished metal lane with straight polished sides above our heads. We walked together a long way side by side, the lane constantly veering to the right. I wanted to take her hand, but a shyness—me?—prevented me. She wore brown brogues. I tried not to look at her face, she hated the way I waited on each word she said, and the absurd devotion I felt for her. We heard an explosion, volcanolike, up ahead. Both ducked as something large passed overhead with a rush of warmth that wasn't unwelcome.

It was late when we came to the end of the lane. We climbed down from the rifling into the breech and made our way to where she had left her bicycle. It was getting dark. I worried she might be in some danger without a rear light.

She believed in endings. I didn't. Nothing was dissolved. Because of the way I was made, she was dominant, whether she wished it or not.

ten

doctor kidd & miss dodwell

Hovering like a brown hawk that had spotted a native mouse, Bill Kidd came, the Sunday of Country Weekend, from the tent of the Church of Prophecy, a portable bastion shaped like a bible in shiny black and blood-red. Zachary Gumes, one of his flock, a man who drifted from church to church, stayed by the local food tent after he'd said his twenty cents' worth; he worked at the Pig, on the slaughter line, as Bill Kidd had done years before. Bill left when the screaming got to him, Zach didn't mind.

As a come-on, an old sulky rested outside the prophecy tent. Elegantly shaped, still in good condition and a genuine work of art, it had enough of the original scrolled enamel left to make it worth gazing at. Everyone who came by stopped to reflect on the past, watched by Bill, who wanted them closer. He was lively and decisive and talked quickly, just like a good half-back to his pack of forwards. A constantly busy, opportunist kind of guy. Jane stood back a little, like a backstop.

Make that a full-back, ready to defend. A PA system sprayed 'Glittering Billionaires' over everyone, the new single from Filthy Child. I could see he'd rather be spruiking to the passersby than watching, hoping to plant the seed in those minds, few now, where Christ's blood can be made to run forever. He controlled the urge, like a hawk suspended, working hard to stay still.

'Plenty of cash around?' I observed, indicating the comfortable crowds.

'We're ripe fruit ready for the tax bird to peck us at its will,' he declaimed. He thought I meant him.

Just to be holding the floor he told me he'd heard poor Leanne Fusby often broke out in blisters, with pus. She knew where the loot was from a bank robbery that got little publicity. He shrugged it off as the kind of mall-talk you hear, but wasn't too proud to repeat it. And the one about Amaza's file being missing from her doctor's office after an intruder's visit. He added that death was a kind of truth.

'So you want to know how I got into this racket?' he said when he'd warmed up. He seemed a paste-up, a self-assembly of a man.

It began when Bill's girlfriend died and met her own truth. She'd made the driving error she often made: dropped a leaden foot on the exhilarator and drove too fast. The Mitsubishi went into a skid that took her into the path of an interstate truck on a two-way section of highway. A little more room and she'd be alive, the truckdriver said.

Bill was thinking that day of those eyes that shone like melting bitumen, with a vague haze over the pupils so that the black nudged indigo. Rather like Darl's, his dog. Thinking made him absent-minded, evidently, and he ducked into the Royal for a quick drip. For Bill, this action was as problematic as driving into a carpark centimetres deep in broken glass. It was eleven in the morning, he wasn't expecting Forrester and his boys to be having a few glass canoes. They were enemies of his lot who drank at the Commercial in Cooma Street. Cornered in the toilet, he managed to swallow the toad of fear in his trachea. Expecting to be left in a heap on the tiles he began to talk quickly and earnestly to Forrester, sincerely lying, whatever it took, like a desperate politician. He was going fifty to the dozen thinking he'd be interrupted any moment by resilient obscenities, then fist, boot or iron bar; instead, after five minutes he was selling Forrester a used car. His own V8 wagon. He made a few hundred on the deal and Forrester invited him round any time for a drink, thinking he might have a future use for Bill Kidd.

Bill was outside on Coronation Parade and round the corner into Ladysmith Street before he realised he still needed that drip. Radio 2LR was opposite, so he went in their ground floor toilets. As his prostate released the flow he thought: My future's in talking. What'll I do? Sell garlic Australorps?

He passed St Matthew's in Market Street opposite Anzac Park. The signboard preached: I am the Way, the Truth and the Life. Jesus. Why not? It's my lucky day. It was meant to be. Start my own church. Got to be room for one more. He'd seen Jane Dodwell, barmaid at the Commercial, reading books in her lunchtime. She'd have the only book in the bar except the Breakages book. Jane was the best barmaid in Lost River, though barmaids were few enough now that men had butted in to a job where drinkers preferred a woman. She never forgot an order or made a mistake in the change, always on the ball, ready with a smart reply or a putdown for those who earned it. She could handle drinkers in the pub, she could handle anyone. Jane was saving up to become a road pantry operator.

'You show me a church and a full house and I'll consider it,' she said. If there was money in God, it would help her save more.

Bill got himself a bible and books from the library and spent months reading. Up to then he'd worked for Lost River Ford selling cars, then for Borderline Case, the driveway and garden edging firm. And, fresh from school, at the Pig. It was a new world. He set himself to learn all he could about the God business, mainly from America, since that was where religion was a business and business a religion. He wanted his prospective sheep to get a benefit they'd be happy to pay for.

What sort of people would he attract? He could start with the people who hug to themselves the idea that they're here for some reason. Would they want to agonise over the souls of the plants and animals daily sacrificed to feed them? Over crimes against the soil? People were increasingly afraid of death, so death was a goer. Would they want sympathy? Flexible pardons? Power of some sort? Interest and support? The questions came and went like Urinalla shed swallows, which are notoriously unsettled and nervy. He saw a letter in the local rag, the *Bugle*, about the future of Christianity. Future. That was it. People were suckers for the future. Church of Prophecy. A natural.

He read a prophetic miscellany, and having saved enough to give enterprise a go, gave in his notice to Borderline Case. He began to practise speaking in front of a mirror to get his face right, and the gestures and body language. He read Billy Sunday's *Ninety-nine Short Cuts to Hell* for the fury of it. He applied, paid, did the course and in short order was Doctor Kidd. He framed his Doctor of Divinity diploma; it gave him weight, he felt, like other professionals, such as the vet or the accountant.

The first Church of Prophecy was a warehouse previously used by a distributor of confectionery to clubs and shops. There was seating for two hundred and a strong smell of liquorice near the door and of aniseed at the back where he put the platform, lectern and microphone. He and Jane door-knocked together, to look like a couple.

On the first night he was confident, confidential, persuasive, and landed two converts. Later, they appeared unsure why they'd come out to sit at the prayer table, but Jane was there to take their names, which bucked them up, and to offer a small prayer, though to whom she wasn't at all sure. Later she counted the collection and noted the figures in a notebook purchased at Mitchell's newsagency and having the virtue of a black shiny cover and red-edged pages, so it could be left with her bible and hymn-book in a kind of spiritual–financial alliance.

Jane thought the congregation had been helped by Bill's talking, which was based on 'Come to me, all who work,' and since most people feel they do work despite evidence to the contrary, they felt included. She felt Bill made them feel good about themselves without them having to prove anything; he gave them confidence and a chance to unburden themselves they got nowhere else. The TV didn't answer when they spoke to it, or swore at it; talkback radio rubbished them. For them, religion wasn't founded on the wonder of existence, but on daily need.

After they'd gone she didn't join in with his crass revenue-oriented comments on his brand-new flock and the obvious relation, to his mind, between those who, in his car-selling incarnation, had worshipped cars whose past they didn't know, and those prepared to worship a god they couldn't even see and whose past, and present, whereabouts were unknown.

His message stressed that freedom was the inner core of each person and painted attractive pictures of how best to use that freedom. Many search for inner peace and happiness by adjusting to those round them and to themselves, but a far deeper adjustment was needed: to be in tune with the spirit that vibrates through the universe. Out of tune in the centre of yourself, and there can't be peace where you touch the world. The intoxication God brings takes you from a so-so life to a brilliant success of a life, whether you're rich or poor. Jane thought he was on to something, and in those moments almost forgot the way he spoke to her in public in front of strangers. She hadn't yet tackled him about it.

By the time there were eighty in the tainted warehouse and she had closely monitored the faces of them all as their ears dogged his words, she had begun to think of Bill Kidd as altogether more important, and gifted, than he himself knew, and he had little modesty. Even his bounding confidence and ebullience were a help to those with little or none of those commodities. Several requested a house-visiting and she went, to be what help she could, but alone, not trusting Bill's effect on them close up. She thought the distance of the platform gave him something he didn't possess face to face.

So Jane was a partner, making the switch from spirituous to spiritual as deftly as a mermaid ant takes to water. They began to travel the country when they had elders and carers to look after the locals. He was inclined to be uneasy and suspicious on the same principle that thieves, lurkmen and gangsters have the most locks and alarms on their doors, and didn't want helpers that were too smart, but she persuaded him that the helpers' intelligence wasn't dangerous as long as he played squarely with them and kept them faithful by giving them his confidence. It worked, so he began to trust her too.

Jane was halfway a believer. The sacredness of human life. Calvary. Her childhood had been without any of the doctrines Bill handled so glibly and she had a hunger to hear them. One life can inspire others. The worth of each human being. To lift you to your full potential. The words said themselves in her head, they had a kind of life.

They moved to a disused church south of town, fixed it up, painted it pale and lemony colours: Jane loved primrose and Snowy River wattle. Bill's restless mind came up with all sorts of ideas, most of them impractical. It was enough, Jane felt, that he had been able to put a degree of happiness into people who had very little of anything except the social delights of the Eureka Mall and the vacant and repetitive television which, like the salt in the beer she used to pull, increased thirst but never satisfied it.

On the road during a campaign, he would begin quietly after the first songs, the equivalent of birdsong before a storm, his voice low, kind, confidential. Then more vigorous winds would blow, a minor thunder, then a lull and more confidential talk, like a real conversation. Several brief storms of feeling, each successive squall more powerful than the last, and another lull. Next, a muted start, restlessness, a minor storm, subsiding, then mounting again, higher this time, fireworks, darker colours, lightning flashing, threats, punishments, pain and misery, the displeasure of a loving and inoffensive God; till a sudden turn from thunder and vibrations brings back forgiveness, joy, love.

A sacred sweat runs down his face and shows in damp spots on his shirt. It's all entreaty now. The audience is urged to benefit, to accept God's republic within them. They come, they confess, they pray, they cry. Faces swell, tongues inflated with sorrow fill mouths, handkerchiefs are out. Helpers help, names are taken, promises made, the night extends.

Not all are wrung out. Doctor Kidd and Miss Dodwell hurry to their motel, tear off their clothes and make furious love, both possessed by the power of the words and their own power over the simpler souls whose lives they have affected to a greater or lesser extent, for a greater or lesser period of time.

Waking in the night she feels the motel air like fine nylon sliding over her skin, with that touch of harshness nylon has. Jane thinks, I don't really know him. Always so busy rushing. Does he believe it all, or is it for the living it gives us? It's time to know who I'm with. There he is, not snoring yet, his face blank, but not innocent, even asleep. His shoulder smells of motel soap. He still had that way of putting her down in public. Didn't dare do it in private. Wonder where they get it from? Probably have to be aggressive to survive among other males. Makes it easy to distance myself from him.

I suppose life wouldn't be much different with that new preacher of the Church of the Kingdom, Marbuck Jones. To Bill he's as welcome as sand in the salad. Bunyip from the hinterland, Bill calls him. He's a good talker too. Funny how I like to sit and listen to men's words flowing over me, so different from the way women talk. Grass is greener in the distance. He's got good shoulders, though, I love good shoulders on a man. But men are funny, they don't realise how much time a woman needs to herself. Men are too strong, they swamp you. All that energy.

I'm sure he doesn't believe what he says to the people and in a way I think that's why he's so convincing. Uses all the right words, believes nothing. Good actor. One thing he does believe. He said, 'Any rough diamond at the cricket yelling his head off for the Aussies is a better man than all the politicians, urgers and knowalls in the world.' The way he said it. In that tone of voice I'd have believed anything he said, even if he was selling transgenic pepper-flavoured beef. Splinters of Bill stick in me and come out in words I say. Wonder if Marbuck Jones makes a funny noise when he comes, like Bill, who sounds like the Swialligo hooting swallow.

Do I believe? I thought so at first, in the aniseed and liquorice days. To see people being persuaded before my eyes, and changed. Believed halfway, perhaps. Now, I don't know. What does it mean to believe? How can you believe unless you check, and then it's not belief, you know. Just the same, those folks with shining faces and new confidence have something we haven't, though we gave it to them. What they haven't got is the money. We're making a fortune. I think I'll stay with the cash. Shoulders are only shoulders. Any old road has shoulders. Looks like the road pantry can wait.

Bill wakes in the starlit hours and shivers sometimes to think how it might have been with Forrester, and the fragile chain of decisions leading to being a preacher. Shit, I'm lucky, he says and goes back to sleep. Unaware that he might be said to have attained a kind of salvation by his life of pointing others towards it.

I wanted to think of colours for Jane and Bill's flock, for their fibro-cement faith, their shiny new plastic hope. It was easy to kid myself I ought to be among people rather than alone in a church that echoed only me and my doings. The John Curtin bar at the Workers' had never thrown me out. The shine of glass, labels of bottles. Splendid. Too much alone. Pack too much time into doing, brittleness masking emptiness, avoiding life. There had been three weeks of wind, a blunt blade rubbing at the church. The red dog had the hide to enjoy it at first, as it brought sharp fresh scents, but ended by barking at it.

Looking into this glass. So far to the bottom. The Australian soul, down there somewhere under clear liquid. There's the soul, funny leather-brown bubble. The bar is brown, bubbles aren't. This glass is empty. I drink from full glasses.

What I needed was more people. Good people. Cheerful. Not miserable as the Mordialloc moaning duck. A bit of singing. I bought a drink for a country poet and gemstone fossicker.

'Have a drink. Get your laughing gear round this.'

'Rider O'Neill.' He sported a jaw like a square-cut glass ashtray. Hearing his name I was reminded of Yarrow's voice. Why did her voice lumber me with the guilts? I didn't ever tell her about stealing that brass cross from a pew-end in a

Camden church, did I? I felt it contained something of all the generations of people it had seen and heard for over a century, and had to possess it.

'I suppose you think Lost River's heaven on a stick?' the poet said, drink or no drink.

'Up yours too.' Combative weaver meets combative poet. 'Do you perform with a bottletop songstick?' In company with men I'm almost immediately on edge. Dislike becomes enmity. Is it a hormone I detect?

Across the window between us and the flickering world outside, a large chesty cloud crawled. I remembered standing with her watching caravans of clouds passing. My hand on her arm, for once. A moon like a dollop of butter. Egocentric, she said. Means I didn't always agree with her pronouncements. If you disagreed you had to be wrong. A side-effect of her strength, I guess.

The poet was lean, his skin shiny as a wooden handle you use every day. What colour would I use for his ego? Black, like a chimp's face? Or the concentric wrinkles of a horse's rectum in action?

'Do they call you Clock, for that tic?' Why not? I remember hearing that a thought confined in poetry is sharper, but where was poetry? In someone's back pocket? There was a delicate turning of the fossicker's body. But not away. His lips moved.

'So you reckon you've got balls?' Why do I expect poets to speak differently? To use a voice which venerates words?

Thombe! The deep crooming thombe of low-frequency sound from the music machinery gathered in me. Packed tight in my head, it expanded. Fluttered like clumsy fat birds in my chest. Blasted penguins jostling, rattling and shaking my liver, lights and lungs. Engendering a murderous rage.

Those not deterred by punishment don't worry about laws. Not sincere, she said. Didn't she know I could love and dislike at the same time? That was half the torment of her.

I decked the poet to indulge the aggro, accidentally trod on his right hand and left smartly for the outside world without waiting for eager escorts. Not sincere, she had said when I told her I found her character less than admirable. She had loud problems whenever the word truth came up, though if there was no truth how could you tell? But not with the truth of whatever she asserted. What did she want? Whatever wasn't in sight? I loved her brightness, her strength, her quick mind, her work. I didn't like her character. Did she want something more? I didn't have it to give.

Feeling hard done by. Just the moment to wish, among the mall-creepers, for an expanse of that skin applied like a poultice to my lips. Would I ever escape her hold on me? Passing a pink Wendy's. Perhaps the white skin near that neat navel stretched that one time she reached up and put her arms round my neck, perhaps that could be the magic salve. Could a navel be unconsciously regal? Again, in the mall, I felt the strangeness of Lost River and its people's apartness, as if something had dispersed them. A Feynman effect? Or was that reserved for Yarrow and me?

eleven
shoey mortomore

Ambiguous colour, blue. The sky's cheerful enough, but blue's a mood. Shoey had blue sad eyes, which nevertheless had a sparkle. A last skerrick of youth, perhaps.

I ran into him at another of Lost River's steam rallies organised by Sprocket Man, as Shoey called the skinny, eel-like individual in blue oiled overalls. They'd been at school together. The eel clambered around, over and sometimes in the machinery, there was something in him that bonded to flywheels, belts, pulleys, pistons, steam governors and jets of white steam. He carried an oily rag half out of his pocket like a certificate, and paused in his snaking around to wipe things with the certificate, which he whipped from its holster like a gunfighter from the Wild West. It was a hot October Saturday, the sun hammering down hard on us soft-bodied organisms. I was glad of the marquee.

Tiny Tim Mortomore's advice to Shoey was brief and didn't amount to much. 'Son, keep away from thieves, talkative women, salesmen and fanatics. You can purchase popularity but you can't buy dedication.' Shoey, with a head like a loaf of fat country bread, was eleven and puzzled. Dad was sharp and fierce, like the fabled thick-skinned rhinoceros fly, and Shoey never knew what to say to him. No more than Mrs Mortomore did when they shopped for clothes and Tim looked martyred if he had to wait five minutes.

Shoey once asked, he was six, if fish ever got old and if so, how old, but Dad thought it was a leg-pull. He didn't say much when Shoey at ten asked why people didn't keep records right back thousands of years so we'd know who we were. Nor did he say if the same clouds we saw came round the world so we could see them twice. Shoey didn't quite believe his dad didn't know.

Shoey grew tall as a cliff, apologetic that he dwarfed his dad, a fidgety little guy who smoked like a chimney, always regretting that he no longer smoked 'roll-your-owns' but had gone over with the mob to tailor-mades, with their saltpetre content to keep them alight to the end whether you puffed or not. He knew men of ninety who smoked and were never sick, but he wasn't one of them.

On his deathbed, with Mum managing a few tears and Shoey and his younger brother Brian not knowing where or how to look—though Brian tried to tell a joke to cheer Dad up—Tiny Tim was passing in and out of wakefulness. Then he would wake and say something about the football, a dying father again who hadn't dropped the thread of meaning, and knew violence went to the heart of life.

It was Sunday, the match of the day over, its second half obscured for the dying man by another period of darkness in which he didn't know his family from a bar of soap.

'Who won?' he asked when he came round, and begged for just another cigger to make fragrant the minutes before the end.

Manly had won a game closer than the 18–8 score indicated, but there was no way they could tell that to a dying Saints supporter. Shoey was as innocent of experience as an unused toilet roll, so Brian picked up the ball, he knew about football.

'Saints, Dad.'

'How much?'

'Forty-seven to seven. Annihilated them.'

'Aaaah,' triumphed the dying Dad as the great Referee in the sky sent him for an early shower. Like a stale lettuce letting go its limp hold on life, he sank into coma. There was a smile on his face. An hour later he was out of the coma. Dead, the final expression of need. No more breathing stale tobacco into the atmosphere. His eyes were open, their look softening, as if he were quietly thinking.

It was a colder world with your father dead. Shoey and his brother, two monumental non-achievers, weren't sure how to be sad, as they hung about doing nothing except to inhale their inheritance. For some reason Tim stayed in the house two days, pale as those shop fowls you buy, bred and presented to look as if they'd never done anything so grubby as to live, but had always been meat. When Dad was carted away to be processed, Shoey felt some of himself was gone, he was no longer the person he was. For some reason Dad always wanted a nice burial, not to be shoved into an oven like a burnt offering or a solution to a problem.

As a younger boy, when it was apparent that he would be a giant and therefore a great deal different from other people, Shoey kept away from other boys. The jokes they played on him. And the punches from Zorella, palpable as lumps raised by a baseball bat. People noticed him and kept noticing him, he never blended with the background. Not with a face like an abandoned sculpture.

Older, and a real giant, he got work in Ivan Sherack's new

plant nursery off the highway south of Lost River. There's a big green sign that Ivan fought for five years to get. Shoey took over the house payments. He was a slow worker, but never stopped, big hands bandicooting endlessly around among the plants. Young guys would come by and chiack him about chewing gum on his boots and offer to work for a few dollars less than Shoey got, and some came from his year at school, claiming they could run rings round Shoey. Times were going to be hard forever. But Ivan was no fool. The sarcasms and talk of grass growing that he heard from the hares didn't disturb his faith in his giant tortoise: Shoey would be working long after they'd got bored, chucked the job and run off.

The year after Brian went blind and became known as Batty, Shoey took his annual leave in the experienced Fairmont he'd bought from Wayne Mitchell Ford. He travelled straight to the coast, going south, stopping often, standing on lookouts and odd beaches that caught his eye, turning his big serious head this way and that, sweeping the featureless ocean. Cann River, Orbost, Lakes Entrance, he enjoyed Australia with the careful abandon of a company auditor on holiday. He left the highway at Sale to get closer to the sea and at Geelong did the same, getting onto the Great Ocean Road and joining the highway again at Warrnambool, and so on to Mount Gambier.

He drove up the slope, the brakes squeezed motion from the wheels, he parked and stood on the rim looking down into the lake. But it wasn't November, there was no change, no blue lake. He drove round the town, was attracted by a bluestone church with buttresses. Its door was open; he went in. The pleasant dimness greeted something in him. He smiled, looked round, then lowered his two hundred and eleven centimetres as quietly as he could into a pew. The floor creaked under his weight, so did the pew, smooth-worn and polished from generations of bottoms. He sat silent as the Darwin ghost-worm, which has an enormous workrate but whose mouthparts can't be heard in the toughest timber of joist or floorboard. He looked round, listening to the stillness. The tapestry kneelers reminded him of when cousin Delvene got married in St Matthew's, all the blue and gold, and the red bits.

He picked a leaflet out of the rack that rammed into his knees. On prayer with God, plus examples. He read it and put it down, his slow thoughtful brain gradually encircling the words he'd read, rather like a natural feature of the landscape digesting a large and complicated plantation of trees. Being a Christian seemed difficult, like tucking a cello under your chin to play it. He read the leaflet again.

It wasn't his, so he put it back. He looked up and round at the leadlight windows with their unfading beauty, some of the words he'd read gathering together in segments appearing in his head in a random order. Yes, he was free to need a god, there was no need yet to apply to opinion police for a permit.

Did God have him, Shoey Mortomore, in his grip? What did it mean to go from the unreal to the real, from darkness to light, from death to life? Could he be a child to the god who fathers the family of mankind? How do you become a little kid again? What did that mean: be silent, still mind, and reach the void from where all things are possible? Was he near the dedication Dad said you couldn't buy? He picked up the leaflet again to refresh his eyes. 'Heaven is a true family, we will no more be isolated from each other. This will be our joy, to see each other with new eyes, to see God shining through his creatures. In every person we meet forever we will see the love and beauty of God; first in one's self, then in the selves of others, finally in the world's self.'

Beauty of God. What was that? How did a person find rest and peace in a god? And about death. Death is a going into, not a going away from.

He knew how he kept within himself. In a funny way the world inside him was the world outside him too. Strange to think that further out than all the worlds was a god that could be part of his inner world.

Shoey drove back the way he came, just like undriving, peeling the trip back, rolling it into a ball back where he started. Asleep in a motel at Lakes Entrance he dreamed he was in a small boat on a cold sea among dangerous icebergs with pink interiors, and because highway traffic woke him at the right time, remembered the dream all the way home.

More words from Mount Gambier drifted through his memory as he did his patient work for Ivan Sherack, rather as a gas drifts over an undulating landscape, settling in places. They began to mean something more than words casually encountered, like ads.

Then one day as he worked in the chromatic scents of the morning, among the tomato plants and the corn, he found God and didn't need to worry any more about people, or being different, or jobs, or bad things that might happen. God looked after everything, for that was the kind of god he found: one who spoke out of the cornsilk, the yellow blossoms of the tomato plants, the pretty lavender and white petals of the potato flower, the strong fluted celery stalks, the shiny leaves of the different varieties of lettuce that were protected without pesticide from slugs and things by something miraculous inside them.

A voice without a mouth spoke to him without words, and Shoey heard the voice, which wasn't exactly a voice, but more a light, or perhaps a tide that filled him and somehow completed him with thoughts he'd never had before. He didn't know how, but he knew that now, like the plants, he had something miraculous inside him.

The modern cant of accepting and loving what you are had never reached Shoey. He was incomplete, unsatisfactory, he needed God. Now God had found him. God made him happy. God was company and completed his life. More than that, he shyly understood that God loved him, and in his own tall, humble, clumpy way he tried to do the same for God.

Others might look out into space and say maybe all the answers are out there, let's go and find them; but Shoey had the answers he needed right here and now. In a way, God was like death: both brought outer space into perspective. And sometimes, among the plants, he felt the whole of space above him became an eye, a gaze which knew him ...

Shoey went to St Matthew's and sat among the other parishioners, his shaven face shining expectantly. The priest told of the noble rabble of martyrs, the many-sided character of God, how poor scared humans, like sheep, look for higher ground as night approaches. He spoke of unrecognised and uncanonised saints, one of whom might be sitting near you, and Shoey looked round, in case. And when they stood and turned to their neighbours to shake hands and say 'Peace' to each other, he felt he was part of a larger family than the Mortomores, and with a different father. As time went past him, he felt his dad had come to somehow live in him, and blind brother Batty, and his mum.

He felt awed by this, but important too, and began to smile a lot. Those smiles changed him. People began to turn their heads and reconsider him.

Life seemed to be a kind of curtain, an outer layer; you couldn't see past it. Just as daylight is a bright, even dazzling, curtain masking outer blackness. When day was done, of course, then you'd be able to see, but only a bit. Patches of light, never the whole of the brightness that must lie beyond.

At least until then his soul was safe in the womb of the Computer, he was a registered member of St Matthew's and beyond that of the body corporeal of God's church in Australia, his name and details recorded electronically and saved on God's hard disk. Many times a day, and always before he went to sleep at night, he pointed his mental mouse and clicked on God and the window always opened.

He's learning bell-ringing under Amanda Mitchell, the captain, who manages Mitchell's newsagency. Amanda loves tall men.

Late at night another call from Yarrow.

'How can you ever know me when you're so full of passion? It's a wrong reaction.'

I knew about reactions. She was the kind of woman, at first meeting, who makes you wish you were rich, or at least taller. The bed I slept in felt as empty as the pale amber husk of a cicada, still clinging to a tree. It was years since she had walked away. I'm still not reconciled to never seeing her again.

In the garden that day, with wattle-dust on her shirt, the smell of wild thyme where her feet had trod, I knew she was made of elements common to earth and plant life, gases and minerals and awash with complicated chemical compounds, but I didn't believe it, there was more to her than that.

'How did you know how to get in touch ?' I asked.

'You know I exist, you think of me. That's how I find you.' As if it were all straightforward.

She was gone. I imagined her flesh caressing her little bones, snug and in their right setting. And when she walked, the rhythm and rhyme of her stride harmonious. I never knew or cared what she felt about me, I knew what I felt.

Why did the curve of her cheeks down to that little chin seem so valuable? Was I born to be like this?

twelve

lord henry ball

There's so much I don't know. The feeling I have is of being a prying centipede looking for knowledge under rocks that are off to one side of the road, and once under a rock not quite sure if I'm looking for anything but refuge. Are there studies of the resolution of varieties of chords into unusual or comfortable harmonies? Is it the case that when layer after layer has been peeled back from the music, that there's less and less of interest underneath? Or is there more? Are others in a state of wonder, as I am, when I reflect that a state of mind, a feeling, a belief—things that don't show in the mirror—can affect what we do? Little controllers inside. Or irresponsible children playing with the buttons and levers.

I sat in the Holly Tree, Juniper Grey's coffee shop, waiting for Irene Ball. The warm spell was still with us and Irene, when she arrived, sailed into Juniper's with two large cake boxes held out in front of her.

'I make their Black Forest cakes and a special carrot cake,' she told me. A fine-looking woman, substantial hips and two of the most advanced bunions I'd ever seen visible under the straps of her sandals; she seemed a person who worked steadily from daylight till dark and when she was old she'd have to be stuck in a rest home to get her to have a good lie down.

Irene Ball, of Yabbie Street, had one subject: her youngest son, Henry.

It's hard to tell about babies and their concealed impairments. They gurgle confusingly, apparently with the best of intentions; their families gather round, paying the utmost attention to the new human's actions and supposed needs, even holding their breath during the baby's pre-sneeze stillness, hoping he gets it right. If the infant has an ancestor in family legend who tried and failed to pinch the Crown jewels from the Tower of London, this isn't held against him. If a dog bites him, it's no more than originality if he bites the dog, even if he develops annoying symptoms because of originality.

If he's given the rudiments of a religious education, in this case a Christian one, it's not altogether surprising, on a day when the big boofheaded school bus is packed and tempers flame up and the driver pulls over to the side of the road because of the noise, disharmony and riotous confusion within the vehicle, if a small child declares into a sudden silence, 'Jesus should be on this bus.'

The other kids' mass rejoinder to this remark didn't shake Henry. He smiled at them and they turned away. Only Henry Ball. Brain like the head of a match. No more important than a back-and-front lizard. He didn't understand that God or gods exist only for certain people, and then only at certain times of the week. He went back to wondering what's hidden behind the blinding light of the sun. Must be something they don't want us to see.

He asserted himself, he wasn't determined by others' customs. He ignored all criticism, just like a superior person who might say, 'From dills criticism means nothing.' Older, he began to make his mother a new kitchen cutting board out of a piece of beefwood tree because of her muttered complaints about the old one, not knowing that her complaints were a kind of therapy that made her feel better. And once he tripped and fell in a deep 'AA' carving in the concrete of a gutter.

His father called himself Q; he sat at home after being told by Meesner Construction not to come to work anymore, working out on sheet after sheet of paper ways of replenishing the country's artesian water without causing sinkholes or landslides. He'd worked at it for eleven years and still hadn't got it right. He still had the habit of work. When not busy, he talked of comic-book heroes of his past: Springheel Jack, Keen-eye the Tree Boy, Tarzan, Brick Bradford, Buck Rogers, Rockfist Rogan, Speed Gordon, Tim Tyler, Joe Palooka, but for some reason omitted Mandrake and the Phantom. He chewed gum recklessly. Flashes of pink and an indeterminate bone colour showed his teeth intermittently becoming unstuck and roaming the wide shores of his mouth. Bubbles appeared at the corners of his mouthparts. He was blind to Irene's wife-look that showed a persistent, though patient, lack of trust in the husband.

After some years of shame and sympathy, and Henry's habit of confidence without sense, and having him worry the soul-case out of her as she put it, Irene took him along to the doctor, to see what he said. Like many doctors, Doctor Armor said very little, but he did say something that helped her for a time: 'If you feel you're hearing nonsense, it may be because you can't hear the accompanying and unexpressed thoughts.' He raised his eyebrows when Henry said he heard gunshots in every house in Yabbie Street, though when you think of it ...

Henry liked being the object of attention. His childhood and its incidents were pulled out and displayed as if they were important. Like his saying that God's miracles were mad as potatoes, or his schoolwork where he wrote of seas that speak, trees that count aloud, birds with human voices. And of the birds picking the nose of the statue in Anzac Park.

Sent on to higher authorities for assessment, his slightest gesture was recorded, so he made more gestures. But suspicion attached to his most harmless actions. Was there some reason why he knotted his socks? Why did he sometimes drag his knuckles as he walked?

The tests were inconclusive, and Henry at sixteen left school and worked for the Pig, for three minutes, for a pest exterminator, a tombstone maker, the live bait supplier, the trout farm. Sometimes, as he worked, these enterprises would grow tense as the dinner table when old Uncle Ted was eating beans: they didn't know what he would do, or come out with next. He applied for a job with the fireworks manufacturers, but they didn't need him, nor did the ostrich farm. He did some trenching, attempted success in singing and acting telegrams, but though he was always clean as a cockroach's chin, his employers had to be on his hammer all day and he wasn't fulfilled in any of those jobs. Each time he got sacked or fed up he left immediately and went to sit in Anzac Park. There he spoke, usually quietly, about the leaves wringing their hands, and branches in the wind going up and down like pistons, or levers pumping the trees. He would walk from one end of Budawang Street to the other, dropping words at random: Avoid triangular people. Don't walk under the cattlebird. There was sense in this last, since its droppings were foul as well as wholehearted. Then he'd go home to his room, dying to get a grip on the white pudding.

Sometimes he gave a few strokes to the cutting board, but was in no hurry. Anyway, Mum had stopped muttering about cutting boards, when she saw what that led to.

He fell in love with an Arab soldier in the news who, when commanded to torture an Israeli soldier taken in a skirmish, killed himself rather than obey. The gentleness, the self-sacrifice. He sat up late thinking how admirable the suicide was, watching the blue and orange lights of the town, and thought of this man while he watched the sunset and its high clouds of spun sugar with a gold the colour of sparkling urine.

'That man was better than Jesus,' he ruled sincerely at breakfast.

'I don't think you should sit up so late,' his mother worried. Would he ever keep a job? What was his future? God, don't let him become a dribbling idiot, a face-wreck, a lunatic who'll live long after I'm gone with no one to visit him. She went for support to the Relatives and Friends of the Mentally Ill Association and told them how he shaved cautiously, afraid of a fist behind the mirror. Her death, the nth term in the progression of human mother love, was a long way off then. He had a habit of opening his hands in turn to see if he was concealing anything.

He had almost decided on the final dimensions of the cutting board. He was out of work, not yet accepted for an invalid pension. He read, and showed some interest in a story of an early convict on work release working for a magistrate and hanged at sunset for giving cheek. He was particularly interested in the fact that it was at sunset. His life was full of complex observances, rather like the complicated rules and regulations laid down for employed persons generally and which, if followed to the letter by all, paralyse whole industries and cities.

He discovered what the world knows but no one does anything about: that packets of tea command you to lift the flap to open them, and when you do, the flap tears off and you need to rip your way in. Ridiculous. Henry thought it ought to be fixed. Irene knew his suggestion was mad, the flap had unfailingly torn off since she was a child. It was part of life. The learning process, the way things were. Henry was absorbed by this conundrum for months.

He was frank, always mentioning what was on his mind. When Auntie Val came for Christmas dinner, he mentioned one of his own farts, as if its history had importance. 'Like a big pile of vegetables on the turn, with onions. Vegies on the turn smell far worse than meat, or a turd left in the bowl too long.'

They weren't quick enough to fill the brief pause with a suitable interruption and he went on. 'And everyone knows how a turd looks when it's been in the water, all furry round the edges.'

Eventually, after he had taken to becoming other objects, as actors do in training for their profession, such as a chair, a peppermill, a waterfall, or a tree, some unexpected clothes containing able bodies appeared at the door and he was taken to Butterdale, where many of his actions were no longer voluntary. Butterdale seemed like a holiday place, and he still woke as a saltcellar or a pair of argumentative boots. People asked him questions and seemed intensely interested in his answers. He'd always liked that. They listened and wrote when he showed them blemishes on the calendar called yesterdays. He'd have fitted in well in any comfortable country where people talk, all their lives long, to people paid to listen.

A nice woman asked about his bowels. Bowels were one of Henry's hobbies.

'Have you been?'

'Yes.'

'A big one?'

'Ooh massive. Lovely. I go funny thinking of it.'

'Thank you, Henry.' She made a tick on a chart. He was disappointed it was just an ordinary tick. He mentioned that he breathed better in his room when the light was on, but she only looked. No tick.

At first the only work required was reflection, reading or conversation, but when he began running through the grounds pushing a mower repaired in the workshop, they put him in the workshop with the quiet man who had killed seven people, and had himself been rescued from apathy by carpentry. He was building a sherry-coloured ukelele to present to the canteen manager, Mrs Mummo, in return for culinary considerations.

Since it was an institution run to rules fixed by no-nonsense people, inhabitants of Butterdale wore summer clothes till June first, when the boilers were lit, the buildings warmed, and winter officially began. Henry was often cold before June—the year before there had been snow in April—and felt the need of what he called his woonter willies unless he worked with a great deal of energy. He figured in the great escape the second May he was there. He was an emu that day and ran wildly with great emu strides and elbows flailing waywardly ahead of the rest of the rebels who were scattered across the road, all running after a fashion up Barebottom Hill, and looking back, expecting pursuers.

The staff watched, then trooped back inside where it was now much quieter and they could get on with their real work in peace: sitting at desks, moving papers, tapping keys.

The drama of the escape was spoiled when punctually at ten to one the escapees turned up for lunch, forming a queue outside the canteen; not speaking, not looking at each other, like a beaten team. Many were loudly amazed that the canteen staff seemed to be expecting them.

Where others heard sports and excursion announcements from the PA system, Henry was riveted by announcements of the triumph of death and the imminent end of the world. To enter the kingdom of reality you must become as a little child, so he ran about telling everyone of the end of the world, and retreated under a tired and very old banksia tree to pull his pud, as the saying has it, to get a last bit of pleasure before everything stopped.

The staff referred to this activity as 'jerking the gherkin', 'tugging the forelock' or 'whacking the witchetty' and weren't greatly disturbed by it. Not one of the more vibrant vices. From the distance Henry stood bent over like the humped camel worm performing this operation, the PA system shortly after announced that all was well forever, and he knew he had done the right thing.

Little Jim, a boy of fifteen, passed without glancing at Henry. He walked a little way, sat down and untied his shoelaces. Before he got up he tied them, and repeated this operation all day, every day, year in and year out, for no pay or any further aim, just to keep busy till the end. He had no visitors; they had dropped off after foreseeing that the future was no longer uncertain.

At lunch that day Henry remarked to the shoal of enigmas at his table, 'I had a universe once, it tasted like this wine trifle.' When lunch was finished he brandished his genitals, which were white, but not very white, and commenced work. An older and more dignified person at the table, with a face like a truck checking station, began to say his word, which was endless, but sounded vaguely mechanical and went like this: 'Fuckafuckafuckafucka ...'

Henry, busy below table level with the rigid candle snake remarked, 'Did you know my full name is Lord Henry Ball?' His career as titled resident pud-puller had begun. He had life, liberty of a kind he appreciated, and happiness in the enjoyment of public and private property undisturbed.

Treatment also began. The most recent of a succession of abstract theories was grafted onto his live body to see if it would take. And why not? Our increasing knowledge of theories places a tactful and orderly veil over the disorders of life as it is lived. Carpentry had to go. Henry spent the time between his spurts of activity in thinking, he said, with a little reading thrown in, plus the occasional storm breakfast full of odd flakes of the oat and the corn. In group sessions, with his hair looking like a willy-willy, he told his story of where thoughts come from. The original pre-human race, driven out by us, invented death as our punishment. They try to come back, but the best they can do is mental promptings, which are the origins of our thoughts. Good or bad, we're not responsible for them, a conclusion which fitted well with the prevailing fashions of treatment in Butterdale. Now and then, numb outcrops or symbols of sexual emotion sprouting from Henry's body would approach passing female flesh, but never once registered a hit, or a 'contact' as the military like to say.

In departmental drives towards rationalisation, which happen regularly to please political masters and cut costs, Henry is not one of those considered for return to the community of the gutter or as a reactant plonked down without notice among resentful neighbours. He still attempts to wash Butterdale's flock of alarmed and haughty sheep, in the rough paddock, when they get dirty, and to measure the vegetables in the patients' garden. He speaks familiarly to and is very critical of Butterdale's eucalypts, for slouching so informally and with such a cynical disregard for symmetry.

He loves the grounds, which are watered to a lush greenness even when the surrounding honey-blond hills of summer are dry as dust. Trees speak to him, cats sing in his ears, cubby-houses grow in gardens of uncut grass, ice on the birdbaths rings with a clear tone, the conversations of birds wake him each day before the sun's loud light. He understands raindrops, perceiving that water is poured into little containers in raindrop shape, and, when full, they fall. In the early morning he catches snails, lifts and looks, puts them down and they go about their business. Snails don't appear to worry a lot. He has discovered that, like moths, there are always more snails.

Days often stop while distant towns chat to him, the river and its moods he can taste on his tongue. There's a damp smell about him. And a dribble from his bottom lip sometimes reaching for the ground, like a donkey eating apples.

When he was taken to the beach he gratefully drank water from the sea's toothed mouth, and thanked the urinating fish and defecating crabs and other yokels of the sea for their input, and thought the sea-wet rocks, mooled by the tide, might be bread of a darker kind, but no one in the party had a bread-knife. He squinted for a long time at that distant margin where the sky is wrung out into salt water, and asked what shape is the wind, which fingered the water in patches, and whether, way out there, waves reached up and tickled the crotch of the sky. White-coated healers, grave and calm as trees, combed his waterhair and held his hands of glass, while he, comfortably tranced, watched everywhere closely, in case he could see time passing.

On weekends yobbos from the town drove through the grounds to look at the loonies, many finding their faces and actions as arresting as watching big city drunks cross in front of heavy traffic.

If we put our hands between our knees and begin to play our instrument, slowly a transcendent chord swells and soon the music is in full symphony; at its climax is an emission of glory. Which is gone as soon as it happens. Loneliness and desolation are reinstated. We must begin again to construct our gorgeous personal palace knowing it will vanish at a stroke and we must work harder immediately it collapses, for each day is different and there's nothing to hang on to. Reason and foresight come in handy at the end of each day. We must get a good night's sleep ready for the rigours of a new day called tomorrow. Why are there days? Why are they all separate, like fragments of life? Is it because fragments are the best things to convey the constant movement of reality? And why do we actually do anything? I mean, we're born and start eating, but why do other things? And when we do, how do we know what to do? Sometimes night expands to push the days further apart, the long night hours hanging like debts round our necks, and we must wait a long time for morning, but after a flint-hard dawn sky, daylight, like death, eventually comes. It always has, so far. And death itself is only frozen art.

Are we unnecessary?

Little speeches, like seashells, tally his impressions of the world as he sees it within himself.

Irene clings to a faint hope, and has preserved the beefwood block which, if things had been different, would by now have had a fine cutting-board career in the kitchen. The potential is still there, in the wood. And had her child decided to become what he was? She'd been a mother long enough to observe that children are not empty buckets waiting to be filled with whatever learning others decide to put in them; there are many things they prefer to learn, and some they learn with no apparent prompting, almost like needs. She had no time for psychology and its cousins. They might explain this year, but next year the explanation would be different. There was no healing in knowing what was wrong, and they could fix only the simplest maladies. She had lost faith in her century.

And yet. Sometimes the light in his face, the beautiful smile as he recognised her on visits, hinted at something far more blessed within him than the behaviour that kept him in

Butterdale. Was it possible that he was in touch, in his clearer moments, with a reality denied to many? Or was the fact that he had taken to plucking all the hairs from his face instead of shaving, a sign that there was less hope than before?

Irene put this question to me, but since I'm no good at calming fears or cheering people up, but usually think of horrors they haven't thought of, I didn't answer. I spoke to others and got several minor anecdotes. I don't know if they add much to the tapestry.

Once Henry carried a portable window, a sort of demonstration thing. He opened and closed it, wondering whether he was on the inside or outside, and also which was the inside or outside. There were the papier-mâché mock-ups of friends and rels that he talked to, kissed, and finally ate. Once, swimming with a cousin, he said, 'I'll rescue you and you rescue me.' Both had to be fished out by his brother Dennis before they drowned. And there was his job at the Pig, but only for minutes. He saw the killing line and ran out screaming, and didn't stop running or screaming till he got home. They said it made the pigs themselves scream louder, confirming what they half knew.

I got to see Henry in Butterdale. He had an exact face, firm and strong, the kind of direct eyes that made stern demands. His expression was one of alert seriousness, like a car passenger suspicious of the brakes. As we walked the grounds, he kept imagining he was trailing things stuck to his shoes.

Henry's was more than the usual queer isolation from other Lost River people that I'd noticed in the town; the buffer that soundproofed him was thicker and more efficient.

Yarrow said accusingly that it was love, but why was she pressing the point? I've said I'm reluctant to say the word.

Times past I've felt the letters sliding off the substance of it, falling to the ground, and the thing itself needing an entirely new description. I'd said it in the past to get things. I regretted violating four harmless letters.

In myself, all right, I admit to it, also to envy, fear, desire. Once or twice it's felt like need. How pathetic. Far better to have the leopard's strategy: capture, render helpless, stroke and lick the inert body tenderly, then begin the heavenly part, of having that body enter me.

I think of that navel, the slight roundness of stomach, the translucent flesh above the bent knee and above the inner wrist. The angle of neck to shoulder, seen from the rear. I shudder with delight. But she wants none of that foolery. Her bag is intellectual victory, unqualified agreement. Leader of a gang of two. I was to follow, never question. One doubt and you're out. Just by being herself she took over. I sank into her ways a little. I would have trimmed myself to fit, perhaps. But I'm not a natural gang member. For one thing agreement and compliance come as easily to me as impetuosity to mud.

How did a continent of feeling fit into such a little island of regrets and talk?

thirteen

lumpy van tran

Female relatives tried for years to get him matched with a suitable girl and always failed, never aware of their mistakes in judgment about Lumpy. The girls took one look. His rellies did no better with his brother, who, when spoken to, gave the impression of a mind on hands and knees scrabbling round collecting spilled thoughts. There had been a lay preacher in the family way back who gave up praying and pleading for demanding with menaces and became a bushranger till he was hanged in 1879, but no one of note since.

Lumpy's brother Humpy, christened by realists at school for his posture, found his refuge from the world in radio. He was now a real ham, Lumpy said supportively. Lumpy once had a job at the Pig, on the packing line, but having as much idea of continuous work as when he inhabited his mother, he couldn't keep up with the women, who roasted him in the street about his slowness. And no wonder. He loved sleep, and resting. Perhaps a new breed of analyst might assert that he had an

Endymion complex, after the mythical youth who was made to sleep long hours by the moon, for her purposes, on account of his beauty, a commodity Lumpy lacked.

I met him at the Woodcraft Expo so we could amble side by side and he wouldn't feel an interviewer's eyes boring into him. Be more relaxed. His face was a montage of features you'd see in any crowd. I said the usual warm-up things, the proposed jail, the incinerator, the new civic centre, the tapestry, unusual happenings in the town. He struck like a marlin on the last one, his body momentarily electric, his voice loud, the montage on the point of disassembly.

'She's got a double garage up the back, keeps the door shut. There's more than that Chev in there if you ask me. And a Rhodesian ridgeback big enough to bite your leg off. Snuck into town in her other car, did the magic lady over, snuck back. Got out the Chev and off she goes to the Show. And ...' he paused impressively, 'she's going to write a book about Lost River. We'll all be in it. She'll cut us to pieces.'

Poor Leanne Fusby, she was the one in pieces. Once the story was out, Lumpy's interest collapsed, his voice subsided, his mind wandered and he wanted to wander after it. I had to stabilise him with eyes, attention and prompt-words to keep him with me.

For any other subject he didn't like or dislike, wasn't for or against, he had no views. Maybe he was seeking the wisdom that is said to be in the vast deeps of all of us, or he loved living innocently with no aims, no attachments. Or he really was an example of portable slumber, as kids at school said. It might be he was one of the large pool of people who possess abilities nothing in our civilisation has tapped, like still unknown forest plants with wondrous and possibly useful alkaloids. Maybe crucial cogs engaged with nothing.

You'd know him if you saw him: he walks as if his next step is problematic; any synchronised centipede has lessons for him. He's twenty-six and suffers skin eruptions, at the moment has an anthrax at the base of his nose. Apart from that, the face is common as concrete, though in profile I could see a resemblance to the Dead Sea trout. The nose and laid-back brow. He comes of a family which can make no sense of the world. They float along, do the easy things, take the line of least resistance, life being a kind of organised formal mirage. His mother is obsessed with the house and cleanliness, his father one of the poor who are inert and lacking character, energy and initiative, but unaware of this lack and fiercely self-righteous about his dole money. He too has the hook with life in general. All of them were vaccinated by early fears and scares against caring for others.

You know how you wake every morning and read the day and your surroundings? Lumpy gave the impression he didn't, as if his juices and sap had gone to sleep and he crept from day to day without recognition or interest. He was either deficient in envy, which usually gets us up to the mark, or it was so powerful in him that he was paralysed by it. Whichever end of the stick he grabbed was the smelly end. His only wisdom, that a watched boil never bursts. He had a tendency to breathlessness when confronted by work, and was at his best sharp and decisive as suet.

Don Love, proprietor of Love's Locksmiths, next to the Junque Shoppe in the Hawk Arcade, once when drunk as an amiable wombat among the flabby spontaneity of his business cronies, described his employee as having a mind as large as the smallest room in the house, and at the same time as a Shpos, a sub-human piece of shit. 'Needs a sharp stick where the sun never shines, but I'll get him up to speed or he's out,' he said, but he was lying. He wanted someone not too smart, a bit of a log in fact, not quick, alert and intelligent, who might soon know the business better than he did. Lumpy was no threat, he worked and thought with all the speed of the Parramatta River bursting into the Pacific.

Don called Lumpy his employee, but thought of him as his parasite, like Lasseter's riding wren, which gets a lift from unwary ibis as they take off. He regarded with grim amusement Lumpy's time sheets, tax certificates, payroll tax return, superannuation provisions and the multitude of state and federal overheads created by his generosity in employing one of the dependent poor. Still, there were times when he had to be out, he couldn't very well shut up shop each time; and Lumpy was honest, nothing had ever gone missing. Lumpy was temperamentally reluctant to see money leave his hands, anyone's money. But it would have suited Don Love best if he'd been able to summon Lumpy when needed, like a genie from a big green bottle, and stick him back in it when he didn't.

Not that Don Love treated Lumpy in any way other than with cheerful friendliness, but private thoughts are just that, and the equality taken for granted in public assumptions was mostly cant. The businessman and his servant lived in different worlds. Even though Lumpy wasn't really a Shpos, to Don Love real human beings owned their own businesses.

Don was convinced Lost River was going backwards, but that was a common perception up that end of the main street and in the Hawk Arcade, well away from the bustle of the Eureka Mall, where the town was said to be rocketing ahead. Don didn't mention around town that Lumpy shaved his pubis in an attempt to get more feeling in that area, nor did he tattle about the objects he'd found in Lumpy's desk drawer; one an appliance to maintain an erection, the other to oblige a friend when he was spent.

Lumpy, despite his slewfoot mind, got pleasure from simple things: the ornaments and decorations in the Soldiers' Club, the new blue-patterned Workers' Club carpet, the green of the snooker tables under their low lights, the shining rows of spirits bottles behind the bar. He had no craving for power, no strong hates; he liked to stand alone, where he didn't have to compete. What fantasies he had were small and mostly to do with the area between his legs. Only a small proportion of slaves really want to be free, and Lumpy's freedom consisted in a different kind of confinement. He knew he'd never succeed in the world, even with the most extreme effort. His dream was to live away from the traffic and disturbances of Budawang Street. He wanted the life of a child, or a gentleman of past centuries, or royalty, being waited on by slaves, robots, nurses. And where? In Butterdale, set in large tree-filled quiet grounds, ideal for those trying to reproduce inside themselves the apparent peace of the park outside.

Usually you had to have something wrong with you to get in, perhaps a mind that wouldn't stop, making you alarmed, then desperate, then sick. His difficulty was in getting his to start, then to coax it out of first gear.

He had a voice somewhere between reluctant and strangled, like the transgenic Sago Hill animal bird, whose oesophagus was said to be malformed in the genetic experiments. I think of him as the endangered Mallacoota blindfish, which hides under banks in the Inlet and lives up as far as Gypsy Point, and sometimes has to make do with jellyfish for lunch. Lumpy lived in a world which had no future that he could see, and outside himself saw a world where even the poor were greedy, where even if they rose to the top they'd be as mean as the rich.

He shared bread with ducks in the park, ungrateful pigeons, bad-tempered seagulls, reasoning that a female might be interested in a man sharing his bounty with lower forms of life. What about a dog? Females were said to be soppy about animals, but the expense and having to walk the wretched thing turned him off the idea. If only he had money, which would charm birds out of trees, make nightingales sing and young tits fly about all over the place. He had very little money now he was paying off his little unit in the new block Don Boobiak built in Galloway Street.

He wasn't game to go into the instant withdrawal business. Besides, he didn't have a shotgun. And there was that fatality where the young robber was squashed, like a pistol-packing fly, against the ceiling by the security window in that building society money shop. Poor Lumpy put another picture on his pornograph.

Then he met Henrietta, who immediately became the love of his life. Dimly he intuited that there were things a male had to say or the process couldn't proceed, but what was love? He ducked the question and went for lies and flattery. Eager as a greyhound in a Saturday night race, his tongue hung out for her, with a broad yellowish channel down the middle of it.

She was rapt when he found her beautiful, and seemed to be easily convinced of it. In Anzac Park he liked the feeling of being with someone; he was no longer by himself in the world. Another human accompanied this portable slumber. They had a scowl in common for the kids kicking a football on the grass, and sharp advice for the toddler smilingly beheading poppies sitting up straight in their neat council beds.

For some months Lumpy and Henrietta Stamp stuck together like Jaffas left in the sun. He was as concentrated and engaged as a thirteen-year-old let loose in a sex shop, and didn't need his magazines with their pictures of girls who needed money so badly they had their private bits photographed in close-ups for men to find inspiration, comfort and guidance in life. Not even the one of the American with a mouth wide enough to take a watermelon. Not even the videos.

So this was a relationship. He jumped on Henrietta like a parachutist landing. Though some details worried him. Like the first time. When it was finished and she'd sucked the goodness out of him he felt he'd died, but he soon got used to dying. He was not a worldly man, and began to sentimentalise what was mainly a sexual matter. Eventually, imagining this was for keeps, he made the mistake of confiding his deepest fear to Henrietta Stamp, and his deepest fear was, to ears other than Lumpy's, stupefyingly ridiculous.

It was that he had a lump inside him, and perhaps was entirely this lump. Just as a pimple when squeezed yields its goodness, or a blackhead its whitish paste, so Lumpy feared that he too, if squeezed or punctured, would deflate, drain away, leaving a wrinkled bag of skin. He let each pimple live out its self-contained but sordid life unmolested. What if he had an accident and leaked out, or spurted all over the place?

Television had shown him this kind of confidence rewarded with words on faith and the future of the universal loving family accompanied by kindly and uplifting music, but he was nowhere near the end of his story when Henrietta Stamp was on her feet—they'd been lying on Lumpy's bed, afterwards—shouting about crazies with xylophones in the attic and wrenching at her clothes to get them on in the shortest time. He pulled his horns right in like an offended snail. She wasn't fully dressed when she flew through the door, still full of uproar. With the door hanging open he saw how she was still dressing as she accelerated up Galloway Street, the commotion accompanying her like a cloud of something alive and ferocious. Galloway Street? But she lived over in Nerrigunyah. She was heading for the Shearers Arms. It was after eight; he hoped she didn't attack anybody.

Dingbats? She had no right to say that. Everyone has fears, though now he came to think of it, Henrietta didn't seem fearful of much, or anything for that matter. This was failure, the last refuge of the weak. Lumpy was among the large number of people who don't find the unclothed human form attractive, though he could have looked at naked women longer than at naked men, so that when he caught sight of himself in the wardrobe mirror awkwardly, miserably starkers, he turned his eyes away, not wishing to look.

He felt he amounted to a lot less now she was gone. He had failed in love. Just going on, the way he was, seemed like flogging a dead horse. He wished a new man was inside him, so the old one could be thrown away like a cicada's shell, hollow, stiff and lifeless. If only his inner lump was better than he was. Getting to work on Monday, registering the sight of the white plywood hawk flapping weakly in the low-velocity wind tunnel that was the Hawk Arcade, he saw for the first time how sad it was.

He's been Lumpy since Henrietta Stamp spread the story all round the town. It even spread to little kids, who laughed at him and pointed and said, 'Hey! Zitface!'

He visited Butterdale the next Sunday and sat in the day room where paintings hung on the walls; one of a black woman with green lips, one of a still lake surrounded by shadowy trees and misty mountains, and a hot dry Heysen print of majestic old river red gums with no grass under them, but sheep there anyway, which was peculiar. Pretending he belonged, he picked up an in-house leaflet on parent training. Successive headings were 'Thumb Suspension Courses' and 'Rack and Pinion Operations'. Puzzled, he replaced it among the *New Ideas*, *Woman's Days* and two copies of *People* featuring well-nourished and generally outstanding young women. He'd read them in the barber's shop, but dived into the pictures to perk up his memory.

Other visitors sat. Patients came, containing unmapped jungles of the mind. Lumpy breathed in the mood of the room. He got game enough to wander, taking a good walk through the grounds, noting the ugly communal facilities, walking slowly, very slowly, almost not walking, hoping to be mistaken for a patient. Trying to do what they did. Some were sitting, reasoning tirelessly. Most were inscrutable. He could do that expression. The grounds were lovely. He could even detect the faint November perfume of clover in bloom. He could imagine making love here, a morning glory, say, in the pink of the dawn. He remembered Morrie the Magsman in town one day telling someone those dozen rhododendrons were for the laughing academy. Lumpy heard no laughter. He was within the grounds, but not really in Butterdale. He practised standing still, as dead trees stand.

If he'd known about old myths, he might have reflected that here he was, searching for the thread that would lead him to the labyrinth, not out of it, but to its heart where he would be finally safe and valued for himself and settle down with, or in, his very own minotaur. He had no voice in him saying: Fight free, Lumpy! His freedom was a burial in which he stayed conscious, as in a kind of heaven, or a womb where you breathe air.

He saw a woman who had been crying, another woman digging worms from a garden and carefully committing them to a rubbish bin as pests; he saw Lord Henry in the distance. He thought he heard the PA system say, Wait where you are. Someone will find you. He saw people moving about, no two in the same direction, staring into themselves. Some seemed stunned, with not a movement, standing still like trees. Others, like flowers, unfurled their petals to take the sun. In a goldfish pond was a set of drowned teeth fixed in rigid pink gums. At the back of the kitchen block he noticed bins overflowing with scraps of the past.

He wasn't disturbed, as some are, by the sick people; if anything he felt safer. He could have fitted in well. He could offer to tend the new trees. After all, he didn't desire that life be a journey; it was quite satisfactory as a predicament. He could go along to meetings in the meantime to get to know the right way to talk. People accept you if you have the passwords.

'I'd like that,' he crooned aloud, and looked round to see if anyone had heard. From nearby paddocks came the hoarse call of a cow in heat, roaring in tongues. Feeling bolder, Lumpy began to talk aloud, as if he belonged there among his own kind. A pavlova wasp zimmed at him, hovered, and danced away. He liked that, too.

Could he make himself different? Do things that might qualify him for Butterdale? What did others do? Make cuts in their minds till they bled? Bind depression to themselves like an armour? Did they know something he didn't? Was there a secret he could nut out? You didn't have to hurt people, just say things differently, do things they didn't expect. Lots of things were sickness now that once had other names, and opinion had become a kind of schizophrenic theatre. It would be steps in self-determination.

He sat in the shade of a grevillea hedge. Several transparent people passed, two embracing the warm November air. A jaunty cockroach, black and shiny, hazarded a few darts towards a distant part of its territory. 'I really like it here,' he marvelled aloud. The hedge was spiky, but he didn't mind. Ants with their own histories patterned the ground. So little, and they were up all day, like people. Such a long time for them to be awake and their tiny legs going so fast. Cats and dogs have a few naps, at least. What good little ants. He felt well disposed towards ants. The black cockroach cerebrated, remembering an intuition of chaos under apparent order, and a deeper order under chaos.

It would be good here. Everyone sort of equal, though different inside. No one getting above the rest, thinking they were everything, when we were all only animals. Money didn't count here. Luck didn't matter, or being clever, or having rich parents. There'd be no bosses, no employees, no problems. People were interested in you here, for your own sake. It would be perfect. His inner voice was defiant as the tone he used to the sneering waiter in the Burning Log when he ordered the cheap wine.

Might even be some girl, with worries, and they could talk. Plenty of places for it where no one could see. The cockroach disappeared under a mat of leaves, remembering pressing business. The cow called again in an agonised manner. Lumpy had no questions to ask of order or chaos, had no pressing business, had no instincts to produce his kind: he was a natural spectator beside the inarticulate animals; his only need was to be fed, and what better place for it than this quiet backwater away from the stormy boisterous sea of competing human destinies? Apathy's muffled dullness enveloped him already.

I was about to ask him something about the futility of human aims, but stopped myself. For Lumpy, simply having aims, the dream of a perfect future, that was fulfilment.

What the hell? Why not help him? So I told him: hear voices, and he'd be admitted immediately, without question. If he couldn't make up the words he heard, he didn't deserve Butterdale. The doctors and carers were as suggestible as the patients, they wanted to believe. They'd label him a schizo, zap him with medication. Play his cards right and he'd be set for life. When they wanted to return him to the community, all he had to do was go over the top, they'd get the message and keep him in paradise.

For some days I hadn't felt the unease or dissatisfaction that had plagued me earlier. I played music while I worked. It helped. Why do some tunes stay in your head? Why does some music not stay? Sometimes it's a kind of relief to hear a tune polished by time, a melody that's smoothed by having rubbed up against so many past days. You feel a gratitude as it takes you along with it again on a familiar flight.

I thought of Lumpy at first as a guide to imaginary destinations. It was too active a role, and besides, I was that guide for him. He became a discarded boat buried in slow deep sands. Tides he would never try to comprehend nuzzled his inert structure.

Yarrow late at night again. Her mystifying question. 'What's important?'

She was important to me. I know she was trying to point me to deeper, or higher things, but she was my height and depths. Where was she? How did she get in touch? Why not tell me how to reach her?

Getting information from her was like drawing off a glass of Guinness from a gum tree.

When I met her first I thought my life had been provided with a new music. The fingers of her right hand parallel, her hand bent at the wrist and resting on her book. I was hypnotised, helpless. I felt my life hanging out of me, on display. I had no strength to cram it back inside. I was hopelessly gone, but she was nothing of the sort.

All I ever possessed of her were my own thoughts.

fourteen
the old couple

At their place tomato plants, potatoes, vigorous broad beans had spread from the backyard beds along the side of the house and were interspersed inside the front fence with rose and geranium, bottlebrush and broom. The old couple loved being in the sun, stretching out their lives under the tall dome of daylight. I'd dug them up in Bogong Street, spoke to them for a while, then arranged to see them at the Antique Fair, at the showground. Yes, they'd heard that the Fusby woman was supposed to have been one of a young gang that hijacked a cab driver, a father of six, and that he'd been on his knees begging for his life, and they'd still shot him, each one having a shot, but the old pair would have no part of spreading such talk. I felt a bit grubby for having reeled it out. I couldn't remember who told me.

Love was the introduction, friendship and tolerance their long conversation. Plain as scones, ordinary as bread, John and Mary have been together since they married each other at twenty-two and twenty-six. For years both thought there must be something the matter with them, because each fretted for the other after absences of only a few days. Eventually they accepted that they couldn't bear to be without each other and left off talking about it.

They still live in the cottage they paid off to the bank for thirteen years; interest was only five percent then. They live in the way they've settled into, the way that suits them, side by side like sardines in a tin. There was no ecstatic happiness then and there isn't now, they just suit each other; life without the other would be an abridgement of almost everything. They do the usual things people do. In wintry weather two side-by-side faces, with the gossamer of years networking the skin, are pressed against the wind. Male and female, nourished by their differences, they need each other. Success in marriage? Who knows? Perhaps it's more than the absence of bloodshed. Earlier, she knew enough about men to know that once deeply attached, men feel the woman is part of them and can be spoken to and handled as such. She put up with it as her sacrifice, knowing there were parts of himself he'd given up to her when he accepted her woman's authority, and she knew that was a real sacrifice.

Number 31 is warm with them, and each year old age seems to recede. Marrying their lives has been like two creeks joining; it's impossible to tell how much of one life is in the other. Mary is plain as a granny, her top teeth come down to keep her bottom lip in order as she sits with her silent hands laced together, some of her fingers painful, and each one with its frown at the bent knuckles. Her dauntless husband, wrinkled as raisins, looks like an Adam living in equality with an Eve, with equal charisma, equal ordinariness: head for head, arm for arm, leg for leg, tongue for tongue.

In pinched and brittle weather, in times of hump and grump, like testy koalas bickering patiently, or pandering contentedly to each other's momentary eccentricities, they tell me growing old is something you have to learn, and it's as well to keep a little green in you as you do it.

Both shake their heads at the latest discovery by some male child-engineer who imagines that things which can be done ought to be done. Why would they shop from home when they love seeing people they know in the street and in the warmth of the mall? Why miss the sight of goods on the shelves, goods they can handle, and in the windows? New brands? New displays? And the warm bath of familiar sounds, with voices, registers, music and movement? And in other towns, other malls, the squadrons of shoppers with faces strange yet not strange? The calm bustle, the kids' new crazes, babies in pushers? Life warm around them? Town kids and nieces on the checkouts? They wonder at the experience of life that can advocate sitting indoors hunched over a screen rather than touching, comparing, talking, meeting, and keeping their aging bodies in motion. And the calm joy of contact, walking arm in arm.

On shanks's pony in Eureka Mall with the crowds round them, or in Budawang Street, they make one shadow. Alike as two Mondays, one will speak and almost finish a sentence. The other understands; there's no need to finish sentences. They know that two may not see the same hill, but both can climb it, name it, and describe it so others can find it.

He apologised once for not saying 'much love', after reading something in one of her magazines, but she knew men. 'Don't talk love, just show me. I'll settle for that.' You get the feeling they have no unpaid bills.

You wouldn't know, looking at him, that John refused the call-up in 1944. Hauled before the beak he said, 'Defend the country? What do I have to defend? I own nothing but a few clothes, a Malvern Star bike and a cricket bat I've had since I was twelve. I'd have them no matter what happened. Let them defend the place who have something to defend.'

The magistrate replied that at any stage, in any change or conflict, the poor have a good deal more to lose than their few possessions, and John, though he didn't accept a word of it, was taken and put into uniform anyway. When he got out in 1945, he got a job with the wool store, and after he'd had his eye on her for a month or two, Mary looked at him.

For John, at that impressionable age, when the eye loves, the whole woman speaks: knee, foot, fingers, wrist, even the overlooked elbow is eloquent and has its own language. These unusual feelings didn't last, and he fell into a kind of quiet love, but even that led him to do all sorts of crazy things, just as greed does or hate or earning a living, though love's effects are different. All his life long he has kept that look she gave him. Sometimes he takes it out and looks at it again. There it is, as fresh as ever it was, her brown eyes looking straight into his, one look out of many.

Mary, who had often felt loving towards people in general, now had an actual object to fix on. He would be the man she would love. He would be the man she would marry herself with. Each dealt with the other from within customs and ideas of what was right and wrong that were shaped by a long procession of events no two individuals could know of or imagine. They stood together where others could see and hear them and made a promise: your motel will be my motel, your breakfast my breakfast, your dog my dog. Well, something like that. There were many things they knew they didn't know, many things they had never heard of, yet they were content. Neither wasted much time hoping that civilised and peaceful behaviour would suddenly break out over the planet's surface.

Both felt that adding children to themselves was increase, extensions into the future, so that only part of them would die. As parents, their job is long done. They made themselves servants for a time, and four good people had life because of them. Four extensions, without the sorrow of creating a single one unable to bear the burden of existence.

So there they are, still in Bogong Street. He's seventy-four, with ears enlarged like ear trumpets. They still go to help in Trash and Treasure in the Hawk Arcade, and this gentle work has given Mary an informal insight into the wonderful workings of trade, for she said, 'I don't know for the life of me what they do with the things they buy, but I don't need to know, they know what they want.' She spent a little time helping distribute secondhand clothing and gifts of food to people in need and had been dismayed to find many turned their noses up at fresh fruit and vegetables, and preferred Big Macs, KFC and pizza. Rather than cast-offs they expected new jeans, fashionable tops and Nike or Reeboks. She limited herself to T&T after that, knowing she'd never understand. On the other hand, she startled me by saying she looked back on wartime as the best time: the government told you what to do, you did it, and knew you'd done the right thing.

They try never to mention Barry now, for when the old grief breaks out, things like scars open in their memories; they avoid the subject as if it's a place where something vile and smelly rises from the ground. John has forgotten all his own babyhood and most of his childhood and a good deal of his youth, but remembers every detail of the son they buried. He can't see naked bone in the butcher's window without thinking of the son they buried.

'No use saying it was a stupid thing to do. Been over that. Climbing up a power pole to stand on the top and have his girlfriend take a photo. Out along the Western Road this side of Gubba Dam. A westerly gust tore him down and spreadeagled him half across the T-piece and the live wires.'

Mary remembers the children that lived and the one that died and the knowledge falls between them like the blade of a guillotine. Each knows when the other thinks of it, and a silence starts up. Twenty years ago, but like yesterday. She remembers when the boy was born, washed, kissed, given breast and warmth, a name and a beginning, and the few short years of growing up, then mostly out of the house, returning to eat and sleep.

When they talk of it they say things they've said before, and don't apologise. They know their continued sorrow is as useless as a car's blinkers still going after a fatal crash, but they can't help it. They think what they've thought before, they know no way forward or round, and are too proud to try to escape the whole confusion into an easy understanding.

Death, their death, when they think of it, is a way of looking at ordinary matters, sometimes coating them with sublimity, but not that other death. With that death in mind, even the eventual death of the planet seems a kind of justice, a final comfort. End of story. All together, and all done.

I needed company. In the big bar of the RSL I ran into Morrie the Magsman, a hairy man with washed-out eyes. Owns the Root and Branch nursery. They say he'd talk under water. He was the sort of middle-aged dead male you see everywhere, last alive when he was young. Years before, on the roads, on holidays, at the beach, on the sports field, among other youth, at the popular spots they were winners, on the crest of every wave. They were royalty, and the best of them, the winners among winners, were gods. To train, to excel, to be shoulder to shoulder with others at the peak of their physical capacities, was to be a resident of heaven. A heaven far beyond the weak and unimaginative dreams of religion: it was here and now.

Suddenly, one by one, each male reached his expiry date, could no longer hack it, and dropped out of heaven, falling to earth among the other dead he had so recently looked down on. A grey and bitter life stretched ahead, among decrepit men and among females, to whom he had never granted full human citizenship. Females were useful, like mothers; valuable as trophies to be worn on the arm; or handy, like receptacles. At ground level little had changed.

By the time Morrie retired from active sport he was a regular at the Loaded Bushranger in Burunguralong, a quiet, heavy village not all that far from Lost River. He hadn't married, or, as he put it, hadn't bought a roof to keep the rain off a live-in female downsizing engineer who would give free estimates of male dimensions—of body, mind and spirit—with consultations at any hour, which always left you smaller than the previous estimate, the miserable shits.

Morrie had the intent gaze of a portrait painter, as if he could see your face in detail but wasn't aware of the you underneath. He belonged to the old clan inclined to solve severe disputes with a scoopful of termites or a house fire when you were on holidays. Late at night he would sling an affectionate arm round the boys of the football team, pat on the back, arm or backside those who went well last season or last week. He turned up at games religiously with bandages and sticking plaster, Dencorub or horse liniment for a joke. He would put a bandaid on a head cut, help a player move his leg after a bad knock, tenderly support an elbow for a player whose clavicle was in two bits, listen with sympathy to grievances, tales of unfair refereeing. And when the team left the field for the showers he could be seen gazing after them; in his eyes a faint sadness, eloquent as a sigh.

The players tolerated him. He was old, like the publican, and the old were peculiar, like Mum, or strange, like Dad. In the off season he'd take a stroll to the park and saunter across the grass, watch the kids play. The soul of summer sometimes seemed to throw over the children and their parents an invisible net, a kind of frame which gave them unity. Their laughter sounded notes white and wistful as a wedding dress. He was caught by no net, no unity embraced him. He often wondered at the gentle and inarticulate sadness that had overtaken and surrounded him when he left his nursery and walked alone in public. Something had disarmed him. There was nothing he could do. There were even moments of that peculiar emotion, that oddity, that joke called male pain.

But Morrie had something many other dead men didn't have. A different love had taken over an empty life and filled it out. He propagated plants from seed and from cuttings in igloo-type plastic shelters. He planted out at the right time to ensure the young plants became frost-hardy. He transferred his seedlings to tubes and the plants which outgrew tubes he potted. He supplied pines for windbreaks by the thousand, ordering them from forests.

They said he hated selling a single plant; he wanted them for himself, to enjoy, talk to, watch over. They were his children. He had some plants that would shrink and grow poorly if they were touched, and others that flourished with contact. He lamented when blossoming trees were knocked about by August winds. When they weren't, October's often made up the deficit. He dreamed of forests of imaginary trees, sometimes at the bottom of the sea.

Mornings, back at the nursery, his thick brown fingers with their layers of heavy skin delicately separated small green plants for potting. He hummed, whistled, sang to the plants. He told them stories of the world, about likely customers and faraway gardens, about companion plants, and smiled a welcome each time he checked on a new melaleuca or grevillea hybrid, or a hakea he hadn't seen before.

The baby eucalypts in their black sandy mixture put up

slender branches and tender, translucent leaves, and each shape—all were different—seemed to Morrie to be the infallible sign of a different personality. He didn't believe in beings without natures and consciousness. To him their existences could never be exhausted. He had thousands of babies, millions of seeds ready to become babies, and was happy he had so much to love, though he wouldn't have put it like that.

Back at the church I drank plenty of water, to rehydrate. The RSL had been like a lukewarm sauna. As I worked, Yarrow's question came back to me. What was important? It was important to know what my intermittent uneasiness, sleeplessness and miserable feelings were about, for a start. And, of course, she was. Before she left, I so often wanted to launch myself at her. Why didn't I? Was I scared of her?

She'd say I had cancer of the commitments, but it wasn't so. Commitment to keeping my distance? Was that the desirable thing these days? I get annoyed when there are things I want to say, but can't say them. It's as if I'm being told that what I'm feeling is wrong and can't be allowed. She says love has changed. Her love is like dancing and never touching.

I suppose she meant big-picture importance, cosmic stuff. My cosmos was smaller, had face, shape and voice.

fifteen

boobiak's waterfall

It was the last week in November. The uneasiness, the hard-to-pin-down dissatisfaction gave way to something worse. I began to wake again at two or three in the morning with such a punishing heaviness pressing on me that I found it hard to breathe. There was a presence, this time in me, taking charge of my muscles, bending my ribs in its grip, holding me firmly, while before my closed eyes, in the colourless dark, in the silence of a church, I was forced to view scenes from my past. No words, just actions paraded in detail, and me lying there unable to move or to stop them. There's something discouragingly final about actions you can see in exact detail, when they're your actions, and when you know them so well they're set in their shape and sequence for life. As if burned onto your mental screen. They seem to grow into your organs and tissues. You're surprised others don't mention them. Sometimes you try to cover up, thinking people must see. And all those things you got away with. At the time.

Other animals perform many of the same actions as humans, but I don't know if they have a category of unpardonable deeds. It was time for Don Boobiak to make his appearance. I tried to leave no gaps in my days.

Life starts with an act. Boobiak closed his eyes. Thinking: the progeny of events. A little rest, just for a moment. His eyes were strange, the colour of sapphire pebbles straight from the creek bed. Once or twice he woke himself, sleeping loudly beside her.

He remembered clearing the block, Teresa helping, the large, gently sloping piece of land for the house plot, a fraction of the three hundred acres they'd called Teresa Valley, with little Banana Creek running through it. The house itself would stand to one side of the water, the creek curving round towards the front of the house, trammelled by rock walls, then would fall down a two metre cliff he was going to blast in the underlying rock. The water would pool in front of the house under the waterfall, there would be fish, the creek would be led away to resume its life in the original creek bed further down.

Ever since he was apprenticed as a carpenter and joiner to old Bonaccio—both had agreed that the meaning of human life was putting one stone on another—he'd dreamed of that waterfall. He'd come across a picture of a bush waterfall in Mum's *Women's Weekly* when he was sixteen and cut it out. Still had it, pasted on cardboard, shielded by plastic. Teresa fell in love with the idea the moment he mentioned it. That was the second time they'd gone out. She was the only girl he'd heard of who collected stamps. At the wedding it was her idea to have an exploding cake—before they brought out the real one.

Working together, they burned off the accumulated branches, fallen trees, debris, and cleared the few patches of tea-tree and the odd biddy-bush in instalments one winter between May and October when fires were permitted. She was like a delighted child when fires were lit, eyes bright, feeding more branches, skipping back out of the way when the fire made a sudden grab for her. Watching her, Don felt content as a cat with seconds.

They used old potato bags, wetted, to beat out the little spurts of fire carried by sparks to nearby tussocks of grass. Her fair skin was pink with the heat when she got too close; her face stayed pink for hours. Part of the house was up, and they camped in that while the preparation of the block was done, so they could be handy if the embers caused fires at night. Otherwise they lived in the old house in town. They held hands watching the wooded hills to the east turn pink in late afternoon, and he thinking of her undressed body, neat as a circuit diagram.

The waterfall was built, the house too, but Teresa was dead of cancer at thirty-two. He was holding her hand when it went limp and floppy as the neck of a shot bird. They had no children, having left that little task for after the completion of the house in which they'd grow up. Was it some sort of judgment? Couldn't be, they'd done nothing wrong.

She was now three years dead. He worked harder, the business did well, but he remained alone, visiting her grave every Sunday in the Catholic cemetery that was separate and distant from the council graveyard. Theirs was on North Arm Road, old John Klay kept the aisles mown, and there were flowers on most of the graves. Boobiak had discovered that whoever he met, not only did he not feel the slightest tug of attraction, but he wanted only Teresa. He was still married, but to a corpse. If he had to travel to a job, or attend a function or conference in another state or country, it was Teresa's grave he left, and when he returned, her grave was home. He'd never planned to live with himself; the days were dull and passed through him like gamma rays, he noticed nothing about them.

Shopping in Lost River year by year, the inhabitants seemed like ghosts, tenuous somehow, as if they had no substance. As if life had been lived in the town once, but had moved on. Boys he grew up with, fished with among the water-rancid boughs dipping in the river, wild heroes and roaring drunk in their twenties, were now carefully pushing babies round the town. The girls he knew were married, pregnant, in business, or gone. The men who'd been fathers when he was a boy were old and changed and grey, led about by determined women who had lived in their men's shadows years before, but now seemed, in age, to have a reserve of life, energy and zest the men had lost with their youth and the sports they could no longer play to an acceptable standard.

In his mind he did as he did every day, went back to sit by the waterfall and remember. It was as practical as sweeping the sand off Ninety Mile Beach, but the memories of what they'd had together were more real than anything he saw round him; gave him more nourishment, too, than the living. He'd considered getting out the waterfall picture and framing it, old as it was, newsprint and all, to have beginning, event, and aftermath all round him inside his concentric circles of grieving, but not now. To see it every day would be too much.

When they sat knees-up side by side in the sun he used to grab both her knees suddenly and bend over them to smell the sun on the satiny skin, and give the skin a lick to taste the sun-perfume. Everything about her was constantly on the move inside him, reaching into every organ, every vein, every recess, and lodged as a permanent deposit in his bones.

It couldn't be a judgment; the very thought was inhuman. Life starts with an act, begins anew every day with more actions. Continues in stillness. For Don Boobiak there was no ending.

He woke suddenly from his half-dream and found himself on the big bed side by side with Leanne. The partial intimacy of books in a library. Sex now was a kind of workout, love-sex lay in the past. He could hear a clock chopping up time into separate seconds. The word noggings came into his head. Funny old word. The first house he built.

When he got out to Darkwood, Leanne Fusby's house at Woodpigeon Neck, Boobiak was full of juice. Felt like a five-legged donkey. He paid and mentioned a hellfire, which was a fast and furious bout with rolling and bucking, lots of energy and sweat. Crotches really beavering away at it. Leanne welcomed it, it would take the kinks out. She went at it like a drummer in a frenzy. He found her a rather loose fit, though not to the extent of the fabled well-worn wellington boot.

In the quiet time, Boobiak took his usual rest. Always paid for the hour and never left early. He'd never been a fast man with a dollar, but always gave value as a builder and expected value from others. He did right by the town when he landed the contract for the civic centre ahead of Meesner Construction with all their connections.

It was a good two-rounder; he was puffing when he finished. Leanne's face was impassive as a Bungonia bird-lion, without the fur and yellow eye. He didn't believe the talk that she'd got friends from East Sydney to have that old woman done.

Boobiak had turned away to lie on his back. He closed his eyes. Only a moment more. It was a November spring day, the temperature calm, almost turquoise.

Up in the hills, on Teresa Valley, there were spiders whose names were unknown, whose pictures had never appeared in books, whose fingerprints had never been taken. At home alone, Don Boobiak felt anonymous as a field-spider. Needed someone to know him; he felt that knowing would be a validation of his existence. The one he really belonged to didn't know him anymore. As far as he knew. Do the dead know, when you think of them? When you remember them? Do things come back to life, a little, when they live again in your head? Is death a larger life, a projection enlarged on a screen we hadn't noticed?

I headed back to Babel where people would be exchanging other data in bars, later in cars, and elsewhere after that. In the pickup I imagined myself working on a Chinese cut-silk tapestry, but of the long graceful tresses of a waterfall, rather than a princess riding the skies on a ho-ho bird.

Boobiak was holding his life together, start and finish. It must have taken real strength. I suppose I should have wished he'd leave some of it behind and get on with something new, as the modern cant called commonsense would dictate, but I couldn't.

He was a stiff, isolated figure in a Seurat painting of Lost River, alienated by his pose, his orientation, from all the other figures, each of which was a little episode, a fragment, of their town's life. Not one had an overview of the whole of Lost River, only a narrow segment within each one-directional gaze.

In Babel my new acquaintance Panzo Potts had a faint voice, like the Warrumbungle weakbird. Most of his conversation rotated round his wife, as he'd like to have done. Pamela, in her late twenties, had just wanted to be a married woman. To her, males with their noise, clumsiness and leaping about were all much of a muchness. Yet, better to have a harmless manageable man, however boring, with her when she went on holiday than to go about alone and be prey to men she couldn't control and were far from harmless. Like a lock on the door, he was some defence, unless the predator was sufficiently determined.

Panzo made the big decisions in their household. The future of Africa, how to banish poverty, the international movement of funds, national debt, global warming, balance of payments, global cooling, fragmentation of nation-states, the future of the party system, the coming wars of religion, how to limit the power of the executive, the ozone layer, competitive federalism. All weighty matters.

Pamela's trifling decisions prescribed where they lived, what they ate and when, where they went on holiday, the colours of their cars, the clothes he wore when with her, who their friends were, the kinds and places of their entertainments, how their house was furnished from dining room and bedroom suites down to the kind of extractor fan in the toilet, what colour changes occurred and which house alterations, what gardens were made and where, the kinds of plants and trees, what rules were observed inside the house and in company: little details like that.

He'd had one life-adventure. Elinda and Sharn wanted babies but not men; they approached two males of their choice. Sharn enlisted a football hero, Elinda picked Panzo, who'd had a name at school for original thoughts, clever use of words and interesting opinions. Panzo enquired a month later if he could be of further assistance, but he'd done enough. Elinda expected he'd be pleased, but the urge to help was strong in Panzo, he'd have been more pleased if he'd failed, as the football hero did, necessitating further efforts. Perhaps he was smarter, after all.

Pamela's mother was a Gleet. He said, 'I think trying to understand your life is like trying to follow the music back through the sounds into the violin, and beyond that back into the overarching mind of the composer.'

I met Pamela. She didn't answer to any of Panzo's descriptions, looking awkward, disorganised and graceful at the same time, a combination hard to beat, her long fingers ibising down into her handbag for some reason of their own. Probably to look awkward, disorganised and graceful. I couldn't take my eyes off her. She compelled your attention like a single performer on a stage.

She told me later that on their first sex, there it was, the eye of a big schlong, open and looking at her, with a droopy sad-sack of a ballbag bringing up the rear. She laughed and had to pretend she was laughing with relief, happiness, expectation, hoping he'd swallow that. She wasn't going to. She asked about the church and how it was furnished. She seemed a private world where the unexpected would be touched with a lubricious strangeness. She mentioned Leanne Fusby, to give me time to chew over her proposition, and while she dished the dirt she smiled and laughed and made herself so attractive that I thought, Why not? Keep my mind off other things.

Yes, I'd seen Leanne Fusby once or twice. A flattened face, her cheeks rounded out, eyes slightly puffy, reminding me of a cat's. Was there any truth in Pamela's report that Leanne had been in Silverwater Prison for murder? That she'd changed her name from Fubs by adding a 'y' and the clerk on the desk made it Fusby instead of Fubsy and she let it go? It was all about a cab driver on his knees begging for his life, pleading for his kids, seven this time, but the group put the rifle to his head anyway, then all had a shot so no one could say they were just looking. They'd planned to kill someone to liven things up for the group, and thought he'd do.

We got on like a house on fire. In the kissing fields of our private ecclesiastical jungle binding playfully together, my mouth full of hers, all her tastes and flavours, lips brushed by her skin, her sternum never far from mine. After each necessary parting, to see her again my innards struggled and heaved in my ribs like caged wildlife. I wondered how it would have been with the woman to whom I was connected by a cord twisted from strands of more things than desire for surfaces.

sixteen

pursey & etrog

Just nicknames given to them when they didn't join in a group game while they spent three weeks at a health farm in the Blue Mountains eating plain food, pale juices, raw vegetables, and he, Etrog, drinking milk to ease the stomach pain of the sudden change of diet. Unpeeled cucumber, raw carrot, raw onion slices, shallots, capsicum, zucchini, made his 55-year-old stomach feel older than that.

They met in Sydney when they were young, she an accountancy student of nineteen stepping as prettily as a mermaid ant along Pitt Street, and he an arts graduate of twenty-four whose parents had just died. He worked in advertising, writing copy, spreading burley on commercial waters to attract fish who didn't mind being caught. They became attached; bonded, grew together. A hand alighted on a hand and an epoxy relationship ensued.

Pursey became a practical, passionate and assertive woman, and the stronger of the two. She called a spade a spade and cellulite fat, and liked a slight melancholy and unconfident reticence in others. Her love was so consuming that she gradually forced him, by power of affection, to live in her image. His food, habits, exercise were hers, it was the way affection took her. As individuals we're not in charge of our selves: cells and autonomous systems take care of us. But she was more, she was a virus subverting his ways for the purpose of making a new self. Was she some kind of Narcissus? I daresay she became all she was without understanding it, as he did. He was faithful as a weathercock, I was told. He looked like an ancient verger when I met him at ninety. I thought of her as headmistress of a one-man school.

They were people to whom the business of earning a living came easily; they more or less thumbed a ride to affluence and hardly noticed upsets that tended to throw others. Tacitly they agreed that no matter how well-off everyone starts, the world divides into haves and have-nots and felt comfortable with that.

Lost River Pets was a good business in a prime location. It had been a cake shop distressingly called Pandora's Box before his parents passed it on to him when they moved to smaller and cooler premises. The corner of Budawang and Market, opposite Anzac Park, was ideal for pets, not cakes.

Etrog found in Pursey a home and a sanctuary. She supplied what she knew he needed. He subjected himself to her rhythms and was lost when he had to be away from her. She wasn't a mother, but more than a minder. Maybe once or twice he imagined, from his cocooned security, what it would be like to be a crumpet collector or even a garish gay. And maybe she dreamed of love with a more male man than he was, preferably big, possibly rather brutal; to have to do certain things, to be compelled to come up to the mark. Mere musing: Etrog was hers, no matter how many times he failed in her missions.

He could never fully participate in the household. The woman's needs, the furniture, the frequent cleaning routines, the changes of curtains, the china, the discovery of dirt or fault where he saw nothing, were incomprehensible to him. They filled him with wonder, since they seemed largely unnecessary. Nevertheless, he submitted to the lot as he'd submitted to the similarly incomprehensible rituals of his own family and his school when he was a child, and the ins and outs of the constantly changing tax laws devised as traps by bureaucrats. It was the way the world was.

They say the loved one can't know the one you love. They say all sorts of things. I don't know. All I know is you're neither what you love nor what you eat. Wait. I do know something. People can live together for years and know practically nothing of each other. Observation and contact don't lead to knowledge and accuracy. Here's a steal from Pursey's diary:

October 19

It's thirty years since I became Pursey at Mountain Farm health resort and had to admit belligerently that no, I don't put him on a diet. He can eat anything I give him. Since we were married I've cherished the husband I was given, though it's painful to know the object is just as irritating and evokes the same criticisms I tried to silence in myself years ago. I do try to be tender and conceal the underlying seam of granite I feel round my heart. When I took him he had no family. I did my best to be a virgin again for him. I took him as husband and servant and in return I was his servant. I'm a tough old thing. Twenty-five dollars worth of fruit and veg used to cut my fingers getting them out to the car, now I do it easily.

I think of our thermo-cuddles in cold weather. How I made him drink my tears after our misunderstandings. The nice sound he made as he came. As a cook, am I really a sergeant-major marshalling, parading and drilling the food? Do I really have a nose like a direction-finder? We don't hate each other, do we? We may well do, but we get along because we both benefit from it. Lovers quarrel more, the nearness does it.

That man at the Open Day. Is he a good man, he said. Yes. He loves you? Yes. Take no more lottery tickets, you've won, he said. I suppose I have. But I still wish I could feel free to change my mind every time I want to without attracting criticism. And I still don't feel easy talking about certain things, like serious riches,other men's ways, stray sexual desires. Makes him uneasy.

Getting ready for widowhood. Implicit in marriage. A few years of grey abandon left to us, I hope. Long love's like a road in hill country. I must remember to be understanding, men live shorter lives. But all the mistakes he makes, hardly remembers a thing I tell him. Still, to err is human, but to forgive divine. And to forget bloody impossible. I will be more understanding. But where there's a will there's a won't.

When he goes, will I join the Friendship Club? Or Civilian Widows? I'll miss him, I think, unless death is just hare-brained gossip. Won't miss that nose, though, making its own music. Or the deep and meaningful burps. Thank God we're both farters, always free with our wind. It's a strong bond. But you can't have a high fibre diet and dormant bowels.

When I'd read it, the old man closed the book and put it carefully away. 'Some brothers stick close. But the best treasure is a wife that sticks like a limpet. Why were we suited? Because I'm me and she was herself. Professor Motherly's theorem: psychology's bunk, a good woman knows best.

'She was always there for me when I came back to the cave, in bad weather or sickness. And the shelter, when I needed it, of the A-shape a woman can provide. Absence makes the heart beat calmer, but she was half my life. I don't mean household things: she trained me well. I do fine. I mean having her around to check on me, to care whether I sleep well, care what I eat, to see I buy new clothes instead of sticking with old comfortable things, to pick me up if I made mistakes. Such a pity to have to die when life in old age seems better than ever.

'In the last few months she didn't know if she was a Korean rubber fly or a Numeralla blue sheep. All those years, a separate death in our veins. First the benign lump, like that peculiar cousin from Adelaide. Tiny predators no filters can keep out and no poisons kill. And then the stroke. So sad to see the bird-bones of her chest showing, under her diminished breasts. I remember saying to myself before we got married: Where you go I go, where you stay I stay; my house is your house, and us sitting in the old Bijou when it was still a picture theatre, amid the alien corn of an American movie.

'Thanks for giving me the chance to talk about it. I'm still here, breathe in and out, life stumbles on.'

I remember losing my mother, the one who knew my early years. When she died those parts of me died.

Pursey brought her man another blessing. Making him live the way she did kept him an active and healthy man. He neither went at things like an enraged bull nor lolled about. Something about the constant, gentle activity, the moderate meals, the cheerful, orderly, practical outlook of the female preserved him in a comparatively youthful state while other men were greying, stooping, creaking. His face was often smiling, his digestion and arteries in mint condition, his alcohol intake the same as hers, and she would rarely take a third glass of white wine. So she was a benign virus after all.

Her grave was magnificent, with a steel railing in the old style, except it was stainless steel. The borders marble, the headstone polished black granite, there was room for him beside her. Welland-Smith, the spare-time blacksmith, had made, also in stainless steel, a bunch of freesias, her favourite spring flower. It was concreted into the slab near the headstone, which read: 'Half my life, for all my life.'

He's happy to be an Australian, though he never makes a fuss about it. Content to be different, to speak his own words, revere his own past, to walk an Australian track, to stick to the habits he formed that made him what he is, to follow Australian laws and value Australian treasures in his own home, among his remaining friends. He feels no need to be the same as the rest of the world.

He still goes to her. She holds him tight, though he doesn't have to be held. He didn't throw her away with those things that had to go when she no longer needed them.

I had an appointment with Pamela, which went off very well, turned up briefly at Babel's Whispers bar just to be near people and hear voices, then home to church to work.

I slept well, didn't wake till around four, to find my mother's face in the darkness looking at me with her old way of letting silence increase the pressure of her look. Since she had formed large parts of my conscience it was fair enough that she should play conscience again. 'Put yourself in other people's places. Look through their eyes.' After so many decades, still saying it.

seventeen
leanne fusby

I'd caught sight of her at nearly every local function I'd been to, even Jazz in the Bush. Hair red as a rusty tank. She was against new jails and had no opinion on incinerators. Didn't need warming up with crap questions, see me at the house. I could tell she didn't like me one little bit, but wanted to be in that tapestry. Those who'd been to her as clients told me they'd found her as seductive as Eve, and for the same reasons: she was naked as soon as you got in the front door and was the only woman there. But that was business.

She had a commanding presence. Dressed in electric blue; a blue and tuneful dragonfly, with some acid thrown in. Front on and close you knew she was the kind of person whose life had never been trammelled by the word don't. So was her dog—not a Rhodesian ridgeback—whose liquid caresses implied there were places I hadn't washed.

A secure woman, she barely mentioned her work for the town. She'd started off the 500 Club for the heated swimming pool, was behind the push for much of Budawang Street to be paved for pedestrians. There was fund-raising for new fire-trucks for the bush brigades; an assertiveness class for men and boys targeting the jobless, to teach them to use words and to dress for job interviews less like members of rock bands. She helped start police girls' clubs, with weightlifting, boxing, martial arts. As an elected member of council she'd been popular and envied. After the Show last March she'd noticed a cooling. And then the stories, whispers, fictions.

When she arrived in Lost River she was interviewed by a kid from the *Bugle*. Why Lost River?

'Best state, best town, best people,' was her answer.

The local rag only just stopped short of recommending her for honours on the spot. A perfect election speech. She had eyes that could get angry as a hot gun barrel.

She picked Lost River because it was small and Darkwood within her price range. Outside the town at Wood Pigeon Neck, it was just right. Darkwood was the only house on a rise with a straight kilometre view along Jinglemoney Lane to the bend where the lane starts as a spur off Forest Road. It was built of timber milled on the site in the 1890s, stringybark mainly, taken from what had been a great forest. The cottage was painted red outside and the timbers varnished inside, walls and floors showing grain and original colours. It had an all-round verandah with hundreds of pots: herbs, geraniums, native plants, roses, daisies, mock-orange, wallflowers, freesias, daffodils, grape hyacinths, jonquils: everything that would grow in a pot. There were gaps in the ranks at the front door and the back.

Her money came from the restaurant she bought, managed and enjoyed, tucked away in a small arcade and patronised by Sydney legal people. She put ten years into it, then sold. The money for the restaurant came from practising her profession—making a living from nuance—from the age of eighteen, a profession where love was at a premium and the rates published.

Her face was puffy round the eyes, like some boxers' faces or the Tighe's Gap balloon bird. Her chest pushed forward; if you've seen the Shoalhaven seaduck you'll know what I mean. She could fight better than most men and would tell you about it, but no one asked for a demo except an uncle of Wayne Door's who lived in the hills among a crew of people who lived rough—they'd told the world to shove it . He got drunk easily, he wasn't wholly committed to a New Age way of life, challenged Leanne and got done. She said he wasn't worth a bucket of warm spit.

She'd worked it all out when she was a Granville girl driving for Buttercup Bread and saving for a flat in the city. At eighteen she commenced her twelve years 'on my back' as she put it, 'hawking the fork', and saved the money for the restaurant. She was a body builder long before it became popular. As a girl she felt like one of those quivers archers hold their arrows in; she was sick of getting the sharp points all the time and wanted something better out of life. She was far too equal physically with most men to want one of them hanging around looking for freebies.

When her work for the council tapered down after the Aprahamian death, she got back into bed. Mainly for the company, but also to fill the time. And there was also a tiny, shy feeling that she was giving something highly valued to men often unable to approach other females in a civilised manner as sources of satisfaction. She adjusted her fees to the client and the service, but overall kept any fluctuations in line with the service costs on her restored 1957 Chevrolet.

In the queue at the bank or talking to Doctor Armor's eagle-eyed receptionist, she looked like any stocky, well-shaped woman getting cash for the groceries or checking in for a Pap smear. She had recently made friends with Delvene Mortomore, cousin of Shoey, who runs Bubstop Kiddies' Clothes and on Saturdays and slack days helps in the shop.

I found her as responsive as a concrete borer, but after the array of men she'd known I guess she'd find a weaver a wimp. She said the business itself was more interesting when you were new to it. After the first five hundred there was a sameness.

'I remember with the first one under my belt I felt pretty good. Just like a woman who's finished cleaning the house. Boys came for their first, expecting a roaring cow in heat, ready to swallow them whole. Went at it like rats up a drainpipe. I remember that first customer. There he was, naked as a willow in winter. I cleaned his rod for him, watered Dettol in those days. Just a young kid who thought he'd have a horizontal lunch. Reminded me of the kids round Granville when I was a girl and we had fun making the boys come; it would get all excited and throw up, and we laughed. The boys didn't. Some used to go down if we made jokes like calling it the gimlet. Boring tool. Get it? Some came for a quick root, just to get the dirty water off their chest. The cowboys gave it a muscular shake and up it came like an obedient dog. "Get your labia round this!" they'd say, and in quick as a mongoose after a snake, and stiff as a bank's resolve. All sorts. Even those who expected to neigh between wind and water. You know, yodel in the canyon.'

She has her reception room done out to look like the bedroom of a fussy suburban woman; she found men liked nice things round them, even frilly bits, as long as they could escape later. On her mantel is a photo of her with a resplendent tapestry-backed frog on her shoulder. She's looking sideways at the frog and the frog's looking sideways at her.

Her steel chimney stack was brown from burning wattle logs, wisteria hung over the back corner of the house. Away from the house a patch of grevilleas hummed loudly with bees as they populated the spidery flowers. A red wattle bird, its throat so mobile that its neck was bent round double, sucked nectar from flowers behind it. Uncertificated builder termites tunnelled their edible dwellings in her fence posts, leaving tiny piles of spoil.

Something about her made me feel virile as skim milk, limp as the bun on an imported style of hamburger. And not just because my one joke went down like curried razor blades. I wondered what it would be like to be a partner to such a woman. A unique blend, probably, of karate and kisses, with an effect like that of the sphincter-tightening beetle.

She said something that struck me. 'Every failed relationship makes future success more unlikely. Every client I have pushes further into the distance the possibility of a future partner.'

She exhibits her classic tangerine '57 Chev in Classic Cars. At the end of the interview she showed off the car and kept fluffing at its glittering surfaces with a bright yellow polishing cloth with a border of a single red thread. Her voice was different, she was more alive, and not just because I was leaving. A new energy surged in her, her face shone, her voice softened, her eyes glowed from point to point over the pampered body of the extravagant vehicle with love and pride.

She was no longer a dragonfly, to me: she was a Sisyphus. I don't know if she had a history of fraud and avarice, as Sisyphus did, but she had slowly pushed the rock of respect up steep Lost River, hoping to set it firm and stable on the summit, only to have a woman's death roll the stone back down a bit. She was still pushing. It would have been cruel to wish her luck. I didn't know then who was behind her season of adversity.

Her mutt gave me another wash before I left.

There's no one best way of explaining anything. I found that when I was busy, or had company, my insides felt light and mobile, but when work was done and I was alone, each silence was full of happenings, and my ordinary self seemed a fragile shell trying to contain a heaviness and apprehension that pulled me down and threatened to break out and spill into the open. In my better moments I resented being dependent on company and public places to cover the mess inside me, and each time I came away from some bar or meeting place I felt an extra guilt at having dumped there more used and useless hours that could have been better spent. Like, but not like, a competent chef captured by savage enemies in the nineteenth century Pacific and forced to cook a dish of ears, a delicacy for which he had no taste.

And yet. The shambles lying about still in my conscience, the unhealed scars left by my own half-forgotten deeds, plagued me all the more if I tried for a more decent and temperate way of living. Rumbling out of the past. Trundling their pictures and scenes into view. Intruding on dreams, waking me with vague fears. I don't mean silly stuff like selling fitness programs that hadn't made it to existence, selling portraits to go in a time capsule for the future, taking deposits door to door on house robots—that one really enlarged the exchequer till the killjoys killed it—or selling a few cars from a house address without a permit. I mean the baseball bat and the security guard. Or retaliating for a knife attack with that kicking in the car park. Not proud of that. Still, I could have lost the use of a hand. Though some were funny. Like contributions to famine control, hypnotism courses for smokers, the special foods for arthritis and insomnia. They were lean times. Weaving commissions didn't grow on trees. But taking that gambler's girl for the fun of it wasn't right, nor was letting her go straight away.

I could have recalled these peccadilloes easily if pressed, but they didn't wait, they rose up and confronted me. What had given them such energy, at such a point in my life? Was I becoming tired, ripe for the remorse that comes when confidence ebbs?

In addition, they travelled to my arms and legs and set up quarrels in my bones so that often an unexplained pain overtook me and wouldn't go away no matter how I rubbed or warmed the parts.

My latest acquaintance, Carlotta, had chosen a path of slight austerity to fit with her membership of the Party. She'd wanted a system of belief stable and permanent; to serve truth in a hostile world. The Party's network of people, branches, activities, youth clubs, functions, rallies, formed a forest of meshed, interlinked vines, bushes, trees and scrub: self-validating, self-supporting within the cyclone fence of belief. The years copied this forest into Carlotta's circuits, the edifice growing within her in miniature.

Then it was all gone: collapsed, discredited in the socialist subsidence. But a strange thing happened. The whole belief system, the vast thicket of tangled trees, branches, vines, shrubs and undergrowth, though cut off at the base, didn't collapse entirely. It slumped, settling heavily on the network of branches and tangles that supported it a little above ground. Her own mini-forest was dead and brown, but still there within. Often as she walked through her mind in her quiet times, she was scratched by dead and broken branches and prickles. Some of the abrasions were painful, and drew blood. One, though, was still glowing with a beauty she can never forget; it was her memory of strike action, the warmth and closeness of common purpose, common danger, and the union of human souls in closer bonds than the rest of her life had known.

I met her in the Curtin bar of the Workers'. In talk she was interesting, as her conscience squirmed and dodged, trying to find a way to plug the hole in our practical philosophies, that gap she identified as the entry point for the worst of the world's horrors. 'I think that living by the murder of animals, which are our kin because they live, means that we will never live at peace,' she said. It sounded like a quote. I too spent some time in useless talk, but the problem has defeated better people than we were.

At her house she had a habit of walking on her toes, perhaps to feel taller, or lengthen her calf muscles. Peculiarly, she didn't open her mouth to be kissed. When she raised and lowered her eyelashes, it was done quickly but inexpertly. A performance, but under-rehearsed. She sometimes felt that everything was slightly possible, saying this in the same breath as she spoke of how people interpret the world in different ways. 'But the point is to live in it,' she added, as we sank into her rather soft bed.

A brief call to Love's Locksmiths and no Lumpy. Taken ill. He'd done it. I felt a little bad at helping him rort the system, but if it was so easily rortable, why not give him a free ticket to paradise?

I wished there was some way I could speak to Yarrow, without having to wait for her to decide to get in touch. Nothing was quite as magnetic as the unreachable. If I could, I'd always drink from her glass. She wanted big things. I'd happily settle for an everyday life of the feelings. At least for a time. Certainly at least for a time.

eighteen
nurse pain

I'd heard crazy gossip about her diverting spare body parts on their way to the incinerator, making attractively patterned lampshades from leftover human skin, cooling fevered patients by injecting ice-water. What sort of woman was she? Before our meeting at the Old Steam Mill on a warm December afternoon, I felt like the nail-biting wallaby. In the distance, the Christmas carol practice from the Pyramid Church. Did she really need, at her age, a substantial weight on her just to get to sleep? Yet I'd heard that pressure on babies relaxes them.

She carried her arms in at the elbows, wary and aggressive. We walked past the plump old machinery, the worn timbers, adzed ceiling joists, as she talked. Somewhere someone was burning pine bits. Fragrant. Nurse Pain had a nose like a convex slippery dip. Her mouth looked stuck on, not quite in the right place, her eyes candid and innocent as an STD receptionist. Duke Jensen had told me, after praising her main virtues, to expect a face like a horse, with the lipstick, mascara and powder spoiling the effect, but I found her more like a Roman centurion, though with the sudden asperities of the arrogant snapping-cat. Knudsen Boult said she was sharp and nasty as a parcel of used needles. Morrie the Magsman advised me to take no notice of Knudsen.

She seemed uneasy. Dressed in grey. An erect ewe with seedy toe. Her father went away to the war when she was little, and didn't come back. She had no memory of him. His mate in the unit, a nineteen-year-old from Wangaratta, brought back the short story of how Jack Pain died. 'He was sighting dead ahead; the Nip's bullet took away the rear sight and went clean through his eye and head. Didn't know. Too quick.'

Her mother was a kind of bouncer at the retirement village in Dalgety Park, had a laundromat face and was as full of prickles as Saint Sebastian was of arrows, except hers faced outwards. She only laughed when others cried, her children hated her. She had the ability to arrange her words witheringly, throwing a net of resentments over everything in sight. When in repose she held words handy, like a quirt ready to slash. Even thinking about her raised a slight alarm, like finding half a grub in your apple. The only community value she owned was the necessity for public lavatories, because that was what the public did best.

The only teachings of her mother's that Nurse Pain remembered were that feet in expensive shoes were more valuable than feet in cheap shoes, and that it was better to sell a house than put a tenant in unless you got someone old-fashioned, with morals, and scrupulously clean.

Nurse Pain grew with her hackles up. From childhood she divided all she saw by two and all she heard by ten. The household had no affection for living things: not plants, not horses, not each other. There was no sympathy in distress or loss, though food was never lacking, or money for necessities. No one who came to their door ever took away more than they brought. Not so much nastiness as complete lack of interest. She never tried hard to like anyone. She was proud of being as caring as Hitler. Icecream wouldn't melt in her mouth, Morrie said, though that must have been a problem.

There was an exception to the family's detachment, and that was sulphur-and-treacle Granny, who was loaded. Oddly, Granny was an old and wrinkled kindness with runny eyes, who used to go to sleep on the toilet, and wasn't long above ground. A smell of discreet old clothes, a breath of quietness from a cupboard, and a faint smell of lavender, were all that remained of her with Nurse Pain. She wasn't sure who was to get the money, she said.

She had no religious education, had never seen the inside of a church until Granny put on the wooden overcoat. In church she wondered why she had to stand and sit, then stand again, like a jack-in-the-box, but in the course of the service grasped that some guy called Jesus was an hypothesis who imagined he died in everyone's place. Well, it had to be crap: there was Granny, dead as a doornail.

Not much from school stayed with her, only that owls see in darkness but not in light, horses are fast but can't catch mice, a demolition ball can wreck a building but can't plant seeds. She disliked soft girls, with their ambiguous flesh, thinking them useless as cut flowers, or chihuahuas. She was proud boys said the more she was stroked the more venom dripped from her fangs. They used a different word. She and her friends waited for the boys at River Beach, and when they came Nurse Pain, in her briefs or out of them, would have her hands full of some steamy youth who, after a brief paroxysm of excitement, would be putty in her hands. To cover her intense interest in the boys, she developed the reluctance of—well, if you've seen a jeweller handling a refund, you'll know how it was. She went on a lot more about sex, but I found her about as sexy as an argument about tickets to the grand final.

She made the decision to be a nurse with so little emotion that when she left to commence her training in Sydney she omitted to say goodbye to her mother and brothers. The training she enjoyed, glad to be away from the suburban atmosphere of Lost River in which the tracts of houses with gardens seemed to her like a vast lawn cemetery full of memorial flower beds. She preferred straight-out streets and big buildings and no silly nonsense with flowers and stuff; loved the institution feel of the big city hospital, the authority structure, the uniform, sense of purpose, the status of an elite. Certainly nurses were inferior to doctors, matron and the sisters, but the profound gulf between nurse and patient was as satisfying to Nurse Pain as food and drink. She was above those she felt she ought to be above. Away from the patients she missed them as a retired sheepdog misses her flock. She even learned to feign tolerance and patience, which didn't come easily to her. Her natural attitude was the manner of a madam to a client without readies.

She filled a vacancy at Lost River and soon became known as knotty, cross-grained and difficult. She didn't so much fear the matron as hate her, which raised her in the eyes of her peers. She revelled in enforcing strict rules. To have her burst, starched and hostile, into a ward, cross as two schoolteachers after lunch on Friday, was a terrifying experience for those who had to be there. Like successful climbers in an organisation she found everything others did was at least a little bit wrong.

She developed strong opinions on the 'bloody public' she dealt with, opinions shared by most of those she worked with, but as in the case of police, doctors, solicitors, teachers, engineers, shopkeepers, government servants, never publicly acknowledged. To precis her point of view: waste kills, we know patients are full of shit and that's what makes them sick. Suffering? We all die. Some illnesses are as painful as any police torture, but most patients were born whingeing. You fragment yourself for them, a bit for this one, a bit for that one. The more kindness you do for them the more it turns to shit. Useless to themselves and everyone else, most ought to be put down.

This contempt for the public was strongest in those who dealt most with it, just as in some race relations the closer the contact, the greater the manifest intolerance, and the more the interdependence, the louder the call for segregation. I suppose she meant that the more contact and information the greater the fear, as with HIV and AIDS publicity, and the greater the prejudice.

If she had believed in a god, it would be one without compassion, to whom all life was unimportant.

She looked at me as if she had caught a suggestion of sewage, and as if, skinned, I wasn't even worth making into a lampshade.

Her strong nose is the sort to smell out with a raptor's accuracy any unauthorised sounds and activities in a ward, even though she's long retired. There is a milky-blue outer rim to her iris. The hairs in her nose have gone grey. A wen on her left temple shines pinkly, with a patchy translucence. Her cheeks are soft as withering petals, and on them in the light can be seen the covering of fine hairs that in a man would grow long and tempt the razor. I was an item on a trash and trivia table. I was thankful I'd never had to feel the whip of her compassion.

She told me of her way of beating sleeplessness. She imagined unimaginable things. She dismissed my question on unusual happenings, meaning Amaza. 'I think a person should be able to bury the past, even if you have to kill to do it.'

She was tougher than I was. I found her too much. Like having the same tooth filled on Monday, then again on Tuesday.

nineteen
doctor clitterhouse

My next tapestry subject gave me the choice of an outing with the Wanderers' Walking Club, the New Year's Eve gala, or the vintage car rally at the showground. I chose the cars. I've never had a really good car, but I enjoy the look of them.

I was peering into a fine old green de Soto when the doctor assembled himself from a triangle of shadows at the corner of the big stand. He liked the Studebaker and the Nash. There was no '57 Chev; Leanne liked the word classic, but not vintage. We walked along the rows. Buick, de Dion, Terraplane, Whippet, Oldsmobile, T-Model, Lancia Galaxie, Rolls. His bearded face was coated in a thin shallow smile; I felt he'd rather have been in the company of a woman. He had a square jaw like a mashie/niblick, and the big soft brown eyes of a rocking horse. When he spoke, that jaw released into the world oddly corpulent vowels.

Debonair as a new car in a showroom, he had rooms in the medical centre in Afton Street, the converted Federation house with the white trim round doors and windows and the patterned arrangements of lighter coloured bricks at the corners highlighting flush windows and large bay windows on either side of the building. As well, lighter bricks were set in bars and rectangles in the walls. It had been a wonderful old house, one of the biggest in Lost River. Wealthy families, dispersed now, brought up their children in its many rooms and its half-hectare yard. A newer building, housing other doctors, stood where the old tennis court had been; some of the original weeds from more than a century before and which a succession of gardeners had combated, still flourished round the back of the new building.

Doctor Clitterhouse, who considered all care merely palliative, preferred open and public country life, even in a one-dog town, to rusticating deep in the anonymous forests of the cities, which once had promised comfort and a fuller life but couldn't deliver and now were pest holes spoiled by the muck inseparable from humans. Completely alone, or among too many others, the individual had no significance, he felt. Even cities' tall buildings he pictured as standover men ready to put the inhabitants on the knuckle. And the peasants of the big cities, if they could get away and earn the same living elsewhere, how many would stay in the metropolis? He thought cities attracted many whose freedom blossomed only in anonymity.

He thought of himself as just another gyno scraping a living and looking for shadows. When the X-rays were ready. There was a salvation in helping others, even if all he could do was turn agony into discomfort. Mind you, if they could afford it, his bill was like a pelican's. He wore black socks with white dolphins. Because he'd cut himself once or twice, he felt he empathised with all those he cut with his steel.

I found his vestibule rather sardonic, but the waiting room held a mist-and-haze Turner and a Constable getting ready to rain. He wan't an insatiable surgeon, simply liked his work, and in some cases, loved his patients. He took as his motto the name of the street, it suited his temperament. Flow gently, sweet Afton. He would flow gently, in work and in life. Lazy and lascivious might describe it. He would live without anger, that subtle poison of the arteries. But with love. Well, he tried. He liked women and tried to make good judgments on which ones to like a little better. Usually those willing to be nearby when needed, overseas when not, and unobtrusive as a bedside clock radio at all times. He aimed for an involved uninvolvement, rather as the UN manages. Like the UN he was largely front. Women noticed his beautifully kept nails, and long, careful, respectful fingers.

Some years before, having decided to remain unattached because all the women he knew had carefully made themselves unsuitable for marriage, companionship, or dwelling in the same house with a man, he felt his life needed something. He made a list of his unacted impulses, lusts, secret desires, deleting the more exotic and unthinkable, and opted for a life of sexual fulfilment. He thought of it as love, but then he thought of the aerial views he'd had in spring of nearby sparkling farms as glimpses of an Arcadian world. He had a wonderful manner, I was told. His patients could dwell on their lancinating pains, relate every resilient symptom, riffle through their compendium of anxieties, and be sure of receiving comfort and assurance.

When babies came, he was very good with the mothers. It's easier to be decent on a good salary, but he was a kind man, anyway. What mother doesn't dread giving birth to a monster, an alien thing?

They tell me there's a club of his exes that meets to have a laugh about it all, show each other the notes he wrote to them and recall the tongue-in-cheek endearments they wrote back, but 'they' may be laying false trails. Whatever the truth of it, Doctor C had no roots in the community that might have sensed this possibility and carried it to him.

When Sylvia Thorp entered his rooms with questions about uterine cancer, so did his downfall. She had heard through the grope vine of the doctor's little adventures, which all ended, as is the way of such things, since he chose carefully. Sylvia reckoned she had his measure. To her sex was as unremarkable as bare bodies among nudists publicly airing their differences. It was a utility. He thought, Here's another dying for a devoted doctor to palpate her jolly old purlieus. And since she seemed to agree with most of what he said, he thought she had lots of commonsense.

He knew little of the life of Lost River, the life that went on in streets and houses after dark, apart from what he picked up during his stints on the hospital board and occasional talks to the Red Cross. He said he knew no more about how information got round in the town than he knew about how neighbouring cells in the embryo knew how to become breast and nipple. He had lots of patients, but was strangely alone.

Satan flourished in the hearts and houses of a select few in the town, whose members followed a local mixture of Aztec and Celtic rites tacked on to the Satanism gleaned from picture books in the council library. They sacrificed animals on an altar welded by the man who made barbecues to order, and often hinted at the next step. Sylvia was a luminary among them. She patterned herself after the women she knew who'd had a little fling with the doctor, and presented as a quiet, quick-witted woman with a comfortably worldly attitude. She judged correctly, fitted the pattern, and he went ahead with this attractive humorous woman. He had no idea of her usual persona. Sylvia was much sharper than an angry tongue, she was violent and domineering and filled with hate, and scared the daylights out of the other worshippers. Her idea of seduction was to walk up cold and ask, 'Feel like an exchange of body fluids?' But this was business, and she didn't flinch or sneer when he was gentle as a Snag in getting to the subject of sex.

She was a bridge over sallow water, did everything he could ask for, and volunteered more. It was permanent Christmas. She flooded him with what he craved, knowing very well what happens when little boys gorge on chocolate for long enough. She even managed a kind of piquant sauce to her actions that smacked of innocence.

Her initiative in organising Flowers for Prisoners, and leading a hesitation of kind women to visit the 'motel', as the jail in a nearby town was called locally, deeply impressed him; after all, his own kindnesses had a cash value. She was elegant in tact, dress, speech. With a little woad around the eyelids he thought she was a drool come true, though not strictly beautiful. Her nipples were of such a pink that his head swam to see them move. And they moved, as the poet says, in more ways than one. The nectar that received his wand flowed like a comforting honey; there was even a triangular hood over her clitoris that could be lifted to display the tight little head that always seemed to be erect for him, whether for finger or tongue. Once or twice he lost his balance and thought he might have fluked someone who would fit the almost forgotten pattern of a godly, right, and sober wife. If only he wasn't addicted to pleasure.

He had no feel for the percussion of poetry or for its rhythms; nevertheless he wrote a fragment of verse for her and stupidly presented it to her. As an adolescent he'd read poetry of the past, and those honeyed words of romance and love preserved in him a kind of sugared silliness. He'd believed them. Far better for him if his verse had been studded with the puzzles of physics or mathematical mnemonics, or even the craggy vocabulary of anatomy or physiology. As he wrote them he told himself he wasn't entirely responsible for what came into his head. Like a driver to whom the oncoming traffic just happens. He'd forgotten most imagination belongs inside and should never issue in action.

Touching you is handling flowers
At night when I think
Your flowers rise before my eyes
Petals with tender wrinkles
Stamen with sensuous bulb
Dishevelled fringe of hair
And I want to prescribe you
For myself.

The next verse continued this drivel with pulses, hands, heartbeats. She was absent yet he was never without her. There was a third verse, and no better.

It's at such a stage
That I can't face each night
The thought of flowers alone in the dark.
Feeling lost, I prescribe
You for me.

She had other prescriptions in mind. Already he was helping—he had insisted—with a little money for her child, a boy of eight who was a problem at primary.

Two years later, in a moment of what had come to be increasing weariness, not to say the onset of a punishing boredom, he said he needed more time to himself, and she knew pay day had arrived. At the beginning she was interesting as wet and shining coloured stones in a rock pool, but now dull as dry ones. He thought the most that could happen was that she might be a little aggrieved, like an aunt left out in the rain. He explained about time and internal dialogue and thought the words right, the tone plausible. It sounded right.

Her opinion dropped with a thud like a feared and weighty name into a conversation. In an instant she became as sociable and open-hearted as a police commissioner when corruption is traced close to his desk. She thought it sounded like a rent payment each month plus a lump sum to show no hard feelings, the alternative being to be struck off after a withering blast of publicity; and was amused to see how he appeared when his mental pants were down and his mind round his ankles.

Her eyes, when he looked, were two villages of hate. Nothing had prepared him for this. Even the most brutal, violent and turbulent teachers and academics didn't show hatred as nakedly as this; they covered theirs with a decent coldness. He had to agree with Sylvia, it was too horrible to picture himself in the hands of official persons, cliff dwellers of the bureaucracy sitting at authority's comfortable desks, to whom he was merely a messy and inconvenient idea. He sat late in his office, thinking, while sudden neons made the office furniture jump out of the dark. No way out.

Checkmate. Life had become austere as a convention of accountants. Previously he'd thought of his women as so many concave collectibles, like surfies with their grommets: little rubbery things with holes.

For Sylvia the new security, the slightly higher plateau she had won, seemed to curb if not cure her temper and irascibility in the same way as sudden prosperity relieves many of life's maladies for a fortunate few.

The doctor still liked country life; the space and the sight of green hills ringing the town fed something in him, but he held himself even further from the risks, limited opportunities and tyranny of community life. He'd always thought of it with distaste; now he feared it. For a while he was as shy of people as a failed financier. Perhaps Sylvia would write a book. *The Art of Cooking and Eating the Human Head* would be suitable.

Some weeks later the medical provider was on the bed of a sexual provider for whom the world had never been a noble place and rarely generous. This was his golf day, and the kind of lunch he liked best. Off his eighteen handicap he had that morning shot a birdie on the short par three third hole, so it was a day of satisfactions.

On the whole I prefer a professional, he thought, and again remembered the city. The involved shadows of high towers questioning the light. At ground level no familiar faces among the thousands. Streets and air jammed with mechanical toys. Wind blowing vertically downward on your head. Weird. Better here. Everyone's unhappy at times, he ruminated, but mine's not the deep unhappiness of having to do what others want. He began to talk. He'd paid for it.

He'd travelled, developed a kind of travel blindness from too much moving around. The habit of the quick glance, the eye that sees nothing. Each tiny village would require ten to fifteen years to begin to understand its intricacy. The monument cringe; cathedrals, markets, plazas, Knossos, dusty Delphi to dowdy Olympus, trying to imagine a magnificence that's long gone to live in books. Could write a guide to the airports of the world, queues of the world too. Discovery that discomfort, inconvenience and stupidity can be raised to art forms. The babies: that's what it's about. Honorary father of thousands.

He subsided; thought. A vagrant memory of the obstetrics lecturer and the words, 'Born with the amnion over its face.' 'Caul?' interjected a student up the back. Rutherford. Anything for a joke. 'If it did I couldn't hear it.' And the time Rutherford asked, 'Do doctors weep over lost patients?' Entire lecture theatre rocking with laughter, hysterics. Put tears in your eyes. The value of education: to teach that some problems were insoluble, some diseases ineradicable, some questions unanswerable. And old Ogilvie: 'Some physicians keep alive future patients and the old who can be made to linger, generating wealth for the comfort of their declining years.'

Mrs Fusby gave the appearance of support, or listening, as any wife does a dozen times a day. Or can do, if she wishes.

Again Sylvia surfaced. Triumph he could understand, but why hatred? Most days this sneaky rhizome of a question, reaching underground, spreading, pushing down roots and up stalks, compelled his attention. But what a mistake! To try to graft a theory, an adolescent form of love, onto a real person with a separate life and her own agenda. How could he have done it? Now his feelings towards her were cold and lifeless as a dead man's dick, and he felt sorry for himself for that reason.

As he lay still he could hear his heart whispering its message and wondered what dark threads mazed his heart, creeping onwards, and how far the normal sclerosis of his arteries had progressed, and how long it would be before he ceased to live as an individual and in one moment forgot self, patients, world, and became again part of the material inventory of the planet, to be used for its future. If the universe indwells us, he thought, perhaps we all possess qualities common to the universe.

All at once a familiar joy filled him. He smiled widely. At least he'd never married. He'd never sworn, however lightly, 'In sickness and in wealth, in change of personality, change of mind, altered aims, mutated behaviour, in unpredictable desires …'

His smile was so noticeable from her side of the bed that Leanne asked, 'What's tickling you?'

'I'm lucky. If you ever hear me grumble, remind me I'm lucky,' he repeated, with this request unconsciously treating Leanne Fusby as the wife whose absence from his life he was so happy about. Shortly he would go, and tomorrow, Thursday, work a long day partly to support a mother and child, unseasonable allies to whom he was uncomfortably tied. For life.

Forget equality, forget enlightened attitudes; what a pity he couldn't keep a woman like you keep a pet. Take her out when you want her. Idly he wondered if the more recent exfoliations of feminism were bringing with them a recuperation of woman's supposed civilising role and rule-making behaviour.

Once upon a time he felt he was some sort of hero because he regretted nothing. Now he regretted the wrong things. He resolved, if ever he returned to his old ways, to be as circumspect as the wimpiest Snag approaching a militant feminist with drying scalps hanging from her belt.

Before he left, there was an incident of donger renascent. Leanne didn't like you trying to sneak seconds when the transaction was neatly over, so he let it die.

I drew him as a failed Theseus. Not that he was devoured by a minotaur, but that he'd failed to put down the Sylvia rebellion and find a way out of his dilemma.

As for me, I've done some miserable things. Some so ugly, so mean-spirited that I push them away when they gather round at two in the morning to gloat and point the finger. Hammering that idiot against the post, banging his head into the concrete. Executing the black dog because it annoyed me, and still in a blind rage when I buried it. The axe. I wish I could forget the axe.

I was alone in my church with the whole of my past, but banished it in an instant because all I wanted to think about was that I wasn't able to tell her how much because I didn't speak that language.

She had the idea that others could see what was in her head merely by looking at her face. I couldn't. I saw other things, but she didn't want that kind of attention.

Why did I take notice of what her attitudes seemed to be? Or what she thought they were? Attitudes can be changed. Why have respect for every person as if they mustn't be disturbed since they're in their final form with no likelihood of change? What was wrong with a bit of push and persuasion? What kind of wimp was I? The point was, what did I have that a woman of the future might value? And how do you persuade a woman whose fixed principle is that to be her friend is to agree with her?

twenty

angel zuccalo

I'd had no more attacks of what might be called my panic at night. Some centre in me had faced the fact that it was bare guilt. Guilt surrounded me like a thick quilted atmosphere. I breathed it. Strangely, I felt comfortable in it, almost expansive. I felt it supporting me as I went to sleep. I had a word for it. It seemed to be true about me, for I remembered well enough the invigorating joy I felt when I stole, years before. The intoxicating pleasure of getting away with something. The satisfying superiority of walking away a victor, leaving someone else on the ground. That watchman and the baseball bat. Bricking the jewellery shop. The untraceable knife made from a file.

I'd empathised with victims and the weak, in my time, but also with oppressors and killers. I'd loved representations of death and destruction, and the parts in me that loved them were those that could have committed the same acts. I'd not only been the man tied to a kitchen chair waiting to be shot;

I'd been the one with the finger on the trigger. Never once did I turn my eyes away from the gory scenes in film or book. I devoured them, savoured every last slosh of blood, every spatter of brain on the wall, every dying groan, especially the last one, the last shudder, the last flicker of nerves in the corpse. I was there watching, I was there dying, I was there killing. No censorship! Suck it in! Bits of bodies, slaughter, laughter, buckets of blood, satisfied smiles, money well spent.

The same person would look, listen, imagine, draw cartoons, apportion colours, and peacefully weave other people into tapestry to give their lives a brief permanence. How many of those terrible things I savoured were in me? Did I enjoy them because they were in me? What of family and children abandoned, loving friends smashed to pieces, putting themselves together, then smashed apart again, into smaller pieces? And Yarrow. At least she was someone I couldn't smash. She hadn't let me get close enough for that.

In the little white office at the rubbish tip on an island between the in and out tracks for traffic, Angel sits breathing the heavy musics of the radio, his life intangible, indirect, as he waits for utes, trucks, cars with trailers, to stop at his red and white barrier before paying to tip their rubbish. Trucks left, down to the landfill; domestic straight ahead to the tipping bays.Crows overhead call like hoarse babies. A tiny personal fan wings left and right crookedly, a bird with one engine on the blink. A glossy picture cut from *House and Garden* is stuck on the wall to decorate his workplace; it shows a landscape filled with quiet irony: a mansion overlooking an ocean somewhere in the universal suburb. Plates of baked potatoes come sailing over the eastern ridge. Good idea for tea tonight. He loves eating alone, can use a spoon for everything, lick the plate, get away from the table as soon as he's finished, fart when he feels like it, scratch when he itches, rave and swear when the spirit moves him. From the west, on prevailing winds, hate-spores come from other continents, leaving no tracks in the air. Angel sees them clearly.

Angel looks out at Bob Penny bulldozing big stuff towards the far slope of the landfill, and his dog Archimedes that accompanies him everywhere, scattering ibis and seagulls newly retired to the easy pickings of the tip, but what he sees happened years ago. The family taking the train to Sydney to gape at the verticals after the country's horizontals, and to see the Zuccalos at Hunter's Hill, and Mum falling between ferry and wharf at Valentia Street. The pictures are in his head until he dies and his memory is wiped, he thinks. He wears a poor reluctant smile that looks as if it cost money he didn't have.

His face is as remarkable as many of those you find at seven in the morning in a city early-opener. The responsible nose and calm mouth of a neurosurgeon, the eyes of an itinerant knife-grinder, a prizefighter's brow. Yet he'd gone straight from school at fifteen to a job with the council. Nothing about his appearance fitted him any more than sunburn on a fish.

Mum broke the surface, wet as sharks' teeth, and yelled non-stop at the ferry driver. Water pushed and sucked, she couldn't get a grip. Her tough fingers, cut by mussels, beat like hammers on the aged turpentine decking as she tongue-lashed everyone in sight and called on the Deity for vengeance. Not that she had much truck with deities, but the Catholic one was familiar and respectable enough to swear by. The nearest to a real deity for the Zuccalos was the promiscuous bank that inculcated indebtedness then threw them off their land, and it was in fact cast in the same mould as the ancient deities: splendidly got up, constantly trumpeting virtues it would like to be known by, but also capricious and vengeful and at times given to disastrous mistakes. Angel was the eldest child and made up additions to the story for the younger kids, Maria, Tony and Joe. He loved them and looked after them at school and in the street and at home, where he dressed up the dog Mike in a frilly skirt for Maria, his little sister; but they were the only kids he loved. He still loves them, but as they were then. He's stiff with them now, resents them being strangers, with all the changes of the years.

Angel had the usual boyhood and youth and dreams of dipping the wick, and even in manhood was conditioned to shout 'C'mon, Aussie!' at the slimmest provocation, the provocation usually being some sport or other. But this tune was accompanied by a deeper and stabilising bass which boomed 'Roll on the weekend!', which was the real national anthem.

'No family,' Angel says. 'Never have kids. Horrible bloody things, kids, specially these days. Sacrifice yourself for kids who forget you before you die, who will sacrifice themselves for kids who will forget them. Self-made eunuch, me. Bugger the lot. Had a few birds here and there but no closer than taking them out, spending money, a bit of sex. Every man's his own judge. I did what was best for me. Either the steermaker and a few minutes pain, or in for a life of the Emsie Emasculator or the Colless Castrator. Great sometimes, but not to be your jailers. Bloody nuisances. All the stupid things they want, bloody bowerbirds. Like another race, another language; all the words mean something different. A man can't ever say anything right. A word's wrong, or I ought to mean something else, or I said a word someone said that they don't like anymore. Jesus. They think they want this. When they get it, no, they meant something else. Always something more, not what's here and what they've got, but they can't say exactly what. So whatever you get, you can never be right. At arm's length they're okay, but let them in close and you cop the whole shit-list of married life.

'What I mean is, look around. People get married. In five years they've changed. Diverged. Both changing, getting further apart, and there's still forty years to go. Who needs it? Times have changed, and so have I, but not the way the times have. I'm a man of the old style, but without the patience and dedication to be a husband. Nothing in it for me. No, I couldn't come at the other thing over on track two. Being gay is a male dream, all the sex you can take. Some do both, foot in both camps, but I couldn't come at blokes. Know too much about blokes. When I told Sharon and Georgina I wasn't interested in women they dropped off like dried scabs, not even a mouthful of hateful words with jags of flesh hanging. All over. I bought a few rings to wear for company. Got this tattoo "M" for mother. Had a few nights on the slops, woke with a mouth fresh as the bottom of a drunken cocky's cage and a head big as the house and felt all the better for it.

'I think of babies a lot, just like they reckon birds of the desert think of water, and inquisitive fish come to the surface to take brief looks at the sky. In town I see babies in pushers, faces like fruit; girls with mouths like flowers, body shapes like music. I love living things. Trees. Little bunches of ready-shaped leaves in buds on the oak branches in Anzac Park waiting all winter to come into leaf in spring. Marvellous. Funny how you always come back to the start of things.'

Angel seemed unaware of the jewel within him, which was this: knowing he hated children and that females were unintelligible to him, he kept away from both, thus avoiding the twin evils of marital misery and the senseless propagation of his own kind.

'Wonder where the stuff goes when the sperm-cords's cut,' he said. 'Must put a strain on the clean-up system in the old bod.'

Failure was in the family, way back. Grandpa's car, that he bought with money his mum left him. With his round head, grey hair, wide nose and funny ears he looked like a disorderly koala. The car gave Angel his first insight into the ruggedness of natural objects. No matter what Grandpa did to it, the vehicle persisted in going. Motion was its nature, ingrained in its design, its materials, its heart and lungs. It resembled something alive that you chop into bits and the bits keep wriggling. Finally he had it in so many pieces that it didn't go. He didn't assemble it, just left it. People thought it was a wreck, but it was no wreck. He just let it rust.

Angel looks out over the town. 'It's a good place, Lost River, like any place that comes to live in you. Big on participation, small on big city alienation. The memories of mankind are embedded in the shape of hills like these, the rounded slopes, the slow rise up Casuarina Rise, the flats spread out with plots and roads and trees, bends in the road, bends in the river. Roads like these all over the world, sudden hills, narrow bridges, walking paths that recognise you.'

Outside, a long grey bird uttered a metallic cry and slammed into a tree, damaging the bark. Angel nodded as if he'd been expecting it. Objects, processes, happenings, weren't placed here for us to fit into a pattern, his face said. It wasn't a test, this planet, not a problem, just a home. We all just popped out into life, they put clothes on us, give us a push, send us to school, expect us to take it from there. We just have to play it out to the end. Life at the tip. Always room at the tip. My life would make a good joke.

At one stage a fly with a hyacinth-blue backside dropped in and stood on the desk top, feet planted purposefully. Angel watched as the fly extended her tongue and rubbed it vigorously with both forehands for twelve seconds by the clock, then stopped rubbing, reeled her tongue back in, made a half turn in a businesslike manner, then stood stock still and did nothing. There are things in me, Angel thought vaguely, that might make me a genius if the world were different. Wonder which things.

Towards five, when business had dropped right off, Angel, who in the morning had given a virtuoso performance of being one of those grublike souls who crave to be shown their cubicles and told what to do, grew wings and flew round the other side of the world to his mansion on a ridge overlooking the cheerful blue waters of the Caribbean. He changed into fresh gear after his shower and passed slowly along the white flagstones that paved the extensive patio. It was idyllic autumn, right after yesterday's pleasant winter. He loved the comfort of Italian shoes, silk socks and underwear. The maid would bring cocktails the moment the sun dipped beneath the ocean's threshold. Sharon or Georgina, who was on duty tonight? It didn't matter who was on, they both looked alike and both were the nearest any two females had ever come to resembling Maria, his sister. Who, for her own reasons, had remained single.

The hills surrounding the tip looked as if they had been born exhausted. One tip section was where statues die. I was surprised at how many there were. Many concrete, some plaster. One of the workers had turned them to face each other. You could imagine them saying meaningless words to each other, just like people at a formal party where time is ritually sacrificed for other reasons.

I made Angel a kind of Ajax, without the heroism. All he had was the defeat, then the symbolic suicide. He didn't mind heaving a few stones at Leanne Fusby, either. She'd been a torturer from South America, was on the run, Amaza had recognised her so she had to die. Fusby had stolen a police diary with so many incriminating entries that they couldn't touch her. He heard it from Bob Penny.

While I worked on him, I had a thought about death. Is it

sometimes a gradual thing, like dark particles falling and covering your world bit by bit?

And a thought about my twin Jonathan, born dead. Is there a world to one side of this where he might have lived an interesting life? And in that life, might he too have put on people like coats, lived in them for a time, then taken them off and thrown them aside? Had he lived that other life full of resentment that I was the one born to this world?

There were times in Lost River when the streets were empty, as if the town had died. Also at night, with lights in the streets and in the blinded windows, a TV flicker here and there, but no sound. Peculiar. I suppose there was life going on behind those blinds. Were they in touch, were they on the phone to other townspeople, or was it the Feynman effect, where they'd got too close to others during the day, and been hurled apart, to lodge safe and alone in their separate rooms?

twenty-one

carmen mummo

I'd heard she was the town liar and would lie even if the truth was more interesting, or easier. A caution was added by Edward Cuttlebone, the retired spy: even if all Cretans were liars, he said, who's to know whether all they say is lies, or whether the lies are sprinkled throughout their speech like sultanas in a fruit cake? I broke off from straightening the heddles, which had overlapped, to ring her.

Try to keep her talking about herself, I was told. By Juniper Grey, actually. And you'll get a network of stories about Knudsen Boult, Saint Salivarius, Borry Blow, Crasher Coy, maybe even Hollywood Hossan. She has stories for everyone. I transferred a kiss from lip by finger to the photo of Yarrow I'd pinned where I could see it as I worked, and in the pickup, floating down to the town, I reflected on the coming meeting of liars. I'd lied to myself so often I don't believe myself even now. How many others run out of credit with themselves?

She took shape at her door with a washer cold from the

fridge held to her forehead. I didn't ask. Even so, she did it so well that when I came away I received a picture of the headache colour, a washed-out yellow with grey flecks and sharp blue electric sparks. Her eyes were surrounded—defended—by a stockade of eyeliner, her expression steady as a coracle in choppy water, her hair straight-out-of-bed dishevelled. Since her education at a private school in another town she had worked for the vet in Market Street for fifteen years, giving pleasure and immeasurable reassurance to thousands of dog and cat owners, who, because of the way she spoke of their pets, loved all the more the absolute treasures she convinced them that their animals were. So there was a utility to her words. The vet was sorry to see her go. She started Puptrim, Care for Dogs, out of her house in Macquarie Street. She had a defiant look when she closed her lips round those full rows of slightly prominent teeth. My first impression was that she had expected more from herself, hadn't thought she'd be as ordinary as she turned out.

I'd been to see her in *The Robbers*, a contemporary play against the new universalism by a young black playwright. Under cover of life on a remote camp, the writer's message to the world was death to empire-builders, whether of language, customs, or political systems, and long live tribes, minorities and individual cultures and peaceful co-existence of the most diverse forms of national life. She insisted we wouldn't achieve community without nation and pledged to accept others' differences while swearing to maintain her own. I didn't like the use of the wobble-board, its chuckle sounded too laid-back in the circumstances.

Carmen played Kunzea in a fluffy, pink and sensual sari, of all things, who had a snout on the red-headed Mouse Spider, and told harmful lies to the Native Indigo about the white powder on Ghost Gum. She produced a tinkling laugh, silver rain. The play was set in the days when possums and koalas were roasted by white as well as brown folk. At the end Kunzea was put out like a fire. With hisses. Carmen, with eyes closed, was able to push out tears you could see in the fifth row.

She took the washer away from her head; she was wearing the empty smile some women hold out in front of themselves to ward off strangers. She had the kind of pretty face that makes lechery rewarding, for the trivial reason that the lecher goes away with pretty pictures in the head. In summer sandals, her toes kept anting in a group, never still. Perhap their movements were an accompaniment to her thoughts.

Most babies look innocent, though they soon learn. But are they innocent? How much are they born with? What is the reality? Do they at first expect the ground itself, as well as steps, to move underfoot?

Carmen began to wonder about reality during the time it took to tell her first important lie. After the first, all the rest would be easy, that was clear, but during those seconds she could feel a fuzziness of words, of descriptions, of objects, of happenings, even of people, and certainly of herself. A kind of intuition of the universal grammar of lies and concealment told her the best liar is one who feels the truth of what she says. And feelings can be trained.

Grown-up, her friends said that where reality was concerned, Carmen didn't have a strong suit; they didn't know her. As someone said of a famous American diplomat, she didn't lie for gain but because it was her nature to lie. Sometimes a forefinger helped her think. It went to her chin, or her cheek. Perhaps it was a substitute for the whole hand, behind which she'd like to have hidden while she lied, to give fewer indications of what was behind her face. I didn't know what was the status of the information she downloaded about Mrs F having been part of a car-stealing ring, and as a master of martial arts having beaten up a politician in Sydney one night, and that now bad people were spreading the lie that the Aprahamian woman died in her sleep. This time she didn't need the finger's assistance.

Back to when she was six. She'd been angry with Washington, their agreeable spaniel, for wanting to look through the fence at the neighbours' children and their noisy game, when she wanted to pet him quietly and have him to herself. When her blood was up it seemed reasonable to paint Washington, but when the work was done and the time approached for confrontation with the parental police, it did seem she ought to be prepared to suggest alternative explanations of how the paint got on the dog. She could see that any number and sequence of events may be given a meaning and interpretation, or, with more imagination, any number of different explanations. Carmen didn't need Leibniz to tell her that.

So. Washington whacked the paint with his clumsy tail and knocked it down over himself. The dog was not well placed to contradict. For policy reasons her parents accepted this story, hoping the responsibility of being trusted would induce her to be trustworthy in the future. It works, with some. But she remembered her father taking a walk over to where the paint brush, still wet with green paint, reclined in the drip tin. He said nothing, just put the lid back on the paint, and cleaned the brush. That he believed her was as unlikely as the disciples not recognising the risen Jesus.

As she was telling the lie with their eyes on her, she was surprised how easy it was to keep her face open and sincere and to look first one, then the other, straight in the eye. She was too young then to know that such a look is often an infallible sign that the truth is on holiday. It was a peculiar feeling.

More than that, it was wonderful, as if she were lifted above the ground by a power outside her, and she was speaking assurances to a vast audience, the world perhaps, and somehow becoming more than herself as the words came. And certainly becoming more than her audience. It was power, changing the history of what happened. It was also like crossing a dangerous bridge, doing it cleverly, and arriving safely on the other side. That was the moment she decided lies were right for her. She wanted that feeling of power repeated as often as possible. She would think carefully about her lies, take them seriously, spruce up the faded patches with colours. It took some time for the paint to grow out of Washington's coat, and the whole world of objects, words and actions had become plastic, shifting, blurred at the edges.

It was a little later that Mum had conceived an ambition to become a physicist. 'I can sense and almost see the sort of white coat I'll wear, and the colours to go with it,' she said to anyone who would listen. She was serious, you had to give her full marks for that, and as busy among her books as a Coolangatta henfish with her brood of chickfish.

Carmen was terribly unhappy at fourteen, at the first blood. Cried for hours, she said, though that's a lot of tears. Not so much at the blood, but because others were right and it came as they said it would and the future was there and rigid as walls. Was she adopted? She was so different from the family. Maybe she was conceived in a dish, she thought. She was then at the age when she was mad on horses, admiring their huge muscles and proud heads. She loved being astride and in control of such power, such magnificence. She was good at hockey, too. As she ran with the ball two large objects seemed to be taking swipes at each other under the front of her school uniform blouse, I was told.

The English teacher went on about words, hypocrisy, truth. 'You must look at what's actually there, whether actions or words. See things as they are, as far as you can. Get rid of humbug, deception, cover-ups, try to arrive at the truth.' You could only attempt this, it appeared; it was impossible to achieve perfectly in practice, though you might sometimes get close. Cosmic truth about the universe may never be known; you may have it yet not know you have it, but to strive for it was an honourable aim. This was the official line and it suited Carmen: truth was somewhere, but out of reach and unknowable. There was a large, vague comfort in that.

So reality had no hard and fast borders. At the level of atoms, everything was a whirling, dancing, vibrating—who knows?—mass of movement. The surface of her tennis racquet was a mass of movement too small to be felt. There was no fixed edge. Nothing was still. So her inner conviction was spot on. Nothing was still, fixed, true. She stood slantwise to the world and was right to do so. Perhaps even death was a set of agreed falsehoods. And already she accepted into her world objects that had no existence, such as the golden mountain of the logic class. In addition there were objects with only a slight existence, but that thought was her secret possession.

The world was so big, so much in it, that it was a kind of darkness. No one could know or understand it all. Everything might be different from what we think. And in fact she began to see so many positives in negatives, such activity in immobility, such strength in weakness, such waste in frugality, weariness in rest, achievement in sleep, such presence in absence, such filth in beauty, so much love in hatred. The list was endless and could be reversed with similar results.

'Everything,' she said, 'seems ultimately, at the base level, to be unreal, or at least phantomlike, though for practical purposes and our short lives, it's the only reality we have. Even our buried and half-forgotten memories aren't graspable, yet they make up what some call our unconscious, which is at the base of our crazy little unstable selves. So who do we think we are? And why not be different tomorrow? I suppose truth exists, or there'd be no lies, and it matters. Inside, I know it, I think. But sometimes I'm convinced it doesn't, that all is provisional, all is flux, and truth is a thing that existed momentarily in a past constantly moving away from us and to which we have no access. And the past itself is equivocal, you know, growing at a rate faster than the flow of time.'

I didn't feel equal to replying. She rather took my breath away. I'd thought I was to meet a common liar, and I got this. I couldn't even think of a question.

'There's a larger world enclosing this one. Nothing true in that one is true in this. I can't express it, but I've seen little flashes of that larger world. Everyone there is like me. It's my real home. It's so different from this world where people take the straight line they think is so simple, but get disoriented and lost among its subtle changes of direction.'

I drove home to the church, still thinking of her, and halfway there realised the pickup was travelling at much the same pace as the grass-counting slowbird, few of which survive nowadays. I speeded up. A cow's face followed me in small shifts of her head. I didn't know at any moment if she could see me now, or had seen me before, of if she'd realise in ten seconds' time that she'd seen something, and wonder what.

One of Carmen's friends mentioned Wally Welland-Smith, and Carmen's fascination with this rough, self-taught man who was straight as a die and didn't know he'd made such an impression. Often she was cheeky enough to try to date a man with his wife listening, the friend said. Carmen was looking for something a little longer-term than what she had, but none of the men who took her out had her on his list for something permanent. Her core acquaintances kept asking about her life and she always had a different story. What Carmen was seeking was a companion to whom she could reveal anything, everything. 'Someone who wouldn't bring it up against me later. Like a god or something. I could talk about my parallel worlds where life is richer, people live superior lives, where there are different attitudes to conflict and power, where confident self-affirmation is the preferred option rather than this slinking around within boundaries others police.' It was as if a tyrannical empire of truth locked her into fixed positions, when she loved freedom to say things that appeared to fall down if you prodded them with a word, or other object.

She was honest and realistic about her lying, but few wanted the bother of having a liar about the place: a potential trouble-maker, a Pandora. You'd never know, Knudsen said, if there was a joey in the pouch.

Some thought she wasn't so much a liar as too careful about how her words would be received, so she discounted or marked up what she said. Others said the idea that truth was what isn't hidden, truth was openness, was anathema to her. I think she loves lies, variable truth, because she feels things don't have to be this way, they can be that way, and is drawn at a deep level to having things the way she wants them at the moment. Expanding her horizons with a wish. She feels her truth is superior to the truth of others. There is so much in her that detests obedience. And I mean obedience to anything. I'm still thinking about objects with a slight existence.

At the performance of *Knife in the Eye*, a flower-thrower each night directed his blooms to Carmen, who played the murderer. In the *Bugle* he claimed she was a great actor, unrecognised.

In the cartoon I made for her she was a cosmos of good things. The key to this cosmos was a word she kept under her tongue. In the Eureka Mall today she was leading her cat Springfield with collar and lead. She wanted Springfield to feel the interest and affection of an audience. Edwold, at the magazine stand, doesn't know what he's talking about: she doesn't keep a python in her laundry.

I still kept dreaming that Yarrow and I might be together somehow. What would be the correct distance apart to keep us in double orbit? Or would we push apart if we were any closer than we were now? At that first meeting my eyes felt like fingers that had a tongue to taste with as they wandered from her face and hair and tried to catch her hands in flight. I remember it was an autumn day, the sun asleep above heavy woollen cloud. It was no surprise when that mouth uttered words about the unreality of history, though later words indicated the apparently fixed reality of her own history. I felt like dancing when I saw her, she fitted everything about her, but she wasn't a woman you dance for, she was only slightly more demonstrative than my father Jackson Blood.

twenty-two

macaterick black

In Rugby Park where they hold the Highland Gathering, I caught sight of the old writer, not yet terminally marginalised, watching some strong citizens, King Khan among them, tossing the caber. It was orange weather, with leaves of shining green. He withdrew and I saw his long eyes searching west, then east, and remembered some words he'd written. 'East and west, the long warp of country waiting for our lives' weft to bind and stabilise to it,' from *Land of Thieves*.

I'd looked him up in the library and seen the comments that he needed a moat round him, that he avoided city people high on distractions, people in whose company he leaked away in harmless trivia. I didn't feel competent to interview him, but it had to be done. Oh, and one picture of him in company with a brawl of intellectuals. In an anthology I found an early play on politics, *The Bucket*, and an early line about reaching into the songbird's mouth to touch the song and finding the words of its language were single letters, and a confession decades ago to having set fires and walked away. Another line on how the word becomes flesh on the reticent page. A lament about mistakes: 'I was wrong. I didn't believe arms could make war less likely. I'd forgotten the schoolyard and how you defend yourself against the bully.' An aphorism: 'We must find the treasure before we can search for it.' And one I didn't understand about having to die to the world before your best work happens. On the way to see this difficult old guy another quote repeated itself in my head. 'Life tears at us. Goes for the spirit and wrecks the flesh on the way in.'

I made a list of questions, without the unusual happenings question: too ashamed of that. A sign on the fence next door said, 'Emus for sale. 6 mths. 18 mths.' And on the other side of Black's house a notice about Ostrich and Alpaca transport. Reminded me of Black's 'Australia is not a melting pot, more a coleslaw.'

They told me he bestows words as if they're donations to a failing cause. Maybe he was soured when some clown made a fuss about his 'valued birthstain', an ancestor in the early convict lists.

Mac Black lives in Monash Street and talks mostly to his cymbidiums. He's a lean, laconic Australian, though no spartan, simply a writer who values isolation, obscurity and open spaces. Deserts, too. You only need to read the experienced guardedness of his watchful and well-watched face. Just the same, I sensed that his real isolation consisted in others not understanding what he was saying, as when he wrote of trees and people full of windows, rocks and concrete growing in ladder shapes. I think he had come to believe evil begins with the presence of other people. He has Iron Age skin and the slightly impatient eyes of a mathematics lecturer.

'Love for a neighbour increases in proportion to the square of the distance between you,' was quoted by past interviewers, who questioned him about the ascetic distance he keeps from others. They speculated on the deep north of his personality, the permafrost of his self, and his publicised fear of having to spend time with the young, to suffer their poised, confident and loquacious ignorance.

Last book he brought out he said miserably, 'Life would be fine but for social occasions and the distractions of company.' He needs the silence and room in himself that allows him to luxuriate in books and to think. He regards published interviews as takeaway food for thought. I think he wanted to communicate, to get into minds, but feared contact with bodies. He said, 'I was blessed with an appetite for a minimum of possessions and have a taste for simplicity, self-effacement and lots of uninterrupted silence. I have no need to win, in any sense. As long as some of my lines breathe. Usually, after energetic, laborious work, I arrive at very little.' This is the man who said man is one of God's quarks, who maintains that awareness of other cultures prompts people to resist change. He asserts that Australians are not yet real people, not used to living, he says, and certainly not used to our present modernity bursting out of the old boundaries. In the Vermeer print above his desk a calm clock was about to strike one.

'When people get too close for too long I feel I've been hammered flat, smoothed of natural bumps, polished like a mirror, and to be compelled to listen is misery; I feel like the uncomfortable frog which eats centipedes. My life is largely in me, where my thoughts circulate like a gas. I like to learn constantly. What I do among others is makeshift, artificial. I'm convinced I won't find life, the pulsing real, in talking to others. It's too far beneath, well hidden by the mist of words we spray out even when we're being as honest and accurate as we can, and no narrative can be trusted.

'Solitude is difficult at times, but it's the lesser of a number of evils, one of which is company. In cities I'm a lover of alleyways, worn steps, slums and old warehouses, and dead Sunday mornings. I think I need no friends except the dead.' His dead were closed and silent on his bookshelves.

'Isolation gets the work done. Disturbing no one, and undisturbed. Inhabiting other consciousnesses, other memories, working on scenes that can't be caught in pictures, using words for which there are no pictures. No, I can never be integrated into this society, I don't accept its degraded values and don't trust it an inch. It's crowded with people who'll follow any leader because they have no ballast in them; they've abandoned poor old God and now will believe any thing. Folk who simply haven't the moral authority nurtured, practised and developed within them to be responsible to themselves.

'Another thing. I love no one. It was a hard day when I faced the fact that I've loved only the once. For the rest, I was drawn to opportunities to get something I wanted, even if only a new milieu, and annoyed by the other things I had to do to maintain the contact. Now my pet image of love is of the lion licking its prey, before dining. Just as you touch, look at and clasp objects, to make them yours.

'I was afflicted in youth by poetry, and, like herpes, the virus never left me, but I have no talent for it. A few pewter poems when I was a student. All I'd be capable of now would be a poetry of anger and despair. Much verse now is like bran without milk. I made myself a writer; I had no discernible talent. I guess I'll never do as Poe did. Remember how he solved Olbers' Paradox on why the night sky isn't full of light, long before Olbers knew he had a paradox?

'I knew when I was young that I would never do well in hierarchies of males, I lacked an interest in the rubbish they go on with: their symbolisms, their little tests, their balls-oriented attitudes and prides, their juvenile banter, jokes, teasing, all designed to check group morale, mood, attention and solidarity, and at the same time to put down any who can be put down. I needed a work outside hierarchies dependent on physical size, self-importance, aggressiveness, ambition, the desire to rule and dominate. I couldn't take such things seriously.

'Yes, I withdraw myself from experience. I'm not separate; my consciousness is part of the external world. I adapt the Burns prayer: 'O would some gift the power give me to see others as they see themselves.' Not a loss of identity, but a recovery of the identities and bits of self I hold in common with others, which usually aren't allowed to appear or that have broken off me somewhere in the past. I regard what I do as an escape from this one self, sometimes even from selfness as such.

'Why keep on? Because I decided to. Poor naked watcher in a clothed world. Decades of work have honoured me with obscurity. Following a will-o'-the-wisp, a mysterious fire leading to foolish hopes. It makes no difference to the world, a matter of character now. I give thanks for my failures, which taught me to put no value on popular success. However, I must keep on. I have a conscience which will not allow me to rest if I try to suppress what I know I ought to do. It's the long line of my ancestors, who judge by the strictest standards. They're merciless, not turned aside by sympathy, fellow-feeling, humanity, deference, pity or any other thing. They're not dead. They live today in judges, referees, measurement, accuracy, examinations, mathematics, rules, auditors, laws, keeping to the right side of the road, and such.

'Daily my main toil is achieving simplicity and freshness, which entails constant reworking. Language is, amongst other things, an instrument. So that when I write of choosing freedom and losing security, choosing equality and losing self-esteem, or gaining self-awareness and losing peace of mind, I aim to produce an effect in the body of the reader.

'No, criticism doesn't bother me now. The world is all rough edges. When it privileges the academic and marginalises the writer trying to exist in the marketplace it seems a threat, but when the gusts of wind blow themselves out the work remains, though by then it's off the shelves, so criticism can affect sales. Beautiful writing? Ah, if I could define that, I could define a dog. But I can recognise both, and about dogs I'm usually right.

'The thought of death makes me work harder. The body is weaker, but the will is stronger now. When I sit at this desk to work is when I'm doing something real, and I'm almost real myself. Yet still I feel like a child trying to carry water in my hands.

'My great disappointment was to live in an age corrupted by doctrines false at a casual glance. For instance, only force can give equality and while that force exists, the state can never wither. And if stealing is wrong, there's a right to private property. States founded on such dogmas have run aground on the rock of centralism. Reason dreams beautiful futures which usually turn out to be disasters, because the future has to be built brick by brick, by a lot of different people, and not created at a stroke by a few like-minded ones. I was never inoculated with the paradigms of the day when I was young; I refused the Marx injection, and spat out the Freudian serum.

'I am for maximum freedom. It will bring human fragmentation, that's its price. And government will be desperate to clamp a lid on it all: their aim is to have us dependent, and helpless.

'Christ's religion? Ah, a gentle beauty, but corrupted by the churchmakers. He was of the East, spiritually, you see so much of his teaching in the Tao. Treating others as oneself can hardly lead to a prosperous state in a world of large populations and electronic funds transfer around the world; besides, it would require a dictatorial world government to bring it into being by force. Yet I'm still troubled by whatever it is that underlies all our queries, intimations and inklings. Perhaps God is the accumulated past in us, and perhaps death is life seen through a mood, a certain way of thought. I confess that I have a little voice outside me that talks to me and gives me hints, reproofs and answers. I ask questions and talk back, and often say thanks.

'I have other voices too. Things done and said years ago, acts, omissions, defeats, embarrassments, fears: all recur, act themselves out time after time. Plague me. The past is in my ears always, floodlit in memory. Friends, insults, enemies, family, failures, mistakes: reliving everything until the past is alive and all its inhabitants. The older I become the more alive the past is in me. It kicks like an unborn child, out of my control.'

He looked old. He turned back to his desk and pulled a paper from a pile.

'Here, take this with you. I must get on.' He handed me some paper and looked so relieved to be seeing the back of me that I hurried out. Sitting in the white pickup I read the old man's words:

Burying the dead is difficult.
No sooner is the earth in place
And you walk away
Than you hear them beside you
Or ahead.

They revive a past they were in
With you. You know it word for word.
Answer back
Or try to shut them up;
They don't respond.

They never go, talking to you at night
Waiting for you round corners.
In your last moments
You hear their voices still
Talking of that past.

Safely dead, you too
Must leave your grave and do duty:
Over their objections
Constantly remind the living
Of their past.

Stuck to the back of this sheet, in the way paper sometimes clings, was another sheet. Perhaps he hadn't known there were two. Or he felt more comfortable giving me a piece of writing than a few minutes more talk. I read it:

When I was young I thought that in literature and the arts generally I'd found a domain of directness and honesty; of people who loved the simplest things, who treasured life and beauty in object, word, artefact and animal; who loved the world with humble hearts. An enclave of the enlightened to whom the invisible speaks, for whom eventual or even unreachable truth, not a comfortable life, was the light on the hill giving direction to the lived life. It was a shielding wall consisting of a special and especially sensitive morality separating and protecting from the slime and corruption of an acquisitive, self-aggrandising world, but within which a kindly love for all inside and outside it flourished; a relaxed unselfishness that would promote others before itself, that would endeavour to live by the best rules it knows in the light of all the inspiration and examples deriving from the long past of humanity.

I would be part of that, I thought. In my innocence I was honest, my face open, concealing nothing; prepared to love and value others. I was punished for my open face by those with several faces, derided for taking a back seat, suspected for letting others go first, sneered at when I hated no one and refused to be partisan, avoided when I tried to live by ideals of gentleness, fairness, tolerance and what kindliness I could muster. I am an old man, but I carry these ideals like gold in my heart, and like gold they never lose their brightness. I haven't lived up to them at all times, but always I have tried my best after each failure.

Bit by bit, lie by lie, hate by hate, greed by greed, I was pushed away and isolated from that artistic domain of selfishness and self-promotion, that enclave of compromise and dishonesty, which merged indistinguishably with the acquisitive commercial world. I do no deals, I feather no nest, I want no seat on the board, I desire no riches. I will be no one's man and no one's judge. I cannot live among the place-seekers. I will not sit with the lost leaders. There is a world of things I will not do for a handful of silver.

He had given me his testament. What could I do for him? I jumped out and went back to his gate looking for something to tidy up, something out of place, some pruning I could do. Nothing was out of place. The letterbox. I took three letters up the path and pushed them part way under the door. Save him a walk. One was a phone bill, one a circular, one addressed to him via his publisher.

Back at the church I thought better of it. I raced back to town, sneaked up the path trying to be as unnoticeable as the Gunnedah grass dog, put the letters back in his box. At his age he needed his walk. A man like that didn't need help from anyone.

A red Falcon station wagon with a trailer pulled up next door, perhaps to buy an emu. The sun was hammering a message on the roof of the town, a message I couldn't decipher. The flaxen light of summer thrashed the footpaths, pointing to greasy dust. Why would anyone want an emu? If the sun spoke, would we understand? What might it say? Would it ask, or tell?

The colours for Mac Black were a problem until I remembered some dust motes tinkling soundlessly on the table-shine in his office, in the morning sun's beams. He became for me a bell with a clear tone. Reminding me of things I valued years ago, but which seemed now to be grubby and neglected. In memory I heard the voice of an old teacher walking the school corridors at Archerfield school, saying Black's words.

I am different from old Black. For a start, my thoughts begin well, then seem to slacken like seagrass drifting back and forth in shallow currents.

I didn't want to talk about mine, so I didn't ask about guilts, but he'd told me anyway. For me they'd risen up like a ninth wave, but for him they seemed just as bad. But wait. Others have done things publicly judged as worse than anything I've done. The world has called them conscienceless psychopaths, since it's unwilling to see that some have tastes, needs, compulsions shared by few, and these characteristics arise from within. Many shrug off their pasts, call it a new start. I did that for decades, but they were still attached without my knowledge, and when the years slowed me down they crashed into me from behind.

At that first meeting with Yarrow I could see she was so much cleverer than I was. I drew back a little, wary of her warring mind and the incidental brutality of her stronger feelings. 'We need more metaphysics,' she said. I suppose she meant fresh doctrines. Like a great gloop my mouth filled with her words as she let them free.

I was composed of desires that feared nothing. I wondered what her desires were. At the time of our one hug I remember how the smell of her hair moved mountains in me I didn't know were there, making visible new landscapes.

twenty-three

merle bird

From a distance she struck me as a brightly coloured sun umbrella. The 2LR Skyshow was forcing its attractions on a day that started out like hot breath in your face and got muggy and closer as the horizon tilted eastwards. She arrived first, in her red Daewoo, waiting by a corner of the showground stand in the shade as if she expected to pick up a mysterious strangler. Well, stranger. I wondered if my atomic intuition was accurate or merely smartarse. Particles that attract when apart, but repel when too close. I felt her pulling at my eyes. Would I tell her the story I'd read, of transgenic trees with haemoglobin instead of rubber? Better not. I wouldn't want her telling me about weaving.

Last night I looked at the planet from out in cold space. I was swinging round the earth, which was actually me, and watched recent events on my surface. The slaughters, hopes, extravagances, poverty, that made such a messy pattern on me, gave way to the same kinds of things, in different dress, in the recent past; then I saw back and back to the deeper past, way back at increasing speed beyond the Greeks to the earliest life on the savannah and up into the trees, until the past was too dark to see. And the pattern was all the same. I woke convinced I was descended from dogs.

I walked up to Merle Bird without barking. She came to the point. Merle was a published writer, one of those who vend their spleen and anything else they think will sell. She had a fine supply of even teeth, so that her lips hardly met. Her arms were folded, she hugged herself tightly. Her mouth was wrinkled and dull in the January heat. She seemed in a funny mood, a sad tiredness, and kept coming out of it then going back in again. Occasionally her eyebrows levitated, like a bouncing fakir's. Perhaps it was a writer's temperament, a pose, boredom, irritation, something about me, the weather, the town, a habit, or any other thing. For experience she had worked as shop assistant, cab driver, meat packer, fruit picker, live-in teacher on rural properties, and once as a 'working girl' for the money. Adding bitter cherries to her sexual life. She called it the 'revolving door' phase. Her rule then was no kissing, she didn't want to feel dirtied: 'she' was located in or near her face, not down there. She still has her T-shirt: 'You can't be first but you could be next'. Her pet dislikes are milk and the feeling of being sucked. She approves of the coffee in the Holly Tree.

She couldn't navigate the sea of poetry, she said; the wordfish fighting savagely just beneath the surface put her off. Nor had she been an orgasmic revolutionary, she didn't believe in progress. Her face was a dead ringer for that actor's who played often in Groucho Marx movies; you could imagine Merle's blanched face beneath a frivolous tiara. Margaret Dumont, that's the one. Merle's voice was hot, with a splash of wetness. She had always been promiscuous. 'I've seen more moons than any landscape,' she said. In Lost River her name had been seen with the usual list of men who made a point of being prominent in the town. She liked to taste and try.

Alienation's not for everyone; she was at home anywhere. She had the kind of chest that looks complete when it has a gold crucifix flat against it.

'I wanted to be a writer ever since I was a girl and wandered in Lexico, land of words, and wondered if you could choke back a gush and have it come out as ordered prose. Ever since I began to notice things, like how ugly birds' feet are, and that human feet are uglier. Or looking at rain-rods and wondering who broke them into lengths. Or seeing my Auntie Lyn freshly dead and feeling death was a unique manner of expression.

'Feeling ignored, I kept a diary, following the injunction to find my own soul. No, all I found was some common old apple and blackberry pie of a soul, crushed round the edges and with blurred flavours.

'From the time as a student when I was involved with a vendetta of poets I detected and detested egomania in others, especially males. Apart from that and their mendacious idiom I had no opinion of them; they were just another animal, except they carried their tails in front. Since then I've seen the confident, the boastful, the undecided, the sulky and disobedient, the permanently pendant. Tails, that is. Mind you, I dream of a chorus line of men on stage displaying their pretty pink dicks and dancing desperately to please an audience of one. Males taught me faith, which is taking your pill and going right ahead.

'I was educated—well, lectured—in literary engineering, hydraulic poetry, by vinegary academics in pepper and salt threads, whose egos demanded they live in interesting times; who loved, studied and supported disorder, which they christened change. Peace and stability were boring to them, had nothing to teach them; they felt prosperity yielded no interesting situations and problems. In the name of fighting prejudice and repression they taught disregard for moral institutions that had helped us survive so far. Well, I survived them. I knew I had to keep afloat in the world as it is, not look for isolation in a city of women, and that their often single-issue politics didn't fit that world. In effect they elevated and strengthened the bureaucracy, since their goal was policy.

'I taught myself to read; that is, to read the street: faces, shopfronts, gestures, clothes, patterns of traffic and sky, and to notice all the things that don't happen when you turn a corner or walk in busy places. I tried to think of it all as text, but the metaphor was unstable: everything kept changing back into the forms I first knew. Lost River is about as sinister as a stadium full of child gymnasts, no noisier than a creeping fistula. Apart from the rumour factory. My theory on the murder is that Leanne tried to seduce Aphra, failed, and systematically frightened her to death, but I owe that to Borry Blow, and he was joking, I think.

'Oh, the diary? I soon discovered intimate journals are edited before being written, only fashionable crimes mentioned. Concealment and lies. I daresay we all long for significance, and permanence, and reality, but there's nothing to answer that longing, so we fill the gap with fiction. I'm a soft-shelled crab in the crevices of literature.'

The tired sadness welled up from her skin and spread over her face.

'Why did my father die? We loved each other. Moments when he was specially affectionate I felt bathed in a glow that covered me like a golden liquid, without sticking to me, but somehow roomy, so I could move freely within it. He gave me so much. So. Here I am, with one book out, but not a real writer yet. Old Black lives here, paid his dues long ago; probably soon cap the well of his verbs. Told me to just write, stop trying to live my books. I'm a nomad travelling the world of stories looking for sustenance and opportunity, seeking nourishment in nouns and verbs; a double agent working for opposing sides. I hope you don't take the slightest notice of my pronouncements. I often don't speak for truth, but to try out words and see how they sound. Sometimes the words resemble a truth, when it's a small, domestic, everyday truth. Most thoughts are the reflections, ricochets, or hints of other thoughts.

'How do I write? A special part of me comes into operation, or another person appears and does the work, or a natural ability comes to the fore, or a certain configuration of brain software comes into existence when the brain apprehends what is required, or I go into a dream state and the past or other people write through me, or creative sectors of the brain overwhelm others, or I use parts of my knowledge that I feel fit with what I intend to write and ignore the rest, or desire is so powerful that it carries me along. Or something else entirely. That cover it? Or is it all a woolly wrangle over words?

'I admire writers who say something. Sarraute claimed "Life is full of sentences". Isn't that big? And Whitman: "I contain multitudes". I wish I could write things like that, but I think I haven't got them in me. I dream of one exact sentence, but at the same time I want to write as if I'm making love to the world. Instead, I'll probably become the kind of writer who dreams up her reminiscences, keeps her vendomat smile for the interviews and under her breath swears revenge on all tropes.

'After my book I wanted to be part of a crime so I could do a book on jail. I got in with a gang, took the van where they told me, had it loaded in the dark at one in the morning off the highway, drove it back to town and left it. The cartons were still in it a week later; I'd been dudded. Borrowdale said I was lucky they didn't "off" me. I did a story about it, but was annoyed to find it labelled humour.

'I feel literature is a vast flower growing petals from inside, different petals exfoliating to become things other than literature. When you talk of it you soon find yourself talking of other disciplines. The great books of the past often seem as romantic and far away as the Hyksos, and my little ideas as tedious and pedestrian as a description of the double Matthew Walker or the Turk's head knot.

'*The Taste of Applause* was well received as a first book, but where I dreamed of reviews praising my lissom syntax and graceful intellect, I got comparisons with *Ruthless Rhymes for Rotten Kids*, phrases like "The Indian Trope Trick", and accusations of wandering off into description. One said it was plastered with neologisms and plodding pleonasms, another made a joke about the taste of apple sauce. Reviews have the function of ads; many people just won't look at slammed products. At the moment I'm working on a series of stories: "The Glass-bottomed Girl", "The Pauper's Guide to Food", "Black Flames", "The Natural History of the Coffee Table", "The Iambic Geometer", and two untitled. One is of a boy's little cock dropped by a crow on a lawn during a barbecue, the other of aliens landing on earth and trying to make sense of the language of a population of cockroaches, spiders, ants, bees and flies, all organisms the same size as the aliens.'

I couldn't resist another caramel and walnut slice from the canteen's food bar. After a while she fired a question at me. I was the interviewee.

'Do you believe in a golden age to come?' Was she a socialist? A dinosaur?

'Where the problems of human life have been solved?' I parried.

'Yes.'

'No.'

'Why not?'

'People have different aims.'

'Is that all?'

'It's enough. It's the key.'

'To what?'

'Individual liberty and social equality are incompatible. There are no common aims.'

'So?'

'If there are no common aims, and if liberty and its self-expression can't live together with equality and its supposed social stability, then an ideal world is a myth.'

'Oh.'

'Take you.'

'Why me?'

'You decided to be a writer. No authority decreed it. No meddlesome government selected you. You made your own aims, and your own values, to some extent. Moral freedom, plus our variety of cultures, that's the rock on which the golden age is wrecked.'

She leaned across the canteen table and thrust the last wedge of walnut and caramel slice into my mouth to shut me up.

'I've got some recordings. Young Australians, new composers. Like to come round and we'll play them?

'Probably.'

'Are you ignoring me?'

'Are you weft or warp?'

'I'm the finished product.' Abruptly as a bright idea she fished out one warm breast, as if producing a miracle, and picked up my hand to feel her warmth. It seemed time to go. Several onlookers thought so too, while several more seemed to wish we'd stay.

Some of the music she played I found very strange. There was a piano piece like a dream you have when you're awake, and a quartet which, as I entered it, put me in mind of a camisole of the mind with intellectual embroidery. I can't explain it, the memory flutters and wriggles as I try to pin it with my mind while I fumble for words.

In the weeks that followed I was drawn back to her time after time, but just as often I felt something pushing me away. Yet she was often soft and agreeable as spring air. She thought of us as both artists, but I see myself as artisan. She had a penetrating kiss, like a new style of toothbrush, though the kisses themselves, peculiarly, had no taste. Not that I mind. She decided years before not to be a breeder, and had her tubes cauterised.

One thing I did take away from my times with her was a growing conviction that the guilt I felt was part of my make-up. I had noticed that she made a show of guilt feelings when she'd done nothing to reproach herself for, and that gave me the hint. But if in me it was a disposition why did it have to make me feel worse than the life I'd lived warranted? Why the amplifying effect? Was my early religious training, that I'd thought I'd cast off, still attached to me and catching up? Perhaps I wasn't so bad after all, punishing myself for things others might smile at. On the side of the angels? It seemed a fine and positive thing to convince myself of.

Merle made me laugh with her stories of student fashions when her hair used to stick up like a forest of garden stakes; of student parties and how by the time she got the joint it was usually the size of a splinter wrapped in soggy tissue paper; of student poverty and food thrown together like a pile of dirty clothes waiting for the wash; of when she had so little money she lived on dates in a freezing basement where she was reluctant to get up for a pee once she'd found a little warmth.

She studied how to dismantle value systems, and came to grips with the doctrine that language is the only reality. I noticed she was clean and well groomed as a new car; she stole nothing I could see, told no lies I could detect, never spoke ill of others, was often considerate and mostly polite. The value systems she dismantled were of the paper kind.

Tapestry left her cold, but she tried to show a slight interest. It wasn't necessary. I didn't need support or supportive noises. Perhaps friendship, where it's neither feigning nor performance, consists more of a puzzled inadequacy. Her bodily shape was a graceful poem, with interesting highlights, melodic surfaces, and prominent rhymes; easy to memorise.

I didn't dream Merle: I dreamed Yarrow. We were children, both in kinder. I stopped at her house on the way home to play marbles. We called them mibs. She had a bag of mibs of all colours. My favourite was a sphere of glass with swirling white over a blue–grey translucence. Hers was red. The afternoon was filled with light, just as later, looking at her, I felt I was filling with light: organs, veins, bones, the lot.

At the end, when she left, she could have healed everything. One word would have done. I folded my dream, tucked it away where no one could get it, as a person at risk in a hairy town folds a few high bills to put in a cunning kick.

twenty-four
knudsen boult

He had a big head, the spitting image of Giacometti's, but the face was the puffed landscape of a cauliflower ear. His tall, tilted frame presented me with the picture of a lean and roughened soul. The picture may not have been accurate. He had a way of talking to you that included a momentous hesitation, as if he held an important piece of language in his hands and was deciding on which shape to mould it. It was known in the town that he was ambivalent about incinerator and jail, but was loudly for the angora project, which put him onside with the powerful crafts lobby in their drive for development funds and permanent space in the civic centre.

Our first meeting was at the Australia Day celebrations in Anzac Park. We stood under a full-grown elm facing south, and though I was prepared to be sparing in my liking for him—I get on better with women, I find men lack warmth—I was taken with his eyes. I'd been thinking that morning of a particular blue; it's the blue in the William Morris woodpecker design of

1885, and there it was, twice, stuck in Knudsen's head, lubricated and shiny with eye-spit.

Lost River had been well washed with a diligent January rain. When the summer sun reappeared it seemed blindingly bright and hot, as if an oven door had been opened. I didn't envy the locals, riding floats along Budawang Street. Only a hundred metres away yet strangely muted.

He'd had to battle to get started in the world of sculpture. At one stage he sold off ornaments, war decorations, old books, thirty albums of photographs taken over sixty years by dead Uncle Sven, collections of hand and garden tools of antique design, to set himself up in his first studio. Thieved, cadged, conned his loved ones for the one he loved most. They lost that battle. He made trips abroad—so much is meagre here, he said—and when he got back implied his work was done while he was away. He had no opinion of fellow Australians. 'They'll only respect you if you've been over there, and work done there has a mystical sheen.' He married, too, but didn't take that seriously either. He said, about being a husband, that everyone knows what to do, but how do you keep it interesting for fifty years?

His work was well received, and his autobiography written at thirty-five drew surprised attention. Physically he was a large man, but early on, in order to gain admittance to the company of those he perceived as the ruling group of artists, those who could put his name forward at the right time, it had been necessary to be well to the left in politics, so he did that without turning a hair. Those same artists did verbal obeisance to the dwindling number of 'workers' while their own lives were dedicated to interesting, and producing works for sale to, those who could afford to pay high prices. He regarded his hypocrisy as an entry fee.

He was divorced and set up in an old house off Tantawanglo

Lane in the hills, extending, renovating and using mudbricks. He called the place Scarebezilski, but no one else did; it was Mudbrick Palace. He was at one of those stages where a new direction was beckoning. Some incandescent critic was convincing the art world there was a new spirit of the age, whatever that was. His own spirit of hostile creativity welcomed the challenge.

He had wonderful energy, and gave informal parties to which he invited anyone remotely connected with the arts, marking their names off on a jotting pad of vellum. He was surprised at the numbers who turned up. The little knot of people from the 1927 Cafe who hardly mixed with others and talked incessantly of social change, several theatre groups, music schools, schools of dance, weavers and spinners, sculptors, artists, musicians, pop groups, and at his first bash the parking took up a hectare. A notice on the neighbouring property said, 'Warning—Ostriches!' and an answering sign in the parking paddock advised, 'Do not read this notice if not parking.' Near the house a long-eared mountain songbird yawned in a small yard. A black dog joined in the yawn, then, seeing visitors, began waving his tail like a conductor of orchestras. Three portaloos stood in a triangle, facing inwards.

Knudsen was a funny mixture. At one time he was all sticky niceness, smothering a nest of women weavers in a thick web of confining compliments, sometimes a conservationist wanting to fit locks to a swamp to save it for our children, and at others a towering petulance like a prime minister with his nose out of joint. Then again he could be cheerful, open, outspoken, laughing like a coven of drains then cursing jovially and inviting the assembled ones to 'curl your egos round this' as he began a story. He dressed fashionably in black. Some of his tales were enough to wring your sternum, if you were inclined toward sympathy for others.

Moving from one group to another to direct, gymnastically, their fun, he would wave his arms about and bellow in his viscous voice, 'The wine's on the wing! I'm here!' He certainly had a place for the wine. For initiation, everyone had to go and find a spider, drop it in their drinks and drink it. There was no difficulty finding spiders on his bush block; miles of mulch prowled the house plot, and paddocks were dotted with neat round spider holes. He himself held aloft a Windang whisky beetle and drank that, and told the story of the hard-headed sake spider that no alcohol can make drunk. The next event was the measuring of tongues. Then he played 'Rhapsody On Three Portaloos' on a brown upright. He presided at the barbecue, reciting a poem, 'Antique sausage, be our saucy saviour', written for the occasion, he said.

Around the barbecue the shape of the conversation was that of a spade. A small cross-gabble of talk led along a strong connective queue to a large, flat, edged surface that rang loudly when you knocked it. Tactless, testicular, short-tempered, he was a wonderful addition to the art world of Lost River. To see him pick up a glass, taste its contents, grimace, then throw it self-importantly away was almost worth the time taken to visit Mudbrick Palace. Daniel Dogstone said he talked through his balls and that balls have few brains. Of his performance he said Boult was supported by a cast of hundreds and thousands.

Knudsen was tall, bronzed, and continually mistaken for an American. He made a large number of connections with women of the town, and said he pleased them with his fierce lovemaking, which he described as being sweet in the mouth, like revenge. To hear him tell it there was no other side to the story. Carmen Mummo told me he considered coupling an act of altruism, on his part. There was a look about his head, or perhaps his neck, a suggestion of the lewd. I thought of the almost obscene and hairless neck of a vulture protruding violently from thick feathers.

'Didn't begin to do any good till I realised the old metaphors were bullshit. It was the landscape made us. Paths and roads, hills mounting in front of us, vistas to make the senses bounce, valleys dropping away beneath us as we round mountain corners, caves dark and dangerous, holes in the ground, restive rocks in creeks, rivers to cross or fish in: landscape is in our brains like the figured grain within the cassowary tree. Casuarina, I mean. Our forebears, who didn't mind working themselves to death, balded the hills west of here for their damned sheep; I still wonder what effect that new landscape has on us.'

I was about to make no sensible reply to that when he resumed, like a tide of meaning that expects to engulf and possess the century. There was a feeling of hurry, as if silence was an irritation that would be salved by his next words.

'Last time I jumped our Pacific pond into the States I brought back a wizened bag of family jewels cut off and tied with a drawstring, result of a mutilation murder. I did a series on death. Might do another, with those kids in mind and what they did. Also that woman, the earring found at the scene, the head back in that funny position. Mind you I don't believe the Fusby woman did it, mainly because the town's turned against her. The public's never right.'

I caught sight of Juniper Grey. She was radiant, but it was a bothered radiance. Rivals? And Batty Mortomore being asked if he'd been blind all his life and saying, 'Not yet.'

I tuned in again to hear Knudsen saying, 'I'm more at home with the young, their minds are more like mine. New people, bright faces, wider sympathies, it's good to be my age.' I watched as he strode off towards the party scrum feeling easy in his riding boots and conscience. I wondered if he was heading for Juniper Grey; I'd heard something of the sort. It was only circumstantial, but they'd been uncovered in bed together. She felt she'd like him to do her a still life, but wasn't sure if that was ideologically sound. Perhaps it was better to be one. I also heard she'd complained about him. 'I just don't like being in a minority. He shouldn't laugh at me. It's well known that a woman likes consensus.'

'Mudbrick, like Semiramis' walls of Babylon,' Knudsen boasted with hefty pride at the next party as he showed us round his new studio. There was a severed head in terracotta over the front door, Knudsen's head. In the hall photos of the Mount Beauty bottlebird and the threatened Murray River watergoat. And over the toilet door a notice of sheet brass with black lettering: IGNORE THIS NOTICE. In the food room I saw him unobtrusively put a fork in the sugar bowl.

In the centre of the studio a builder's plumb-bob swung slightly, a wizened black scrotum was suspended against a black glass mirror, there was a large grainy photo of Knudsen as Chips the Carpenter. On the walls pen and ink cartoons. I remember a sky full of unstable bats flying in all directions. There were sculptures: weird celeriac shapes, a blue fox flying, the frozen tints of a dunny with rudder, the *Hand-wrought Tool* in silver, the *Hand-tooled Vagina* in gold, the *Man with Wickerwork Teeth*, a complicated wood carving from tree roots of what appeared to be a lock titled *The Invention of Linus Yale*, and a clockwork, wood and sheetmetal construction called *Time Bird*, which sang every half-hour. My favourite was *God's Golden Codpiece*, crazy as a wriggling highway, though it wasn't clear where Knudsen's hermaphrodite deity would have fitted the thing. Then there were the paintings, dozens of them. The man was an energy field, unless they were leftovers from previous exhibitions. He had two Christs: one scourged by Satanists, the other overturning the moneychangers' tables in the National Gallery. There was *Mind at the Fingertips of the Senses*, a man of the land trying to peer into the earth, an eye with wings poised like a hawk above a waving sea of cloned human faces, with more faces coming off a distant production line. And a nude with cobwebs in all four hairy places.

I asked him more about his shapes of the land ideas.

'I look at the plains and hills and think of waves in a vast sea of land, it speaks to the deep sea of my mind. But there are no words shaped, used and run-in to speak of gullycool, hillfeel, cresting landshapes, slow billows of land, earth-rills, mountain ranges that look like folds in a curtain or limbs under a blanket. It torments me that I can't speak of those forms in their own special words. We glimpse, we feel briefly, then look away; we don't mine deeply.'

But he wanted to talk about stone and I didn't. I went to commune with the wickerwork teeth. From a window I saw porpoises bobbing up and down in the back of a pickup. Boy and girl porpoises. Fragments of party had taken root in the car park. There was the occasional ostentatious scampering to retrieve clothing.

Later I found the host surrounded by a crowd of those amiable, gentle souls who love to gather and talk and sprawl about, and to listen, earnestly admiring from a restful distance someone else's constant application to a task; who go weak at the knees as they pronounce the word discipline and speak of single-mindedness, words that are real goers with the indolent and those who can never make up their minds, and also with individuals who passively worship passion and violent emotion in others. He could have recited a shopping list to them as poetry and kept their devotion.

He was enjoying himself, pacing back and forth on a small section of floor which acted as his platform, while they listened to his words on fools' reviews, how the imaginative die many deaths but live more lives than one. His audience was hushed, like an assembly of clocks with deceased batteries, all showing a different face.

'... and now no aims except the artist's expression of himself, his feelings, his desires, channelled by fashion to catch a gallery director's eye. But I'd like to approach a new point of balance, yet each time I reach out for it, it's gone. I see the edge of it, not enough to hold on to, the dream tails off. I feel I must look, listen, taste, pull earth, space and star into me so deeply that they can be seen in me, and I will taste of them. Then I may make a statement such as has never been made, so that the innermost detail will be present in a gesture. I want to show a fruit, with flesh and skin, in stone, so that all there is to be seen in it can be seen in shape alone. And throw it at the critics, to let them weave their malice around it.

'No more dodging this way and that, no more wordy theory learned from ideologues with both feet firmly planted above ground. We humans are creative, we think, we make, we foresee. We shape the world's materials in ourselves, then shape the world in the patterns within us, we transform the given world, and our selves, within our limitless imagination. In human hands even death becomes poetry just out of earshot.'

It was wonderful the way his imagination's spinnaker was fully filled out by his own breath.

'I think of the future and know we are astronauts, we have no permanent home and few possessions apart from our instruments. We travel faster and faster towards destinations pictured in our telescopes but which may no longer be there. One day we will leave this planetary camp and travel outwards long before earth is cindered by the sun. We will seed the universe with our life, our ideas, our plants, our breath. Then the crocodile, the cat and dog will be the citizens, birds will inhabit the airy buildings and cockroaches the floors, ants will control the soil that our activities have left bare. Our cities, which by then will have become conscious, will die, not understanding that they needed humans as a kind of humus to feed on.'

The audience actually clapped this vision of Knudsen's as if he'd lifted them above the usual earthly level of thought. He appeared a little overcome by an emotion generated either by his words, his whisky or his listeners, for he turned and marched from the studio. They watched him go as if his tread on the floorboards echoed in the pits of their collective stomachs. Momentarily, along with the shadows that slid up the wall and out with him, his body suggested the shape of a giant bird, the side shadows his wings. I thought of the Delacroix lithograph of the winged and flying devil-figure, wings sprouting from his back, in effect a mammal with six limbs; the wings, though, too small to lift the great muscular bulk of that naked body off the ground.

I left early, reflecting on the great number of people, actions and intentions in our world that remind us of more powerful and pregnant images from the past, though without their content. Our images are strangely empty. Are we searching still for that elusive question which will illuminate the basic problem of our existence?

On the way out I glanced at the cleaned-out food table. The fork was still in the sugar bowl. I've known people do that sort of thing just to have you go away shaking your head. Not satisfied with that, on the verandah an empty rocking chair was rocking. Something else he'd rigged up? Night beetles clustered on the flywire in an image of decay. As I drove off, the flamboyant lights of Mudbrick Palace glittered like a lone supermarket in a dead suburb.

Knudsen later set up Monthly Events at the palace, to which the different kinds of artists and craftspeople brought their music, artworks, pottery and poems. I went along to one and heard a fistful of poems recited, poems which, if not tinged with talent, were reasonably short and spoken in subdued tones. Once I gave a talk on weaving to women of assorted ages, who seemed like a montage of my past. Knudsen seemed suddenly older, heavier, as if hung about with worries. I saw in those blue eyes the falling of an oyster-coloured rain.

Knudsen's section of tapestry was colourful. I was kept busy with other matters then, and slept well despite the heat. The attacks from inside had slackened off, disempowered by my discovery that guilt was as natural to me as the shape of my face. I worked like a demon, allowing myself bits of time off to enjoy the company of women like Merle. Between us we had a joke about the times each was unavailable for reasons apart from work. Mollocking the one, the other bollocking.

I'd have exchanged the lot for one of Yarrow's impatiences, such as a loud 'Shut up and let me think!' when I got too close. With her head turned away, so all I could see behind the curtain of hair was a cheekbone and the fist it rested on. Or even a derisive snort when I admired her hair, a sarcastic sentence when I touched it. I suspect that if I'd put my ear to her head to hear her thinking she wouldn't have laughed. I guess my kind of affection was too childish for her.

twenty-five

leon undermilk

On the first of February I found him worshipping a '67 blue Mustang at the Classic Cars exhibition. The Mustang was next to an Oldsmobile from the mid-'30s, and past that the tangerine Fusby '57 Chev surrounded by a crowd of shining-eyed admirers.

It was a day when waking up was an escape from trauma. The night-miseries were back in full colour, bastardries of the past playing behind my eyelids. They hounded me even when I worked. They seemed to be worse, but that may have been because of the respite I'd had. They came with bone-pain; the bones of my legs and to a lesser extent the bones of my forearm and wrist ached in bed, and when I got up my neck was stiff, as if I'd been in a scrum all night. It wasn't arthritis, and my diet hadn't changed, but is there a special diet to ease guilt?

When the world was naked and without colour in the blackness of the church it was a particular distress to feel so guilty and to know it was partly because that was the sort of person

I was. If getting even with Richardson under cover of that big brawl was written off as something anyone might do, there was enough, without a natural affinity with guilt, to keep my conscience shredded and painful. Taking those deposits on kitchen robots when I had no money, pinching Billy's girl for the fun of it then ditching her to see how she took it. That truck with the explosives. Still happening. I couldn't think of that episode with the chemist without squirming; getting rid of a baby with a supply of bombs. It was alive. I murdered it. Poor Elspeth. Then pushing her away, feeling nothing but relief. And had I killed while I was still in my mother? I was glad to be out of the church.

The day before I'd ducked down the highway to Canberra with the Bird, and before the theatre eaten at her favourite restaurant. Larks' tongues? Birds on the menu ruined everything. Maybe they lived their whole lives in a tin, I didn't care, but whose job is it to execute small birds? Do they shoot them? Dynamite them? Bite their heads off? What was the matter with me? Once upon a time I'd shoot anything that moved. It was a relief to see Undermilk and be back looking inside one of the real worlds.

He had the suspicious eyes of a loss adjuster. His unconvincing moustache had never done that levitation through the horizontal lattices, vertical fissures, and snakes-and-ladders drainholes of the Company that is called 'going places'. He didn't have the confidence or aggressiveness to dominate meetings, the cleverness to undermine or talk down colleagues, or the ruthlessness to plot, trap and bring down those above him. He was not executive material. He was battling to break even with the covetous agrarians he dealt with. Organisational viaducts far above his head carried a traffic he could only guess at.

Nor was he a young man in a hurry. He was plump and pink-faced as a middle-aged liquor sales rep, his edges all chamfered and sandpapered, no abrasive surfaces remained, and in effect he had become a filing cabinet. Not the kind with many megabytes of memory, but the old metal sort that clanks as you slam it shut and has original pieces of paper in it, legally enforceable promises to pay or deliver, together with signatures which can't be accommodated on hard disk. Leon was godless as a triangle. No star to steer by, no cultural interests or attainments, no sport to obsess him, only his car, which he revered. He worried uselessly about the state of the world, but a whole media industry was in existence to keep those fires banked. He had no loyalty to anything except his Jaguar. Not even to the wife, for whom he and his earning power and eventual superannuation were a kind of carapace, and she the hermit crab who would move on when he crumbled.

He stayed with the Company, even going to far as to imagine he was giving his life to it as he'd heard others say, and no one to contradict them, because it fed him and without it he had nothing and was nothing. Having little idea of the reality of a slave's life, he thought he worked like one: his reward was his car. He had lusted after a Jag since he was a boy.

His sleep was poor, he had pains he thought might be a playful ulcer, but didn't mention them to Mrs Undermilk because he feared her tongue on the subject of hypochondriacs. Aggressively critical or dismissive words from a female were extremely cutting and humiliating to Leon, not least because custom, training and manners forbade the physical or oral reply to a female that custom, training and pride demanded for similar aggressivenss from a male. Maybe we could invent a Zeus complex to slot him in, after the most powerful of the immortals who nevertheless quailed at his wife Hera's tongue.

To the sort of male Leon was, females seemed to go on with so much talk that was irrelevant, or plain crap, that he was forced to ignore most of it. This appeared to be disengagement. What the female called intimacy seemed cloying, repetitious, trivial, unnecessary. To Leon, in a very real sense, being there—not having gone—was love, loyalty, intimacy. They were in the same house, weren't they? To Sheila, his bursts of levity and inconsequential anecdotes were just as trivial and useless; she didn't recognise them as a male's social lubricant and group medicine. There was no bridge between the male and female cultures. To him she was a different life-form, to her he was a failed woman, a joke, a reason her nose was always casting about, fishing for untoward odours.

The house, its work, furnishings, routines, were built around the woman. The household appliances dignified her work; she decided what work was necessary and how often it would be done. She selected the twice-weekly cleaning person, one of the Prewitt boys. If Leon helped in the house, it was with the same sense of strangeness and being on foreign territory as she would feel if once or twice she had volunteered to hold torch, ring spanner or feeler gauge while he tried to adjust the Jag's tappets. Both unlikely, he said, but you know what I mean.

He chose his car, she chose hers, and in all else she was queen of consumption: stomach, display-case, clothes-horse. In the house all he made was a mess and a noise. In most things, life and genes had given him the fanfare bucolic, the general fart in the face.

Leon worked in marketing property, vehicles, equipment and accessories used by the rural sector. Rationalisations and retrenchments with the savagery of pogroms, of those incapable of holding several incompatible points of view at once, followed each other in nerve-rattling succession in the Company; he had no idea when someone would say, 'There's the door, mind the step,' or what else the future held, but then neither do birds, farm animals, sharebrokers or policemen.

At night he sweated with fear and woke pale as a dead man's tongue, with his scalp sodden as if he'd come from the shower rather than his single bed in the second bedroom. He indulged in phone sex and had a variable speed reliever.

No one remembered him for long. He lacked the ego that might have been put out by this; instead, he was vaguely amused. The future wasn't amusing, though. He saw a world filling with more billions of humanimals packed closer and closer like so many picks of weft beaten down and jammed together on to the previously woven weft. Just the way Hamlet saw his time—'The age is grown so picked'—which Leon remembered, when I reminded him, from high school English. The horrors of crowding, a world village, its pressures and lack of privacy, its torrents of gossip and useless information, its hierarchies of powerful groups looking over your shoulder: madness, he said. Civilisation kept such things at a distance. We were entering a phase with no name, but it wasn't civilisation, he was sure of that. And what about here, where federal power increases daily, where legislation has gone mad and weaves its immense blanket of regulations, laws, intrusions, which descends over us daily, stifling freedoms, weakening us as individuals, all in the cause of keeping us easy to govern? He took another pill.

His great break came when he overheard a conversation that contained information valuable to a rival company, and therefore to his own. But it was with his stomach newly unstrung and croaking for help that Leon took his information to the MD, a businessman conspicuous among the conspicuous, a man of Byzantine cunning and fabled connections whose lightest word stung his inferiors like the bite of the forty-millimetre Gundarong alligator fly. You can't feel it alight, but when its glistening black jaws take hold pain travels instantly throughout the body. They have such a grip they can be killed where they stand, and are known to suck blood in the act of dying. Leon was deeply afraid, like a citizen between two lawyers: tissue paper between the blades of shears.

The MD had authority. He said Come, and people came; Lie, and they lied; Do This, and they did it. He didn't ask, Why do they? He knew. The balance sheet was the only check on his personal power in the feudal organisation he ruled. Luckily he had great ability, for he was surrounded by yessers, and heard few ideas that weren't his own.

Leon sat in the waiting room, comfortable as forty soldiers on a flight in the bowels of a Hercules. From that door to the MD's desk was the length of a bowling alley, but at last Leon stood on the thick carpet, pale as a blood-drained pig. He was sure the great man could hear his stomach's throes, but he was mistaken. Mike Hunt was delighting placidly in Leon's discomfiture. It was sweet to him that the increase in 'democracy' in the workplace meant that the underlings' grovelling, writhing and generalised terror was half concealed beneath a desperate first-name mateyness.

He received the information in silence, saw its value immediately, arranged a raise on the spot, and had Leon report to him in future and directed he commit nothing to paper. Leon promised, but Leon was a liar and kept the written information in a safe place, happy as a flea on a sleeping dog. Leon left the presence, a new industrial spy. As he catlike brought new trophies to lay on the doorstep of the MD he was given a position as Special Projects Officer to the Management Services department and licence to roam as far as he chose. He bought golf clubs, his first foray into sport.

On the domestic battlefield he enjoyed a giddy elevation from verbal punching-bag to a position slightly above contempt, though far beneath equality. If the automatic error-detector thought of him before as an insignificant Murrumbidgee guppy, now she promoted him to a bigger river, the Murray, and adjusted his status to that of the cod, of which his large protruding eye, and jowl, in profile, reminded her.

His file grew. The mutton duck saga, making sheepmeat more saleable by altering its flavour; meat with no cholesterol content; the compound exuded by the common tree frog and its uses in medicine, staph and herpes being only the first discovered; the new uses for eucalyptus, and many more. The MD presented Leon with a monogrammed poserphone to call in on, and listening equipment in which a sensitive recorder was activated when you took a pen from your pocket, plus a bugging device of phlegmatic appearance but omnipotent faculties which could monitor phone conversations from anywhere in the world.

Leon began to find life thrilling. By finding one company's bottom line he had enabled another to undercut it in tendering for a contract, and soon had a respectable list of such triumphs to his credit. He would like to have tracked money movements between countries, but lacked opportunity, and it would have cut across the MD's own interests. He envied those spies working for state and federal government who kept an eye on protest groups, environment and animal rights organisations, trade unions and the like. If he'd been younger, he'd like to have been a real government spy, having heard of the CIA inserting its agents into other countries' law firms, banks, computer companies; and chuckled at stories of all the various nations trying to steal secrets from their big, rich and clumsy friend, America. Life had never been fun before.

Home was hell. Divorce? She wouldn't agree now they were well off. Besides, at least with marriage there was someone else in the house: even that would be gone. He imagined himself and her sitting in court with their situation laid out before strangers, and the results of honest discussion, which breaks up more marriages than reticence, in full view, and the lawyers silent, unable to disagree. A hopeless case. Perhaps she'd score more than half. Divorce was definitely out. He was stuck with Sheila. Very likely she was a woman of a future in which maleness was not only a curse, but unnecessary.

Once he had a thought that said, Murder her. There's no law against it, only against being convicted. Even if you're caught the major penalty is gone, you only pay half-price for crime now. The foetus and the elderly may be despatched, but not murderers.

His beloved kept him from murder; there was no XJ6 in jail. Who would care for her if he was away a few years working in a library? Though he was attracted by the idea of living in the exclusive company of lawbreakers and criminals; he admired them as being the epitome of those who reject utterly the power of all who would restrict and set limits, and that included women.

Even the ways of speech of Sheila and Leon were different; they were often at cross purposes out of basic politeness and reserve. Though he got her full attention with the story of how Mrs F once pushed a man's head down into the oil in a fish-shop boiler. Long enough for the eyes to float free.

He met Sheila when she was sleek and presentable as a rainwet horse. Not knowing how to compare women he had judged her by her face, her legs, her general shape and appurtenances. To any other less obvious and puzzling features he had shut his eyes before marrying, and opened them only later. It was a disaster, he should have kept them shut. He noticed that she would never tell the matters that lay deep and close to her. And she, when she heard the simple tales of his paltry concerns, was convinced he was covering up too. And this would go on until he was old, walking stiff, and three-footed.

After forty, when so many women get their second wind,

Sheila met Amanda. Both tulipomaniacs, they used their men as shields, backstops, ladders, tools to fix little things that went wrong, and also as badges of their suffering, to be displayed at the right time, taken out when needed. The men were to keep quiet and out of the way and keep the money coming in for the privilege of having their delightful presences about the place. Life was a lottery which she would win with its natural outcome, his death. He would go by seventy, with luck, while at eight years younger and with long life in the family, she looked forward to over twenty-five years of life after he went, with twenty of those being good, active years.

She had stopped working after she married. She was one of the old school who looked to the male to be a servant, and go out and bring back money. She devoted quality time to bridge, and her Cactus and Succulent Society, and needed regular tennis. A varied and interesting life. Work was less than interesting, and fit only for men. Her life was a bourgeois personal equation in which comfort was a fixed term.

Amanda came when Leon was out. Each had found a companion for life. They kept their men apart; they might get on famously. Better to keep them separately confined and tamed with the sting of judiciously administered criticism, relying on the male code, supposedly out-of-date, of not retaliating. All that remained was for these two obstacles, both provided with good superannuation, to leave the stage, when the two women would sell up and go gratefully to the coast, where so many from Lost River slowly brought their autumn days to a close among others for whom the stress of getting was over and who now could afford to be pleasant.

If Leon had been a thinker he might have reflected that the tensions, aims and conflicts of life can never be integrated into an ordered synthesis, that human values and aims are more often incompatible than not. In his own case he might have perceived that however incompatible and disordered they were, the aims, tensions and irreconcilable values of his own life could at least be resolved, and that each day he was being approached by the instant when they suddenly would be. And he might have had the warm humanity to see that just beyond that instant, this resolution would afford another human being, one whom he had sworn to love, the most gratifying freedom and happiness of her life.

I guess he was lucky. A woman with more fire might have got her freedom before the natural resolution of his tensions came about. He must have been a dull doll for her to play with. Move his arms and legs, arrange him, shift him and he'd stay put, do what was suggested.

When I first saw Yarrow walking I imagined I could judge the weight with which those little feet touched the ground. Estimated how it would feel to lift. The feel of it on me. I felt engulfed.

twenty-six

alastair pryde

At the Show he looked the part, a tall man in a neat Gloster shirt, moleskins, riding boots and country hat. He'd seen the camp-drafting, talked to a young Eden guy who won the overhand chop, and won a prize at one of the sideshows for pegging a ball at a face. He gave the prize, made of small coloured lollies, to a short boy in long shorts. At the shingles exhibit he expertly split several shingles from the snappy-gum round sitting on the block, but onlookers suddenly materialised and embarrassed him. He'd planted a small forest, ten thousand pine, and had no good words for 'shit eucalypts that muck up the soil with their damned acid. Rubbish. Lignotuber. Can't kill 'em with an axe. Mighty beech forests here once, gone now, killed off by the fire the black people used to control the undergrowth.'

He was a long way from home, even if he was now a local. Born not far from Leongatha, he had an early memory of a corduroy stretch of road. His father, the icon of his life, grew potatoes and was friends with Sol Heable, of Heable's Hogs. As a boy, Alastair followed Dad everywhere, watched his face, imitated his ways, copied his phrases, wore his old hat. At three he was photographed in Dad's workboots and hat. As if he tried to climb into his father's head to see what he saw, into the man himself, to be him.

His father was a 1914–18 war hero, one MM and twice mentioned in despatches; he kept his slouch hat but got rid of his medals, never went to reunions and all he would say about war was, 'Out of empire, all legal ties broken, now we can pick our own fights and be grown-up.' He had long arguments with Sol's pigs about it, and threw them handfuls of beggar's fescue. He discerned an admirable frankness and innocent open-mindedness in one sow's light brown eyes as she looked up from her pen, and addressed many of his arguments to her.

It was a great disappointment to Alastair that he was not going to be like Dad: different heights, different natures. Dad was quiet; the most he would assert was that Gallipoli was a mistake, Phar Lap a gelding, Ned Kelly had no kids either, and Lawson couldn't make a damper, knocked round with tramps and wrote painful poetry. Though Kelly's 'Such is life' when about to be killed impressed him. Dad was quite happy never to see another woman apart from Mrs Pryde, who would drive into town at the drop of a hat, had a large ring of acquaintances, played in theatrical productions, sang at weddings and in the church choir. Alastair couldn't get enough of the sight, sound and smell of pretty girls, any girls. At school he played silly buggers and made them helpless with laughter at stories of the Cocklebiddy cow-horse, so he could chase and catch them easily.

It was a blow not to be like Dad. The realisation left a little depression somewhere in him, a concavity. Perhaps in the soul, whatever that is. Older, he and his mates drove round the state, shooting, discovering. They shot bush dogs, wild cats, kangaroos and wild pigs for farmers, and goats where they were a nuisance. They married young, and in a bunch and it was 1939. They rushed to join up and fight Hitler. Away from home Alastair felt the presence of the slight hollow in him and thought danger and driving transport trucks for Australia might fill it. They didn't. The concavity became a hole, he tried not to think of it.

On discharge he let his brothers, who'd worked the property during the war, buy out his share of the potatoes. No land for sale there, so he went up into New South Wales with Eileen and the four kids to fifteen hundred fairly level acres, quite a decent bit of country, outside Lost River at Doctor's Creek. The hole inside grew.

Later the boys moved to Queensland and Dad died back in Leongatha. The girls got married so he and Eileen were alone again, but he didn't miss the kids the way he did his father. Spoke to Dad every day, even at the cattle-crush while marking his uncomplaining calves with the sharp knife and throwing their bleeding testicles to his quick-as-lightning dogs. The hole was a pit. Nothing filled it.

Once, at a neighbour's place, he, like his father, met and talked to a pig. She looked up at him and in her eyes there was, he swore, a human expression. Those were human eyelashes. In her expression beauty, intelligence, affection. Was someone trapped in that pig? She could see more than the wind, he said. He felt he was on the edge of a discovery. Then he caught himself, stepped back and called it nonsense. Illumination had escaped him.

He had his land with the sky above and the warmth of molten rock below, though, being Australian freehold and inferior as title to freehold in other countries, he owned nothing under the land. Maybe when Crown land was gone, things might change.

The cavern within began to echo with voices, with boyhood thoughts, names from the past, places and habits that were his companions in boyhood, glimpses of the river back home, calm as a deserted highway. And over all, through all and bigger than anything, his father's face. He would go up into the shed and pick up the old brace and bit and the ball pein hammer that his father had handled for a lifetime, and run his hands over them. Perhaps some of his father might enter him. He didn't want to move on, he wanted the life of years ago and the same people forever. If he had to die, he wanted to die with them. He knew them, felt comfortable with their faces, their voices, the words they used, the places they talked about. And the times they'd talk of them. The hills in their minds were his hills, he knew their ways to town. Dying here would be not real dying, but the apex of fiction. Beneath the shining aluminium surface of the big dam he saw the ghostly river back home in flood. In the face of one of his trout he saw Uncle John's face, Dad's brother, with the flat ears. Remembering the horses he rode when he was young, he knew the dogs and cats which had eaten their flesh were dead too.

Fifty years had passed since he'd come back from the war, and he was lost. No one travels to look for home, he said. He'd left his native place and the loss crippled him. He felt empty as the Murray River taxi fish which, they say, blows itself up to enormous size and can never again submerge until it vomits up sufficient air.

He'd love to have had something in him. A real purpose, say. But purpose was one thing he lacked.

'If emptiness persists, see your doctor,' he gloomed, and talked of the valley inside and the threatening silence that boomed up at him. He'd even laid aside his earlier goals of gaining admission; of assertion and insertion. His prostate had grown: it had little exercise. He was too empty to humble himself and ask, or discuss it. He still had some crazy idea of mutual desire. But Eileen hadn't changed with the times: the man had to make the moves. She assumed he'd lost interest, and said nothing.

The shed was a refuge for him, as it was for his father. Protected from the harsh western afternoon light he fiddled with truck parts and tractor engines, often looking for minutes at a time out to where the horses stood about, half asleep, and the cows lifted their heads slowly, as if they too were trying to remember something. And the clouds forming, swelling, dissolving, gone. His life seemed to consist entirely of two-in-the-morning thoughts, impervious to hope, trying to forget so many things.

Growing away from life. Like most men he would be well on in years before he came to grips with the pressing need to die. Even then it would be a surprise to discover that life's long summer contained the seeds of winter, and almost anger to find his body so determined to make an end in spite of him. How strange that we approach death as if we're being asked to read aloud in a foreign language, yet any animal does it easily. As far as we know.

On weekends it was pleasant to potter in her garden with Eileen, who was now a very different woman from the laughing, casual girl he married at eighteen; like his mother, full of purpose, blazing with energy, active and engaged with Lost River affairs. Her days were stacked closely together, solid with reality. She had echoes where she expected echoes. He felt as useless as a man in company with two women, both dying to talk to each other in private. For a while she took him along to functions, musical performances, plays, church anniversaries, until she saw it was impossible to interest him, at which she gracefully and without reproach gave up. He didn't feel comfortable belonging to the whole. He felt separate and couldn't see how absurd that was.

He felt she would have laughed at internal dips and hollows, vacant caves inside a man that grow to be valleys capable of echoes. He kept it to himself. And had an afternoon drink with the dog. Wondering if the trout in the dam came up to the surface at night to look at the moon and wonder. Listening to wasps making mud nests under pallets and in the ends of black poly pipe, constructing little apartments for their kids.

Youth had been the high point of his life. It had never occurred to him that youth was only preparation. I drove past his place and admired his high-backed Friesians and big round bales of meadow hay like thick sausage rolls. He never drives heavy equipment on bitumen if he can help it. Gravel is better for rubber, he says.

When I last saw him he had retreated inside himself, scared. The abyss was so deep there was no echo. I sat in my church fixing on colours for yarns, altering his cartoon, and thinking of Alastair with only a foothold on a narrowing ledge, fingers trying to persuade the sheer rock to afford a handhold, the space in him black as doglips, waiting silently for the moment when the ledge is narrower than his foot and he begins the long internal fall to the floor of his personal abyss, his cries swallowed and absorbed by an impenetrable darkness more frightful, because conscious, than straight-out death, which was years away.

Once, I grew into a religious faith and from its safety began to look askance at a helpless God on 24-hour call to anyone who cared to cry out. No payment, no effort required. Not even thanks were compulsory. My meaning then was fixed in a context I hadn't chosen. I wanted freedom to do my own choosing. My childhood context seemed drab and something to be ashamed of, tagged with a word I joined with others in spurning: the past. I wanted a freedom where I was the only subject, where there was no One to bow to. I wanted no restraints on me. I trusted myself, proud to think I would have only myself to fall back on. I gave myself that freedom. I felt strong. But there were effects I hadn't foreseen. Gradually, people and aims, past and future—everything—became mere objects. And I treated them as objects. Freedom had spilled a wash of sameness over all it touched. Freedom emptied the world of meaning. That was fine as long as I had meanings to bestow or construct. There was no obvious direction to take, no guide to what I ought to do. I'd thrown guides out. I was the guide. Yet I didn't, alone, have the inspiration, the creativity that would produce a replacement. I wandered, I inhabited a bare planet of solitude and silence. I would break the silence by outrageous acts. I would fill the solitude by doing what I liked to other people. Anything I liked. I was alone, but not really strong enough to be my only support.

Faith in nothing was a starvation diet.

Now here I was, years later, finding it was no life to be constantly disgusted by what I'd done, imagined, thought. It was better back there, when I was inhabited by a childhood divinity, which, like radio waves, penetrates everyone.

Another thing. There really were restraints on me. I hadn't completely freed myself, whatever I thought at the time. Restraints so native to me that I wasn't aware of them. In customs, habits, ways of thinking, things I'd been brought up to do automatically. The past bore me up, in spite of my rejection of it. It protected me, preventing me doing things too absolutely atrocious.

I'd seen Alastair Pryde as a statue, frozen and immobile, his still active body carrying on a kind of stiff outer life clamped round a hollow space once inhabited by a home, but now eaten out by that home's absence, and rigid in a gesture of loss and hopelessness.

As I thought of ideas for his cartoon, a picture of my own life seemed to be reflected from Alastair's, and that word gesture' struck at my life, right into the inmost parts of me, for it seemed there was another frozen gesture, and it was me.

Simple. Like one plus one. Why did someone like me, with my history of deliberate cruelty, my cheating and casual violence, dither and complain and mewl like a sick kitten when a few coloured and bloodstained pictures from the past attacked my resting hours? I had no intention of doing anything about the past. Wrongs can't be righted. Why the fuss?

My guilt, my precious writhing and squirming, my aches and pains, my diseased conscience, were gestures.

twenty-seven
helen welland-smith

At the gallery exhibition of Wearable Art an imposing woman bore down on me, traversing the polished timber floor with better success than did a blue cattle dog with an other-worldly expression, who had entered without paying. She introduced herself and answered a few questions as we paced the gallery and dodged the dog. No, she didn't think there'd been a murder—'Though I do think Mrs F was very afraid of being attacked in one of Aphra's future shows'—and suggested I come out to the house with further questions. When I did, much of what she had to say was about her husband.

Wally Welland-Smith took to reading like a camel to sand. In high school a book on Wayland the Smith gave him the idea of becoming a blacksmith. He wanted to be a maker, and was later apprenticed to old Albert Strong whose blacksmith's and farrier's business in Gold Street was the historic premises so often photographed by tourists, and used for occasional fillers in the *Bugle*. He read a lot, and began to take an interest in the wider world when he read in one of Albert's periodicals that egalitarianism was a danger, since despotic power was needed to watch for inequality and stamp it out. This was interesting; he began, Helen said, to follow the strange currents that swirled in Australia's political rivers and creeks.

Fatstuff, one of the 'roughies' of Lost River, got his attention for a while, but her sexual aims seemed to branch out in directions young Welland, as everyone called him, didn't like. Some years later, just as he was beginning to sign little notes and letters with 'love, Welland,' Helen Bent had been getting ready to drift away from the pairing. Marriage seemed so final, at least for a time. He wouldn't have picked Helen for romance, but he could see she was wife through and through, and that was what he wanted. He knew that no man is a hero to a wife, but a good woman would never let a man get above himself. Oh well. She married him after he'd asked her twice.

She wasn't much of a talker, even when it came to curtains and furniture, but he was. In her ear constantly. She was a big woman, with a comfortable, quilty disposition and alarming eyebrows winging capably above strong eyes, who worked happily at the post office and did all the talking she needed there on the counter with the other girls, and larking about in the mail room, but she felt that a husband who talked often to her, as Welland did, was at least noticing she was there.

She made with the words sometimes. One Saturday in Eureka Mall a fortyish man danced crazily as he walked—ten in the morning—with legs and arms flinging off to the sides, two steps forward, one step back; shorts and bare legs in winter, a red headband restraining long straw hair, white shirt open to the belly-button.

'You can see he hasn't got a woman to look after him,' she explained placidly to Welland. 'A woman would soon knock that sort of shit out of him.'

After three years of marriage she reminded him it was time to start a family and wasn't surprised when, after she'd worked out when her next fertile days were, Welland settled to the task, and her next period failed to arrive. He was satisfyingly healthy, would have been dismayed by sympathy in any minor disorder, and needed no major repairs. The family began, and he was happy. Made for it.

He loved ducks and built a duck pond and duck palace, enclosed against foxes, bought three birds which produced a crop of offspring, his favourite being an infant duck devoid of beauty which he called Bradman for the relentless way it pursued its aims. Bradman reminded Welland of the forest of pressure groups on government, so thick and noisy in their scrabble for scraps that the citizen couldn't be seen among them. That was his kind of reflection. He trained Dog, the dog, descended apparently from basset, setter and spaniel ancestors, to pick up a mat and lay it on the cat. The cat often didn't move, and slept under it as a blanket of a rougher kind.

Helen liked goats and planned to assemble a small flock when they moved, as they soon did, to a house on forty acres off the Western Road, on the town side of Gubba Dam. Welland now had a large shed, part of which took the overflow of books after Helen refused to have more than six bookcases in the house. He built a blacksmith's shop close to the road when Albert Strong died and the family sold the Gold Street premises. He worked as blacksmith and farrier for eight years, until he accepted a good job with Kimberly Konkrete. His furnace still spoke, people still got him to do farrier work and blacksmithing in his spare time, though the new music in his head was that of soft diesels.

Just as in the days of Wayland the Smith in his forge in a barrow on the Berkshire Downs, and very likely in the forge of the lamed Hephaestus of Greek antiquity, swords had names, and steeds too, so objects at the Welland-Smiths were named. Her jelly-mould Mazda was Portia, his square Volvo was Hannibal; ducks, goats and even the children had to answer to names not inscribed on their birth certificates, pedigree papers or bills of sale.

He made tools and tines, helped with the little inventions farmers nut out after tea at night, and had a special area set aside for scrap metal, with its fascinating and eloquent likeness to other, more familiar forms, such as statuary and art objects. The quiet growth and silent rust of this garden of shapes was a subject of Helen's dry tongue now he had a well-paid job instead of the fluctuating income of a dying trade.

He built himself metal- and wood-working benches, hammered out horseshoes, made trampolines, designed sports armour, made dew-catchers for campers, a scimitar, kris or kukri for the odd collector. He turned wood, designed and polished wooden bowls, wine racks, trick boxes. He had a feel for the grain and architecture of the wood, his work suggesting strongly the dignity of the tree it came from.

Stands for bird houses, tree houses for the kids, enclosures for the goats, a gazebo for the garden, ponds for fish, bird baths, brick paths, feeding trough. His energy and ideas had no end. His life was like a rather large wave that rolled on within the little sea of the Welland-Smith family, supporting ducks, goats, horses for the girls, odd work with the forge, the job with Kimberly, the progress of children through the entrails of the education system, the constant making, and his talking.

He talked to everyone he met, but the main set of auditory receptors at which he aimed his words were Helen's, since, like Everest in another connection, she was there. She heard how we lack watchdogs on government, how the dinosaurs may have expired from constipation as ferns were replaced by flowering plants. She wondered what to do with the information that there was a minimum temperature but no maximum, and that coral can make new bone for humans since it's not recognised as 'other' by the immune system, information elicited by their daughter Sarah's recitation, 'Of his bones is coral made.'

He had many original thoughts: original because he'd never heard or read them. If he'd read even more, he'd have found that almost nothing he prided himself on was his own, all had been thought before. It wouldn't have stopped him. He speculated that humans might be a life-seed that would spread our kind of life through the universe, but six months later others were saying it in the newspapers; it was in the air.

But his strongest expressions were kept for government. 'When you fight for freedom and justice, you find your main enemy is government. In moderation it's fine, but unrestrained it becomes a predator, a cancer on the society that feeds it. If the cancer takes over, government becomes society: everything an expression of the state.' You see, I know it off by heart, she said.

How he'd love to be among those privileged to spend their lives with ideas. If only he'd had the education. If only he could, then the pressure would be off her to be chief listener, sometimes getting up so close and so enthusiastic to show her things that he couldn't help clonking her with his great head.

But what if this science stuff was all so much talk? A few years later shown to be rubbish? It had happened before, she thought. The respect, the fame, the honours; then nothing. It was no use asking me. What would I know? Helen was restless. Days of discontent trudged over her; she felt their weight and imagined their footprints on her skin, just as she detected the tracks of those things she'd meant to do for years but never got round to, prevented by her years of love and slavery to a family.

She felt she came about midway on Welland's scale of love, somewhere below his beloved old forge and the big lathe, level with his power tools and Volvo, and well above the cement-mixer and the lesser tools. She wasn't so far out of the world as to imagine someone better than Welland might come along; she knew men were pretty much the same. People were basically incompatible, but with a few dozen major adjustments could get along. Yet they shared a good deal. There were the kids. They both tacitly agreed that being a parent was only accidentally altruistic, it was really a display of power, enabling the unspoken triumph, *We created you*, to be implied in every proud parental look. And to give up the power inherent in parenting was not worth it, so their kids would be brought up with the discipline that had stood people in good stead in the past they felt they knew.

There was their shared dislike of a sudden descent of relatives, sometimes a deluge in which they felt they were drowning. Both valued their cash retention program. He was always willing to chauffeur people to meetings of the Arthritis Foundation. There were reasonable holidays. He played cricket with the boys and only last week there he was batting and boasting, 'Not a feather duster yet!'

She'd only seen him once in drink, while his legs were in contention as to which should go first and which to the left. Tight as a vain man's shoes, he was. They got along fairly well. Perhaps that was all she could expect. Her guess was that he got married to have all the things people had in the past: wife, kids, house, hobbies, family life. He hadn't run away after the children came and her body slackened. Some women had Caesarians to keep things tight down there, but she would never consider it.

She'd never said so, but she was interested in some of the things he said. That set of ideas, that family, locality, religion and language were more important than states. Especially family and religion. She liked him for that. He said they were two prime defences against the state. And always that other one about no real democracy till power is decentralised. She liked him defending her parents, who still spoke of England as home despite the derision the ex-English suffered for so many decades. 'Let the smarties try putting down migrants from Laos, Vietnam, Africa, India, Bosnia for talking of home,' he said.

He had an ancestor who had been at the Eureka Stockade. History got it wrong, he said, they weren't workers, they were gamblers and opportunists. And his refrain, 'The voice of the people is soft, slow and hesitant, until it's ignored too long.'

It might almost be addressed to her. Speak up for yourself. But what did she want? To burst out into words just to be asserting herself? Or was there something specific? Going or staying? In company she never spoke up to defend him, she felt that wasn't cool, as the kids put it nowadays. He did defend her, and it made her feel like a child. On the other hand, if he didn't defend her, she'd be long gone.

But he wasn't a bad man, he was a good man. A rarity. He hadn't married her looking for a mother, just someone who loved in the same way as his mother: businesslike, not cloying, keeping a slight distance. That's me, she said. But if only there was a little more quiet about the place. He was a whole noise-works by himself. All that energy. Do I want more attention? I get talk, that's his attention. He wouldn't be himself if he was different. If he mixed more he might start drinking. Or other women. Women liked him. His face, his size, his strength; he was like a rock. Rocklike, they said in the *Bugle* article on black-smithing. And that Carmen Mummo always fixing her eyes on him, willing him to look at her, and he hasn't noticed. Yet.

Going. But would life be any better if he wasn't around to say that all cats are different but they're still cats? Or that Ireland was the scene of attempted ethnic cleansing? Or that if you knew which children would be the psychopaths would you put them down? Or, if the dog spoke the whole town would understand her since the underlying grammar of existence is universal? She was forty-four, the kids growing up. What was puzzling her? Was it those addresses on letters? Mrs Wally Welland-Smith, for God's sake! She was Helen Welland-Smith. Bloody lawyers and relatives living in the past.

It was starting to be dark. There he is now, coming down out of that shed of his. Several swallows playing with the air, making quick strokes in space. He stops to talk to old Indy, the neighbours' ex-racehorse. Indy moves painfully, nursing his arthritis. Welland made a stall for him with a heating pad he could stand his offside rear quarters against. They always say hullo. Indy comes up to the fence every afternoon when he's due home. Welland had taken to fighting Helen's new pedigreed billygoat Shagforth every day and the silly animal seemed to like it. When he came home from Kimberly the flat, straw-coloured eyes of the goat would be watching for him, and when they faced each other they'd square off; the goat would charge, he'd grab the horns and swing him round and round like a razzle-dazzle. This, in addition to the usual male madnesses.

When the ritual fight was over and Welland came inside, taking his shoes off on the verandah, the goat would wait expressionlessly for more combat. Even her own goat liked him. Why the discontent? What do I want in place of this? She could think of nothing positive, she had no answers to her own questions. And dimly she was beginning to feel that she never would know, for the thing inside did not want the roughness, the violence of being expressed and left out in the open to dry and perhaps shrivel. And maybe die. It would fight her to the end.

He's coming in now. Look at him. He's happy and, as far as he knows, the whole family is.

Welland saw the white pickup, knew what was what, and strode masterfully across the concrete verandah floor he'd laid with his own hands.

'Ah, the weaver bloke. You sure they won't change the room size on you in that new centre? Never know with bloody councils. All that uncontested power. That'd stuff you. No? Listen, you'd be interested in this. You too, Nel.' He'd abbreviated Helen to Hel, and that she would not tolerate, so he reversed the last syllable. 'Just thinking in the car, and Indy and Shagforth Splendour III gave their approval to the idea: Have our attempts at altering ourselves by means of religion been promptings towards a destiny our forebears intuited? That is, eventual flight from this planet to another heaven for the race, and then another, as we keep the race alive, while successive life-giving stars go out long in the future? Is religion's eternal life'—we had both taken a step backwards, blown by his words, or something so powerful about him that it was impossible to resist—'a foreshadowing of an eternal life for the race? There wouldn't happen to be a pot of tea on, would there? Mind you, some would say we'd be the ultimate pollution. So should we stay here till the planet runs down, and die with it? And is death itself no more than a dance to the music of memory?' I dare say we both had our mouths open, for he laughed explosively, like the crack of a wet sail.

'You bloody great big dope!' Helen ejaculated and ran at him, giving him a monster hug right in front of me. Two massive bears wrestling. One in his socks. And one not entirely comfortable in anything. The hug, which was returned, forced from both of them two very piggy grunts, striking notes a third apart. So there was harmony, of a kind.

Helen's cartoon shows her as an anchor to the Welland-Smith ship. The anchor is beginning to drag.

All day I couldn't get that word gesture out of my head. All the fuss, the feelings of guilt, and I had discovered it was gesture. Was the discovery gesture too? But only gesture? Well, I was easily convinced of it. I've always suspected myself. Token, half-hearted actions, rhetorical devices, partial inclinations.

I left that and ran away to thoughts of Yarrow and the warmth I feel between us even now. Two distant particles still in contact despite the distance. The first parting scattered dead leaves and dying in my path everywhere I walked. Half a person, unsatisfied, like one mouth kissing. But that last parting, with no address given, left large holes in me. I retreated, walking back into myself, since her shadow was in there, and I felt like a walking wound.

twenty-eight

sonya ergot

In the Holly Tree she presented, to my eyes, as thin and long like the Taralga toothpick mosquito. A complexion like the white of an egg. I realised I'd seen her at Jazz in the Bush and at the Busker's Festival. Juniper Grey had cooled the Holly Tree only slightly, but that amount was welcome after the February heat outside on the bitumen.

She was hard to draw out at first. Came on so abrupt and jittery she seemed scared enough for her shadow to run back inside her for refuge and to get there before she did. She was of an age—I remember—when you feel your self is setting around you like concrete, only it's not concrete, it's habits and skin that feels more than ever the roughnesses of the world. She looked pinned, like an experimental subject in the grip of a magnetic flux.

I told a crazy little story of the coat that ate into people who wore it. Passed from hand to hand it had unusual effects. Some complained of a little civilising pain, some of an acid-drop pain with a hurt then a sweetness, and with others the fabric drew blood. It gave an imaginative jolt to another, who felt she could hear the despairing wails of wheat and the lost cries of corn as they died for her at breakfast. A little excursion in a vegetarian direction flushed out the comment that the meat-eater is a client of the abattoir. She was ready to talk. The kids at school had served up weird theories about the murder. Leanne was on the run from her family. Someone saw her leave the Show early, someone saw her come back, no times mentioned.

Sonya loved old-time dancing, liked the variety of men to be met at a club dance, liked to dream about them and speculate, and had what she described as 'terrible orgy-imaginings'. She couldn't stand the smell of fish. Her skin felt like iron filings. Was she about to lash me with her wounds?

Her face is a narrow elegy, shaped by prominent bones. Just pencil in powerlessness and anxiety. Without lipstick her lips are not red, but like veal killed yesterday and drained. She admires people who live with a classical cool, but confesses that in company she stops thinking, can feel no longer a separate person, goes with the flow of talk and settles into being with, an extension of, the others. Submerged. Emulsified. She can't explain it. Didn't need to, I've often done it. Cowering in summer sandals, her toes are crouched over, meek mice. She has yellow ochre hair, a pink scalp, two thin lines of dark hair roots.

'This is my life: my father kills me, mother eats me, brother and sister sit under the table picking my bones, which they throw out to our skinny dog Jones. It started years ago. I'd always wanted to help people, so when I didn't qualify for medicine I went for teaching, became a counsellor. I thought the highest, noblest life was one spent helping others not so fortunate. There was a memory from when I was eleven of going underground, finding small pale people living in darkness. I took them torches, matches, anything to give them light because light fed them, it was all they needed, even light they couldn't sense. It became part of my conscience. I couldn't not help, without doing violence to myself.

'My work exposes me to the running sores of our school civilisation. And I don't mean just avoiding the nerd-gas when the air is green. They give me nightmares which sentence me to summary depression, dreams of neglected children with verdant teeth. Wind and flowing currents of air wear away rock; no wonder I'm worn down. There's no nourishment in tears.

'Why won't the kids cooperate? Am I the fractious child? They've been told the universe has no ruler so why should they? It's not that I don't wish to eat, just that when they're like this all appetite is gone. Very well, sometimes I starve myself. I see starving as a psychopump to get the waste emotions out of me. I'm skinny as a schoolboy's excuse but not terminally thin. Hidden scripts inside us choose for us in some matters and no rubber hose, steel blade or alkaloid can erase the deep troubles written on our brains. It may be possible to make sense of life, but only in small increments.'

Was she a masochist? Did I hear the jingle of handcuffs, and intuit the presence of the leg-spreader?

'I'm too exposed. No skin. I'd be more relaxed filleted. When they see me so thin they might—well, it might make them think. Some hope. Changing my name made a difference. Sonya Ergot is more vital than Dawn Doble. I'm like a flame, I change constantly into strange shapes, warming no one. Or a dry leaf in a forest, falling in stillness, and no one to notice. At least I don't shout and slobber on the floor, frightening the gentle kids. I try never to take pills and retain my habits, but calm down and do the work myself when I'm anxious or angry. But I wonder if it's all right to take that much responsibility for yourself.

'I don't want to become one of those whose only exercise is throwing the book at the class, or one of those who ape the next generation. This is really a cultured nervous state, not a common inability to cope, you know. At least I'm not like my mother who was terrified of wandering interplanetary sperm. But right now I've had too much exposure to children. It's as much as I can bear. I wish they could all be put on a spacecraft and sent to colonise planets of distant stars, as people once were sent to America and Australia.

'In the staff room I try to smile but it hurts and I see them looking. Anxious or superior, as if mine are only freshwater tears. And I feel my smile, all verve and no content, wilting. In company I nervously examine my silences. They must notice. But I can't reduce myself to an eye, I must feel.

'So thin, yet I feel swollen. Tits like a malnourished mouse. Wary and self-protective as a nervous echidna. Collarbones like whipsnakes under a threadbare blanket of flesh. Where are the oils and lotions in the beauty bar for the soul inside, for the speckled spinsterhood that's ahead? Where's the help we're supposed to get from our infirmities?

'The kids even came with me when I took long-service leave and boarded the plane with the other cultural cringers for French cathedrals, Italian towns and Greek isles. I try to enter through their words into their minds, but there's a gap I can't bridge. Are their minds blank sheets of A4? Or rusted shut? A lot of the trouble is class-based; those with books in the house play with their kind, the rest feel inferior and play up. Boys and girls tend not to mix. Some talk entirely in slogans—right on, way to go, cool. They love to be cool. To be enthusiastic is uncool, so what hope do they have?

'This second facelift seems to be working. Only thirty-nine, but the next stop's forty. I feel I'm drowning in warm water. Are the poorer kids the trouble? Or the hillbillies where the man's tea is sent in on a pole: "Don't say a word till he's had his tea!" No, the ones from better homes are more insolent, they look down on me. The poor families are often bottom-dwellers whose lives go on the same no matter what fuss there is way above them at the political or social surface, hearing nothing of passing fashions or superficial change. Some have never heard of the fuss about smoking, and only know one variety of greenhouse.

'But even though I feel all my inner rivers and tributaries flowing in the wrong direction I try to feel calm, to rejoice once a day, to say: I am. Yet really the only time I feel safe for five minutes is when I'm locked in the toilet. Years ago when I was told to talk it all out, I did. The words I used became rigid bars caging my memory.

'I'm at the mercy of an education bureaucracy's official theory of the moment, couched in their flabby analogues. I have to carry out untrue policies made in the valley of the shadow of theory, that I had no hand in making, which change this way and that without notice. Their makers retire unscathed even if their theories explode and do damage. The bureaucrats are helped to their official opinions by intellectuals of varying temperaments who never face a class, voices of power from the low moral ground manipulating versatile facts and observations which go to bed with any number of hypotheses. And once I hoped for a society of sustained cognitive growth.

'At the end of the line, when the behaviour, irrationality or dementia of the child gets so they can't be kept in class without the others suffering grossly, there's Sonya. Out of the way for an hour or two. Maybe they'll calm down. For the bad classes the older hands tell the young teachers, Don't get these sleazoids to do anything, they can't do it; just read to them, show videos, give puzzles, get them to copy from the board. Some can't even copy, they've been to remedial teacher after remedial teacher all the way up from primary and they still can't read or write. They tell them, Don't bash your head against a wall, you can't improve them. Fifteen and can't read? So don't ask them to read. Violence and constant action are the only things to get their attention.

'I have to listen to the verbal pus that comes out. Often takes weeks to get them to talk. They'll appear to, but a lot of it is rubbish, stuff they've picked up from hearing adults talk, muck from the dramas on the box that reflect their own idiocy back to them, or jargon phrases they hear from other kids who've been through the system. It's no picnic getting down to what they really think. Usually it's disordered or childish. Well, they are children, though you doubt it when you hear them in a lane saying, "Not in the skin, get in the sewer," when they shoot up.

'Why do I think I can work it all out in words? At least I've got the car, so much to see in the country. Polo on the weekend at Lilly Pilly. I leave sex for inservice courses. The obligatory warm wrestle. Then I live on the memory of a look, a gesture, a feeling. Or a lick and a promise. What a ghastly life. Who wants a Spotted River panic fish for company? The rest of the time all I have at night is the elegiac fingerbird. Though I'm aware that with too much fingerbird the instrument performs poorly for other players. How long will I survive? I suppose when I've outgrown hope something mild like sadness will settle down comfortably over me like a house and I'll live in that. They say freedom is the thread leading you out of the six-billionfold collective, and sometimes I've dared to want it, but when it came to the point I decided not to choose it. I'm stuck where I've always been: up to my chin in shit and I haven't even climbed out of my own navel.

'Perhaps I'll be free when I'm old and have cats draped over me. I'll wear men's shirts for comfort and men's long pyjamas to keep my ankles warm. I'll drive to town with my old cat in her baby seat and the dog on the roof-rack. I'll do my garden most of the day, read for hours. I'll pee on the compost heap when I feel like it, my nieces and nephews can ride my donkeys. I'll swim naked in the dam and sing at the top of my voice whenever I feel memory making a lunge for me. And write a book on the universal grammar of need.'

The narrow elegy was smiling at this cut from the future, but the brain behind the facebones struck me as being full of outraged letters to the editor.

In her early twenties she'd had a kind of weeping eczema which left her when she learned to cry.

Under the blank February sun on the drive back to the church I thought of her as a sculpture sculpting itself. Remember the drawing of the hand drawing itself? Like that.

When I got back there were practical matters waiting. A girl of between fifteen and eighteen—I can't tell anymore—was sitting in the shade feeding a baby. There were several bruises on her face, one at the outside corner of her left eye. Someone had caught her with a right hand. Other marks of being knocked around showed high on her chest and above the left elbow, on the muscle.

'Ssssh,' she told me unnecessarily. The baby sucked vigorously and loudly. No amount of noise was going to separate that boy from the breast until he was good and ready.

I got busy with Sonya's cartoon. Funny how with thin and miserable people you get the urge to warm them up. When the girl was through feeding the next generation she didn't threaten me with her wounds and abrasions, just told me she'd come in a taxi, wouldn't be in the way, and I was elected because I had all this space to live in, wasn't with anyone and lived on a hill. She'd brought a bag with baby things and a few bits and pieces for herself.

'I'd like a spare blanket in case there's a cold snap.' In February? I fetched a spare blanket.

'Any spare beds?'

'Only a camp bed.'

'I'll have to take yours, then.' I'd been about to offer. Well, I was considering it.

She explored the church, found a place to put Jack down, and consulted pantry and fridge.

'Can you cook?' I asked. I can, but I'm not sure about young women. She didn't answer.

She stayed until her bruises faded. It was a hot summer, but she was constantly concerned to see that Jack was warm enoughly dressed, as she put it. I didn't like to ask her name.

The time of weaving Sonya into the tapestry was full of gestures. Gestures everywhere, artificial, double-faced, dishonest, casual, all the way from the red dog's dealings with the cat, visiting birds' scuffles with each other, to little Jack's arm-waving and the nameless girl's sidelong glances at the meals I prepared and her surreptitious wiping of my knives and forks between her fingers before eating with them.

In the town my eyes caught gestures in almost every movement, even of the traffic, certainly of the mall people strolling or just sitting there to look at other people, or to get out of the heat. The placement of meat in the windows of Mountain Meats, the advertising displays, the cruising shoppers: the spurious, the counterfeit, the suggestive. Even the demons in short pants that clustered round adult legs were someone's gestures.

Would I ever have met Yarrow if I'd met someone like her when I was young? I thought of all she had kindled in me when I saw her. What had I kindled in her? The emotion you have on finding a toe in a park?

twenty-nine

fatstuff

I was winding on to the tapestry roller, thinking of my next subject and of how motives and private designs arose in all parts of Lost River. Looking down from Wiradhuri Hill you can see them as vapour plumes twisting together, rising, attenuating. Dissolving, flowing free and finally invisible. Do they remember their shapes as they settle unseen on other places and people, having their effects?

Perky as a Snowy River armadillo chicken, Fatstuff had helped fight the last bushfire west of town, thought to be started by kids, and got a run in the *Bugle* for heroism. It wasn't the first thing you'd think of when you saw her slumped in one of the side booths at the Holly Tree. I thought of a travelling con-artist selling cures for imaginary diseases, then of a circus fat lady who'd lost her nerve and given up, to retire in a country town.

Fat-covered muscles like small pillows parked themselves all over her expanses. Dips and hollows, whole valleys were pulled together under her little dress which I immediately congratulated for its valour in holding so much and so many together for so long. Unpacked, that body would overwhelm. A lover's first survey and reconnaissance would be like finding your way round an inflated rubber mountainside with few handholds. It was the eyes that showed everything in order in that ballooning body, from calmly cascading blood at her temple to the heroically pulsing blood at the bottom of the mountain, raising itself to the upper interior under who knows what pressure. Her eyes were so bright they seemed to have an extra film of glitter on their surfaces. After a little sparring, in which I got the verbal bruises, she agreed to give her version of herself, but at her place. On the Saturday, in Jacaranda Street, she received me in what was a real performance.

She answered her door without the confining dress, her feet and ankles pussycatting on the carpet, and I thought of gestures. But the things you noticed were her hands. Those fingers. Delicate. Eloquent. My face discovered that her cheek was smooth as stainless steel. A white fan prowled the room in horizontal arcs.

In a large china cabinet she kept her sex aids for training purposes. There was a deflated and folded latex three-hole doll with fingers that gripped, and full lubrication; the other items were more ordinary.

I am fat and naked, as you see. White, smiling and unbelievable. Sensual, funny and a complete waste of time. But what else is time for? Look at me and see the temptations I've surrendered to; I refuse to say no. I've mastered guilt and fear and engineered my own salvation. I carry a lifebelt at my waist. Look at me and who can resist laughing? I certainly can't. But remember, the tree is more than leaves and branches.

God kissed me when I was fifteen. I saw clouds made of blood, which the wind streaked across the sky. Not a warning, but a confirmation of the body. The mountains of air were part of me. Blood clouds came down and ran through my veins. I opened my legs, which were intersecting mountain ranges, and God kissed me there, blessing me and my life with his big mouth. While he had me in that position he spoke into me a kind of music, melodies I couldn't understand entered me there and echoed through the arteries of my life. They sing in me every day songs of feeling without flesh and blood, songs of death without decay. I remember especially each time I undress in my sunroom and feel the blue eye of the sky looking at me.

I'm a planner in Lost River's town planning department. No, I can hardly believe it myself. Positive litter control was my idea, but council refused permission to shoot offenders. Pity. I dress for work with the Empty Ones, as I call them: interested, busy, but no souls. Empty as new-built houses. Obsessed sometimes, but no heart. Nostalgia is impossible to them, freedom a foreign language. I say to them, Be spontaneous, be free, practise every day; a minute a day will change your life. Do they? Like hell they do. Know how you test for freedom? You say, You're free now to do anything you wish, the meaning of your life is the meaning you give it by the way you use your freedom and what you make of yourself. If they say yes, then it's for them; if they say wait, it's probably not, so they choose by being themselves. Like Snow White fast asleep and the seven dwarfs restlessly awake.

Here in my castle with the turrets in Jacaranda Street, when I relax and rest my large white feet on a pink and grey pouf and think of love—well, it may not be love but it's the practice and outward signs of love, who can choose?—I'm grateful to chance and choice that I'm suited by my sensual nature to enjoy and increase its pleasures. Here we worship sensation, our actions are plantings and produce results. For me the stomach too is an erogenous zone, and capable of loving. The surface area of my extensive skin, rounded, undulating and hilly from my gluttonous habits, multiplies the feelings persistently provoked by lips, fingers and other means as my young and little lovers, boys and girls, show their teeth, set in motion what can't be stopped; they oblige me and soothe my soul. Which I carry displayed on the back of my hand along with the motto of the month: never abandon excess, never make do with enough.

They love my pride in myself, my young lovers do, and laugh at my dog Greedy, and at my castle Vanity. I give my character in one hit to everyone I meet and my character is freedom to pursue my own aims subject only to a few thoughts about the rights of others. One rule is to be completely played-out sensually once a week, my recipe for spiritual growth. You should see the young fry when they hear such things. As interested as dogs outside a butcher's shop. Even those incapable of thrilling moments unassisted. There's no room for hate here, only satisfaction, in our mutual aberration society. Room for laughter too, when a waterbed leaks, or in humid weather when thoughts begin to pong.

Oh, the noisy climaxes, piecrust promises, prayerful debriefings, primitive groans and purple gasps, some as poetic and catchy as a Fortran program. Sometimes a confusion of doubt and hesitation with innocence. And all of them clothed only in the words of songs. Here, individuals who would never approve the use of whips, chains and harsh restraint on the beef-brained public, will use these aids in private for fun and sex on themselves and their intimate friends. Humanity is fully consistent with cruelty.

When I give food to my lovers they come rushing holding their temporary hungers as if a headless horseman were in pursuit. Sadness doesn't belong with eating, even after many chocolates, and cursed are the poor in spirit, for they cannot know full wildness of joy. Hunger is a terrible thing, also a delight. Often I delay its consummation, dressing in fancy clothes—damson dinner suit or crocus cowboy chaps, spurs and hat, sometimes a sable diving suit, or Santa Claus uniform—to delay matters of haunch and raunch and sharpen desire. Then I look at a new boy who shivers at my look as if a carnivorous tree turned its attention on him. Let there always be a corner of your desire unsatisfied. Absolute satisfaction, beyond further desire, is the enemy, no matter how completely you have been exhausted. I teach the young to be desperate for pleasures sharper and sharper, wilder and wilder, till they graduate into seeing red. I teach them death, in fact, which is the understanding of spiritual things by means of the material.

We were a fat family, breeding spherical smiles, carrying conviviality at the waist, not so much consumers as absorbers. I was always fat and sleek, full of cholesterol and happy. I could never reach my feet. Goodbye feet, I said at eighteen, is this forever? The new morality is slimness, while I hunger for third helpings of everything from russet roasts to alabaster ice-cream to burgundy with its elusive shades of colour within the glass. When I'm old and my roots withered, suffering the vengeance of time, my memories will be more specific, all prudence gone, pretty boy and girl love-partners flown, grown or dead. The best of friends must stiffen, but let the young come back to instruct the old. Bring back the young, I say. Alone I'll be, under the narrowing mornings, the white-washed clouds massing higher than ever before in my life. My life's blue-bordered map will turn up at the edges, be torn at the folds. I hope I'll remember what's missing from the worn places where towns are rubbed off, population gone, whole shires missing. What escapes time's demolition will cling all the harder to my emptying auburn skull. I'll feel like a new puppet gloved on the hand of old events, like an old music no one wants to play, an ancient singer of a lost reed-green and distant country. Still, misery passes. Joy takes its turn, or nothing does. Unremitting gravity, gentle at first, pulls me down and back. All round me the traffic is faster, while I'm islanded in an eddy to one side, looking every day for the rainbow bird. Where do you hide in this heat? You don't. You wear it and suffer the climate-induced lassitude that made us casual. Careless is the word.

My little lovers, did you ever love me? I still have the belly-folds, I'll say when I'm old, but you have forgotten me. My angels have grown older. Will they really wipe me from their lives? Do they still have the maps I gave them, their personal maps of imaginary treasures? When I have difficulty walking, I'll buy a duckhead stick of ebony, the head of heavy polished brass. I may want to hit out at people. I love shiny things, and better still, shiny colours. They put such a gloss on the members of this world, almost cover the miserable half-patched pasts, the thin greyness, the untold poverty of the human soul.

An obscure blue future dizzies me, I can't imagine myself different. No, I won't join the Gastric Partitioning Association, they can stop inviting me. I'll still be me in spite of weird dreams in which fragments of my life's episodes are knitted together in fantastic patchworks, words go crazily multiplying each other, and everything turns into something else. Dressed in my favourite hyacinth-red I shall dwell in the house of food forever. My approach to death will be like finding your way around a strange room full of furniture in the dark.

She moved to the door to see me off, lumbering like a dray. No photos of her young lovers adorned the walls.

'Take a chocolate, it will make you feel pleased,' she said.

I did. It did.

In the front yard a small dog emerged guiltily, as if recently suborned, from the shade of a callistemon, to welcome my departure.

Fatstuff's cartoon began with a heavy white cloud, icecream mountains against the Pacific blue of the late February sky, which was how she lived in my head.

Was I really a gesture, like Pryde? The idea, with the equivocal, many-sided connotations of the word, puzzled and fascinated me. I couldn't leave it alone. Something simulated, faked perhaps, invented, assumed, artificial, dressed-up, pretended, fictitious. Or even bogus, half-hearted, ineffectual. I searched for more words to hit myself with, like a pinball going out of its way to hit as many obstructions as it could find.

I wished I could have seen Yarrow, contacted her somehow. That first meeting, when she sat on the edge of a large flower, or perhaps a tree that opened for her like a flower; her stillness put me on edge. She was poised, I scrabbled, feeling like a boy. When she left me, she took all my good days. I saw them go, in a swirl around her head. And my first resentful dream of her, with my head in the basket, her hand on the lever. Didn't even stop to set my head upright.

When we talked, that time, we narrowed ourselves down to arguments in which I could see no merit. So everything was political, she said; who could disagree? Everything we do or think affected by our interests, and we can't stand to one side, apart. Fair enough, but what that told me was that we needed as much detachment as we could manage, or even real politics was useless. She maintained we couldn't tell the truth about the world, but seemed to feel that what she said was true. And if no particular discourse could be privileged, yet she presented arguments in a rational, orderly and logical way, assumed I could understand what was said, and obviously believed I would change my opinions if her words were persuasive, so she certainly favoured that kind of discourse. I wasn't there to hear her when she said by what right her discourse was to be judged correct. Perhaps I missed it.

In the end I had to pick up my own head. A few drops of private unease fell as I lifted it.

thirty

juniper grey

In complete control of herself, she was calm as top fish in the dentist's tank. I'd seen her face often in her restaurant. The Holly Tree was popular for coffee and lunch, and had taken off in the last few years, I was told, when Juniper opened for dinner Tuesday to Sunday. She favoured black and pink, with grey booths, white cloths, and a mixture of hard-edge townscapes and pretty-pretty watercolours for the walls.

She particularly wanted to see my church, the loom, the view over the town, and the way the surrounding hills looked from Wiradhuri. The topographical map showed it as being a whisker above the 800-metre mark. Her quietness invaded me like a daydream you're in before you know you're daydreaming.

Juniper is around six feet tall, long-legged and long-necked, and smells like sandalwood. She says very little at first, though she did remark that everyone wants a long life but no wrinkles. I put the chairs and table out on the grass where the view was best. A considerate gesture? Or a devious one? Perhaps routine. Later I looked back on it rather as a half-hearted suggestion that she was entitled to special treatment. What response had I intended to evoke? What intention did I want to convey? I suppose sitting in the back seat of my mind was the memory of Knudsen saying her kisses went straight to your Richard; in the same conversation he released the hot news that Leanne's second lips were wrinkled and soft as the petals of a pale hibiscus. Juniper gave the impression that all her senses were unlocked and let out, but under supervision. Her skin showed pale pink and warm under thin cotton.

She was interested in the topographical map. Apparently she'd only ever seen road maps, which showed most of the country, including vast areas of private forest and green country, in white, and only national parks in green. She didn't realise how many forests there were.

Happiness is possible under any regime, and Juniper was happy. From childhood she'd had a profile reminiscent of aristocratic stereotypes as they appeared in cartoons of the past, but which is best seen these days in the Snowy River paddlefish, if you can land the beast after it's dined on too many carp. It's a challenge, with those meaty paddles batting at the bait. You think you've got her but she loops the line round a paddle, then lets go near the surface. I wonder if Knudsen, or Carmen Mummo, discovered this resemblance.

Juniper finished school but didn't qualify for veterinary science. She wanted nothing else, so when Niobe Waxman, her friend at school, inherited smilingly enough money to start a coffee shop and asked Juniper to work with her, she accepted immediately. The Holly Tree did very well. Perfect position.

Seven years later, when Niobe's two children were killed in a car accident on a two-way section of highway, Niobe was inconsolable, didn't eat, just sat hunched over as if turned into a woman-shaped stone. Juniper didn't burden her with bothersome sympathy, but saw to the burial of the children, and the husband, who was also in the crash. Gradually Niobe let go and slipped into a state in which she was still alive, but no more than that. Juniper ran the Holly Tree, and over the years *was* the Holly Tree.

Some years ago she was prosecuted for planting edelweiss in the Southern Alps. The town didn't consider it a crime, and ignored it. It was at the time of another green drought, just enough sporadic rain to green the grass. Farmers had to shoot their five- and six-year-old sheep, but they were mostly water at that age and their teeth worn down too far to feed.

The beauty of living in the tablelands is that you are given the four seasons and there are good things in each: autumn with its long afternoons, spring's soft air unravelling garden perfumes, winter's snow and cool sunny days with the rushing cold of the hills and the solid cold of the valleys, when you blink to warm your eyes, and summer's two or three bursts of dry heat. Of them all I love spring's regular demonstrations best, when I'm Wisteria Woman. I watch little flies searching the oak leaves, birds hunting the spear spider, or notice ants wandering indoors from the world. I think about the pond covered with a mirror the same shape as itself, about the way the river moves and how the currents seem to have intentions, and sashay in their constant dance. I wonder if the metallic starlings in their hundreds will come here from the town. They haven't yet. I search the morning grevilleas hung with masses of small webs outlined with tiny dewdrops. The sunlit day gives the impression it sings to itself and is sufficient.

Many years ago something happened. At the river, where it bends like a knee, the water swirled at different points, the current disturbed, moving as if large bodies were struggling underwater. As the water moved, all sounds stopped. The breeze towed in perfumes I'd never experienced. From a new planet? I felt I'd come from somewhere else and was a stranger. It was morning, and morning seemed a sacred rite. The swirl of water mounted up, its strands of water twisted together like hair, or cables formed of promises, thoughts expressed in movement, secrets, enlightenments. They twisted and rose, became a flow, then a kind of wind which caught a floating leaf and carried it high in the air, so high it saw a world where all humanity formed one global brain. Dazed, I went into town and saw riches everywhere: bread in the gardens of Anzac Park, wine in the bubblers, gold in the dust of the streets, and pedestrians wealthy with happiness. Everything came alive with an inner, more powerful life than showed on the surface. As far as I could see, glass, metals, bitumen, street trees, concrete, were all moving and quivering with their own current, their own life. I felt I'd seen into the world, not just its surface, and the strength and intelligence that made everything move.

I have a small property in the hills north of Lost River, north of here, and spend time outdoors. The old rail lines glide in a curve and disappear under a bullnose hill. The mock orange is in flower; the white syringa, jonquils and daffodils in July and August line the access road near the gate. The trees I planted, black sally, white sally, ribbon gum, cider gum, Argyle apple, have extended their arms, their wrists sprout leaf-covered fragile twigs. I love walking in my native garden surrounded by the components of poems, insects and dead leaves included, and spiders in their geometrical kingdoms, and think of cures for imaginary diseases. I leave one pretty Paterson's Curse plant; it's too blue to pull out. I stand often among the thickest growing shrubs, with their thesaurus of leaves; I straighten up after pulling stray weeds round the kangaroo paws, and am pleasantly dizzy with the weather's thunder. Even the bitter touch of winter frost has its place.

I enjoy the sweet smell of the acacia chips I've spread on the earth, and watch adult rosellas in the mearnsii nibbling acacia galls and dropping their scraps on the steel roof of the wood shed, with loud clangs. I enjoy the smell of rain before it arrives on the westerly wind. Sometimes I think of the end of things and how it will be to have quiet forever and not to hear it. To be a part of the universal poem which includes a canto for each death. I turn back to my garden, which is a lake of blue and white fire, and bathe in its living quiet. I stop, I look. The marvels of life are all around and constantly passing in and out of me, as clouds, encouraged by a crinkled wind, fill the dome of sky in shapes always new and interesting. I think we are marvellous, and so is everything that lives, from kingfisher to kangaroo. And so is the soul of the smallest flower.

I know I'm lucky, each day to wake happy, grateful, as in peace the day rides forward. And at night to look at the stars that gave the chemical elements that form us. I think of the republic within me that is untouched, unreached, by other republics, other powers. The hills reach out to me and smile. I cuddle Maximilian, my darling little cat, and all my mummy-juices flow, restoring health and balance. In front of the fire he holds his head up like a figure on the bow of a sailing ship, and in his mind sails for destinations I can never know.

I love the birds, even the alarm bird with its harsh shriek, as well as those that pass through. The flashing little water swallow. Birdsong sounds cheerful, but sometimes I think they cry out in anger, grief, frustration, though their morning conversations in their nests, before sunrise, speak of nothing but family matters. And I don't find the barking spider funny; who's to know she hasn't got a pain in her binjy? A gloomy uncommunicative tiger snake mooches past the back door with somewhere in mind.

Perhaps they all cry out at us in their hearts, since we're the animal that leaves a desert because we take everything. Birds take a bit here, a bit there, don't exploit systematically, leaving each patch with enough left so it can recuperate and be visited constantly. I've seen them do it. I rejoice when I see a quoll jumping up a low bank, like a heavier cat, on her way west to forested land.

I enjoy the conversational rain, its talk, its whispers, sudden enthusiasms, confidences. Before rain the sky is sprinkled with birds, and after rain, or after pellets of frozen rain, the light enters shouting and laughing. Big beaded waterdrops sit on leaves, and light sits at their heart. The koel calls along the valley, the pallid cuckoo sings its scale, the currawong, generalissimo of the treetops, watches and swoops. A smart magpie mother dressed in spotless black, and with her snowy white collar, patiently feeds her disreputable infant in its brown–black and dirty-white rompers, though it's nearly her size. Gangs of choughs mewl and rasp, walk and run. Suddenly the quick welcome swallow is here, with long low swoops startling me, coming close and low over the grass. Where have you been, cheeky morsel? Have you been where the little jacana bird walks on leaves in billabongs up north? And the crocodile toad? Perhaps only birds can hear the shapes of the land they fly over. Like that dip in the line of hills, and that slow rise whose curve is so slow, so elegant, that it speaks. Though never loudly. Sometimes I feel I disappear and only these things exist.

At night the lighted rooms of my house narrow the eye.

Like most places in Kippilaw County there are belts of trees on the ridges and sketchy undergrowth. I walk my own little forest looking for owls and find a deserted nest with oval indentations where eggs were, in the high hollow of a dead tree fork. There's down, loosened twigs, owl pellets. Smooth, no smell. I break them open, finding a tiny skeleton. Mouse. In another pellet I find teeth, the shiny shells of Christmas beetles, the whole splayed foot of something. I lift a stone and pick up the creamy grub with concertina skin and throw it to the fowls. One less Christmas beetle to shred the eucalypts. And was that a singing dragonfly, with its two notes like a plucked mandolin string?

Waterbirds make wide sweeps over the dams, checking for interlopers, then come in to land gracefully, calmly. One wing of the breeze ruffles a patch of water. Always it's thrilling, again, to see the swallows arrowing across the grass, around the house, power-diving, climbing steeply, and at the top of their climb spinning off with a flicker of wing and away. We're a constant threat to the joyous anarchy of other life. Even watching them play perhaps I'm a threat, though that's to be too sensitive, I think. I still buy up pet birds, keep them awhile in my bird area, acclimatising them. Then I free them, say goodbye and to take care.

On my hill, past the wire-weed and the windmill grass, I've found native holly. Tiny plants. And a plant I don't know yet, with little red fires on the end of each flower. Near the wombat holes.

The Holly Tree is mine now, and I'm on the council. I try to stop them further uglifying the town centre. I give little talks to schoolchildren who come round on getting-to-know excursions, that there's no salvation but by our own efforts. I try to get in my little message: examine, criticise, outface your rulers, oppose. You know what you need, they don't. I have sympathy for Mrs F, she has good ideas. She's an example of my motto: from each according to her inclinations, to each according to her abilities.

Being in business has taught me that trade, transactions and money unite people, you can do a service to others without even knowing them. It's a moral thing since my customers and I go about our common business knowing what behaviour is expected of us and what we can expect from others. And where you have commerce you have easy manners and comfortable, pleasant customs. When I serve in the Holly Tree or shop in other establishments I usually feel more welcome and at ease than with relations in a private house. It's less personal and intrusive, but to me that's preferable.

That's my life, briefly. Sometimes it's slightly strange and unreal, as if I've wandered into another person's dream. A shop with words for sale might be better, but this is what I have. I did take over part of Niobe's life, but it's mine now and has been for a long time. I suppose I've attained salvation, to be doing what fulfils me. I don't mind not being a vet. I'm lucky to have this life. I'm glad I don't have a husband making a doormat of me and accusing me of being slow to decide and slow to think and talking me down.

It's good here. The only alarms are sudden fierce thunderstorms or an explosion of choughs in the fowl house. Days are always too short, night and sleep hunt me down each day before I'm ready.

I sometimes catch myself in the middle of a feeling I didn't know I was entering until it's all round me, and I'm surrounded by impressions, memories, words I've known and loved and lived in since I was a child, hints that form in me, promptings that float into consciousness from outside me, perhaps from outside all this. I believe God is unpredictable, wilful, sometimes savage, and not subject to any reason we can learn, but also that there is eternal life for ants and bees for they too are children of God.

Her eyes seemed to flinch away from the Church of the Good Shepherd, from the expanse of valleys round Wiradhuri Hill, and to take refuge upwards in the random patterns of the heavy clouds masking a bright blue we both knew was there but couldn't at that moment see.

When she looked at me directly as she was leaving I had the powerful feeling that she was telling me something she wouldn't put into words. I watched as her white Camry moved off. I waved, and stood turning over and over that look from those grey eyes with the lighter circle just outside the area of the pupil and the black spots in the outer grey, one at four o'clock, the other at nine, until I thought I understood. It was: life is not enough. There's more.

I put it into the tapestry.

After dark I turned up at Club Babel. There was a new bouncer, I didn't have to do any talking to get in. In the Whispers bar I sank a beer with Ray Keirle, a tall and interestingly ugly ex-policeman. Before he became a detective he loved foot patrol, working behind the stick, trying for more arrests than the other young officers. He would go out of his way to find misdemeanours. Shop his granny, I heard. Bad as the early convict police. Other police avoided him. They called him Laughing Uncle Ray because he sometimes smiled—a terrible sight. He loved music, especially the fine tenor voices of villains when their tibias were tapped with teak. As a young constable he had found the wallopers a great excuse, for a tall man, to put the arm on those smaller, cheekier blokes who had been so irritatingly clever at sport, so quick-moving, so quick-brained, when he was younger, in high school.

Ray brightened up pistol practice with such words as 'Backs to the wall, I'm here!' And with some of the politicians' and criminals' names he gave to the targets. It was impossible to shush him, he was deaf to pleas not to call female officers dickless Tracys.

He was tall, like the sonorous Seriema bird, which preys on small snakes that waltz by. And dangerous to meddle with, like the razorback crab. When he reported in and regarded his fellow officers with those hurly-burly eyes, he lent a Donnybrook expectancy to the project in hand, even on the graveyard shift.

Ray was no show pony. Shot through the thigh he used two bandaids and didn't even limp. He had a left hook that began as he turned his wrist to look at the time, and a state-of-the-art Liverpool kiss. He once took out a crim he'd known for years as he was walking alongside him down an empty city lane.

'Retired. Nearly seventy. A mug copper paddling in the shallow sewers of life. Risking your skin every day of the week on a walloper's pay. Called out, check your weapon, run for the car. Never knew if you'd get back. The few I killed? Well now, you wouldn't want to retire with no notches on your gun, would you? And what do you do for a crust?'

He wouldn't believe me when I told him. Not that he chucked a mental, but I'm still trying to think of a way to make it sound interesting to a knockabout copper of seventy with death adders in his pockets.

thirty-one

chainsaw

I rolled up at Pat and Mick's Tyres to see Chainsaw about his place in the tapestry. He bowled his eyes sideways as I edged into his field of vision. He had just picked up a new Michelin radial, delicately, as if it were hot. The indentation in his head, with its scar tissue like a river-bed at the bottom of a shallow valley, showed beneath the front edge of his blue and white Dallas Cowboys cap. The pale skin glistened, the scars were brightly shining. The cap was worn peak to the fore, not the usual way.

A young guy he appeared to know took off then with a triumphant squeal of rubber outside Pat and Mick's. Dust spurted beneath the tyres like routine expletives. I'd heard from a man called Pincher Apps that Chainsaw had planted ferns in his front yard for grass. Didn't need mowing, he said. I was worded up to go easy on mention of his accident, which is what they called the mess that had been made of his head. As I spoke to him I felt I could detect, from the way he spoke, a trail of spots and spills of blood on some pavement in his head. Sounds a bit much now, but that's what I felt.

I talked to him as I went with him and his dog Mac on their lunchtime walk, but got more from his mother and others round the town. There were things he just didn't remember. Like his spider collection.

As a child he was sure clouds were stuck to the sky and the sky moved, because the boy next door told him. If you'd said then that there's life after youth he'd never have believed you. At eighteen he started to lift weights at the Police Boys' Gym and build himself up. Pectorals, latissimus dorsi he inflated and developed. Deltoids, triceps. Spent hours a day, there were no jobs to go to. Abdominals, biceps, all got loving care and attention. Double dumbbells, pushups, bench press, clean and jerk, the snatch, squats with big weights, it was practice every day. Just as if he were in jail.

He added weight, and some bulk, but he was never going to look like the magazine covers. It gave him a charge, though, a certain confidence in his body that in another age he might have gained through daily physical work, but that was something he had no taste for. Besides, in its wisdom, technology had left human muscles behind. At home he had his spider collection. His mother directed looks at that hobby, but he was blind to looks.

He seemed set for a life among the growing numbers of the lost, the turned away, the ones who come down often with police trouble, who don't fit the successful world, for whom there is a barrier, a fierce and unclimbable mountain, between them and an understanding of the wider world. So they take the hint and keep to their little world, pulling it tight around them. The Wangi woolly crab does the same.

Of course, there's always more to it than that. Whether they were born like it, or taught to do it, or their surroundings impressed it on them, many of those who loved trouble and went looking for it positioned themselves with the greatest naturalness opposite the police, the law, the quiet people, the usual ways of behaving, and all the straight and sober customs they had been encouraged by so much of urban culture to look down on. Yet they didn't appear to force themselves or be forced: what they chose suggested strongly a deep need. Perhaps the rapists among them had a powerful and profound urge to make progeny to carry their genes, and were helpless in its grip, and only looked for reasons in the unhappy event of being caught. There was no cultural initiation, no rite of passage which might have channelled their urges. Only a country full of adults who didn't have a clear idea of what being adult meant. Or could mean.

A few years later and he went round armed. He said little. Adults who noticed him thought him surly, or if they were perceptive, slow-witted and at a loss for something to say. Those he drank with sometimes told him he was dangerous, ready to explode, and he felt bigger, but he had no way of interpreting their grins. No one could see into his mind, but that was no wonder. After an inglorious night out, full as an emu egg, he felt he was a hero like the rest. When he woke next midday with a tongue that felt like the feet of fowls in a crowded chook-house, the feeling had gone.

He got his chance for glory one Friday night in the reserve out past the cemetery. A mate of a mate called for an assist, due to a sudden challenge by the Terminators from the next town west. The request should have ended up in the So What basket, but he didn't know the world well enough to file it there or to be deaf or forgetful at the right time. So he went.

As he went into action for Losties against Terminators, the same things ran through his head as did through the heads of soldiers down the ages. A man's job is to fight. All be old sometime, be no fighting then. No crime to be young. We'll win or they will. Death comes to all. All be the same in a hundred years. People may be more rational than other mammals, but it's not certain. The Losties who noticed him there gave him the life expectancy of an icecream at Marble Bar in February.

Freedom of action produces peace and war, order and disorder, winners and losers. One combatant, bald-shaven Curly, a man with grey skin and notorious for the fact that even when naked he was armed—a folded knife in a small orifice—had a baby chainsaw under his coat, and in the moonlit dark of the reserve, lit as well by headlights, pulled it out and started it as he was surrounded by enemies. And friends. What did he care? It was a black and yellow McCulloch, with a shortened bar. One warrior took a quick goodbye like an armed robber with a full bag of banknotes.

In the massed headlights bikechains were going, someone had nun-chakas merrily whirling, there were iron bars and brass knuckles. Most of them loved fighting. The danger, the fierce excitement, the partly sexual thrill of heavy contact satisfied a craving, filled an emptiness. This was living, right out at the limits. Without the courage to put their lives on the line, as boxers and footballers put brain and limbs on the line, and racing car drivers the whole body, they couldn't have held their heads up. And there was the chainsaw surgeon following opponents ruthlessly, his machine no longer black and yellow. It was a massacre, like a butterfly caught in a fan. Chainsaw showed some courage, but not much. Another warrior, Arnold Door, who wasn't much of a fighter and lost his nerve easily, was dead. He suddenly obeyed the universal and wordless grammar of flight, turned and ran, straight into an iron bar, immediately tasting the brandy of life. For Chainsaw there was no chance to use his weapon, it was all over bar the shouting.

Crime creates a moral debt that must be repaid, violence a medical debt. In hospital Chainsaw lay like custard: plain, quiet and childlike. The surgical team had made more cuts and done extensive needlework. He remembered as a small boy holding Dad's hand for a minute when he died. He had been ashamed; dying was a failure. Now here he was, hardly a success, held together by hundreds of sutures, impersonally observed by dizzying, sickening white walls, cut to pieces to oblige a mate. His condition precluded his dwelling on the demoralising costs of the operation. Someone else would pay. He thought of turning over to rest peacefully till Mum came to visit, but couldn't move for the stitches. His eyes felt dull and wrinkled like sultanas. Some of the guys visited later, most as appealing as a teenager's neck with a three-headed carbuncle, but he didn't recognise them.

In a few months he could get about. The slice through his head militated against remembering much. He moved like one of those Windy Flats approximation birds which have difficulty landing in a tree, swaying backwards and forwards. He was now permanently cautious, and thoughtful, as a dog gets each time it sights the dog brush, towel, bath and hose. The guys christened him Chainsaw to help him remember. He wore his Cowboys cap to hide the scars. It covered the greater part of them. His spiders died, he'd forgotten he had them. His dreams were weird, like something from the Book of Revelations.

Eventually he remembered faces and names of those he had helped on the day of battle. He greeted them gladly. They let him hang round, but didn't enjoy looking at him, unnoticing him as if he'd died. He wandered down to Eureka Mall to have people around him. He watched dull grey shadows led by bright wives sound in wind and limb, and strolling slowly, held in the connubial armlock.

He discovered beauty, something he'd never noticed before, often going out into the peach or flamingo dawn. He liked to watch the sunset, which because of a recent volcanic catastrophe was spectacular, as nice as the pictures on Mum's biscuit tins, though not so permanent. He stood and watched the sunset colours dim right down to the auburn sky that remained just before uncoloured darkness washed it out, and felt new emotions brushing past him.

His dog Mac developed a lump on her nose. Chainsaw applied his mum's suncream, but the cancer spread till Mac was a slow, uncomfortable dog. Then one day her walking was over and he was lonely. In the pub, where he sank a few beers on his invalid pension, his old mates saw him glancing at females and knew where it itched.

'Get out there, champ,' directed Dwayne, 'and do a bit of good for yourself. Cut yourself a slice. Nookie doesn't grow on trees. Get it while you can.' Dwayne's other name was Ironbar. Out of consideration he withheld the knowledge that it was his iron bar into which Arnold Door had blindly run.

Since his accident, Chainsaw hadn't thought much about females and their pleasantly bald bodies, but the idea was beginning to take root. Trouble was, he could only thumb through his thoughts laboriously, they felt like a large handful of slippery and uncooperative credit cards.

He met Paspalum Girl in her usual haunt in Anzac Park. She was excitable, which made him wonder: he'd never been excitable. She didn't spill her drinks, so okay, but when she sang, she sang agitatedly; when she talked and got excited, her tongue seemed to boil in her mouth, there was a froth of words shouldering each other in their haste to escape. It takes two to tango, but only one to stop. Neither stopped. The baby was badly deformed, no life for it but operations, transplants, alterations.

Chainsaw stopped. He knew nothing of any baby and kept away from Elspeth, who was volubly shattered and had to be readmitted to Butterdale, from where she'd come with high hopes of coping with the community.

Even the boys back at the pub raised what eyebrows they had at this. Perhaps the sage was right who said social convention and civilisation aren't just veneer, but the essence of humanity. The boys in the bar were ashamed of Chainsaw: like prisoners in jail they looked down on crimes less popular than their own. He kept away from the pub a long time, confining himself to memories and the beauty of natural landscapes.

Then out of the blue he got a job at Pat and Mick's Tyres, taking tyre cases off wheel rims, learning how to find leaks and mend punctures. He's still there, Cowboys cap and all. He looks forward to his team winning the Superbowl again, and has written away to get a Cowboys T-shirt. He loves America. Land of colour where everything's so much better. He'd like to be an American.

He laughs and jokes, doesn't drink much and has few nightmares. The old affray comes back now and then, but less than it did. He finally worked out what he ought to have done with the original request to help. His mum, who brought him up alone since he was six, is teaching him to cook for himself for the time when she won't be there. The owner of the little old house they rented in Waterloo Road offered to sell it to them as long-term tenants; Chainsaw is paying it off. He drinks at the Workers' Club and likes the odd game of pool. In his head the click of pool balls sparks a memory of the click of teeth at Christmas dinners with elderly relatives. He hardly ever sees the boys from the Shearers Arms. He's settled down, and this is how it happened:

Mick's wife Narelle, a big brisk woman who handled husband, four kids, a house, her work for the Church and a yard full of pets with no apparent pause or strain, came by one day and said hullo to Chainsaw. She chatted a few minutes, asked a question or two, drove off, then in twenty minutes was back with a leggy, hopeful-looking female pup. She tied its lead to a stanchion, got it a dish of water, patted the pup, patted Chainsaw and drove back to work. Like so many professionals, despite her twelve hours work a day, she always had time for the needs and woes of those barely able to manage seven.

Chainsaw spent the rest of the day talking to his new Mac while he worked. It struck him that someone might tell Mac she had the same name as a previous Mac, and he worried that his new Mac might feel put out. So he explained it was his favourite dog name, and told her a bit about the first Mac. She seemed okay with that, and waggled a lot, looking pleased whenever he spoke to her.

Mac is allowed to come to work provided she's tied up, and gets an extra walk at lunchtime. Chainsaw explains the world to Mac, along with tyres, the game of pool, good behaviour, the ways of mankind, world politics, sunsets and the universe in general. He even confides to Mac that Mrs F was world karate champion. Chainsaw's got an audience.

Chainsaw's got love.

Alastair Pryde was a fixed gesture, a hollow man living the life of a statue. Was my life really a gesture? Earlier I regretted nothing, I was too busy doing. Were those gestures too? The doing, the lack of regret? Even the desire for freedom?

What if the actions that gave rise to my earlier guilts were no more evil than the actions of fish, birds, animals in the wild, insects? What if they were inseparable from the life of humanity and its everyday atrocities? Yet it was a fact that I'd offended against the standards planted in me, those I was born with, those planted by others, and there'd been no punishment. It wasn't symmetrical. Circumstances had been merciful, justice had bypassed me. But was justice itself a gesture?

thirty-two

zorella

For Zorella's section of the tapestry I spoke to his family. There was no lack of rumour and character-sketching in the town. His mother, Mrs Yoshilo, even added an embroidery to the Fusby saga: the lady in blue was on the run from jail, from other murders, from giving evidence, and in Sydney was the perpetrator of the chopped-body-in-the-pet-food murder. She spoke freely, as if words were only words, sounds propelled by a mouthful of air, blowing away as soon as spoken.

Zorella stood, hands raised in surrender. Deep-set, like holes made in wax with a hot poker, and with all the human expression of a watch-face, the two eyes were pale as early morning sky, black holes piercing their centre. The face yellowish, with three prominent lines, one between and above the eyes, and one each at the outside borders of his cheeks. The shoulders were constructed like a bridge, the head set like a rock plumped down hard on wet cement, leaving no visible neck. A dangerous man, like a butcher's bandsaw. People kept their distance.

It had been a day capped by a magnificent sunset, the sun going down like a burning landscape. They took him in the small walled yard where he parked his vehicles, in Sydney's east. He flicked through his thoughts at speed like a cardplayer looking for the joker. No result. Done like a dinner.

When he was trussed, they walked him to the one-tonner, his gait a kind of lurch as if a statue moved. The night sky was suspiciously perfect, a planetarium sky. There's a harmony between man and the nature that gave him bloody birth. Man is red in claw and intention, dangerous, predatory, yet often calm and harmless, as Zorella was then. The bed of the truck was inhabited by tools of the digging trade: crowbar, pick, two shovels, sharpened spade.

His peripheral vision was so extensive he didn't need to turn his head far to read their lack of expression. Professionals. They weren't there to analyse him, but then evil is a force, analysis would come later. The shotgun wasn't in his back, but a precautionary three paces behind him. Three of them. So who? Maybe up from Melbourne. They put him in the bed of the truck rolled in a carpet and took him west towards the Blue Mountains. He began work on the ropes right away, might as well give it a burl, but knew he'd have his work cut out to undo them inside a carpet.

So this was it. He couldn't see any way out of situation or carpet. Fuck this for a joke. Be better when he got out of the truck.

Maybe this would be a boots-on death, and no more shotguns confronting a Thursday payroll truck in the hot sun; no more hostages pissing themselves; no more jokes like that head on a goalpost; no more pulling apart knife-cuts and shaking pepper in the red trenches; no more removable tattoos as camouflage in armed robberies; no more stuffing the tripes back inside a victim when his timing was wrong; no more using horses to tear in half poachers on MacMurdo's territory, like at Wallacia; no more cutting into strips like Horrie the Skull; no more fun like the carcass in the tree in the botanic gardens; no more injecting talc to see what happened, or detergent, or kerosene, or coffee; no more jacking a split tree apart and putting an ankle in it and letting the tree snap shut like out in the bush at Terrey Hills. He saw again all those victims whose first sight of him was final as a date of death. But so what? The dead were just a branch of the living. He viewed his past as an artwork, a mental impasto of sweat, fear and blood, covered by a wash of hate as natural to him as a reflex.

Still, the future wasn't over yet. He sneezed in the dust from the carpet. He could tell from the traffic flow and the stops that they were on Parramatta Road, headed west. He worked the knot nearer his fingers. Really in a deep hole now. Up to his bottom teeth in seven shades of shit.

He could feel the tyres on the bitumen, an intuition of wearing away. He often had feeling for humans in distress, but that was to enjoy it. Would this be the day when the roof of the world would crash down like a permanent wink and leave him in darkness forever? Well, if it was, it was.

A few hundred million years of lead-up, of training, before each birth; a brief speck of light and life, then underground to everlasting dark.

Thrown up by the unbounded prodigality of life, even murderers were once helpless babies. Most of the time he was a sweet little chap, his mother said, suckling efficiently. She had gone without her evening glass of wine while she carried him and while nursing, and wasn't a smoker. Stepan Yoshilo, fat as spring thunder, who had the boomerang factory in the new industrial estate, didn't believe in hitting children and neither did she; a good talking-to was their most extreme sign of disappproval and that usually ended in smiles and a hug.

Like everyone else, he was different, and by the time he was four was no more trouble than a watermelon flea. The cat Kelly used to jump out at him when he was a toddler, till one day he waited for it with his toy cricket bat. He lasted less than an hour at kindergarten. He walked up to one little girl and floored her flat as a mat with a backhand stroke. He polished off two harmless boys, then methodically felled with a forehand swing the son of a mother who'd just brought him through the door. Other children dodged the juggernaut. The staff got on the phone before he towelled up the lot.

Mrs Yoshilo came in from tending her rose garden. She displayed in the rose championships each year. There was nothing in the rumour that she sprayed her exhibits with rose perfume. She was only mildly interested in the way her boy adapted to those around him. It's always possible to look away from an unwelcome reality. No, she didn't know he hit other children, unless they picked on him, she said. She seemed not to want to know. What she knew was he never gave cheek, never attempted to thwart her agendas. He acted, but used no words. Her hands clasped each other, as if they weren't trusted to be out alone.

Hitting knees with a hammer, flying off the handle if his lightest wish was blocked, taking a flyer at a passing face in a crowd, attacking little boys whose blows were ludicrously inaccurate, he was large as a lion in a paddock of sheep and goats. He was never joyful, but could manage a certain grim pleasure. He carefully taught other children it wasn't necessary to love someone first in order to hate them. Headstrong as the Bialla pilot pig, he seemed to lack the gene for obedience to anything except calls of nature and his own whims.

Teachers at Nerrigunyah reported that he couldn't seem to understand the concept of rules, rejected entirely the notion of conforming—he was eleven then—had a craving or even a deep need for victims and to dominate smaller people, and that only by being kept on his own could he be prevented from doing damage. Yet even they looked for reasons outside Zorella, when it was plain as day his behaviour was him. Warnings he noticed as much as you notice molecular ricochets. What punishment he encountered was in the form of words which blasted him with all the force of a kitten attacking a ball of wool. His silence they took to be the silence of a lamb, a shyness in the face of authority, a lack of words to express himself. They couldn't hear the conversations he had with them in his head, nor could they see the inner face behind the outer face, alight with the heady pleasure of evil.

He was unresponsive as an avalanche, but once his family detected something he liked. A song he moved his body to: ''Taint no sin to take off your skin and dance around in your bones.' For months he could be seen looking at a boy, or more usually a girl, moving his lips to the words, with that faint grin.

They thought he had high endorphin levels; he felt little pain. He played like a runaway truck, a bull kept in by paper gates. If there was an attack to be made, he wouldn't bark first, just go straight in and bite, quick as malice. And stand, swaying slightly like the hypnotic rocking wallaby, while the victim roared in pain.

He was a powerful boy at twelve, strong as a winch. He threw a neighbour's son at a glass door once. The victim picked glass bits out of himself for the rest of the day; it was the most careful and thorough he'd ever been, his mother said. Once Zorella persuaded another bright spark to climb his TV antenna and jump off with umbrella assistance. In another kid's house he pushed the boy against a heater, the boy stuck to the heater where his buttocks touched it, and the mother lifted his flesh away with an egg-slice. Yet boys wanted him with them, just to have him on their side.

Even to his intimates, if that's the word, he was friendly and outgoing as a security guard in winter at three in the morning. He used to say he'd like a world without mountains so his enemies could never hide and get away from him. He was cacky-handed, but no other boys ever said so.

At thirteen he had ordered, bought and used a Sailor's Wife masturbation kit from a Melbourne post office box number, and by fifteen and brimming with a love of beef, he had pectorals he could make flutter like fat birds, and nostrils like bolt-holes for imaginary animals. He boasted to his intimidated intimates that he could see not only with his eyes but with his whole body, like the eagleskin cat. His personal space extended ten metres in all directions.

When he was around, teachers in the playground at Lost River High noticed the print of fear flitting from face to face, though he didn't need to stand over other kids for them to take a lower stance; what they knew of him outside school was enough. He was violent as a kill-crazy volcano. He had a punch like an absent-minded nudge from a reversing truck. What no one knew was the burden he carried.

A kind of pressure vessel inside him inflated and pushed against his internal organs. It felt like an expanding metal that heated up and gave him his parched mouth, made it hard for him to breathe, and a strangling sensation behind the eyes as if soon his focus would be gone and a dizziness would topple him. Unless the pressure was relieved. Bashing gave relief. Violence relaxed him. Then the metal deflated like a kind of rubber, he breathed freely and felt fine. The world felt right when he was standing and others lay on the ground. He was seen once shaking his fist at the sky as if to clobber the cloud that had pissed on him. He was great fun, like a small yard crowded with fasting German shepherds.

He made Gumes' life miserable. Big Shoey Mortomore copped it from Z-man, as he liked to be called. But Zorella had the crippling torment of knowing he would never match Dando. He wasn't invulnerable, he suffered a deep hurt every time he heard someone say there had never been anyone like Dando Rocavera.

In class he couldn't understand why Australia felt so guilty. After one breast-beating lesson on what the teacher referred to as genocide, he said, 'Sure, we been a bit naughty to blacks and Chinese miners, but not much. Other countries done a lot more, never give it a second thought. My dad says why we always moaning?' Other kids in the class knew about the family's black dog, but said nothing. Might make it worse. Old Mr Yoshilo made his money from boomerangs, but lacked gratitude and some finer feelings, for he called the dog Mabo.

At sixteen, in year ten, he thought he'd be a bouncer and tried his luck at Club Babel. He didn't consider regular work, where you were occupied all day; he felt too big, too special, for that. He couldn't understand why he was shown the door. Nor could he cope well with the thought that the man who had the power in the club was a scrawny wimp whose throat would have fitted comfortably in Zorella's big fist.

The music teacher was often at him to sing in the school choir. He had a magnificent bass voice, they told me, enough to quiver your boots, but despite all evidence to the contrary, he considered singing feminine. Some things can't be changed.

When he was eighteen, happily and successfully alienated from dummy, nappies, schoolbag and now school, Southern Security hired him to patrol the streets and industrial areas at night in a little van. By this time his neck was like the back of a pig, his lips like fat rubber gaskets. The other employees called him Gorilla, naturally.

The principal of the company said Zorella's voice had a rumbling sound like the pounding of surf, or even the sound of a shovel through gravel. And a roar like destruction in a wrecking yard. 'I really think some people have impulses for which there are no outlets apart from crime and violence. The space near a select few is distorted, pulled out of shape by the weight of their reputations and personalities. It's many years ago now, but I remember it was a peculiar feeling to be near him. He was one who distorted the space round him, so that you could feel the force of his gravity. In Lost River he was too confined, like a big man's shoulders in a thin man's coffin.'

With a chin like the front of a Mack truck he went to Sydney, confident as a snake in a fowlyard. Eventually he made contact with an employee of MacMurdo, who thought he might have a use for this prognathous poon from the outer reaches. To MacMurdo the public wasn't so much people as idiots transporting guts full of shit aimlessly from here to there, but they had cash he wanted. He controlled many cruel and murderous people, mostly men, who were dying to become 'offenders', feeble word, those who must smash, burn, take, outrage, abuse, wreck, or else they became full of loathing and nausea at themselves and at the flat monotonous, stinking, rotting peace and harmlessness that would otherwise be their intolerable burden.

He was in no war with society; his business was to get hold of its teat. He had no problem with the encroaching powers of government, merely extended his reach, and the world adjusted to him. He hated no one, and like most successful people had long since given up the luxury of contact with the public that supported him.

Zorella received a phone call out of the blue, with a woman's name and address. Get rid of her. What did they want done? She looks nice in green, throw her in the harbour. One-tonner's in the street, keys in your letterbox.

In a small gully down a slope off the Bell Road in the Blue Mountains he tied her body with light chain to a tree and lit a fire. Like a picture in a book at school. Of a martyr. He watched patiently, noting when the bowel contents boiled, the chest opened and smoke came from the mouth. Later, the eyes having gone, the eye sockets smoked. Better than the picture in the book. Yet he'd never taken the new steroids for petrifying human feelings: his were human feelings. When the skeleton had shed the soft bits that made her what she was, it was time to go. He cleaned with petrol, burned the rug he'd brought her in, got rid of everything. At the bottom of the gully, both sides of the creek, thousands of grey stones lay.

He was in business. The money was in his letterbox the next day. He worked for an organisation as savage as a government, and which despised the tame public as much as governments did. He carried a roll that would give a hippo a sore throat, dressed in the latest gear. His life now depended on obedience.

He worked for years in the same capacity, alternating long periods of laziness with sudden savage action. Debt defaulters were treated more efficiently than the law managed, interlopers on MacMurdo's territory and those trying to set up by themselves were discouraged, even to the extent of losing bits. One had his tongue cut out. One malefactor was frozen and pounded to pieces in that condition. Zorella was never able to obtain plastique, but used detonators taped inside a mouth and had to be happy with that. Perhaps his victims were stand-ins for elements of his own nature that he was trying to root out? No, I don't think so either.

I daresay our centuries will go down as they must and no one will mourn either them or us. But if you had told Zorella that no matter how vile, how horrible, how terrifying our world was, there was worse to come, and after that worse still, he wouldn't even have bothered to nod agreement. He knew what many have forgotten or disregarded, that his happiness, what others called crime, didn't come from anywhere else but the unorganisable, untranslatable darkness within himself. And there was more inside.

Zorella had done a job off his own bat. He had disobeyed. It was a disaster. He hijacked a container fresh from the wharves and found he was the proud possessor of an uncountable number of unsharpened razor blades and forty thousand shoes for the left foot. This, together with MacMurdo's new cooperative enterprise with old Melbourne foes, who wanted Zorella's sacrifice, was enough to put Zorella in that carpet.

The truck stopped. He estimated, from the hills and valleys they'd passed, that he was somewhere between Mount Tomah and Bell. He hadn't decided what to do, he'd have to see the lie of the land. His mouth was dry, the pressure within him was the most he had ever felt. He would make his move soon.

The three men didn't talk. In torchlight they walked him towards soft ground. He enjoyed the feel of solid earth beneath his feet. A new moon was swelling, growing more flesh and bone. Somewhere out there in space the unbounded human future was beckoning, thousands of years of adventure and exploration, enough to keep a lot of mankind busy and interested forever.

Zorella felt the slope was familiar. Didn't that ground lead down to that little gully where he'd done his first job and barbecued that woman? They were headed down there. He'd make his break when they got to the treeline. The knot was undone, he held it together ready for the break.

As he started over the ground sloping away down towards the thick bush, the creek, and a valley of grey and bloodless stones, they blew most of his head off from behind, satisfied themselves he had attained the perfection of animal nature and was dead as the tree that made this paper, and buried him deep where he fell, contributing one more secret to the hundreds concealed in Australia's national parks, so handy for such purposes.

The mountain air, bruised by repeated echoes, was soon healed by silence.

The Lost River tapestry knew nothing of mercy or justice, only colour and story. As I worked on the colours for Zorella I thought of the brown earth in that fifteenth century tapestry *Christ Preaching to the Fox*, reflecting on how different our bush soil colours were, with so much black from decayed plant life. And other life.

I was a while settling on an image for Zorella. First I had him as a newly boned skeleton, with red flesh still smearing the bones. Then I thought of the hollow eye of a bullet looking in daylight along the blinding corkscrew glare of a rifled barrel, ready to go where it was sent and do what it was meant to do. I amalgamated parts of each.

I wondered if humans were human when alone. All the time I spent on Zorella I couldn't bring myself to think of Yarrow in case some of him got on her in my thoughts.

Where was she? Were there birds and flowers? Was she on a summit? Who did she measure herself against? Why hadn't she accepted some of the joy I'd felt in her? I guess her eyes were fixed on distances and heights she never spoke of.

thirty-three

duke jensen

It was one of those mid-March days you get in a dry season when the sky overhead was blue and banks of cloud ornamented the horizon like white Himalayas. The day for the phenomenon of the Duke at the races. What would he back for the Budawang Cup?

A distant relative of his was the last person executed in the jail not far away at Goulburn. Some said Duke's grandma used to travel once a year to visit the jail, and look a long time at the window where the condemned woman sat looking out, on the afternoon before the drop. Granny took a folding chair and a thermos and sweet biscuits to help her concentrate. Other visitors, however, left wreaths at the jail gate, with prayers for the revival of hanging, feeling that murderous acts don't come to a proper close without similar punishment to settle the account.

Duke worked at the Pig till he got sick of the sounds of slaughter. That was before he got the apprenticeship as a plasterer. He was a firefighter with one of the bush brigades, was in favour of a new jail in the town, advocated fox farming, kangaroo farming and fish farms, competed at Shows in the bulldogging and buckjumping. He loved guns and did spotlighting in the hills every chance he got. Peewee Prewitt told me that sometimes, half-stung, he would say, looking round him in the pub, 'There's gotta be more than this. The future's gotta be more than a hole in the ground.' And when I caught up with him at the racecourse in time for the second race, Duke's first words were, 'The past isn't what it used to be, mate.'

Way down beneath the concreted and proliferating superstructures of bureaucracy, unnoticed in the pronouncements of intellectuals, there is a world passed on from parents, relatives, neighbours and the past; a republic of deep custom where all are equal in being different from everyone else. In each town, often each suburb, sometimes every street, there's a republic of personal custom for each individual to live in, developed during a lifetime of rubbing along, fitting in, learning about each other, finding in which direction the itch of freedom, interest and desire is eased. And further republics of local custom and history and relationships which can take a visitor years to discover and longer to understand. Republics, with their own presidents, of sport, love, business, of concern, of minding others' business, of thieving, of bikes, of the fist, of stamps, water, drinking, religion, and lots more. Even of hate, where the grey-headed often do the indoctrinating of the very young before anyone else can get to them.

There are invisible schools: family, group, team, street, shop, factory, office, suburb. There are places of worship, secular worship too, temples of obligation, arenas of risk, risky corners, dangerous families, streets where dogs produce their teeth with no provocation.

Order in these republics is not the work of government. Government is the ultimate stranger, the one least welcome. In the wider community gross lawbreakers, including fine and maintenance defaulters and those who swear at police, making up a large proportion of those in jail, amount to no more than one percent of the population, but in these private, self-organising, self-sustaining republics the offence rate is closer to zero.

These are deepsea people, whose lives go on far below the storms at the surface of what passes for civilised, cultured or metropolitan life. For them, examination of their lives is momentary, infrequent, and usually distasteful, since the end of life is known beforehand, and the more contact they have with days, the shorter days grow.

Deepsea people don't need the theologies, philosophies and other word games that occupy the educated. For them, just to live is enough: to breathe, taste, laugh, feel, and enjoy the gentle pull and sway of the seafloor current. The deepsea is their landscape, their peace, their Eden, their inner map, and it lives in them, so that simply to be, or not to be, is the answer, not the question. They know pleasure is momentary and hope not entirely a lie, more a self-administered therapy. Sometimes fashions filter down to them, sometimes fashions live and die before their dust percolates down that far below the surface.

Deepsea people have their own republics of information, rules, correctness, norms, holy words, technology, thought, and above all, speech patterns in which so much of them and their past is preserved. And these republics are the perfect buffer between individual and state. For instance, after seventy years of the most rigorous and efficient repression, they spring back to life the moment the nightmare passes. But that was in another part of the ocean.

Those high above them find it difficult—since they themselves have abandoned community for higher things—to see what the deepsea people see in their lives, lived often in the comfort of beliefs their betters have abandoned but which still have utility for them, but whatever it is engages all their attention and affection: it's home to them. The submerged knowledges of women, farmers, mechanics, derelicts, gardeners, carpenters, give meaning to the power that resides in and radiates from each individual. Every individual has some knowledge that is not common to the educated, or the successful but lonely wanderers on the surface of the sea, but is knowledge no one else has. No one uses it, but it's there.

They have their own hierarchies of influence, power, knowledge and riches. Life is food, survival, children, a small increase, the comfort of the company of families and places they have always known. They have neither time nor inclination to enter their interior, the vast Australia within them, with its distances, illusions, silent voices and protean past. They have a community which is not open to, and often unknown to, those who see themselves as on a higher level, closer to the surface of the illusory with-it world imagined in magazines, but who are peculiarly isolated and have no buffer between them and an empire-building state, in whose grip they are relatively helpless.

Duke's school for part of each day was the Mountjoy in Hereford Street, just across the overhead bridge away from the town centre. It was a roomy wooden structure, painted a peculiarly gloomy shade of blue. One bar was tiny, but you could have played indoor cricket in the other. Usually as dapper as a hairy hippie zonked for five days, he was wiry and fair, with Mississippi-blue eyes. He was christened in the dressing sheds by the under-fourteen team who won the grand final, and won every other grand final up to the under-twenties. He was an inspired football player, he could run unpredictably under pressure, like a liquid squirting from a sudden fracture in a pipe, but didn't go on with it: the grog got him.

His mates called him Duke because he raved about John Wayne before and after the film star died of the big C. The boys got him to say the name just because of the way he said Jahn

Waayne. After his brief and glorious career in local football, he settled down to being a plain-speaking plasterer who liked to work alone, live alone, keep away from people mostly, apart from his family in Dalgety Park and the team in the Mountjoy, and speak freely only to his red dog Rodney. Rodney was tough as a Reid's Flat rock-chewing dog, but so sexed-up that he mounted other dogs without formal introduction. Any other dogs. A lot of Duke's conversation was to do with Rodney's proclivities. You always felt he spoke from deep inside his invisible fortress, his freedom to be himself. His motto was: don't do me any kindnesses, they're like tags clipped to the skin, reminding me, getting in the way. He drove a car which he recommended as handling like a dog on lino, and attended at the bar of the Mountjoy for daily communion beers in remembrance of every mate he and his mates had ever had. Inside his thirst was a green valley with creekwater flowing, a kind of heaven. He'd been taken there on a camping trip when he was eight, woke in a tent right by that creek, which flowed over rounded stones with a sound of music, and first thing got stuck into the biggest and best plate of porridge he'd ever tasted in his life, eating it with his feet in the water, and with treacle for sugar.

In private matters, Duke experimented. Once with Borry Blow, to see what things were like on that side of the street, with Fast Edie when she thought Mississippi-blue eyes went with her hair, Carmen Mummo in a down-market mood, Adora Weller when she was adding experiences to her collection, and good old reliable Nurse Pain, who was his first, as she was for lots of the boys. Plus assorted chicks who drifted in and out of pub life. Nurse Pain was the most rewarding, she liked regularity, and she had a name for a tight fit, and for that reason was unforgettable.

Among the republics impinging on the Mountjoy, rather like the borders of circles in a Venn diagram overlapping other circles, there were those composed of individuals whose principal reason to continue living was Footytab, Lotto, or any of the rest of them, plus the intellectual exercise, social cement and mental stimulation of calculating the odds on whatever objects or organisms competed against each other for prize-money. Betting was a religion; they continued to do it even if they lost every week. The Mountjoy was a kind of feel-good church, in which miseries were scarce as rocking-horse pellets.

Duke was a reader. He liked books where he met people he wouldn't otherwise meet, experienced situations he'd never known, heard things he'd never heard before. For newspapers he was a tabloid man, but often strayed far from the sports pages. He was taken once with the thought that crucifixion wasn't a rare occurrence. 'Polycrates, whoever that was. Whole villages in Africa only a few years ago. So JC wasn't Robinson Crusoe. Shit, eh?' He was likely to turn away from a conversation and say, 'There's no truth being told here.' Or suddenly look up and observe that there was no customs inspection for birds, foreign gases, airborne disease, or, what's this, aero-plankton? Or ask where flies go at night. Or whether viruses have other viruses attacking them. The boys put it down to a slight eccentricity, or maybe he'd been playing the skin flute too much. He was given to emitting odd roars and punching holes in the air after about eight at night, and singing—innocent of bel canto but adept at can belto—about when he was an itty-bitty baby way down south in Texarkana doing something interesting in the green hills of home. Or performing the dances of Taranto on the bar in socks. Late at night he mumbled, as if toffee gummed his teeth. It was Duke who made, framed and hung the text in the toilet: 'Bless this shouse'.

He had an on-again, off-again thing with Dot the barmaid, but wasn't suited to people or to steadiness. Dot had a heart of gold but a face of gunmetal.

'You went out with Dot? Her?' the team asked.

'You should see her after a few drinks.'

'Changes, does she?'

'I do.'

Like the rest, he was happy fighting, and, again like the rest, this happiness was only necessary every few months.

Once he stopped during a game of pool. 'I reckon you can't prove with words that the white hitting the red causes it to move, but it looks like it does. Maybe "looks like" is the best you can do with words,' he discoursed. 'Words are dumb, they can't feel, can't understand doing or hitting or things that happen. They can only talk about how things look.' He did his own philosophical investigations with the equipment he had, his interest in words steadily collapsing all sorts of previously unexamined concepts; he knew he had a long way to go. The others shook their heads. That Duke. What did he say? One afternoon around four-thirty and about to pot the black, he said, 'Things start, things end,' and walked out, the black unpotted. He did pause, though, to drain his glass.

Next morning the milko saw the remains of the fire, the charred timbers and fallen sheets of fibro-cement that used to be the garage-cum-shed that Duke lived in, round behind the old mill in Iona Street near the bridge that led up to Explorer's Hill. The TV morning show flickered on an upturned blue milk container, its plastic mysteriously unmelted. He and Rodney were gone. They didn't see hide nor hair of Duke for three years. He'd gone to the deep north to be no one for a while, among others with similar needs, debtors and lawbreakers, where forced labour was the go: no work, no eat. Where there were no strikes over issues like not enough icecream flavours in the canteen. They all wanted to be no one to the official world, and not one could understand why anyone would be honest with a government that demanded money with menaces.

Duke appeared at the Mountjoy one day in time for a glass of lunch, face red with the sun and a roll of notes you wouldn't believe. 'Rich,' he told Dot. 'Buy the cocky another seed.' In a day or two he loosened up enough to talk about it.

'A place where friends are good, distant friends better, friends in need stay away. Brotherly love scarce as fish feathers. No buckshee. Every man for himself. No cash? Then piss off, no one needs you. A thief had his finger held on a stove till the knuckle burned down. One guy's nuts were pralined in boiling sugar: tried to leave a two-up game while he was ahead. One with his eyelids stitched together and a card on his shirt reading, "I will not look at other guys' women", written out ten times in his own writing. A bookmaker thrown from a cliff, tried to skip owing fifteen grand. A note on him, "This man was okay when he left our hands." Rodney the red dog was dead, tried to consort with a cane toad, then tried to kiss it or eat it, Duke didn't know which. Duke had a secondhand dog, an experienced middle-aged individual named Hap: black with kelpie round the face and a white chest.

Duke had seen on TV the previous Easter a dozen or so young men getting themselves crucified in the Philippines, so when Easter loomed he announced his own crucifixion on that double block of land Morrie the Magsman owned and rented by Horrie Cassilis, in full view of the traffic on the elevated part of the highway bypass just under Big Hill. Chanelle Cassilis had taken a fancy to a concrete statue of a woman in a secondhand yard at Grenfell, put it on the spare block, stuck a slouch hat and ammunition belt on it for Anzac Day, and for Easter it was respectably dressed in black. A black nightie, actually.

The party went all night. At nine next morning the hole was dug, the horizontal piece bolted on, and a little stand for Duke's feet so they could take the weight and he could breathe. If he hung without support he'd suffocate. Duke brought the nails: five-inch because the six-inch looked that little bit too thick.

'Did you dip them in Dettol or peroxide?' asked Dot.

'Christ, I forgot.'

'Will it hurt?' Duke was a small republic of concern to Dot.

'No way. Piece of cake. She'll be apples.'

'Sure?' She thought he was worth any other ten men.

'Sure as a gambler's tip. She'll be sweet. No worries, Dot.'

They put the nails in. A light sweat dotted Duke's flaming red face. Getting him up was the painful bit. Once upright, they tamped the earth and stones with a bar, just like firming a fence post, and turned away towards the barbecue and keg.

'Hanging like a bull's balls,' he commented, but they were busy. The female statue in black didn't answer, either. He regarded the traffic. There wasn't much blood. He was dressed in royal blue briefs with white anchors, looked great against the undressed Oregon post. Now and then one of the boys lifted an opened stubby to his mouth, sometimes he had to prompt them, but for those on the ground the beer flowed like a water-tank used for target practice.

He looked around. Gubba Dam seemed bigger, the river with its intermittent spreads of water reflected the steel of the sky. Cloud mountains were breaking away from cloud ranges. There was Water Doctor Flats, where they mucked round when they were kids. Beyond was Bullant Scrub, Blackberry Patches, the slopes up to Gumboil Hill and Kneebone Bend, right the way to Liplock Hill, where you either had brakes or you didn't. Duke knew it all too well to think of it as his, it was part of their minds, all of them. This was home, if anything was, however much it looked to tourists like restful rusticity.

He called Hap, but Hap turned away and walked in disgusted fashion towards the driveway. He sat down in the gateway and looked out into the street gloomily, like a wife who's just glimpsed her husband's true nature. What sort of a crazy was he with now?

A police car cruised up, two official heads appeared, suspended at the height of the fence palings.

'Pizza on earth,' intoned the Duke.

'Two hours, twenty-six minutes,' came the antiphonal from the timekeeper, as the team got him down.

For the police there was nothing for the charge sheet. They left. Their public had studiously ignored them, but they were used to it; they had left the ranks of the public, which to them now was a foreign country, an object of study, a fount of fear. They carried pistols, after all.

After a few stubbies, Duke was right as rain. Crucifixion was a snack. Dot put the bandaids on and he internalised some barbecue. Saturday morning in the pub, Dot squeezed some pus from the four wounds, and poured peroxide over them. Duke was rapt, watching the peroxide fizz. Usually he paid no attention to cuts and grazes, they always healed in a few days.

'Triple cross next year,' he announced. 'Need two disciples. Poor bugger Jesus had crooks up with him, but I want mates. Get TV crews here, make a show of it. Raise dough for crippled kids or team jumpers.' His vision had broadened, neatly reversing the order established by the historical Jesus, whose vision came first and elevation second. It was the most they'd heard him say for a long while. He was getting used to having people around him.

Between races he went on about words. 'A word isn't the same as the thing it represents, you know.' The Mississippi-blue eyes were wide with emphasis. 'Words can create things that can never exist,' he assured me. 'Fair dinkum.' Whatever he'd been reading or thinking, lumps of something he felt was a kind of knowledge seemed to be pressing to get out, like tumours I've seen, full of the energy of life and unrestrained cell growth, impatient with confinement, emerging through the skin, eager to eye the wider world.

After the last race I could feel he wanted an audience for whatever was in him, so to help it out I remarked that some thought that even the desire to travel, to journey on the open road, leads the traveller into the self. It was interesting to see the way he tucked this thought away inside. Said nothing for a bit, going over the words, giving the impression he was wrapping the thought so it wouldn't get wet and soggy, so he could take it out later and examine it.

'What do you reckon yourself, about words?' he asked. 'Can words grab all this around us?'

'No. They try. But I think your point's a good one. There are realities apart from the language we use to remember them, otherwise we wouldn't have invented the words, and things we often can't perceive, hiding behind what we think is the obvious world.'

He seemed pleased, and headed off to the Mountjoy. As for me, I wondered if thinking was addressed to another person. Or to a self of the future. Or was it an argument with your past? Or an attempt to correct your memory?

When I passed him, Duke was still in the carpark. He refused point-blank to talk about Leanne Fusby. I felt he had another person inside him, carrying on a daily conversation with him. Maybe a kind of Alky Jack in a pub tapestry of the past.

Duke's leaving of Lost River, and his crucifixion, were gestures. If I was a gesture, was I fixed in one attitude like Alastair? How did I come to choose myself, my gesture? When we're little babies, are fed and have slept, we do things. Wave our arms, look around, smile, slobber, yell, maybe sort out some impressions. But why do we do anything? And when we get ready to do something, how do we know what to do? What decides us? Do we know we have duties as well as rights, and freedom to do other things? Are our earliest actions mere gestures? Substitute actions? Signals? Symptoms? Are they designed so we can differentiate ourselves from the other objects and people around us? Or to join them?

I felt I was an organism provided with sticky fronds which I waved around hoping to catch things, or people, from which to suck nourishment. Yarrow's next words to me showed she knew about my fronds, my gestures. How did she know? Was she closer then I knew? She called them words.

'You want to grab me in your words. I don't want to be grabbed. I know about your feelings for me. They're genuine enough, but so what? You wave these words about, hoping to catch me in them. I won't be caught. Once you'd sucked me in, you'd have me around, like a robot, for use.'

'But,' I said, 'you've already sucked me in, without lifting a finger. Just by being you. I'm helpless.'

'It's not a game. There are no rules. No fairness. You want to train me to respond to your sticky words so I'll give you the feedback you want, with minimum effort. You want someone to care for, to touch, to fondle. All that would restrict my movements, immobilise me. You want emotional safety? Get a pet. I won't be a dependant, nor do I want one.'

But how could that be the whole story? There were possible joys she didn't mention. She was looking through the lenses of impatience and anticipated resentment. How could she cheerfully go without things she might enjoy, when she might share them with a little juggling and negotiation? Was she incapable of softness, of warmth, of letting go?

Right then I spoiled the whole thing by thinking of what I might have done to Jonathan in that warm space where we lived together once.

thirty-four

big betty vroecop

I'd started the day of the Easter Fair working on shots of the weft that traversed the whole warp, the day that my efforts would be poured into the mould of Big Betty, queen of the Mountjoy. The Duke had mentioned Betty's youthful romance with Patrick Hooligan. 'We called them the two big-bums. Used to sit up on Explorer's Hill. Trying to hold their breaths longer than the other one. Running away from Mitchell's quarrelsome Jerseys. Sticking their tongues out to taste the snow in July. Betty wanted to be king of the forest, she thought being queen sort of second best, so they were two kings. Then Pat's mum did herself in, and Pat went west with the shearing. Wouldn't like to be that big.'

She was massive, a glorious wide backside swaggled behind her at every step, a bottom divided down the middle into two huge friendly roundnesses. Her prow the same, but higher, and carried prominently, like powerful headlights, though with a hint of menace, which was dissipated whenever the individual breasts took it into their heads to begin ducking left and right asymmetrically. Her wondrous thighs were each as thick as a man's chest, her knees like monuments, her feet big as two pork chops, thick cut, overwhelming her sandals. The rims of her heels showed painful cracks in the horny skin. She had a strawberry and cream complexion, lustrous milk-white skin without a blemish, not even a beauty spot between cheek and jaw; full lips, Arctic blue eyes under virile eyebrows, eyelashes like shiny black insect traps, a blank angelic expression and thoroughly even features. Between black hair and shoulders her neck was creamy white, like lilies, with just a trace of pink underlying the white, suffusing from the warmth of the dynamo beneath. Even her plump fists, used so well in her climb to pub aristocracy, had a morbid beauty.

Men turned in the street when they clapped eyes on that face for the first time. Its beauty was of the kind that you felt altered you. Lifted you out of the mud of everyday life. They regarded her with awe, and turned back wondering to their concerns, wistful looks smeared over their faces, as if the child inside remembered a primitive yearning to be swallowed in those generous folds, perhaps even to slip inside again unnoticed and be completely hidden from the anxious world in the oleaginous dark, safe at last. Well, for a time. Or had they, as grown human males, retained in their ur-brains something of the desire of the sperm itself, still wanting to penetrate and be joined with that larger roundness of the egg, which her shape, from a distance, suggested?

I caught a glint in those perfect eyes warning of what might happen if you ignored her or gave the wrong sort of attention. The sort to rattle your stones with a fifty kilo knee.

Big Betty was receptionist and general filter at Wotan the Wrecker, the deconstruction firm on the older industrial estate at Elderslee. Something not quite right about you? Out. It was a rough place to work, but she was equal to it. She was the only woman in the place, though women weren't ever excluded; they could have done any of the jobs, but didn't want to go there to work in the rusty clang and jagged howling atmosphere of the wrecking yard among screaming steel plate and angle grinders, and sometimes a roar as if from a subterranean amphitheatre with power enough to get in your chest, atomise your blood, rearrange your ribs and turn organs to mush. That's how it felt to me, anyway. I'm a wimp near loud noise, have to cover my ears against fire sirens.

She didn't mix with women who liked domestic and household talk, who gathered round nicely spread tables with quiet china to converse like herbal tea. Her hands had never been encased in the fine leather of infant goats whose throats had been cut for the purpose. She couldn't stand the contentment of gentle women dressed in soft voices, she liked restive female company and often had a deep yearning for things to smash, or at least to tip over and scatter. Her soul cried out for it, she told me, and I better believe it.

She played trumpet in the Meesner Construction brass band for three years, but gave it up for drinking. After her disappointment over Patrick Hooligan, that was. They were going along nicely, seemed to understand each other, laughed at the same things, both big young people, and he had promised to go with her to the Sydney Show. Next thing, he'd left to go with shearers. He'd forgotten her. She gravitated to pub life. Hers was the Mountjoy, with its sleazy ceilings and slapdash beergarden where the defeated in disputes regularly scraped their scapulas off the deck.

She became a notable at the Mountjoy, a communicator, and often had to wade vengefully through waves of pacifists to get at the one she wished to communicate with. She had a hearty manner with the men of the Mountjoy, sometimes putting the hard word on them, to their dismay, greeting them often with a, 'Hullo, pet, will you still love me tomorrow?' or a 'C'mon sweetheart, give us a smile,' or a tap on the rear in passing and a, 'Orh, love your bum, darling.' By the time the sex object of the moment had turned round, she'd veered away to talk. Or if the mood was different, last week's 'pet' would stumble against a bruising cairn of snarls. She often had the heavy gaze of the female Willerong buffalo bird before she attacks. The gentle male attends to the nest and the young, keeps his head down, avoiding confrontations and unpleasantness.

For a while she used Adrian O'Toole for sex, the stereotypical thin, miserable-looking guy. He said that to kiss her was like trying to get your mouth round a plate of peach slices. For a time she was envious of Fatstuff until she discovered Fatstuff's swans were ducks. All those lovers? A lot of them were schoolkids. Big Betty would never come at that.

Then she let Adrian go, and began to spend free time in the open country. Something in her was turning away from her life to date. She didn't need company. She wandered over the back paddocks of hill properties among horsefruit and sheep bullets, or further out in forest land. She began to enjoy wet farms and mud-coloured winds from the west. Way out in her green heaven below tall valleys of sky, she could pee when she felt like it, scream with equanimity and feel private, or be silent as the black and ivory bucephalus beetle. If it was late she could be a girl again and say to the first stars, 'I want to taste you in my mouth. Will you fizz?' A bad-tempered Jersey hassled her, and once she ran from a bull, until she decided to face him down. She turned and faced him. The bull stopped too, turned sideways, eyes on her, slouched off a few steps. 'Are we mates?' she said. She wanted to put her arm round that thick neck, pat the curls over that wide forehead. The bull didn't answer in English, so she resumed her walk, hippoing comfortably, and she stopped, as she said, 'To hoist me jugs and wipe the sweat.' Duke told me she had 'tattoos under the norks', but didn't describe them. The ultimate privilege, it seemed, was being allowed to lift them and read.

She began to love silence, which clever people tell us is the absence of ritual. Though in those hills it was more. It was tense silence, there was a buzzing of unseen movement. There were silent waterfalls flowing with fish, with no water sound, only fish voices. She noticed the grazing animals who walked on, defecated on and were surrounded by valleys covered with breakfast, dinner and tea; the world was food. She watched the retreating backs of showers as they climbed the next hill. She listened to see if she could hear the crops growing, usually oats or rape. She was a different person, and spoke to the shepherd's companions who wagged their tails and kept close. She began to see soil differently, and the insects in the folds of its coat. She imagined the thin topsoil digesting her thoughts as they fell from her head. She found herself thinking people were ugly and they'd made the world sad. Once or twice she looked over the high fence of the kindergarten feeling she'd like to have been a teacher of little kids. She was emptying of one life, filling with another.

More than anything she loved to be alone with fields of grass and go up into the belts of trees that crowned all the ridges, to search out secret places. Once she climbed a steep hill and between two trees discovered a green landscape she hadn't known existed, way down there at the bottom with cows and a house on the flat and a creek flowing alongside. It was so beautiful she cried.

She would lie out in the open like a patient gazing upward at the blue ceiling, fall asleep, and wake to a sky full of grand canyons and mountain ranges of white cloud, and with a nail-biting wallaby anxiously watching her. She imagined she could lift her hand, hold it over blue peaks, valleys, ranges, touching them gently, feeling their folds, textures, warmths and sudden coolnesses with her fingers and her palm, which was big as a shire. Once she stayed out all night and saw at dawn a stand of white-barked gums wet with light, and shivered, while around her the silence and stillness rang with invisible bells. Sunsets entranced her. She walked straight towards them, large vague symphonies of colour, eyes open, trying to enter the radiance, and sometimes seeing figures within the brightness.

Gradually her feelings approached the commitment of words. The nearest thing to God was a kind of in-breathing, perhaps, the basic taste and sound of the world entering into her and feeling at home, making her feel at home among hills and sunsets; at home in the landscape which she felt she put on like an overcoat, which fitted. At home among the leaves of trees touching high overhead, speaking quietly to each other and silently to her.

Was there something she was meant to do? Indoors, the windows were too full of cloud, too little sky; she loved hills and grass and trees and valleys and big rock cliffs. Could she bundle up the past like old newspapers you take to the tip? Often she stared up into the sky trying to get past the blue, and it seemed the whole sky suddenly swooped down with big blue arms to pick her up and take her to a place of music in words and pictures. Other times she tried to read the answer in the writings on the scribbly gums. She wanted to know: Do you tell your self what to do, or does your self tell you?

Sometimes, when the questions pressed the heaviest, she went back to the Mountjoy to be part of the atmosphere. In the pub all was acceptance, nothing questioned, no doubts expressed. She soon got jack of that, it didn't satisfy her. Why were they all there, mixed in together like moving parts of the one body? Had they once felt as she did, received no answers, and huddled together again in the warm? Or were they different to the core? She backed off and resumed her lonely walks. Whatever was ahead of her, she could face. She even began to walk among the shapes of rust in Wotan's yard, looking deeply into the colours and finding their harsh beauty returning to her later so she could breathe it in. At home she emptied one room of furniture so everything could enter.

Now she has a favourite mountain, just a small one. Thinks if it as hers. Hears it answer when she talks to it. She feels she damages her baby mountain when she tramps up it, and more so when her feet stamp on the way down. She feels she must restrain herself, not walk on it so much, look at it more, learn it. She'd like to carve her hill, shape it, make of it something she could look up to. The last thing she said to me was, 'If we're all there is, I mean if there's nothing above us, we're just headless chooks running till we fall.'

As I made to leave the fair, and she turned back for another stroll along sideshow alley and amusements she once loved but now barely recognised, I saw her perfect face full on. When her eyes met mine their clarity felt like a gift. Only in her eyes was it noticeable, but it looked to me as if she felt anchored by something too heavy to lift and carry home, yet at the same time empowered by desires growing in her, that inescapably drew her towards another kind of home, where her spirit might be at rest, and begin to flourish and radiate outwards to the world.

And within that new home, the wonder she had awakened to, the intimate non-human life of animals, hills, rain, winds, the radiance she entered and which entered her, would surround her and for the rest of her life bathe her in their living music, their incipient words, their sounding pictures.

Still I saw gestures everywhere. Most seemed trivial even to those who displayed them, as they strolled, turned their heads, hesitated, went to buy but thought better of it. But trivial? Those gestures were their lives. Who was I to say they were trivial?

Maybe the guilts I'd intermittently felt were fragments of one large gesture. Was that gesture aimed at directing me towards feeling like other people? Had I intuited a depth of shame and guilt in the environment into which I had to fit, so I had to be guilty too? How much of my life was matching up to the expectations of others?

thirty-five
bubba ylisaka

I suppose people survive as long as they do because their components have a headstrong urge to persist. All of the parts together, along with the animal they fabricate, have no clear idea of a time when they weren't alive, only a desire to continue in a present they have always known.

April, and soft autumn days. I was enjoying life. I went out to see people, even briefly to parties, and often enough people came to see me. Usually singly. I got to know by sight the people who sat in the park, on the courtesy seats outside shops, or on the more comfortable seating in Eureka Mall watching private movies of their past.

I enjoyed quick explorations of the tablelands. Some valleys were so wide they casually, but with great power, squeezed your senses into unnoticeable little gullies, to take cover. That's how it felt. The night burdens had lifted, weighing no heavier on me than wet clothes. Even my dead brother, shadowing me down the years of my single life, was keeping his distance.

On the other hand, the thought that all my guilts and night-alarms were gestures, perhaps one large gesture, had me in its grip. A gesture to what? Towards a new behaviour, a fresh understanding of my life? A gesture in the direction of a new honesty? I felt I'd climbed a hill I didn't have to climb, had fallen back, and wondered why I made the effort in the first place.

The tapestry's next space was for Bubba Ylisaka. The family he'd left gave me what they thought I needed. His son's children seemed surprisingly fond of their curly-headed grandpa, and at times seemed to think of him as an inflatable that could be blown up by memory and played with, then let down and left to lie till next time in a corner with the other resting toys.

The youngest of five, he'd always been different. He was the only one of the five who went to Sunday School, he wanted to learn about Simpson and Delilah and Adam blaming it all on Eve and heaven and hell. Hell was when you got in trouble, heaven was when things went smoothly. At eight he was too old to go, he said, and retired from God.

Many actions are performed because no one who matters is watching, so that one day, at fourteen, inside the front gate of the old weatherboard house in Brahman Road a purloined traffic sign appeared. Black on white: 'No entry'. He liked signs, everyone should have a sign. A week later another sign stood there, this time a small rectangle, white on black—'No way'—which until then had guarded the twin shining manganese steel railway lines, glittering against their background of dirty brown railway crust. This sign came from the north end of a neighbouring town's railway station, platform 2. It still hadn't been replaced forty years later.

He was considered a hot and cold sort who could do something daring and outrageous one day and the next be quiet as the shy dancing bandicoot, the one that freezes the moment it's caught dancing, then, if you keep looking, slinks off like a guilty pup. At sixteen he left school and caddied for golfers, trying to subsist on what that brought him. To save paying board at home he lived in the bush behind the course, fishing Gubba Dam on days off, to catch the crested splinterfish, as he termed it. The woman who lies, Carmen Mummo, used to visit his hidey-hole when she was a kid. Bubba told her it would be good if there were money centres so you could go and get what you needed. He didn't need much.

At eighteen he worked for the U-Rect It repair company, but wasn't cut out for repair work. He became deaf under stress, and items were wrecked even more thoroughly when he got through with them. Though he did buy his mum a new dove-grey outfit out of his wages.

One morning by the lake at the fifteenth he was out of his shack at dawn and saw a naked child dancing on the grass. She had hair to her knees, and danced faster and faster to a crescendo of movement, then slower until, hardly moving, she stopped, then vanished. He had never seen anything so wonderful, not even on television, not even the street of imaginary shops he once dreamed. It had been a poem, a song, about what it was to be young. The youth of the ages was in that naked body. To be alive was miraculous, it was poetry with no need of words, voice without sound. He felt he should have bowed, somehow, though he had never bowed to anything in his life. Except at Sunday School, when he'd bowed his head. Perhaps he ought to have knelt down. For those seconds he had a vision of some radiant Thing showing its face into the ordinariness of his world. He had a conviction without reasons that the radiant Thing had a lot to do with the dancing child-vision, and with everything that spoke of life. Just as if a corner of a superior world had lifted and shown itself to him. Like, though not the same as, the light that he saw in his head in the darkness of night when he remembered, or imagined.

He left the caddying at nineteen, left the district, no word for three years, then he was up in court in Sydney charged with eighteen robberies and asking for money with menaces. He drew thirteen years. The Lost River people who went to the trial said he looked bored with the judge's fake horror and practised platitudes. Bubba asked, 'If money's so valuable, how come they don't guard it better? Maybe money should be privatised, security might be better.' Sentenced, Bubba looked puzzled, like an apprentice dog that's just bitten its tail when all he meant to do was chase and scare it. The jail gates closed on him with a receptive clang.

The family was amazed. He wouldn't hurt a fly, even if he was strange. Always so quiet. When the police got him he was living in a caravan park, cashless, car payments and rent in arrears, though the car had lung cancer by then and couldn't even cough acceptably. For the first five of his revenue-producing jobs he'd travelled by public transport. Always unarmed, he made out he had something nasty concealed in his money bag, and they believed him. After one job he saw an old man and woman in the train he'd caught. He stuffed a few thousand in their carry-bag. He'd taken too much from the money centre. He used some cash to live and gave the rest, fifty-two thousand of it, to unknown people in need, and to charities. Once he had to light some to start a fire to barbecue his sausages.

He was a good prisoner, jail was a home from home. He even drank the jail coffee, which smelled of wet dog. Like most of us he started from the premise that no one is all that much better than anyone else, but in jail he found some were a lot worse. In the yard he failed to answer a greeting. It was a phrase he'd never heard before, but the body builder he'd insulted accused him, in different words, of aiming to abrogate the prisoners' most cherished customs and very likely thinking them stupid and the prisoners too, you rotten bastard. Without waiting for reasoned explanation, or any conversation at all, he proceeded to hammer Bubba, and when he'd met the needs of justice, picked him up and threw him against the yard wall. This was really hitting the wall. This therapy ought to have concentrated his thoughts, like having a boil north of the fundamental orifice, but instead it scattered them. Bubba was as much confused by the self-righteous attitude of the body-builder as he was by his array of bruises, his sore nose, his painful jaw and the blood that kept running down into his mouth.

His cellmate was Old Ed, a prisoner kitted out in clean gear, pants pressed under his mattress, wearing a station-master's cap. He'd used the cap in a hijack attempt on a consignment of fifty kilos of used banknotes destined for the flames. He rolled his own cigarettes from what smelled like ignited horse scones. Ed's nature was such, he said, that he was unsuited to work in enclosed spaces, to perform similar tasks for long periods, to get out of bed before eleven, or not to go and have a beer when he felt like it. Prison trimmed this lifestyle somewhat, but he put up with it all in a forgiving spirit and settled into the life as if he was made for it. There was something splendid about the way he bore himself, but it was a ridiculous splendour. Old Ed sized up Bubba in around half a second, noting blood, black eyes and how sorry he felt for himself.

'Can you fight?' he chuckled.

'Not much,' guessed Bubba miserably. This was hell, if anything was, almost like a foretaste of capital punishment.

'Learn quick,' Old Ed advised. 'Even if you're not much good, shape up and have a go. If you defend yourself, they'll leave you alone.'

'Why should I have to do what they do?' queried Bubba, to whom the idea was offensive.

'We'd never grow up if we didn't copy others, son. Don't talk with them, don't bandy words, a yes is as good as a no to an enemy determined to have you. Stick with the ones you get on with, accept no gifts—there's always a price and you might not like the price—and guard your love slot.'

'My what?'

'Quoit, arsehole. Put a price on it, make it difficult to get, lay down conditions. In here, it's not just a gallop on the tan track, it's often real romance, jealousy, all that. It's their home, their town, this is their life.'

'I wouldn't let anyone get in my bum,' protested Bubba, who had never thought of that area as connected with love or any emotions except urgency and relief, and much earlier, embarrassment. Though he vaguely remembered phrases from adolescence where kids threatened other kids that they'd put a 'blossom' on their turds.

'Well, maybe. But the fewer the things you won't do, the better you'll fit in with the other psychos and the less you'll stand out. Cheer up. When we get out, those with taxable incomes will provide, like they provide everything else.'

'Not for me they won't. I'm never coming in a place like this again. They don't even protect you,' he said, nonchalant as an innocent man about to be hanged.

Ed roared, his lined face suddenly finding a pattern of horizontals as he laughed. 'Out there you cut loose and gave nightmares for life to the poor bastards you robbed. In here you want protection. Let's talk about money.'

'Tell me about it,' Bubba nodded sideways, bitterly. Others had told him Old Ed's banknotes had all been perforated, the hijack was futile. Old Ed shook his head and lay on his bunk.

Bubba was out in eight. He took no notice of the talkers in jail, he didn't want to know how to be an executioner or at what stage to shoot a hostage, or technical details of safes and alarm systems, or even lessons on planning jobs by some expert who'd only ever spent three years of his adult life outside jail. Free and miserable, he was released and stood shivering outside the gate in midwinter at six in the morning.

He did more caddying, then cracked it for a watchman's job with a freight company. He dossed down in his office at night, but Midway Trucking didn't mind having someone on the premises all day. Bubba could never see the point in being exact with times, quantities and loads; he couldn't understand why they attached such importance to their goods, which seemed so much junk. The company considerately released him from these puzzlements. More caddying, this time living in a large hollow log and washing in the creek. A simple life suited him.

Suddenly he got married and started a family. He was thirty-six. They lived in the little weatherboard house at the bottom of Fishing Street, that leads to the sewerage works. He did odd jobs all round Lost River. What gentle Beth thought of him she kept to herself, but they had two children who did rather well. They were bright at school despite the poverty and after school got good jobs, and looked after Beth when Bubba left for the last time as if everything had been a mistake. He was fifty-odd and strange as he'd ever been, though everyone reckoned he was sane as they come.

Beth stared after him as he left, her lumpy worried fingers held to her face, saying nothing over and over. She, of all people, as a mother, knew everyone was a separate individual and had to answer for what he made of himself or herself. She shook her head and went into the house. 'He must have a mind like a sink full of dirty dishes,' she told the sink. 'Half the human race is women, the other half kids.'

There'd be a paragraph in the local rag now and then about a wanderer living in hollow logs, who'd send his dog in first to look for snakes, then crawl in and clean out spiders and the big black bush cockroaches.

The son, who identified the body, said Dad was a teacher by negatives; he taught how not to live and how not to die.

'In the old house things fell down, bits broke off, timber split, there were mice till rats ate them and took over, the heater was always on the blink, things leaked. Rain came in, spiders, the gutters rusted through, he didn't seem to notice. He said the Lord had no place to get his head down but relied on charity like any other Eastern monk. Yet he saved enough for a deposit on the house. I think he did love Mum, he often said so, but she'd turn away. I think she thought he ought to show it in other ways, not words. Then he said goodbye to us one afternoon about four and never came back. We heard about Kangaroo Man later. Had to be Dad. Basic accommodation, that was him. I went after him, found him and got this story about the bush, the weather, how to do this and that, and survive. Bush vegetables, snakes and lizards, birds, roots and nuts. Loved it. Didn't need company, had voices of his own. Talked on and on, making sense like eggshells, lucid in patches, sprinkled with mad intervals, child-dancing-on-the-grass nonsense. Looked older than his years, and on and on about the dancer on the grass. Always thought of Dad as an un-hero.'

I liked the word and used a Nile-blue yarn for it.

'I gave up and came back home. Then a call came from some shooters last month, so he was up in the hills again, five years later. There he was, stuck up his log like a tubular possum. Poor old yellow dog needed a feed. We got Dad out. In his pocket an old photo of his mother, my grandma, in the dove-grey outfit he bought her with his first wages. In the photo I think she's got her top teeth out.'

In his cartoon Bubba is a preposition, the colour of kangaroo grass.

In Whispers I met Sordine Hurley, a journalist who said yes to one of the many openings that come a good journalist's way and was now personal assistant to the CEO of Janus Export Import. Loves her job. She walks like hand lotion, dresses like a red Ferrari, and inspires affection while holding you at a slight distance.

Some of the men she was thrown amongst at Janus thought of her as a comfortable basket cat and tried to pat her. Others mistook her for the high-backed fetching cat. Still others imagined she was the low-profile listening cat. All sorts found she had a greater resemblance to the Bald Valley milk snake, which strikes and resumes its former position before the victim knows it moved. And waits placidly for its saucer of milk to be obsequiously placed. It's a popular pet in retirement towns.

She never uses heavy perfumes, instead goes for herblike and flowered toilet waters which give her an unspeakably chaste smell. She reminds me of a capable jonquil that has pushed mini-boulders aside to rise, take the sun, and bloom. The skin below her throat is populated by those tiny raised mounds which our American cousins call goose bumps but which Australians give a grosser name. Her clavicles are shy as bettongs.

She suggested we do lunch at the Battlements on Hollydale Hill, out of town. It's a restaurant now, but was a brothel once, and used to make money. I was interested to see how unpretentious her hands were. She has whorls on both thumbs and both forefingers, her palms are maps of captivating countries. She resents having men over her, but then so do most of the world's males. Just as in many churches there are women who don't want to be preached at by a woman, so the same churches are full of absent men who won't come to be preached at by another man. She recognises the deep insult in affirmative action, that, on her own, she couldn't make it. She could, and did.

Sordine is the normal plateau person who sees heights, climbs them, finds herself on another plateau and discerns new heights in the distance which must be climbed in turn. Perhaps she likes heights, and that may be why she expressed a wish to come to church on my hill. At that moment her clavicles looked a little less shy. I encountered no evidence that she resents having men over her, but it was even more pleasant beneath her.

thirty-six

pat hooligan

Duke Jensen mentioned the legend that one of Pat's ancestors helped execute one of Duke's. I tried it out on Pat at the Easter Cup. He favoured Wassat? for the Cup; the legend failed to interest him. He got set at eleven to two.

He's big and thick. His silhouette, that is. Duke told me Pat had been a solid centre who by nineteen was so heavy he was pressed into service in the forwards in Lost River's League team. He could go, I heard, as fast as a racing wombat down Rowanna Steeps without brakes. Duke didn't say if that was with legs, or rolling like a barrel.

'There's a time in your life,' Pat said, 'when you just go. Disappear into your own landscape. Become a tent-dweller. Find more places than you ever knew to qualify for being the arse end of the universe. You become a cook and sometimes have a team of shearers feeding on a stew with silver coins in it because you wish it was Christmas. Your own life seems unreal to you when you look round on the plains or up at the wide sky with the sun poured out like weak tea and know you're nowhere and nothing. Or you go mad in Menindie and tangle with a diesel dyke over a girl of eighteen and get mangled. You get back to Lost River and your mates think you're going to bring news and excitement out of the west.'

He won on Wassat? but didn't seem all that pleased with his winnings. He'd bet two hundred. He had a piece of land and aimed for a Shetland stud in the future. He dismissed questions about Amaza by saying she probably suffocated in her own bile.

At sixteen he went bush after his mother's accident; he comes back to Lost River several times a year, has the odd girl-friend, sometimes visits Leanne to get caught in the bearded clam. Pushing the boat out at the Shearers Arms and sailing on golden seas of drink in brittle glass canoes gives him what company he needs. He's a tooth man, with a hunger for extra-large fatman pizzas with the lot. Perhaps food is company too. He's never been seen with the social staggers. He chooses his clothes like a tyre picks up stones.

Australian as spotlighting for kangaroos, Pat does a bit of shooting, sometimes converting birds to meat on the wing, and in spare time helps out on local farms laying 1080 baits in chook heads. Hates foxes, and has from the time as a little boy he saw his first newborn lamb with its tongue bitten out to the roots and went home and told Mum how horrible it looked.

Early on he played with little Betty Vroecop from Hovell Street; they always had fun together, she was as good as a boy to play with. Held their breaths together until the person inside rebelled, loved to play in the rain and snow. A bit older, and he felt she wasn't quite a—what? There was no longer a word for it, but she was developing a rougher tongue than the roughest boys, didn't know when to stop. He couldn't come at that sort of girl, so he went to play with the Coy kids.

Later he struck up with her again and she was different.

Went together from about fifteen, even fought together. On the same side, that is. Then she seemed to think they were together forever, and Pat's mum died and he was so baffled he went bush.

He comes home as keen as a six-month celibate for the comfort of his home town and the company of the crew at the Arms, all intuitively sworn to pursue and defend cultural self-determination and, in the groin of the day, that spicy interval between afternoon and the traffic reek of evening, stands like a huge Loddon River boulder-fish at the bar, immovable. His gregarious grin the signal for the launching of floes of floating anecdotes, tales told well, and most looking to precipitate a laughquake.

Out among the sneezeweed, the dust, the Riverina bluebells, he survived as a cook, and so did those he fed. There were silver coins in the damper at Christmas, if they were far out, or he made a cake if he was handy to a town. He kept his mind on the big issues such as fresh vegetables and whether the beer was good when they hit town. At one place south of Nevertire the beer was really off, so off that for once he was glad when closing time came. Though less glad later, when the whole crew discovered a sudden ability to shit through the eye of a needle.

Criticism made him quarrelsome as a slighted ridgeback. He once threatened to blow up the camp when a strident curry of his was criticised. He compromised by blowing up the shouse and staying out in the bush for two days, then came in again, noisy as an empty house. And once, after eggs for breakfast for too long and the grazier's hens still laying like mad, the men became boys again and got their shirts full of eggs. When the first egg squashed against Pat's neck he grinned like a shark and the eggfight was on. The grazier's wife came running with her camera. Pat has copies of the photos.

'Out west the land's empty and silent enough if you bring nothing to it, and at night on the plains you're open to the universe. Day switches on and you're a spot standing among solid blocks of light. The sun shining mad as a meataxe. Leather landscape, dry and hot. Tears were impossible in the heat. The wind scratched your eyeballs, made the dead coolabahs creak and the old beefwood trees. In the distance silver silos floated on shimmering air. Life seemed a parade of vinegary sunsets and insipid dawns. No rain for months, just bogan showers: a few raindrops and a face full of dust. You'd get lightning's blue flash, jolting thunder close behind, maybe split trees, but no real rain. And I found beads of glass that came from space. When we were in good river country and came across a clear stream with its pebbles and lucky stones settled in a quiet design, I'd run to it and bury my face in it, like running to Mum when I was little and burying my face in her lap.'

Later he said, 'Do you think our basic natures contain the natures of other animals, maybe all other life? Bacteria, viruses, the pig, the goat, the tiger, the snake, the bird, the fish? And always the dog? Or water? Or stones rubbing against each other? Or people who suddenly crack like an over-stressed beerglass? Sometimes I used to lie awake and try to imagine a better future, but now I reckon images of a better future are mirages on a hot day: travel towards them and there's nothing there. What do you think? Let's argue about it. I think I'm a public meeting, there's so many voices in me waiting to have a go. You right for another beer?'

I asked more questions. 'Why be a babbling brook? A way of leaving home. Starts with the accident. We called it an accident; campers pulled her out of the river, dead. That flat smell of fresh creekwater about her. She hadn't changed her clothes to do it, just what she wore round the house. Poor old legs missing both shoes, face relaxed in a kind of despair. How could a mum do such a thing? That was sixteen years ago. I relive it now and then, but where before I was sixteen and she seemed a fairly old sort of woman, I'm thirty-two now and in my head she's changed. She's only a year or two older than I am and her face is just sad. And she's rather pretty and looks like my sister Narelle. Why would a young woman do that?

'She loved watching the highway, cars and trucks, used to make up stories for me when I was little about where they were headed. In town she'd just sit and watch, never got tired of the movement, this way and that, while the sun sank like putty. Maybe she wanted to go. But which direction? To stay was maybe just as futile. So now she's where time dilutes, spreads out in all directions, fades from sight.'

When he's seen his mates in the Shearers Arms and had a few words to the King—friendly ones like 'Honky' and 'G'day you black bastard'—he gives a hand in Tum Tums, the little restaurant and pizza place round the corner in Market Street. Bacon and rose petals. Sometimes he sees Big Betty in the street and doesn't know what to say. She just looks miserable.

I've been in Tum Tums and heard him humming and singing in his yeasty tenor voice. He's a great worker, goes like a breadstorm in a bakery. No, like a hot hangman with two to go and late for lunch, but without the impatience and bad temper.

Pat stayed for the full program. I left. I wondered how he saw his life. To me it looked like a journey, a realisation, a confrontation with what was inside. An investigation, I suppose. My own confrontation threw up some weird nuggets. I don't bleed at disappointment, don't bruise from insults, never feel put down, find no strain at partings. When love threatens I hack it out. Mostly, anyway. I have little life apart from work, but that is life. I find few things evil, strange, unnatural. Maybe I ought to book myself shelf space in a pathology exhibit.

Were my guilts phoney gestures? Put on? Mere acts? A kind of anxiety? A desire that acted without words? A vague effort at propitiating powers I sensed but wouldn't acknowledge?

Couldn't be entirely that. Driving my brother Orville away with ferocity, shooting people's pets when they annoyed me, getting rid of that baby with a chemist's 'bombs', expecting fidelity from the wife of another man, that knifework after pub closing, getting even with Richardson under cover of the big brawl at the Southern Cross, driving away the gentle Alana: those things weren't nothing, however grubby they looked now. I still see Richardson's eyes, that bastard, the colour of near-beer, and the full row of top front teeth broken off clean as a whistle at gumline.

Yet, at the same time there was something more, that was evasive, I couldn't put my finger on it. A different-flavoured crime. Deeper.

thirty-seven

twitch mitchell

From their house in Wiradhuri Circuit you can see all over Lost River. It's built on the high side of the street, has four storeys including attic and cellar, and two towerlike gables with a platform between them, big enough for several tables and chairs. A verandah runs two sides of the house, paved with coloured tiles in geometrical patterns, with animal forms at intervals. There's a wide-shouldered scorpion, a gargoyle with a glittering phalanx of teeth, and what Twitch called the black president-bird writing with a pen on a jotting-pad of vellum. Why they were there or who was responsible, none of the Mitchells cared to find out.

They are energetic people, with their fair share of luck. There are Mitchells in at least half a dozen businesses in the town: shoes, hardware, car dealership, newsagent, supermarket and so on. The first Mitchell, old Sep, welcomed time into the town, building the clock tower on the roof of Mitchell's Markets. Wayne, of Wayne Mitchell Ford, has one of the two deer farms in the district, and old Emma Mitchell has matriarchal power within the family and, through the businesses, in the town. She's a leading light in the annual Show each February or March. There's an Emma Mitchell eisteddfod, and she started Street Rescue, for kids with no one. A sincere woman, with the sincerity of a lion guarding its share, she has a smile as wide as empty goalposts, with about as much meaning. No one could ever imagine she came down in the last shower.

She says money and possessions aren't evils, certainly not, but evidence of something more in us than in animals that live from hand to mouth. She made it clear that the history of Lost River belonged to her and the town and not to me. Knudsen said her authority was so strong, her personality so unquestioned, that one steady look at Clarrie, her hub, was sufficient, provided he noticed, to quell any desire he might have to oppose her. She rubbished the wife of the rector of St Matthew's by saying she was too beautiful to be accessible to the poorer people. It was another world, to me.

They say she decrees who will wear the mayoral chain and that it's no trouble to get on her shit-list. She's prominent in the Power to the Regions campaign, now that it's so apparent that centralism is choking the country. The new jail and incinerator are her pet projects. She wants a bigger town, more people, and works to make Lost River a country centre. 'I'd do anything to have this development,' she told the council. 'Whatever it takes. I want a Yes vote in August.' She was a skilled political surfer, she could catch a wave of opinion where others saw only a ripple.

I detected one attitude of the newly rich in her, which is that by their own efforts and possibly with blessing from the Almighty, they had won through to a higher humanity. Their businesses, money and prominence, were certificates attesting to it. If luck was a virtue, they were virtuous. Twitch, her youngest son, was the subject when she talked to me.

He was a pleasant enough boy, which pretty well damns him from the start; harmless and well behaved, who kept silkworms, collected stamps, and ate his food with the silent concentration of the imperturbable putting duck, and would only eat brown eggs, never white, since they looked too uurgh. Emma loaded him with all the frustrations and unspent angers left over from her dealings with the other four children, all of whom handled her managing ways very well—'You'll be there to catch my last words,' she reproached them when they ignored her. 'Your last shouts, you mean,' they said—and took less and less notice of her, having some of her own strength. Twitch had none. He was smart as a headless chicken. And she had wanted him to be something big, like school captain, as she felt she was town captain.

Twitch thought very poorly of himself, and when Emma decided to adopt a boy from another country, and gave young Ezekiel the sort of treatment he felt he should have received instead of constant belittling, his own lack of worth was confirmed. 'As a genius he's a sleeper,' he heard her say, but he knew that. The universal grammar of inferiority presented no difficulties.

Like a dreaded uncle visiting, Ezekiel made himself at home instantly. He was not a disciplined child. The licensed chaos of his room, his very cheekiness and vitality were tagged as charming by Emma, who appeared to penalise Twitch the more as he grew despondent and sullen. Twitch could never understand why a refugee boy wasn't quiet, fearful, and constantly thinking of the bloodshed from which he'd escaped. He ought to be more subdued, more humble, and not give him, Twitch, a quick glance that read: I'm me, but you're not so lucky. Which made Twitch cringe back into his shell, like a snail touching salt. If he'd had more go in him he'd have been as jealous as Hercules' brother. All Twitch heard was praise of

Ezekiel, who went straight into the soccer team, the cricket team, and the top class. He was chockablock with energy, and danced when he walked, like the cat that jumped up on the barbecue plate.

Emma began to be irritated by Twitch, and impatiently picked on him when he looked up at her and twitched, and when she heard that unearthly wheezing silence that surrounded him as he thought and breathed at the same time, mouth open. Or when his nose glugged in choking mode. Was there such a thing as abstract illness? She much preferred the insouciant Ezekiel and his dork-filled expressions. Why were there no psychopruning methods? And psychoplanting, to remedy insufficiencies? How had she managed to produce this failed soufflé?

In class he was willing, but uncertain, like a dog learning. He was unsuited to a bleak and merciless meritocracy. The future looked like a world where gravity weakens and you have to hang on or get thrown aside. Often in high school he felt a midday nap would have helped, he got so sleepy round lunchtime. Maybe he really was a thicko, a vegie. Were there some shots you could get?

He would go home, up to his room, throw his bag on the bed and go into the big backyard to play with his friendly Bullamakanka bangle snake, and later take Basic, his isosceles dog, for a walk up the Hill and along the walking track on top of the ridge, peering at the messages insects scribbled on the nude white flanks of the eucalypts. In hot weather, when the grass looked hot, why was it cool to the touch? He was content to stay puzzled. Could you pick up the highway down there and crack it between finger and thumb? Put your hands out there to the horizon and lift it up? He supposed not. Stretches of river were visible, and swampy places where reeds and watergrass confided in mud. All the Australian trees with long thighs and small heads of leaves. Inside him another person was waiting to get out. Maybe it was a yeti, which could scare people and get their attention. He'd like to be a yeti. Better than feeling like a supermarket barcode beetle.

Would he ever have a business? If so, what business? He hated the idea of kneeling down selling shoes, and the supermarket was a blur of too much movement and too many bottles and tins. Was he no better than some of the servile bludgers Dad had pointed out in the street on Thursdays waiting for the banks to open for their welfare money? He felt as useful as a deckchair floating about in the water after the Titanic sank, as he'd heard about at school.

Older, he took up windsurfing and drove to the artificial lake at the country's porn capital, as Mum described it, with the windsurfer he'd got for Christmas in the car he'd been given on his seventeenth, as was the Mitchell tradition. A red Hyundai. The others all demanded and got European, except Sarah with her RX7. Nothing was as good and satisfying as skimming over a non-resisting surface under wind power. All you had to do was hold on and steer. If only life could be like that. Far simpler and more comfortable than Mum talking at family gatherings of the unseemly behaviour of banks and the frightening growth of executive power at the federal level. She had joined the growing number of people who called it the feral government. 'The jaws are closing, the roof is coming down tightly over us. May take a revolution to reverse it, a middle-class revolution.' When he was pushed to comment, he had nothing to say, just felt like getting free of all awkward questions.

When the talk turned to the town murder he felt relieved, there was no thinking effort needed to attack someone in her absence. Friends in Sydney said Fusby was an undercover agent bent on undermining Lost River, others said she had come to spread HIV. Wayne's suggestion that Amaza fell off her outdoor furniture, broke her neck and someone plonked her back on the couch, was rubbished by Emma. She wanted serious conversation and a proper murder.

It all went into Twitch's open mind and most of it went out again through the hole in the bottom, but he was proud of Mum and how she was a kind of higher power in the family. And the town. He hoped she got her way with the incinerator and jail, if she wanted them so much. Yes, he said when she reminded him, he'd remember to mention Leanne whenever he got a chance. He knew Mum really loved him and had wanted big things for him and tried to have him turned out crisp and fresh as a hopeful young lettuce starting on life's journey. The difficulty was him.

Twitch came close to loving life when he was holding his sailboard tightly, careering across the surface of the lake, seeing the fingerprints of wind on the waterskin. The sun sunned, the clouds clouded, the lake laked. He felt fit and strong as the Kosciusko turnstone bird, and not just a molestone on the skin of life.

He had daydreams in which he ran and never came back, or wandered in valleys so maidenhair cool that the air itself was a companion and touched him with kindness. He sometimes wondered if he was homosexual, since girls seemed so strange. Sort of inhuman. But boys were too hairy, so what was he? He came to no conclusions, though for sex he'd like to have had certain things done for him while he remained passive, receiving.

He was pretty much by himself in the house now. Everyone was so busy. Ezekiel was the fair-haired boy. The chip on Twitch's shoulder had the weight of a plank. The year twelve exam was done, but he had little hope of a good result. Ezekiel was a popular cricketer and soccer player and they had little in common. The isosceles dog was his pet now, charmed away by

Ezekiel's liveliness and effervescent energy. Twitch was now properly jealous, as Leonardo's brother was of Leonardo.

Twitch made the decision easily, lightly. If he had to be in the world alone, he didn't want it to be in competition with millions, he'd be really alone and do what he wanted to do. The morphia of work was for others. He drove round Wiradhuri Circuit past a lonely theodilite stuck into the earth on three sharp prongs and decorated with a 'Save the Southern Panic Glider' sticker, with warm clothes, a few bits of camping equipment, two credit cards and a profound sense of relief and relaxation. A great oppression had lifted.

His first night alone under the stars. He began to detect then enjoy the inaudible but feelable silence of the bush, which made the overall silence of the stars deeper, yet it seemed both might be broken at any moment, he didn't know how. Look at those stars. He was on the edge of the future, so how was it he felt part of the past? Had the world got away, slipped its lead? Did it now live for itself, not for us? Events, discoveries, new things, new people happened so fast they'd become what was important, not people like him, Twitch Mitchell.

'I'll be a new kind of swaggie,' he said aloud and confidentially to the stars, perhaps expecting the rocks nearby to crowd round and listen. He patted the credit cards in his pocket. 'Always room at the bottom. Wonder where I'll head tomorrow.' He decided to leave that decision till the morning.

As he settled down to sleep it occurred to him that now was the time for thinking of all the things in his mind that weren't settled. The effort was spoiled by a full dental yawn. Three hundred kilometres he'd driven. The stress of leaving, change of scene, the necessity of getting a good night's sleep, to shake the moneytree to get breakfast, to be up with first light, it was all too much to combine with protracted periods of concentration on abstract things, on the future, or even the injustices, misalignments and disappointments of life so far. He yawned again. Should he have done something to Ezekiel? Like shooting him? No. He hated conflict, it made him dizzy, not sure where the ground was.

What a great place to sleep. The stars. After all, nothing mattered to the person who lived for the moment; history was superfluous. Whatever road he took in the morning would lead to his personal future. Great. He'd never been there.

Before he slept he remembered Mum's constant urging to believe in himself. He felt that to believe in himself was like believing in air, he needed something better, something higher than that. To look up to. Well, didn't people come to that conclusion thousands of years ago when they looked up at night, saw stars and meteors and imagined gods?

He hugged his big secret to himself. He was glad all those ideas had been put around the town, the little made-up stories, the rumours. They took people's minds off other things. It had been a good idea. If Mum wanted her pet projects she should have them, she was worth all the other mums in Lost River put together. He sometimes had a funny feeling about the thing he did that day last March; if the word hadn't disappeared from use it might almost be called guilt. The only brave thing he'd ever done. Finding that steel knitting needle, the trouble he'd taken to sharpen it, and doing what he had to do: it was all worth it. That stupid old woman would never say another rotten thing about Mum or the Mitchells. It had been easy to dawdle around near Kioloa Avenue, most people were at the Show. Sure, he was dizzy and sweating and shaking, but it was worth it. It was for Mum.

Drenched to her unruffled tentacles in unwanted and unwonted sympathy, Emma was so relieved he'd run away that she got quite sarcastic at Twitch's failure, which was also his triumph.

In the pickup the problem of gesture waited for me. If my old guilts were mere gestures, put-on affairs, stances, postures, what else was?

Pat Hooligan said hullo in Budawang Street. He was walking with Big Betty Vroecop. Neither said much, waiting for me to go. A bit further on I turned and saw her put an arm round his thick neck, and her other hand patted the thick curls on his massive head. I heard later from Pat that he'd been out in the hills working out good spots for fox baits when he saw Betty patting a small hill. Yes, patting. 'I mean, like it was a big sandcastle she'd made. When I got close she was patting it in a special way. Real careful. Kind of tender, as if it could feel her hands. I'd heard she'd changed, from blokes at the Mountjoy. This was a new Betty. There was something about her that went right to the guts of me. Something from way back when we were little kids. As if the years between were stripped away and everything underneath was fresh and clear and she was a big wide column of light, sort of.'

He drove to the nearest fence and walked the last bit, watching all the way. Then he made up his mind. He went over to her. She looked up and watched him coming, said nothing, waiting for him to say it. They looked into each other's faces for a long time, then he said it.

'Come home, softie,' he said. 'Be queen in your own four walls.'

'I will, Pat. I will,' was all she said.

Young Craig Apps, in year twelve with Twitch, told me he saw Twitch come past his house on the Saturday of the Show. 'I'm surprised no one asked him if he'd seen anyone going into that woman's house, because Kioloa Avenue is just down the road from where we live and that's where he was headed.'

I bumped into Craig's father Pincher Apps in the Workers' Club, sunning himself high up on Chifley Terrace as if he'd found the light on the hill, and got talking. Life was puzzling when he was young. At sixteen he met his anti-gambling dad in the betting queue at the TAB. When at seventeen he tried to crash a roaring party at Bret Mitchell's, son of the Ford dealer, he was ordered away by non-drinking Mr Apps, who swayed under the influence of an emotion that had the aroma of Scotch. 'You're not coming in,' Dad explained, 'while my arsehole points to the ground.' And went back inside, set on getting his back teeth afloat. Pincher tried standing on his dignity, but it made him no taller.

At the party, many took their turns kneeling to the porcelain altar, but Dad was ejected anyway when he cannoned his cookies without warning over the loaded food table into the punch bowl. This exploit momentarily took attention from the international joke contest, the point of which was the maximum vilification in the minimum time.

I'd been told by Wayne Mitchell that in those days Pincher managed to look bedraggled and startled all at the same time, as if he'd just been grabbed in the Christmas hold and slung out of some low barbecue. He'd been a wandering satellite since he was a boy, hanging round others' games, having no idea of making his own. He wanted desperately to tag along, enjoy through others, laugh when they laughed, extinguish his own personality and merge with the collective; that would have been his nirvana. There was a look about him of an animal in hiding, a dog slinking around, dull, ribby and empty like a failed and disenchanted greyhound; he wanted to be with the boys yelling and yahooing, full as a Bundaberg beer tick, roaring out verses of the bugger-me-dead blues.

Like the Nullarbor spiderbird he couldn't win. Not that there aren't spiders in the Nullarbor, it's just that they favour the night, where the spiderbird has poor eyesight at night and fancies itself a bright bird of day. The upshot is, it fails in life and has to make do with the occasional wood-tick, the long-faced dung fly, and the uncomfortable beetle.

His wife Linda and he were with-it during the seventies, but not prepared for the shifts of the eighties and nineties. Craig, bright and popular at school, wears coat and tie to his new job at Dalgety's; Dad and Mum still hide in denim and leathers, with the earrings and, in Pincher's case, the gold neck chain.

Pincher loved having company. Too much, though. Too effusive. I got back to work, troubled by that feeling that there was something else buried beneath the banal wrongdoings I had regurgitated. I knew of the free-floating guilt feeling, though it wasn't overwhelming, just a background noise.

Did the buried thing have to do with the way I'd thrown over my boyish religion? After God had gone I saw and felt the mystery of the world for a time, then gradually looked away and let it go. To feel that a tree in a sandy clearing had a life of inner prayer was no longer possible for me. I got into the habit of not seeing.

I thought about this as I wove the colours of Twitch's defeat, but though this latest accusation had some force, the deeper cloud was still there and unidentified. Could these feelings really be mere gestures? Postcards to myself? Where was the software to give me random access to what I needed to know?

thirty-eight

miles blandish of lilly pilly

People I spoke to didn't know much about Blandish; they spoke of the size of Lilly Pilly, biggest property in the area, and what the family had done for the town. There were the dollar-for-dollar contributions to new fire engines, two parks, and steady support for the local Show. They were good for donations, but didn't mix. They supported the new interest in draughthorses, the heated swimming pool, and helped local efforts to train prisoners in the next town's jail in money management, how to get on with people, English comprehension, things like that. And of course the tapestry. Blandish was seen only at the Show, the Gun Festival, the Off-road Vehicle Show, Classic Cars, Rose Day and Anzac Day. He had helped Emma Mitchell get the town tag changed from Lavender City to Rose City of the South.

Morrie the Magsman said their family wisdom was to keep out of sight; they said to each generation, 'If the town people know you've seen them envy you, they begin to hate.' He also said the rich have a secret recipe for their special confidence, but I knew about that.

The third week of April squeezed from the calendar. Lilly Pilly is south-west of town; from Explorer's Hill you can see the delicate fields neatly spread at the foot of the southern ranges. Closer, the creamy-golden roads dance in the sun, the western lines of trees are rooted only in shimmering air. It was a good season, the tablelands were set mouthwateringly with full dams and good pasture. One sown paddock was thick with a white fungus called cockatoos. Those golden roads were the land's arteries, carrying flows, long ropes of sheep, cattle and wheat to keep the rest of the world warm, fed, occupied and away.

I was met by the Blandish eldest son. I found it strange to see a man of the land wearing a tie, but of course this was a kind of royalty, leading a life which carries few reminders of the life of the millions. A caste for whom the present is no substitute for the things they have lost. Australia is not a continent where herding sheep and cattle up-country makes you a peasant. Lilly Pilly is big and rich, their house lawn dignified with a hundred years of care. Even the trees have a certain hauteur, which, however, the family lacks. They are plain people who have been wealthy for enough generations to obey a tradition that wealth is to be discerned but not discussed. The eldest son was of middle height, his shirt was buttoned to the wrists. His voice was quiet and flat.

My name is Lachlan, I have a younger brother, Onslow. Thank you for agreeing to let me substitute for the skipper. I think the project will be good for Kippilaw County and the tablelands in general. Miles is obsessed by ancestors, he hears them rustling, he says, impatient and critical. During his captaincy none of our land has been taken for purposes such as soldier settlement, as in the past, but our previous losses worry him daily. Some of it was bought back when the people failed; the property is being gradually reassembled. There are still near eight thousand hectares remaining of the original block. We're adding revenue-producing pine plantations in the ranges, a cray farm, alpaca to sell as breeding stock. There are paddocks of celibate cattle, the trout farm, quite successful, and Onslow is increasing the worm farm. There are pigs on an experimental block, in addition to our staple of stud cattle and of course the sheep. A special flock in the hills for quality wool, starvation fine. Our way of life is on the up, though the numbers following it are in decline.

The south arm of the river runs through our country, we have very good bottom land. The polo field is on the northern boundary, handy to the coast road; the landing strip with the new hangar is near the river. Piper Cherokee and a Cessna. Handy way to visit friends. There's a house in Sydney, in a Vaucluse with no fountain and certainly no Petrarch.

As you see, there are fine old trees protecting the house, and we're three Ks from the road. Access road in is decomposed granite, stands up well to heavy rain, as it has for a hundred years. The past here was heroic, but it's gone to live in stories, sketches, photographs. Landscaping near the house is by Edna Walling, the planting supervised by her. When visitors say they nearly got lost among the paths and vistas the skipper trots out his joke about Culpability Brown.

We have a dog called Puss. Used to be Priapus because of his long dong and low swingers. Past it now.

We don't put on much of a front. Gateway hasn't been modernised, almost a point of principle. On the coast road the old 'Hawkers and Canvassers' sign is greatly eroded. Above the gate there was once a family crest and motto, but these days the last word Repayment is completely gone and it reads only Scrupulous In. That's as much as I can think of about the place, except that each generation tries to leave it better than they found it.

Life bowled the family a bumper, more a bodyline ball, and Mum died of cancer five years ago. Dad's pretty much a lost soul. She was a genuine partner in the company.

My Grandfather Howard was a character. Bit of a wave-maker. Tremendously hard worker and all that, but big ideas about his leadership qualities. Dad said he bracketed his position in the world and his family and our money with his natural abilities as if they were a whole and he a most remarkable person. He often pressed to get into politics, luckily he was talked out of it. The army didn't see it in him and made him a major. He could never come to terms with the fact that his colonel was the son of a milkman who was employed, not even in business for himself. I know that sort of attitude is supposed to have died out, but it hasn't among our sort. You still hear the words 'of good family, of good stock'. Bit of a hoot, don't you think? Yet I must admit we take no girlfriends from the town.

The skipper says he always felt like a boy in Howard's presence, and on matters of pastoral company business to contradict him was like discussing the frailties of God with God. Howard felt money was a tool and should create, a high responsibility; he said one person with a million dollars could do more for the community than a million people with one dollar. He gave the land for Rugby Park.

Grandmother was a sweetie, sang like a spoonful of honey. Told me once that any government foolish enough to take from the rich whatever privileges money and property confer would be out forthwith, since if these things were taken from us, everyone else would lose theirs. No one would want to be rich, so there'd be no one with capital to produce wealth for the nation. Governments only spend, she said: take, never create.

I wish Howard had lived longer, he'd have admired the present-day Germans with their modern army doctrine that explores when soldiers must obey, when they might not, and when they must not. Had a thing about obeying and army life.

Mother fought the cancer for fifteen years, then it got to her lungs and eventually they didn't show on the X-rays. Terrible blow. Still, that's the way the ball bounces. She said death was the work and craft of humankind in full flower, but that wasn't Mother at her best. She was a person of fine manners. Treated the politician the same as the electrician. Really acid on the SS. SS people were suck and stamp people; suck to those above, stamp on those below. Disgraceful, she said.

She never talked about Great-grandfather James, who raised a company of men after the first war ready to attack Sydney and root out communists, traitors and unionists. He thought democracy was handing government to the mob. We know better now that we've handed it to private organisations. Mother was from the north-west of the state, her family was New Guard. (I thought the private armies of 1930 and 1948 were raised against equality and a better go for those with less, but I daresay Lachlan repeated what he'd heard in Blandish circles, just as I repeat what I've read.)

We settled this stretch of country in the nineteenth century. The family was brave, independent, worked hard and lived long. They were in no danger of getting a pink slip in the pay packet, but were dogged, and worked into the future with no certainty, no commission from others. Had the pagan virtues: prudence, justice, temperance, fortitude. Taught their children respect for truth, reliability, to think in terms of the next generation. Not turned aside by the latest fad or ratbaggery. Would people have us abandon such things simply because they were relied on in the past? Are there more recent virtues? Have they been tested? Do they produce better people? Do they help humans survive worse disasters than these helped us survive in the past? A past which made the present possible?

Old values, are they? These old values remain and are alive; vast numbers live by them, they're in the soil of the great populations, though silent, beneath the surface culture of the cities with their quick fashions and five-year theories. They're invisible to the quick glance. But they can be tasted in the acceptance of reward for work done, shown in the trust that the money you leave with the bank will be there when you come to withdraw some. In the confidence that when you put the key in your new car it will start and its engine not blow up or its wheels burst. The confidence that the horse first past the post gets the money. The commonest transactions of ordinary life are riddled with these old values. They are transmitted in the family, they permeate the vast suburbs, the country towns, schools, sports, street life, marriage, burial of the dead, eating, shaking hands, queues, keeping quiet at night, keeping the dog on a leash, picking up its droppings in the street, being polite to little old ladies as well as football giants.

Playing by rules. The lawgiver isn't in the capital, but in each of us. This has turned into a bit of a rave, but from this distance you get a little stirred by the city nonsense and the presentation of the most extreme examples of human behaviour as if they're standard.

It's a big property, in good order and producing at a rate it can maintain for many years, since it's never overstocked. We've done right by it. We're functioning parts of the country, where nothing happens, except for the vast agricultural machinery ticking over silently night and day, producing the means for disdainful city people to sustain life and congratulate themselves on living where things happen. And if they make enough money they move to the coast where absolutely nothing happens, or to the country to run beef cattle, dropping off their disdain on the way.

My family has given me a freedom to satisfy a basic need: to belong to a group marked off and distinct from all others. We live in harmony as we remain ourselves, knowing our differences and preserving them. Is it some sort of ism not to want to become other than you are? What we have built here is the best we could do given the attention we gave it and the tools we had. More than that cannot be expected of us.

My father is a carpenter beetle: patient, silent, indefatigable; his greatest gift is strength, not possessions. My brother is a Wollondilly water tiger, he's got balls and is aggressive where I'm diplomatic, like the Tasmanian cone beetle.

Oh, by the way, my brother and I were the ones, some years ago, who planted those seashells near Kosciusko's top. Had the media going, didn't it? We half-buried an old anchor too, but no one's found it yet. Great joke when they do.

That night I had no Pam, no Bird, no Sordine, no anyone. My head was filled with pictures of Lilly Pilly. I went to bed in one of those states where you wonder what use your own contribution is. The Blandishes fed people and clothed them. I saw the hills, with the late afternoon sun outlining the bones of the ascending ridges, the V-shaped gullies cut by rain long before living things moved there. Maybe only music could speak the shapes of such land.

I woke at 2:21 in the midst of the worst dream I can remember. I'd been separating small children from the rest of a crowd of people of all ages, taking them from cattle trucks straight to the Birkenau gas. In the same dream I turned and put the piano wire loop over the harmless head of theologian Bonhoeffer in Flossenbürg. In every book I'd read, every film I'd entered, I was a murderer, a terrorist murdering indiscriminately, making life so much worse for the survivors who had to suffer the increasingly stringent laws created to deter such as I was. Criminal of the age. A virus infecting history.

The dream tailed off into a dramatisation of that boy putting the steel lengths between the railway points, an action which derailed a train on Sydney's main northern line. That same boy, older now, betrayed a friend who trusted him and who, had the situation arrived, might have died in his place. Abandonment, betrayal, cruelty. People who had no harm in them. People who loved him.

Could this torture really be a gesture? The images had such power. My conscience writhed. Yet when I was awake I recognised that, yes, I was capable of simulating the worthy feelings that repudiated my crimes.

thirty-nine

saint salivarius

Everyone I asked had something to say about him and his crime. One even said he'd tried his favourite dish raw. He lived in an abandoned house, Knudsen said, litter on the side of the road. He'd boil a child soon as look at you, to have the bones for souvenirs, said Morrie the Magsman. Wayne Door's mother alleged he knew a method of dissolving bones from the inside so the muscles would collapse the body in a heap of meat. Chainsaw sentimentalised, of his crime, that he only wanted to place a flower in that woman's heart. Juniper said God was periodic, only around at certain times, and that day he had gone missing. Morrie said Saint Sal collected dolls from the age of eight, gave them names, had them in his bed at night and at school could never take his eyes off the girls, but his mother hated him and his two older sisters made his life a misery, tore strips off him. Pat Hooligan reckoned the man had a secret, he was tortured, things came out of that inner room we all have where the half-forgotten waits, and attacked him, so his whole life was one of living against the grain.

I was inclined to think the Saint displayed one of the keys to humans: the awareness of the two nothingnesses. He preferred the one he came from rather than the one he was headed for, and constantly tried to get back there. I spoke to him twice; once at his little house, once at the races. Pioneer Cup day, last week in April. He'd have nothing to do with rubbishing Mrs F.

'Let it go, it's a tide. It'll recede. A tide of talk,' he said. He had a habit of picking at small scabs on the backs of his hands. The few skin tags I could see on his neck itched him, he rubbed at them. He was not comfortable with himself.

A tall man with high ears, a nose like the bow of a yacht, wide mouth, thin simian lips—I looked for pronounced fangs, but was disappointed—and carrying a long history between his legs, he'd been through the mill. You could see the machine marks on face and hands as he lit up a coffin-nail impenitently. The way he stood, the self-congratulatory bulge in the fork of his jeans was outlined strongly by optimistic wear-marks. His hands were dry as talc, his skin warm as a summer westerly.

He claimed to have been taken aside by his grandfather when he was eleven and given a talking-to because the family, particularly his sisters, considered him a milk-and-water, nothing kind of boy. 'Be your true self. The world needs variety. You may be saint or slime or salesman, but the world needs you as you are. Inside,' Grandad said. Or the Saint said he said. An ancestor was one of the Gleets in the Jensen bushranging gang.

At twelve he went down to the cricket ground, sat in the middle, and said to the sky, 'I want to be what I am.' A mouth in the sky said a big yes. He went back there each time he needed a spiritual fix. He endeavoured to justify criminality to me. 'Why try to get rid of it? It and criminals have so much to say about the rest of you. I'm a resource,' he maintained, cool as a Christian with a firm booking on a seat in heaven, an aisle seat where he could stretch his long legs while he watched the main feature.

The more he talked, the more puzzled I was. Is anyone quite sane in middle age? Do others have his obsession, his desperation, for the taste of women and the uses to which they can allow themselves to be put? But he went further.

His desire for something miraculous to happen between himself and the female was increased by his inclination to take what he wanted, rather than wait. He belonged all his life to that social class who never ask permission. To him, breasts were a signal. They commanded. They said, Come to me, these are for you. It seemed evident to him, from the fact that women allowed themselves to be seen, or merely glimpsed, that they were making an offer to the world, even a promise that, if you took the bait, you would be caught in a strong current that would transport you towards a constantly renewable—what? Gratification? Happiness? I think it was more than that: a promise of a constant paradise. Well, that's what he seemed to think. As if the world of females was spread out, waiting to be picked over. Did he have no conception of restraints, or laws? Or others' autonomy? I reflected that there were all sorts of laws, some present long before they were written down, and they were the ones he ignored.

He said that no, on his first sex he didn't feel the slightest sense of being privileged when the girl opened to him. He was the male, she the female; if there was any privilege they shared it.

'I'm fascinated by women. They're so different, their juices different, their flavour, scent and flesh. If you were to chew them raw, it would be different from anything else. The look, the feel, the details of their construction, the changes in texture as you travel from one camping spot to another over their paddocks, hills, elevations, their four forests. I can spend a month studying a mouth, or the pattern of creases behind a knee. As for a lip! Two lips together! My God. And I don't mean just live women. I summon women alive or dead, or not yet born. Call them up at will.' He tapped his head to indicate the room to which he summoned them.

'I hunger and thirst for them. When I was thirteen I realised they were lolly all over, to the soles of the feet. So sweet a taste, so good. Stomachs and sides like marshmallow. If only I could eat them without them being diminished. Their breasts have the kind of spiritual nourishment the priest talks about. I can feel the Holy Spirit that lives in their skin, feel its vibration, its religious sweetness, its divine breath. The body is the soul, to me. You've heard their sweet breathing, you must know faintly what I'm talking about.

'I was little when the fascination started. Everything about them was so hidden, protected. It made you feel the invisible bits were special, valuable, kind of magical. So completely different from my own familiar self. The backs of my hands and of theirs were as different as lizardskin and the skin of breasts.

'Every little patch of them is an object of desire, they can't conceal it even if they're dressed to the nines. One finger. The gleam of an eye. A wrist. All magic. And some know it. They give minute attention to skin, hair, face, hands, legs, feet. Paint toes and fingers as well as face and eyes. Special baths, massages, surgery, relaxation, hair removal, just as if they worshipped their bodies to the same extent as I do. Or as if it's natural for them to be objects of worship.

'I had time to think of it in stir. As a mother expresses her milk into the mouth of her baby as it's nodding off, still sucking, so the body of a woman lets its goodness flow into me from the contact my eyes have with her warmth. My mouth and my life point towards the woman like the needle of a compass. Women are my direction, my destination, even in these years of dryness. Everything else is distraction. Work, money, survival—all rubbish. I have no use for their minds or personalities, just the bodies. I don't want relationships.' The 'ship' word was a sneer the moment it hit the air. 'That part is crap. All women, all people are secondhand. What you get is always other people's troubles, other people's damage. The body can't hide anything, it's a fair dinkum wysiwyg.

'Often I think of them as lakes. Deep lakes with magical tension at their surfaces. That skin, that skin! They're my religion. I'm worshipping my god when I worship them. To me, every facet of a woman can correspond to some external object or happening. Maybe weathers, emergencies, natural processes, journeys, enter into women to help form what they become. Earthquakes, too.'

At this point, proud as Napoleon's parents, he showed me his long, heavily muscled penis, with its roots of fur attaching it to some part inside him that he felt was his essence. Did he want me to shake hands with his best friend? I saw the strong, blood-engorged blue-green vein, the smaller red, probably burst, capillaries, and the softly glistening arrow-shaped love-cap, as he called, it as if it were a kind of magic mushroom, standing with a pride he wholeheartedly felt, but which to me seemed faintly ridiculous. Pathetic, even.

'Feel him,' he invited me. I shook my head. I know that without imagination humans are cripples, but this was too much. 'Never felt rubber, this boy,' he claimed. 'Contact is the point. Not so much the getting in, as the mystical satisfaction of feeling the tides of that particular woman, so that the person seen with eyes, felt with hands and bodyskin, is joined with the one sensed by Moby here, the circle is complete and the female goodness and essence flows into him and throughout the male organism. Orgasms are different again, further along the road. Good boy!' He patted it approvingly, in the way you would an obedient dog. He gave it a vigorous shake, as if throttling a tiger snake. It didn't seem to mind. Why the pride? Dogs, donkeys and ducks do the same. I was glad when he put his Moby away, which he did by pulling out the front of his briefs and letting his pet snap back obediently, down where he would do no harm.

His crime occurred in the spring, that time when a man's fancy turns lightly to thoughts of self-gratification. I say crime, because he was only ever up on the cooking charge. But what about all the other springs? I let that ride and asked why he came back to Lost River after release.

'This is my house, my town, my place since I was a tadpole. I was a boy here, the place knows me. This was Dad's house, his tools are in the shed, his old four-pronged hoe, the handles he made from local timbers, his old axe. I know the people, they know what I did. There are no fresh starts, only one start. The place that knows you is always calling, reminding you. Its bitter hills in winter that look down on the town, hills you've run up, streets you've been chased along, corners you've sneaked round to surprise some character you had to get even with: these things are in you, part of you. Even the shops where you pinched things and the trees you robbed of apples. Without home you're only a fraction of yourself.' Yet I'd met people with whom he was popular as a pig in the Middle East.

'I don't want to be unknown. I don't want to get away with anything; I can't. It's with me all the time. It is me. I'd do it again a thousand times if I didn't have to go where I can't see women every day.' He went on to say jail was a sign of civilisation, a sign they don't know what to do with you. 'They keep you in till the public has forgotten. Without police and jail you'd be torn to pieces by the relatives. Or shot on sight.'

He lives alone, an invalid pensioner like many criminals, supplementing that by some mop-squeezing. Something about the directness of his eyes puts me in mind of the Yoogali sideways hare, which gives you the same front-on sincerity just before it vanishes. His little fibro house is by itself on Iona Road, opposite Rugby Park, surrounded by decrepit pines with tangles of fallen branches at their bases. His brother looked after it while he was inside, paying the rates, keeping it neat, even a coat of paint. His kids helped, while the Saint, being a murderer and therefore an aristocrat in jail, lorded it over the armed robbers, the GBHs, rapists and small fry. If you expected to see a little beggar's velvet in the corners of the rooms and house moss under the bed, or ulcerated ceilings, you'd be disappointed. The place was bare, but spotless. With his pants zippered, his dressed buttocks radiated a cheerfulness that showed where his centre and strength lived.

'In front of that abstemious-looking jury of clerks, mothers, shop assistants, fathers and greyhound owners, I could see that if you want trouble tell the truth. Cries of "May your platelets stick like glue!" echoed in the old courtroom, but the atmosphere wasn't right. Old times were best, with me down in the glory-hole, yells of "Bring up the prisoner!" and the prosecutor ready to go for me like the bells of hell, and the defence vague and forgetting all I told them; the jury in a spin, drowning in weird new knowledge, and me giving them all an open invitation of the upholstery kind.

'Constant questions. "What was your fascination with boiling?" When they should have understood that sex acts are responses aimed at getting rid of the pressure inside created by sex itself. Get it over, I thought. Then the judge embarking on a long sentence just before I did. In the van I thought: make a break, all you can do is get shot, death's no problem. I didn't. I read in the prison library death is just a dress certain thoughts put on. So there I was. Jail's a good place to speculate why we're here at all, it's also a place where you survive if you're the kind that lives wherever you happen to be. It was also an education, read everything I could get my hands on.

'Sex? Did it myself. No bum, no thanks, wouldn't touch that with a bargepole. No turn in the barrel for this sailor, no gallop on the tan track either. If the rest want it up the arse like a chook, that's okay by me. When you do it to yourself it's soon over and you can forget it, until the stinking rotten urge comes back that we're slaves to.' He didn't seem to have formed the attitude that urges can be resisted.

'One day a woman officer was appointed to my wing. I had her up on a table, jointed, dissected, in a minute. Studied every inch of her for weeks. Inside her mouth, her body, took everything to pieces. Forgot where I was, so absorbed in being myself. I formed in my imagination her convex white stomach and neatly folded belly-button, her knee, her outstretched arm with those graceful muscles relaxed. The sight, the taste, the feel of it made me dizzy, made my eyes spin sideways, like when you come, and under that wave of brief delight your eye-cables twitch and give you the illusion of the earth flickering.

'But they're a foreign race, women. Can't ever connect, women and men. Even when you both think you've understood what's said, you find later the words mean something different.

'Inside, they christened me. The Saint for devotion, the rest for what I did. He's the boiler, they said. Which bits did you eat? Shut up, you dogs. No one knew that woman had met a man who made her forget, with one touch, everything else but herself. A man whose touch bound her to him, until the touch wore off. She died without fear. I didn't want her to be less, but it had to be.'

A wash of guilt drenched me. I was imagining it. Though for me the meat was just meat. What had he expected? But by imagining it, I had sat at table with him and lifted a knife and fork.

Suddenly, without warning, he was savagely angry, his lips pale and bloodless as a granny's.

'But bum to those professional slimes who rose on my loss and misery to comfort and power; the staffs, warders, police and law parasites, psychologists, and talkers with all their guyver; analysts, carers, counsellors, clerks and understrappers, all with superannuation at the end of a lifetime of handling people who may as well have been farm stock, motor tyres or tins of ham. International talkers of the world, piss off, drop dead!' With no pause he dropped back to low gear and went on. 'In the house of crims it's all frustration. Guys getting round fed up to the back teeth, swearing to make big scores when they get out; so dependent on the feeling they get from doing what others say they shouldn't do, or can't do, or are not game to do, that when they're blocked it's a real deprivation, and they make up for it as soon as they're out. You had to feel sorry for them, most were okay really: only steal when they leave their pads, only fight when together, only rape when they're near a woman or someone weaker. Only a few I could talk to, like Mac, in for writing short stories. His theory: tax is immoral, legally sanctioned theft, a cause of immorality in others. Short stories? Dud cheques, fiction.

'Correction? Only those who want to be corrected. The rest have faults of technique corrected. Glad I was never in the intractables wing, where guards guard and also attack. Mind you, jail deters—not the one percent that's in, but the ninety-nine percent. Nothing deters the one percent.

'Now I'm free of the aggressive certainty of jail, though not free of the call of my inmost nature. Every day it strikes the note that pierces me. I crave women. I have no excuse for what I did, craving needs no excuse. I love women, whether it's Mona Lisa or moaning Minnie, Marilyn Monroe or Marge Simpson. My nature is frustrated every day. One act out of the me that is me, and I'm back where I can never see another one again. Being blind is no solution; memory would be as big a torture. I may be the only one in the world to value the female in this way. I may be valuable in ways the world has never dreamed of. But one act, one hour of being true to myself, and I'm gone. In woman's flesh I can taste the soul of humanity, the shadow of God, the concentrated suffering of the ages.

'The frustration is deep in my bones. I can walk in the street or the mall and see their necks, arms, their little narrow fingers, pink secret palms, elegant wrists, juicy legs, and I can never have one to myself to begin anywhere and chew and taste my way everywhere. Every bit of me, every organ, cries out, my devotion can have no outlet. Whatever made me like this is cruel beyond my capacity to describe it. Others can make themselves different for a day, men can pretend, can hide their more bloody tastes, their desire to rip and tear and drink blood: I never can. Here I stand, I can do no other. Shakespeare was wrong, the fire in the blood doesn't go out with age; it's less than humble and waits for nothing, certainly not judgment. He wrote platitudes for the average, the mediocre.

'Never is a terrible word when you're healthy and have urgent needs that listen to nothing. I've been born into a world where I can never be at home. Never.'

As I drove away, I wondered how much he didn't tell me. Above all I had to beware against allowing theories to form in my unguarded mind. We're too good at finding regularities. I think of hair-raising conclusions drawn from dreams, visions in inkblots, slips of the tongue, straight lines on Mars, lines inscribed on South American landscapes, flattened circles in fields of corn, corpses that are stolen and thought to be restored to life.

What puzzled me about him was how he could have missed the feeling that for all his ascribing wonders to them and their flesh, females are largely unaware of the features about them that excite the bondage of males. Those secret inner thighs are numb, their own curves say nothing to them. Maybe he didn't care what they thought.

I had my own inner room where the half-forgotten waited, but my monsters had begun to come out. And no sooner out than I was finding my response to their presence might be fabricated. Gestures towards responses I ought to have, and wanted to be seen to have; seen by myself, that is.

Why could I never feel more for other people? I'd been taught to, but the tuition didn't take. I had faint feelings of wanting to feel along with others, to be more friendly—but was that just to be accepted?—even as I reserved the right to push away when the pressure or polarity inside forced me to.

At the church I put aside the saint's cartoon and got out the photos of Yarrow. Played the tape of her voice. Scanned the piece of her handwriting that I had. Took out the one object I had that had once been part of her: a lock of her hair I'd cut while she was hunched over her writing, and kept in an empty plastic typewriter-ribbon box. I was required to forget her, and I couldn't. I knew she was really a rather dry human being, immersed in her own interests and at her own stage of development; it was just my misfortune to be so drawn, and to have adhered.

As I listened and looked and touched, we walked in parks we never visited, on grass that never felt our feet. In imagination we passed a tall tree that shivered abruptly with no perceptible breeze, and I remembered back to when I was seventeen and felt the presence of something unexplained in simple things. Ordinary things like skin, mouth, eyes, and the movement-in-stillness of a hand. One particular hand. Gone now.

Half my life I had suppressed, or abandoned, those responses, but now I found I hadn't lost the ability to recognise the stirrings of something, in object, in person, that was worthy of attention, and wonder, perhaps even of something more.

As Yarrow walked with me we came to a place where my childhood waited for me. There was the countryside I'd called mine, with my trees, my friendly sandstone rocks, those blazing white patches of sand on the bush tracks, the valleys seen from the point, and the plants that grew there before words were invented. As we walked together it seemed the years since childhood had been aimless wandering until now, when I'd begun a detour, a bending of the road back round to the days when I saw more than could be touched and felt. On Slidegrass Hill, Yarrow turned towards me, and I towards her. I searched my ragbag head for words, but couldn't find any.

forty

borrowdale blow

His eyes were a clear strong blue. There's such a blue in Jean Lurcat's *Spirit of France* tapestry. A faint penumbra, whitish-grey, surrounds his irises, slightly obscuring their black border.

Borrowdale emerged from a ruck of bettors at the races, the day of the Goldfields Cup. He gets good information, a winner every few weeks, enough to keep the smile on his chops. When Emily's Gift grabbed the lead on the turn and raced away with the cup, he leaped in the air, both feet off the ground, and yelled something I didn't catch. A few women nearby smiled, the men's set faces showed no movement. Betting is a glum business. Look at the faces in the betting shops.

Nothing could make Borry Blow glum. A fine actor, wonderful voice. His mother lived in Monash Road, below Big Hill. He has a flat in a lane off Budawang for when things are slack in Sydney. His last performance I saw was on a TV panel debating: 'Is it politically correct to be Australian?' He grabbed the limelight with his first line: 'Plain men don't get a look in with all the sexes about nowadays.' Another public gay making the TV audience laugh. And not only at his 'stewed prunes and prisms' voice. He loved being as inconspicuous as a swollen and glistening wen on a cheek, and surveyed the world often from the heights of Cannabis Castle. He does work for 2LR and once punned on queens in grass castles, but it was lost on Lost River.

There's something anemonelike in his expression, the way those fighting-cock eyes lingered on you after his head turned away. I remembered him saying in an interview that not only the coward, but the thoughtful, the sympathetic, and the actor die a thousand deaths. I suppose it stuck in my mind because of times I'd been a coward.

'I was taught to obey God rather than man and determined to love my neighbour as myself, provided he was good-looking. In those days I never ducked an engagement with transcendence.' He put his bony, well-formed feet up on the occasional table, a glass slab supported by four naked weightlifters painted black. His poserphone lay carelessly prominent on the glass surface. An art photo of him hung on the wall, naked as a flagpole, his golden hair glistening.

'We're all on. Even the most far-fetched child. All actors. No one can be out of it.' He loved talking about himself to someone not competing with him. 'I'm so grateful I was turned towards the same sex. It has given me a sense of adding to myself, of concentrating my maleness. So glad I'm not one of those men who want to be women.

'Before puberty I daydreamed often that I was a small soft animal hypnotised by a mysterious power, and shivered deliciously to be at its mercy. Later, I became that power and hypnotised small soft animals. What we did as little boys was quite beside the point, just as my interlude with Merle Bird has no significance, though in both cases we were as noticeable as white-eyed ducks. Not that I like women, but they give me an anchor in the community, an ally. My main joy in being gay is that I am accepted by other males in the most direct and intimate way, and I am among my own kind. Women are foreign bodies.

'I'll pass over school friends, our eagerness to greet depravity—as we joyfully thought of it—and our early exercises in owning our desires and being warm towards our sensations. A little cross-dressing, the desire to be called Miss just once, adventures with the all-electric suction pump for penis power. Few of our group had problems with shame, it was mostly with concealment. I was always free, to have my rape fantasies, to look down communally on unresolved heterosexuals, to make jokes about being bi and liking girls as well as the next guy. Other kids, bless their little hearts, said we loved the tan track, they called us freckle pushers, knob gobblers, dung punchers. "Speak to me, O chocolate lips," they said, "shit'll always wash off." They had no idea. I got back at several darlings, taking naked pictures with their cameras. Their mums got the pics developed.

'Arnold was my introduction to the adult future. I was a runner, on Thursdays, for big Jim Walker then, taking bags of cash up William Street to an address off to the left. Steel plate behind the doors, hinges like you've never seen. Good money when I was hard up. Actors are not exactly must-have items in the economy. Arnold was coarse. When I met him he said he was master of his date, captain of his hole. Double minus. Disgraceful as a turd in a punchbowl. Put me in mind of those heroes who feel they're gay just because they find women inferior or unaccommodating. His eyelashes were short, didn't fit my dream. I love long eyelashes, the feel on your lips. And a toe queen too. I don't like jokes in lovemaking, or someone who blows when you say suck. I got rid of Arnold,

'Life was wonderful. Still is. Partners weren't important then, blips on a radar. Some at the tubs, some at parties. So much delight. A different world from your world of waiting for women to be ready. But I'm ready for monogamy now. I think.

'I must tell you about Totem Pole. You know that moment when you can't help looking at someone, as if you were forced? Well, at a party there was this immensely tall Yank. Our mouth parts met, and it was on. Would you believe a name like Hackamac Sinsquat? Neither would I. We fitted felinely, caninely, every way. But personalities? Like two cats with their tails tied thrown over a clothesline. Pretty rough trade, giving head all over the place, but it was what I needed. Only lasted a few months. Well, six. He displayed an heroic indifference to the pain of self-deception and self-knowledge. He went on to bigger orgies, bigger doses of Amy. Nitrite, for gorgeous orgasms. I can't say if I've forgotten Totem Pole or not. He went to Queensland. There are two classes in eastern Australia: those who look down on Queensland, and those who stampede to get there. Then he was off to embrace Asia, but perhaps not if Asia saw him coming.' He sat still, concentrating, still as a Billyrambija basking snake. The music in the next room changed. A large vague symphony finished and a callous and gritty soprano asserted herself.

'At the back of my mind is a picture of a person who is a perfect fit for me,' he said at last. He excused himself and went towards his bathroom. Poking out from under a recent copy of *Golden Rivet* was part of a typed letter. Or was it a page from a loose-leaf diary?'

... the thing to do at the time. We did things to ourselves to choke off that sort of affection. Didn't want that sort of love, we thought it led to incorrect attitudes, wrong politics. What fools we were. Now there's a fully acceptable man coming at

me with this—is it really outmoded?—love and I can't believe it. But I do believe it and I love it. The adoration thing. Every tiniest piece of me valued. I wish I'd left myself alone and hadn't joined in with others, as if personal things can be decided communally. Perhaps life knows best. I don't know what to do. Can I change back? I'm not sure I remember what I was ...

I heard Borrowdale flush and went over by the massage table, with its chin-hole, and indigo covering material. Several black hairs adhered to the vinyl. He talked of his mother.

'My mother is a kind of geisha, sipping her camomile tea in her wisteria-blue tea room. She has a jade coffee room. It is Sunday morning. The citron-coloured sun squeaks when it enters this room, which quietness invades like a daydream, holding everything still. Here are no indoor plants leaning and looking sadly towards the light, her plants love being where she puts them. She knows. They sigh when she passes them to leave the room.

'It is ten-thirty. The hands that I have watched for a lifetime uncurl, the long fingers, with separate lives, caress the sheen of her plants. I can detect the perfume of her thoughts. There are carved obsidian birds on each wall, in the attitude of song. Purple velvet covers soothe the eye, the tail of a golden dragon is in repose. Her hands stop in the air, shaking the room, between me and the black twisted branches of a painted cherry tree in winter. She is always aware, of where she is, who is with her, of what she does and what others do. Each action is fully attended to, all is sacramental.

'Faint steam escapes the silver teapot, is illuminated by a sliver of sun that enters through glass between the branches of trees carrying a whole thesaurus of leaves that inhabit a world outside. Green lights billow from her plants, like successive bubbles that expand, then vanish without bursting. Her hands descend to the white table and the blue bowl of blood plums. Her white teeth show as they penetrate the flesh of summer. I can taste my youth in her mouth.

'My mother and I rearrange the flowers. Amazon blue, Indian white, Nigerian red. I merge with her.

'Her house clasps me when I try to leave.'

When my own mother died after a number of strokes, and months of not being there, I'd had time to get used to the idea of her taking a lot of me with her. The years of mine that she, and only she, knew, were about to die.

I've never mourned. I mean, how do you do it? I'd produced tears at funerals, but that's easy. A child can do it. Or a surface sentimentality. However long she'd been in Australia, she was English, and taught English manners. Perhaps it repelled Yarrow. It could look false to those not brought up to it. Yarrow was so very Australian, even though, as a lover of theory, a Francophile too.

forty-one

crasher coy

He was a big and brown giant, the sort they mine in the hills round Lost River, and happy as bread in a toaster. He looked the way I imagined a Philistine when I was a boy, heavy black eyebrows and all. Crasher got on with everything. Machinery didn't resent him or sabotage his efforts; events didn't seem to catch him with his pants down, pockets empty or jaw slack. On the other hand, when you got talking to him and the words looked like dipping a little under the surface, he showed the familiar face of people who live with and cope well with regular physical danger, mainly in the words he used, but also in his manner and responses, and was by turns clumsily serious, disarmingly frank and quite shy.

At Jazz in the Bush, or Country Weekend, the Gun Festival or watching the Tantawanglo Gift, people knew him and he was happy with that. Never got tired of 'How you goin'?' or 'Day, Crasher!' He didn't react to the name Fusby beyond saying, 'That woman in blue. Red hair.' He loved guns and wondered how bullets felt, pointing at the world, ready to come out when impelled from the rear. He was straightforward as a garage door. He treasured a photo from his elder brother's time in the navy—warplanes on a carrier deck, their arms folded and restrained like patients in straitjackets. I mentioned a human society in which a version of football was considered a form of sacred meditation, but it ran off him like a raindrop off a nasturtium leaf.

In the long flat summer days of childhood and as a growing boy outside Lost River at the edge of town where the forest had retreated and the orderly sheep and cattle paddocks frayed into streets and houses, he ate like a hungry horse, and by the time he was fifteen was very big. Kids called him Crusher then. His dad was big too, until Mum killed him. The admiring look in her eyes for his comforting bigness persuaded him not to get his weight down at fifty when his mates did, and he carked it at fifty-eight at the end of a conversation with Crusher in which he advised him never to do his cruet on the sporting field. Mind you, Dad ate like a horse too.

Crusher's older brother was rich. He arrived in Brazil from the States with five hundred dollars, bought dirt cheap a 1970 bitumen spreading unit, began to make roads and airfields, and coined money. Crusher's younger brother got a pilot's licence and has gone out west of Orange crop-dusting.

In teenage football Crusher had little competition, he went through opposing teams like a packet of salts, and a good future was predicted for him serving that unsophisticated altar the size of a football field. He was fast for his size, like the American giants of the gridiron, and with the ball would go fifty metres like the accelerating watchdog, which is fast enough.

When he was ready to leave Lost River the year the drought bird was seen three times, to follow his footballing fortunes, he was getting to be shy of the name Crusher; already he'd begun to meet players just as big and a lot tougher. He changed it to Crasher. His first publicity in the big time said he was born at eighteen with football boots on and went straight from the maternity ward to play a full game in reserves, was a good go-forward and only gave one hospital pass. He grew to one hundred and ninety-four centimetres and a hundred and twenty kilograms. In fact his weight varied, as anyone's does, but strict honesty in publicity would have looked like uncertainty, brother of dishonesty, so it had to go. Crasher began to believe in a kind of destiny, and his manager encouraged him.

Girls encouraged him too. He was a funny mixture, recalling those days, one minute speculating on the dong and wondering what it would see if it had a miner's lamp on its head, and the next reflecting that there are so many interesting things you can't ask a nice woman to do. And one of them was to go with you to the nymph-pots of Kings Cross. However right or wrong he was about that, deep down he considered it his duty to regard sport as better than sex: more satisfying, more elevated, for want of a better word. And certainly more profitable.

He entered a world of slogans when he began his youthful football, slogans such as: Two types of people, winners and losers; Hot if hot, not if not; We can beat them with nobody; Hate helps concentration. There was no mention of an older one—Fair go—but every generation makes that observation. Still, it was an eye-opener to Crasher when he saw a Superbowl game in which Steelers helped fallen Cowboys to their feet after a tackle, and vice versa. His coaches regarded such gentlemanly conduct as against the spirit of the game.

At whatever stage of his career he was, it seemed lower grades were an ill-assorted collection of poorly matched players forming a distressing whole and all with hands like sieves, and probably engaging in unprofessional flatulence in the scrum, while those above his grade had an aura of brightness round them that invited awe, if not more. Crasher went to Sydney, where he was surrounded by backslappers who assured him he was someone. Destiny looked a fine thing, especially when he'd made a sudden stand-out play, the applause pleasant as the taste of rain in your mouth when you're surfing.

Crasher and his team-mates competed with every strength they had against each other, to be the best, and consequently their team did well. Competition was part of their cooperation, since they competed against each other to be best at co-operation. Having quality players helped, too.

For his first set of trials, Crasher introduced an invention of his: the cannonball tackle. He followed his instinct to go straight up the guts and was the star of the trials, getting on to his manager right away to gouge out a better contract with his club. The cannonball went down so well with the media that a whole sports page was dedicated to photos of it, showing take-off, curling up, impact and horizontal tableau. Players on the sharp end of it dropped like bags of shit, and lay flat out like lizards drinking, then often got up and wandered around like sleepy donkeys, looking at the ground and quietly meditating, and sometimes shaking their heads as if to remember something. Like where they were. The crowds loved it, it sent a Mexican smile-wave round the stadium each time. After two seasons Crasher kept it for special occasions, like when he had the target dead to rights and there was no chance of him flying through the air and landing unaccompanied on the turf to widely televised and more or less eternal laughter. Besides, other players developed counters.

Sport tells you whether and how much you can endure, and players had to endure the psyching-up each week to super-human effort, they hoped, all in the name of football and big salaries and, when they were ablaze with victory, the zany plaudits of the crowd, short-lived as smiles. They repeated the words. 'There is no defeat unless I say I'm beaten', and 'The word for generous-in-defeat is beaten'. They were taught to relax, to meditate, to pay no attention to critics. And taught also that each muscle will think and act as if it has a brain, if it has a long period of being closely directed by a brain.

To see Crasher hit the defensive line with elbows and knees working like steam hammers, grimly grunting at the impact, performing his suite for unaccompanied earthquake and solo cyclone, as one writer put it, was a heartening sight. Straight from Donnybrook Fair. As a player gaining experience he soon gained something like a fighter's respect for a good opponent, and the shared knowledge of how different they were from the watching crowd, who often seemed thick as flies on a dead bullock.

Often the sweetest hits on him were not from other mammoths, but from smaller men with shoulders like cement and arms like axes. Graceful as Clydesdales, the big forwards went in hard and fell separately, obedient to a command that said it's no use having a tough exterior with a bread and milk heart. His specialty was the short run and off-loading to quicker men through the gap, the usual stuff. Ten to fifteen metres out he was quick like a cement truck downhill and hard to stop, but not impossible. Sometimes he looked down and it was a little nuggety half-back who'd stopped him, his two booted feet held neatly—primly, even—side by side in an iron grip.

Crasher wasn't teak all through. In interviews that dismayed some and endeared him to others he confessed to carrying a load of fear into every game. And not just the nervousness that produces a mass shrivelling of penises just before a game. 'I tell myself to go in and get them, but my legs have different instructions. I think it's the femur that rebels. And my agates knock together. Really packing the shits, like the next candidate for the guillotine. I can get my courage up if I get a tackle in first, but the week before the game is torture. One thing, though, I've never played possum, pretending to be injured, and I've never done my lolly just to cover the fear.' Also on field he'd never initiated romantic encounters of the Liverpool kind. But destiny began to look less like a reward and more like a fate to be endured, specially when a pulsating patella throbbed with spirals of pain and the endorphins were slow getting to the site of the panic.

He got a guernsey for Australia, played in Origin games, got used to the shouts of censure and criticism, jeered faithfully at opponents, gave and took hits that brought snot to the eyes, talked of a 'colossal ask', and made sure he was never slow getting to his feet, something that could be spotted a mile away—or a 'kile' as kids say—and tagged with the dreaded words 'getting old'. He was notable for the tears down his face when they played the Australian anthem before a game. The TV cameras featured it every time.

PMT, pre-match terror, still had a grip on him; he was scared it might show. He dreamed his body was glass and the next tackle would shatter something. He began to look forward to his post-playing years. Despite his fear, and despite gradually learning that everyone has a yellow streak and only its width varies, he was bred for a tougher life than constant winning. He was a peculiar mixture. Apart from the noisy camaraderie of the team he had no friends. 'I'm simply the sort of man who has no friends,' he said in an interview, mentioning film star Charles Bronson in the same breath. But there was one. Crasher married. Kerry was his friend. When he saw her his eyes lit up like house windows when tenants come home. He was a family man and took to house and kids as if born to it, retiring while his sinews were still in synchromesh.

To take a back seat to a wife and a house full of kids after years of publicity and prominence and fans braying their hoarse symbolism isn't the easiest thing to do, but he did it, and this huge tank of a man was happy at last. He didn't feel the feminised life of house, garden, children, furniture and curtains a great burden, as so many males do; perhaps his own upbringing and family habituated him to it. But no, he wanted the kids, loved the woman, and cheerfully accepted her blueprints, timetables and compulsions as the price of getting and raising his own family in his own house, in his home town. A fate that must be endured gave way to a glad destiny.

He helped with the littlies—baths, nappies, feeding time, cooking—and didn't raise his eyebrows or drop the corners of his mouth when, at the first accident, burn, bruise or cut the kids ran straight to Mum. It was a man's place to be on the margin.

As he plays with their youngest, he sometimes looks up and sees Kerry watching, or catches her glancing at him as he pushes the trolley in the supermarket. He imagines she might be thinking of one of his powerful plays, taking the ball up to a tight umbrella defence, or a successful cannonball, or his mighty fend. Scenes like that play themselves over on the screen in his head, hundreds of them.

He's wrong. Those years of games are a blur, she hardly ever thinks of them. She thinks of when she first met him, how awkward he was, tripping over his own name; how her brothers laughed at him bringing flowers on their first date. How when they drove out along South Arm and she was sure he was going to ask how about a certain thing, but she slipped down between rocks and hurt her ankle and was in pain and he didn't ask out of consideration. Never mind that she could have been persuaded, and never mind how strong he was, he didn't push it. And the time he told her about his fear.

He feels funny thinking how lucky he is. He wants it to last a long time. It looked to be a good life before he had to face the quiet judge of all the world's creature life. Some people yearned for deeper meaning to their lives. Crasher found being alive had its own meaning, enough for a lifetime, and enjoyed the world he was born into. Because he had never sensed them, he never rejected, as not worth attention, those subtle intimations of a reality behind touchable appearances.

I left the Coy house in Glenrowan Avenue feeling grubby. I didn't stack up well at all against that plain and straightforward young man. I thought of what I had stolen from others. I took years from gentle people, stole happiness, security; ground them down, threw them aside. Let others pick up the pieces, clean up the mess. My needs came first. Supposed needs. Mean, cruel, selfish, hard as nails. Any wish of mine was a need, my needs won over everything. Not a pretty picture.

Were even those habits of cruelty gestures? If so, what was underneath? Real cruelty? If I'd been there, would I really have taken those dream-children to the Birkenau gas? And under that, what? Worse? I swore at the pictures in my head, aloud. My words unheard in the anonymous traffic. The savagery of my words banished the pictures. Good. Ferocity still worked.

I see her now, trying on boots. How many word-clashes would I have enjoyed if she'd never gone? The unrecorded happenings of each day that we were in loose contact would by now have amounted to a satisfying little heap of common history. All the times she caught me in the act of thinking about her would be marked with her quick pennant of laughter and her comment, 'Hopeless, Davi.'

I'd have had times to wander on her shores, minus disturbing head-pictures. Time to sing songs with no tunes, speak brief poems with not a single word. All for the joy of breathing the same air as she did, while she argued for oppression of—whatever—as an objective fact and in the next breath denying the possibility of objective judgment.

forty-two

daniel dogstone

Scraping down a pick of weft against the one ahead of it, for some reason put me in mind of the Highland Gathering, where Daniel had been pointed out to me as he became visible from behind a curtain of kilts. Perhaps the tartan flame-colour of the yarn did it. It was his mouth. His lips, between that black beard, were a stark wet red. A woman might have killed for such lips. Even the savings on lipstick. The beard itself was untrimmed, looking like equipment to scour large pipes. His handshake, which was reluctant, was a grip of a lukewarm fish not yet stiff in death. There was a hurt in his eyes, such as comes from a painful hernia, or ill-fitting truss.

He was a tall, bespectacled rabbitfish given to wearing roomy clothes like shaggy jumpers and fat jeans. His walk reminded me of the large coastal lurching dog, though I heard him described by Knudsen Boult as the bearded foolduck. This might be due to jealousy of Daniel's prominence at the 1927 Cafe, when he captivated his audience holding forth on the human desire to survive, and the consequent need to kill other life, as being a gaping hole in practical human philosophy. Daniel himself didn't mention Knudsen, but there were many things of which he was oblivious. Emma Mitchell said Daniel was the uncouth back-to-front lizard. He was notable for his lack of cheerfulness in all circumstances, and for spraying reason aimlessly on every observation. Being a computer person his gods, he said, were truth, information and logic, in any order. He made no jokes and asked for explanations when others joked. There was a kind of taciturn gruffness about him. If there was something he didn't know, he said so, or said nothing.

At twelve he discovered where flies go at night, and at sixteen stumbled on one of the mysteries of civilisation, marvelling at his mother and sister, at how normal, even quite small bodies, could get through such enormous quantities of trees in the form of toilet paper. He thought the question was no more private than an observation on nose-picking, but the sharp short answer decided him to keep his nose out of women's affairs from that moment. The quest for information had left one scar. He sensibly went back to pondering the mystery of how objects acquire mass, and whether time has mass, a topic not as silly as it sounds. Before I'd introduced myself I had the peculiar experience of noticing that someone who meets your eyes hasn't seen you.

Daniel hated talk unless it was for the getting or exchange of information. Parties meant nothing, they were for those who didn't mind rubbing up against others and talking briefly until interrupted, usually in the middle of something they wanted to say. He manfully ignored mention of Mrs F. He'd never heard of her.

'Empirical study shows that no party and hardly any conversation yields anything worth possessing. Sometimes a one-to-one uncovers something of value,' he said to a dry woman, small and self-contained, like a transistor, to whom he had been introduced at an exhibition of antique eating implements, which because of its description as 'logic at the table' he had attended by mistake.

Her interests were history and gardening. Her philosophy consisted of a question: What do I want? and an answer: Something better than I've got. She had begun to feel the need of quiet company and the advantage of having a male with her in places where a tame male is handy, such as restaurants, on car trips, around the house for minor technical details, and at night as someone who might possibly be induced to deal with thieves and prowlers if sufficiently urged to do so, or could at least be placed between her and the danger. The fact that this one appeared to be sentient, could afford to be present, could express himself in words of more than one syllable, and move without assistance made him a candidate for the position. Daniel, who would need far more notice of her intention than mere propinquity, had no idea of his new status.

Expertly she drew an elaboration from him, brilliantly she listened, and with genius her little conversational prods kept Daniel talking more than he'd ever talked to a woman in his life, and certainly more than to his mother, who knew such intimate and potentially shaming things about him, as indeed mothers do about all of us, that he'd stopped talking to her.

Sandy Blandford's usual starter for these occasions was to remark that people don't really find nuclear explosions obscene: they make jokes about such explosions by calling some swimsuits Bikinis. Something told her not to, this time.

'And why isn't artificial intelligence possible?' she essayed.

Daniel was a follower of Dreyfus, who was strong on what computers can't do, and of Wittgenstein, with his dictum that rules don't contain the rules of their application. He held that there was maybe hope for neural networks, but that computers are capable only of tasks where rules can cover everything that might conceivably happen, and that the only machine that could reproduce human abilities would be one sensitive to context in the way humans are. 'Trouble is, we don't know how humans or animals learn this. There's another thing. The old brain orthodoxy was that high level thought came from a few centres specialised for cognition. The new concept is that thought is produced from the interaction of many ordinary workaday areas of perception, from a distributed array of brain architecture. A most fruitful idea. Can be applied to government. Political method. Complex evolving systems work from the bottom up, not from the top down. Central programming isn't needed.'

She asked a question about mathematics, since he seemed to think highly of it.

'Objects and phenomena are separated by a logical chasm from their theoretical explanations. The foundations of logic can't be demonstrated. The infinite planes and dimensions of the natural world can't be described by any geometry we have. The major liability of mathematics is the way it coarsens subtle distinctions in the data, so that in mathematics you cannot get correspondence with reality, but that's not surprising in a discipline where you don't even have to know what you're dealing with. Measurement is another matter: you can measure time, electricity, gravity, energy, mass, light, without ever knowing exactly what they are.

'There was an heroic attempt to put mathematics on a logical footing. It was futile, the foundations of mathematics are problematic, not indubitable. The best we can do is base it on the intuition of counting.' He didn't mention that the early twentieth century crisis in mathematics' foundations had shaken him so that he still shook.

For Sandy, the only theory she felt at home with was that there's no one point round which all the galaxies revolve. She kept it to herself, and repeated something she'd read, that the universe appears to be mathematically structured. Daniel felt that his previous words should have been sufficient, but kept talking, since she was interested.

'Mathematics is not a picture of the universe. All things, and the universe among them, are too complex to be fully specified. All universal statements of finite length are false. Mathematical waffle. The briefest picture of some phenomena is their entire history. Mathematics has to have well-defined situations. If it doesn't have them, it makes them well defined even if it means trimming a bit here and there. It turns the scientist's assumptions into axioms, then treats those axioms literally. On a trivial scale, think of Aristotle's A is A. So it is. Mathematics translates that as A=A, then goes on to talk of 2A, which is a step into another world, a veiled inference that those two As are equal. Equality and identity are different things.'

Sandy's eyes never wavered, her feet never shifted. She raised her glass now and then, for the exercise. Daniel was in full flight. To be dealing with such matters, to be near them in thought, was to be in touch with God, though he would have rejected the word. Reality, he would have accepted, provisionally.

'Science, mathematics and logic are, like religions, free creations of the human mind and, as such, built on foundations created by the imaginations of those who built them. Science is conjecture and replaceable; maths is beautiful illusion since there is no world it refers to but itself. There's no reason to believe in either, except that they both seem to work. Science came from myth, and every time a theory is superseded, to myth it returns. Science has no end, it's a process, a method, it will never be done. Completeness as an aim is futile, there are no complete explanations. A theory of everything would be an over simplification. One vice of theory in the hands of suggestible humans is that it can be believed to contain everything.'

As for me, I hope I got all this right. All I know about science is what I've read. They say the whole universe inflated from something so small you can't see it, like ten metres to the minus-35th power. Or have I got that mixed up with ten to the plus-35th as the number of angels on the head of a pin?

Daniel looked at his wine in wonder, then realising what it was, took a sip.

'So science, applied to our psyches or societies, must leave a lot to be desired?' Sandy queried.

'Indeed yes. For a start, we can't know the society we live in. No logical system can produce an integral description of its own structure, so we don't know how it works, what it contains or why it has survived. Nor do we know ourselves and all that we contain of conditioning, by ruthless needs and circumstances, that hammered us down the long generations as we evolved towards the human.'

'Have you ever invented anything?' This was dangerous. Her purpose was to build him up, not collapse him, but she wanted to know.

'Well, when I was fifteen, there was the equivalence of life and reality. At seventeen I decided that where infinities crop up in physical equations the mathematics is incomplete. At eighteen I decided that since there's a minimum temperature but no maximum, the universe is fundamentally asymmetric. But no, not really.'

'Do you find mathematics beautiful?' she dared, more or less as a motherhood question. Daniel, who as a small boy had encountered cool algebra, sculpted like jewellery, replied: 'Surpassingly. Mathematics, like reason, pursues an almost aimless course. It's an art, and is the almost solitary refuge of the beautiful. Art itself once was, but now has no values or standards of that kind. It has abandoned the people. It seems to thrive, and music too, on a philosophy of contempt for the non-artist.'

Sandy mentioned history and its task of setting down common beliefs, and elicited the remark that theories of chaos, applied to history, might bring about some interesting observations. In answer to other conversational prods Daniel admitted that the bits of which our knowledge of the world consists may not fit together; not now, not ever. He asserted that we can never know if we're right about what we think we know, since new events happen all the time in an evolving universe.

Sandy was gauging whether to ask if the universe might one day be edible, but decided no: he had no humour that she could detect. She monitored her expression, concealing all cleverness. The empty face was best.

The place was nearly empty, like a big gap in a diary. A jolt of disappointment ran through him, rather like those pangs of his boyhood when he found Arab numerals were Indian, and Indian ink Chinese; or the discovery that passenger planes had no parachutes and Olympic gold medals weren't gold. An unfairness. He hadn't realised he was enjoying himself. This woman was an exception, as rare as a female computer hacker.

Sandy thought she could make something from this unpromising material. She decided to see his initial reluctance to talk as shyness, his obvious yearning for information as evidence of character, his dislike of parties as a fundamental sincerity, his opposition to Artificial Intelligence as a feature of his essential humanity. By the time they left the gallery for the carpark and their respective vehicles she had him bundled up, tagged, signed with her initials and marked with her tick of provisional approval. She set to work with the patience and planning of a field commander to bring Daniel Dogstone to a realisation of his true nature and real needs.

She was present every time he opened his mouth. Like a

horse, donkey or pet sheep he got used to being handled, and to having an audience. He began to take a grim pleasure in preparing things to say. Without knowing what was happening he became fascinated by his listener. The snake charmer was under the spell of the dancing snake. He became a talker. Life was a tide of enjoyment his grimness was unable to stem. He moved in with Sandy in her pretty flat in the new block on the Hill, well on the way to being socialised.

Sandy was well prepared for the relationship. She was satisfied the balance between them was right: she perceived more to complain of in him than he in her. It would be normal, that was the main thing. She didn't mind that he had a negative interest in opera, and ballet horrified him: she had women friends to go to Sydney with her. She said once about a politician trying to save face that he had a double difficulty. Daniel waited while she explained.

Several times he escaped back to his little flat, bare as prison cells used to be except for books and a computer room. Not knowing now what to do, alone, he made sure he didn't by taking to the wine bottle. A retreat from love? From captivity?

A number of bottles of those regional reds that haven't yet made it to metropolitan shops, and here he is past midnight gaping into the bathroom mirror as if he can't make out the image. There is no easily functioning brain in that enlarged and pounding head, no mathematical intelligence, only flames, furry granules of thought, a green glazing of regret for Australia drowning in a sea of green tissue paper crushed and opened out. For the world which is a deflated football with sweat stains. For everything. For not working harder for a better degree, for not getting back that signed copy of *Mathematical Aesthetics*, regret that the total happiness of the world fits into a discarded lolly paper. An indeterminate face swims under the mirror's surface, taunting the dizzy Daniel. If he could breathe more deeply. If he could understand why he does. Things. A blast of strange breath comes from the mirror, misted mirror, a gust of pain makes the earth move for this death's head. Disgrace. Again. Let's recall all the dead who ever lived, but only for laughter. Vague feeling of things he should have done. Too late? Is that a virtual ant? Into the kitchen. Perhaps a chair. Homes are sad. Chairs over, must be giddy too. Look round at sameness. Who was here last night? Left it like this. Look at those flowers. He was. She left. Months ago. No, he left. Dreadful state. Fern above the sink. That bowl. So many dead flowers. Who kills flowers? Life is not being sure. Who said that? Death is comfort. Home like this along nothing roads in Lost Nothing. River hides from sight due to filthy habits. Consorting with sewage ponds. The world's one long funeral. Masochist? Like other takers of drugs. Useful as the top half of a crutch. Be all right? Hardly.

And in the morning a mouth like a rat died in it.

After a number of these delinquencies Sandy gave him up, any more leeway obviously as useful as giving a corpse a manicure. She counted the cost—it wasn't too far over budget—and settled back to wait for another prospect.

He'd fled from order. There was no time to be alone, every space was filled, just as every room in her flat was crowded with furniture that had to be negotiated and sidestepped and never bumped. The future was mapped and he hadn't drawn the map, didn't even hold it. He had no function or status that he could see, apart from being a buffer between her and things that might happen, an intangible insurance, a solution for which a problem might arise. A possession, perhaps, like an exotic vase or ancient Sumerian bottle-opener.

She had become the talker, and talked of history, which is predecessors, and putting faces to stories. He found history as absorbing as waiting for paint to peel. She talked of the crisis in political ideas: there were none, only drift. The thought of those politic people who work for One World and wait Fabianly for their Day, left him cold. His main fear for the future was the day when generalisations were declared illegal and science was driven underground. One of her ideas was the desirability of prime ministers having the services of a jester, who would tell them the sort of truth that would cut them down to size when they got too big for their boots. Daniel awarded it no significance.

So that was that. His universe is largely on and in a computer where he is free to do as he likes. By nature he is oblivious to defeat as he would be numb to success. He goes to the places he used to go to, does what he did before, is the person he was.

Self-contained as a cat, she lives her quiet life, reads her history, attends to her garden, adds comforts to her pretty flat, goes to concerts, openings, parties, exhibitions. She'll be more careful next time. He'll need to have more personality than a discarded shoe. She feels no pain, has suffered no damage, no more than from a bad hair day. She is the person she was. Daniel is a long way in the past.

Can any human be complementary to another? Useless question. Just as fruitless as Lost River people still speculating on whether Amaza died from secret and undetectable martial arts blows, or from the old technique of being held in a head-lock and her neck arteries and veins rummelled upwards until nothing happened.

Perhaps the beliefs I'd wrapped myself in when I was young were gestures too: badges, banners and bluff. Maybe belief was a social act, a gesture of solidarity, evidence of a desire to belong.

Young, I detected in me terrible angers, an ugly aggressiveness, a disregard for others, pushing away from early influences towards an emptiness I'd imagined was a freedom. A disconnected life I'd thought of as adult.

Did Yarrow see the emptiness in me? She was geared to strive, restlessly demanding more, pressing the last drop from the grape. But wanting me not to want, to be quiet, attentive, accepting her authority, a fully paid-up card-carrying sidekick.

That night she asked, 'Why do you persist in seeing all this in me? I'm just an ordinary woman. There are other females to whom your verbal offerings would be music. Let's keep our distance and enjoy the fact that we're in the contact we settled into. Your kind of wanting, if I accede to it, gives you a leverage.'

'And you?'

'It's not a mechanical advantage I want. I have a natural advantage.' Her voice was faint. I asked her to speak up, and she did, but soon her voice became distant. A battery running down.

forty-three
peewee prewitt

He had a long thin face, like that pattern of stains on the Turin Shroud, and, like it, far older than his years. I wonder why no one at the time seemed to realise that something wrapped round a face, then unwound, would be extended horizontally? Peewee is thirty-six and still infatuated with Jo-Anne. It took her ages to decide to marry him, she really didn't know why he was so keen on it. The clincher was the expression in his eyes, it was sometimes just the same as that of her idol, Elvis, who was in fact dead at forty-two. Or so it was rumoured, and not just a smart career move. She didn't believe he was dead, he was in hiding, waiting for the right time to come back.

Those Elvis eyes. She read in them a warmth and sensuality that struck right into the cave of her, where the she that was Jo-Anne really was Jo-Anne. As if they spoke. Their liquid brown beauty directed at her. Elvis was huge in his puce tuxedo, and not just one hundred and thirty kilos of lard in clingwrap, and took up most of her sky. Husbands were nearby and earthbound, and didn't sing flame-coloured songs. Peewee just accepted the fact that a female was likely to fall for Elvis after he was dead, and asked no further questions. Elvis was king and ruler of her world, just as death was king and ruler of the wider universe. Peewee thought the routines of ordinary life would see Elvis relegated to the past, just as the same routines see death relegated to the future. But Elvis didn't go away. To Jo-Anne he was more real than the real world. She sang as rarely as the seldom white-throated warbler, but singing wasn't the point.

As in most country towns, there was all the sport you could want in Lost River, and Peewee had played cricket and football, golf, went shooting, skiing in the snowfields or on water at Wyangala, raced his bicycle and motorbike. The country version of the Australian dream: paddling in the water-myth of sunshine, sand, open spaces and everlasting play. As a boy he was all doing, pushing, grabbing, going, running, talking, laughing, like any thoughtless male, never just being, wondering, remembering and still. Then, brown knew him well: the brown of earth and trees, bricks and timber, animal fur and fertile fields. And blue. Always blue. He thought he was a good sort of guy; his old buddies, that he'd deserted on getting married, thought so too. He was very much a man, he felt, and she ought to appreciate him. She didn't. He was an empty seed-cup on a dead branch. There was no sex on the wedding night; she didn't like to think of everyone knowing what they were doing, she said.

Younger, he'd been an ingenious hunter, as bush-smart as the hermit dingo of Gumboil Hill, and found ways to snare rabbits, hares, goannas that no one had thought of. His spiced peewit was grouse, he said. His traps, wires and covered holes saved having to blast away with ammo and scare everything for miles. The violence of hunting, and his sports, were the only assertions of his identity. He shot duck, and held the record of seven dead ducks in the air at once. He lives in Dorset Street, in the middle one of the three fibro houses together, all painted white and cream opposite the newly heritage brown railway station. Religiously, and not just for matutinal stimulus, he cycles his fifty to a hundred kilometres before breakfast each day.

She lives there too, and when she comes home from working in Coles her first visit is to her shrine, which is the third bedroom, which Peewee hoped would one day be inhabited by smaller Prewitts. There she sometimes dances to her god, clothed only in the music of the words that feed her spirit.

Marriage is said to be an attempt to arrange the future. Many people skate or paper over their difficulties, determined to erect a pre-imagined edifice. Eventually the gaps, fissures, internecine criticism, weak foundations have their effect, so if the building doesn't fall under its own weight, often the Gordian knot of marriage is slashed through by the Alexander of divorce, a mixture of metaphors that might parallel the confusion, frustration and misery of the situation. Or they stay uneasily, unhappily, where they are, as many do.

The railways downgraded more country stations at that time and Peewee took the redundancy package rather than wait for the sack. Jobs were rarer than a banker's tears. Real tears, not tears of laughter. For seven years he was unemployed, and each week, on foot with Hoi Yu the dog, he did the rounds of every shop, business and factory in Lost River, looking for work. There were things he could have made, taught, helped with, but he was innocent of the thought that cunning, enterprise and imagination were more valuable than obedience to an employer. He went down, he stayed down.

One day he got the shrine door open—it was kept locked—and gazed hopelessly at the life-sized posters, the Elvis stamps from US mail, the photos of her god in all stages of his spectacular career, the views of Graceland, the questionable photos of the funeral with those ten pallbearers, the lighted area of the little mock stage framing the coloured cut-out of Elvis in white. He heard a noise. Jo-Anne? He turned quickly and barked his shins on the occasional table that supported a forest of pottery memorials to her idol, which made him hop, lively as too much chilli, and head for the door, never to go in there again. The table, with its glass top, was supported by four copies of her god, arms linked and heads thrown back, but all four torsos ended in a point at the waist. Even Elvis had been emasculated. Peewee retained a sharp memory of quotations, interviews, statements, pasted up on various surfaces within the holy place; rows of records and CDs, fan club memberships, more pottery figures, newspaper clippings, dozens of signed photos, a colour picture of a snack consisting of a dozen cheeseburgers, two litres of icecream and two dozen doughnuts, and most of all the life-sized portrait in colour on cardboard, that stood propped upright, the centrepiece of the shrine, lit on all sides by coloured bulbs switched on day and night as a point of principle.

Daily he had the slightly fermented taste of failure in his mouth; life was like digging the foundations of a house with a teaspoon. Nothing had prepared him for this. The female he married that Saturday in June was a different person Monday. Since she made no approaches and attacked when he advanced, there was no chance they'd get together. She wanted all the choice, to hold the reins. He was yesterday's rooster; today she dusted the furniture with him. The dog was doctored, both cats spayed. He had joined their club, and told them often. He felt he got a year older every week. There was no one to talk to about it. His mates never told the truth about their private lives to each other, it would have been all over the town in a day and the details alive till he wasn't. They gave ritual answers, made expected comments according to the jokes they'd grown up amongst.

He had no answer when I asked him why he didn't choof off. A lifelong suicide of the spirit of affection stretched ahead. He said there ought to be a marram grass to bind up and hold together eroding people. Instead of going, he trained the younger cat, a brilliant animal, to ride the dog, a mixed breed who turned a rather stereotyped gentle and Christlike expression to the world, even with a jockey up. Next, he taught the dog to hang from the clothesline by her teeth, but wasn't so successful in getting the cat to jump for the dog's back and hang on. She'd do it all right, seemed happy to, but her claws changed the dog's expression to one of martyrdom and his explosive vocals frightened the bejesus out of her.

Peewee was never able to travel back through himself to root out something he had acquired earlier in his life, when he imagined, then convinced himself, that he found beauty, a strange grace, and an irresistible magnet of attraction in females because they were females, instead of seeing them as other humans like himself, with a few superficial differences, but in regular, or even constant, need of soap and water, lavatories, toilet paper and sanitary pads, deodorants, doctors, dentists, aperients, and constant maintenance. And that was apart from the decorations and alterations they found necessary on account of not being made by God or the genetic lottery quite as they thought they ought to have been made. All that aside, the one who has something you desperately want can have enormous power over you, if you allow it. He allowed it.

He was an ordinary man; he needed a female to be with, share with, to love and listen to, work for and try to please. He'd looked for this prize on the basis of need, not suitability, though who knew what would be suitable? Jo-Anne was pretty, but to him the shape of her legs was poetry. She had a beautiful white forehead, like a blesbok. The smell of her bare skin put in his mouth the taste of ecstasy. She was good enough to eat, and she could certainly do that. She had been honoured in the breech countless times, but for Peewee his first elegiac ride propelled him to the stars. To him there seemed a faint bloom on all her words, as if they were fresh-picked from the tree of talk.

She was endlessly fascinating to him, he couldn't take his eyes off her. He would go to the bathroom door just to see her wash her hands, drawing those long fingers past each other with what he felt, but couldn't express, was sublime grace. He would stand in the doorway talking as she changed from her work clothes just to catch sight of the way she stood on those poetic legs, to marvel at how spotless she was after her day's work, just to glimpse the expressive arch of a foot that had the texture of pale pink candy. And her waist pythoning sideways as she reached for a towel. The warmth of a world of women shone beneath that satiny skin.

Then two things happened.

Peewee was walking the town with Hoi Yu doing his job search when the town power went off. He was passing the offices of solicitor Mike Gledhill, who had handled his purchase of the Dorset Street house, when Mike, in a tearing hurry, appeared at the door. 'Peewee. Would you run this round pronto to Quick, Mammon and Snip, and give it to old Snip?' It was a long fat envelope tied with pink tape. Mike was captain of the cricket team when they played together in A grade, and a front row forward in the same rugby team. Peewee was a winger.

Peewee was so surprised that he took it and ran, dodging and avoiding the little Thursday knots of hillbillies in town for pension day, and several city tourists alarmed to see a rheumatic rustic run. Hoi Yu kept up the best she could. Peewee still had pace.

He was paid in cash, and with Mike's help set up a message service. Mike circularised all the businesses and peewee did the rest. Hand to hand in five minutes. He'd just needed the push. Did a TAFE course, got loads of advice from the small business bureau. His face and spirits glowed like a new car leaving a showroom.

The second thing was that Jo-Anne turned off her idol. The shrine was intact, but the deity doubly dead, and lights out. She began a habit of crying in the early hours. When he asked what was wrong, she said, 'You don't understand.' How right she was.

'The only thing going right is Prewitt Will Do It. I'm into parcels, pick-up and delivery in a big way: food, groceries, fruit and veg, chemists' scripts; I pay bills, run errands, shop. I scout for home-visiting and shut-ins. I get offers for tree-lopping, water-carting, yard-tidying, dog-washing. Didn't know so many people remembered me. It's like I've been seven years in the dark in broad daylight.'

Hoi Yu insists on doing the delivery rounds. She rides on the passenger seat of the new truck, surveying houses and people with little nods and movements of her head like benign blessings. Peewee is in the full vigour of his thirty-six years and it's a whole new life.

As I shut the gate, a boy in the house next door danced his baby brother on the iron verandah railing, singing some crazy song and both laughing. The little kid couldn't stop. It was really funny. Peewee couldn't take his eyes off them, not even when I waved.

As I drove off, my last sight of him was of a man looking and leaning towards the brothers, as if trying to bridge the emptiness between, on his face the outline of a hopeless smile. I've seen that smile on the faces of people collecting small change for the blind or sick or starving of the world.

The tablelands coolness of a May afternoon didn't strike me

until I got back to the church to start on Peewee's cartoon. His story, too, seemed to cool with the cold westerly that fought me till I got inside to the remains of the day's warmth. Like the Quialligo quickbird, that leaves its cry back where it started from, Peewee's story seemed far away.

Making the fire in the potbelly stove, my head was wrestling with memories of having believed in so many things and believed so efficiently, that objects of which I could have no notion whatsoever were real and present to my mind. Beliefs. Theories. Fictions. I asked myself about those things that could be called non-beliefs. Was it a gesture to refuse to have beliefs in certain matters? Or a pointer to further deceit?

Was Yarrow a gesture?

Her next words to me were about love, of all things. She loved everyone equally, though some less equally. It was a matter of concentric circles; those further she loved better. Was she joking? Having a little stir? Again her voice was clear, though not loud. Again it diminished in volume until it became small, intermittent whispers of sound. Fragments. Was she pushing away?

forty-four

edwold & day

His face assembled itself, the texture of cheap carpet, a beige monkey face. At the Gun Fest annual gun exhibition at the showground he handled himself as if on stage, giving impressions. He was Gun Expert, moving in a cocky manner from one exhibit to the next. The beautiful rifles and expensive shotguns were old friends. People moved away, if they noticed him. He had a tendency to lurch sideways and bump thighs. Morrie described him as interesting as Mitchell grass. Duke said he was useful as a pothole.

He'd worked briefly at the Pig, but lacked an essential commonsense. Went on and on about the individual animals, words like spent feelings squirted from his wide, featureless monkey mouth, rubber lips. Couldn't get the idea of pig as raw material, then finished product. As if pigs were citizens, somehow. It made everyone on the killing line uncomfortable, impatient. The Pig was a business; there was raw material, preparation, process, product, market, meal, garbage.

He was in favour of Emma Mitchell's projects, and a bigger town. More customers for his magazine stand. He was on course in life's transit, a leaf in a flowing gutter. The sort of man who, after deciding, was undecided; he took care to dress neatly, and as well as his money would allow, kept himself clean and made a constant effort to appear well spoken. He had seriously good manners, rather old-fashioned, but not many were deceived: the attempts to keep up appearances covered a donkey brain. Fortunately the ears didn't give him away, but they were long and of a yellowish hue with slack lobes suspended, which swayed forward and back as he turned his head: earrings like small puddings. His nose was flattish, the meathead mouth dominated, though the bottom lip revived the donkey likeness. There was a look about him as unlikely as the plain truth.

He was neither tall nor slim; his eyes needed extra lenses. His name was Edwold. He counted his strides as he walked. When he was a boy he made a ladder so his dog Friendly could climb up to his tree house and see more of the world. He still thinks of Friendly, who died the day before Edwold's thirteenth birthday. He was so upset he wouldn't have another dog for years.

Edwold was without friends; unable, since Friendly, to form deep relationships with anything more lively than the dollars in his pocket and his stand in Eureka Mall. As compensation he had beautiful dreams of naked women encountered in the dark, and often woke at night in the grip of an obsessive and damp excitement.

The drifts of people who passed his stand contained many wild creatures and savage children from the hills, but no females who looked at him twice, unless he was slow with the change. Even the malignant cripple who roamed the mall ramming her wheelchair into shins never glanced at him. His longest conversations were with the young in assorted

American baseball, basketball or football caps who tried to con him they'd given him a ten not a five. Kids, all tits and zits.

He invented a whole past to make himself more interesting, bought trophies and had them engraved in a distant town. A gun collection gleamed behind the glass doors of a locked cupboard, he salted his conversation with the phrase 'weapons of death'. Bats, racquets, boxing gloves lived on his walls. He would casually mention his past prowess to prospective acquaintances, but lacked a sense of irony and had no idea of its possession by others. The statuettes, trophies, plaques, chromed football boot and mounted cricket ball kept his spirits up; the slow poison of hope hadn't yet felled him.

Like a spider, he was caught in that web in the open, in the most crowded part of the mall: stuck. Did others live in full view and ignored? No one knew him and that seemed tragic to him. No one would mourn when he fell off his perch, or dropped from his web. He drew back from the throng, half afraid of them. Yet they were a timid population, not fitted to be conquerors, and many wondering why their ancestors came here at all. If only there were still Someone up there to know him, but all that's gone now. No one who was anyone believed it, so how could he?

He loved the sight of women, they were so different from men. From him. Everything about them was interesting, except the ones like him, the dogs. If he saw one that made him say under his breath, 'Get on that, will you? Bloody bewdy!' his eyes mouthed her like the suckers of a squid. He was still optimistic, as if he lived in a world where any drongo might one day date the richest woman in the world.

All he had was Gus, his second dog. Had him since he was a pup. Used to take him to work, but the mall manager complained that Gus left his linear equations on the footpath outside the mall entrance, or even on the affluent surface of the mall itself. Seventeen now, able only to thump his tail on the kitchen floor, and with a vague cloud over eyes that used to be clear and shining. If the tabby cat got into his basket out on the verandah Gus wasn't game to turf her out. Not able, either, even though the cat too was old and and moulting like a superannuated mat. Gus had no conversation, not even a bark anymore. Once under his chair in the corner, the only way to get him out was to put a dog biscuit a metre away. Sometimes he didn't move for so long that Edwold would ask loudly, 'You dead?' Gus wouldn't answer. Edwold suspected that Gus had never bothered to learn English, yet he'd been here all his life. He'd have liked a strong repulsive dog justifying a loud KEEP OUT sign, but such a dog ate you out of house and home, and besides, he wanted people to come in.

Edwold called in one Saturday after he'd closed the stand, to Christopher Cat's, the pie shop and coffee bar, sat on one of the fixed stools opposite the painting of the winged teeth, and ordered his potato pie and coffee, next to a man dressed entirely in plastic. The plastic was highly coloured, mainly a yachting blue with splashes and stripes of red and white, and embellished with streaks of brown which may not have been part of the original design. The man's hands were dirty as he lifted his coffee cup to his bearded mouth. Edwold saw rather a good but uncertain profile, like a corrupt judge. He thought hard, like a full load of blue metal going up Grindstone Hill. This man could be a future companion. A friend. They might turn out to be similar yet different, like two snowflakes. Might get on like bacon and eggs. At least, they could meet here at Christopher Cat's and exchange views.

With all the tact and circumspection of a coathanger bridge-worm making its way past a pronged feral drainpipe snake, he eased himself forward and sideways on his stool and said in what he intended to be a whisper, 'What's new?' It came out with a slight squeak.

The beard turned towards him and imitated his tone. 'G'day

Oigle,' confronting a sight as frightening as bottle-bottom glasses on an old man.

'It's Edwold,' he corrected gently. Still the squeak.

'What is?'

'No, I am.' That was better.

'Well, whaddya know?' It wasn't a question. The man's eyes were dark, and shiny as mirrorshades, his voice like a child's rattle. Edwold noticed some porrigo on his scalp under the nearer border of brownish hair that grew from it.

'It's my name.'

'What is?'

'Edwold.'

The beard opened. The mouth it enclosed laughed. The red lips laughed, the tongue with its rough edges, cracks and scattered bits of pie laughed, the black edging of the lower teeth laughed. This man was a smoker, yet he had no cigarette burning in the ashtray. Perhaps he'd given it up. Still, it wasn't yet a crime to be seen with a known smoker.

'Bullshit.'

'No, Edwold.'

'It's Oigle.'

'All right, I'll be Oigle,' he retreated sportingly.

'Be Oigle? You are Oigle for Christ's sake. Never seen a man more Oigle than you are,' and masticated some of the pastry and meat still lying about on his tongue.

'Who are you?'

'Just little old me.'

'No, I mean your name.'

'Shark Man. Hey, how would you like them for warts over your eyes?' Looking outside.

'Me?'

'Too late. She's gone' And tried to touch Edwold for readies, without success. 'You've got it, I can tell. You'll be eating three squares a day till cardiac arrest. Wimpoid like you.'

'Me? Wimp?' Edwold protested, shocked.

'J Wellington Wimpey, I presume. Don't do your cruet. Where can I get a shave, shower, shit and some shuteye in this town?' He was more like an Amazonian guppy than a shark, but Edwold was a mere tadpole.

A beginning. Edwold felt hopeful. Shark Man seemed to have more than the usual amount of sebaceous lubrication on forehead, temples and cheeks. Still, we're all different. He recklessly offered shower facilities and was offered gratitude.

'That's cool,' said Edwold.

'Cool! It's cryogenic,' said Shark Man, and humble Edwold felt a faint flush of pride that he was with a man who knew words. His instinct was to flow like water, to settle like water, in the lowest place.

Which was where Shark Man kept him when he'd accepted the invitation to come home and where he stayed while Shark Man stayed. It didn't take a genius to see Edwold was as innocent as a puppy on its first visit to the vet. He kept the gun cupboard locked. He knew the exercise of freedom was based on courage and individuality, but he preferred safety to freedom. Even he could see Shark Man, like some of the entrepreneurs of the '80s, would seize anything not welded down.

It wasn't till an official letter came for Mr O Day that Edwold learned his carelessly befriended friend's name. What did the O stand for?

He soon learned that Day didn't have a pot to piss in, his assets amounted to zip, zero and zilch, his favourite brand of anything was OPs. Edwold was in over his head and cursed himself for a pliable pussyfooter. Day was a beach researcher, he checked the poached eggs on display for colour, shape and poetry, he said.

A fortnight later, when Day got back from his court appearance, Edwold found he'd been arrested for friendliness to his fellow man, his habit of embracing tenderly in public places people he thought he recognised. He was suspected of relieving them of responsibilities, usually credit cards and wallets. Nothing had been found on him, he passed the loot on to other members of his ring. There was a small fine on a lesser charge. Did Edwold have a spare five hundred kicking about? A month to pay. With more hide than Jessie the elephant he pulled out both empty plastic pockets of his yachting outfit. 'Here you see two pockets of poverty, short, fat and blind. I'm cleaned out, like a barramundi ready for the pan.' Paid employment was as far from his mind as a drowning millionaire refusing a lifebelt.

Edwold couldn't possibly part with five hundred. I mean, five hundred, that's money. He smiled, but his smile was even more guarded than his wallet. Their lifeblood threatened, even the humblest organisms fight like viruses.

Day threatened to punch Edwold's lights out, to leave heaps of shit in front of Edwold's magazine stand, to spread the word about his unchanging sheets and how Edwold did weird things to him when he was asleep or drugged. Or how he applied a coating of Vegemite to his dong for Gus to lick off.

He made these threats in Edwold's kitchen as his host was cooking their meal, since Day wouldn't cook. Humiliation concentrates the mind wonderfully, and Edwold was frightened, but he realised he should go on cooking for Day's zinc-lined stomach, for it was as a source of food that he was chiefly valued, though Day was grateful as the beggar who spits at your back.

'Bastards like you, short and shitty, deserve to be worried to death by wild priests,' Day finished. Edwold lay awake at night listening to the noise you hear when you're not hearing a noise. At work he fidgeted, nervous and alarmed, as if his big end had had an accident with the wrong end of a shooting stick. He was one of those few in Lost River who had heard of the new laws against detestation on account of race; he wondered whether there was a law against detestation on account of face, for he had begun to hate the sight of Day from the time Day's bladder sounded reveille and he showered rock powder on the bathroom floor and under his arms, to last thing at night when Day's grunge music, played through Edwold's expensive speakers, felt like claws running through his head. The calm surface of life was misleading, it was a tarpaulin thrown over chaos, over a filthy and dangerous swamp. Even speculation about that magic woman Amaza being done for by an evil suppository couldn't restore balance, order and calm to his days, as irresponsible tattle usually helps to do. He felt out of place in his own house, like a partridge up a gum tree.

He saw that Day was under the spell of things and the money that would buy things. Cash, being the essence of things and of other people, was what he desired. He needed to feel as able as others, and cash was the certificate of this equality. Yet at the same time he scorned those who had sweated and sacrificed to get such a start on him, so to steal their essence served them right. He was almost in the position where it was impossible for him not to steal, and well on the way to the discovery that the exercise of his profession was an important factor in social justice.

Several times Day tried to get him into a condition where he might reveal details of his cash, but Edwold was as persistent, and clumsy, as a woolly mammoth moth from Bogong, his clothes and drawers were as empty as the pockets of a rolled drunk.

'Get this into you and sleep on bags,' he said, offering Edwold a glass of a clear liquid with a bluish tinge. Or, 'Eat this and do your trousers good,' when he cooked something appetising as a glass and a half of full cream golly. He would whisper beerily, amid his annoying guffaws, that all Edwold needed was love, and proceeded to make him perform the appropriate actions. He was so casual about his sexual needs and his candle snake that Edwold assumed he consorted with cats and dogs and any stray life he encountered. To get him to cough up he once undressed Edwold saying, 'This dream's on me.' Edwold coughed, but not money. He knew he needed love, but wasn't about to admit anything to this mentally waterproof and spiritually drip-dry person he wasn't game to throw out. He stayed sober. The slightest communication became as innocuous as an HIV test. Gus was no help, he seemed slightly less dead when Day was around. Day found Edwold's stock of unused condoms, which he regularly bought to show the Coles check-out girls he was in the swim. Day inflated and popped them, like frogs in a fire. Edwold was a late arrival at the sad knowledge that all are incompatible.

The day the fine was due, Day was gone. Edwold's tendons became peaceable and relaxed, he felt like the jubilant storm-frog when the storm stops. He was so relieved that, noticing the walls of his house sulking and in tears, he recklessly promised them coats of paint in the near future. For the first time in his life he realised the law had its uses. It was a utility, like a government ought to be. It had got rid of Day. Two police came in and asked for O'Happy Day, his tormentor, to whom mercy would be misapplied and forgiveness misdirected, and he calmly said, 'He's gone.' He became again a harmless docile oyster, quietly processing the flow of life through his sensitive organs. He felt no urgency and less anxiety about having friends or being a schlemiel without a shadow. He stood behind his ramparts of magazines, his face relaxed and with all the shy refulgence of a jackpot winner's smile. His heavenly dreams returned, all nipples and crutches. Not sheep crutches, not pump nipples. It was rather satisfying to be unnoticeable, like bracken on life's hillsides.

They say death is an imaginary place populated by real people. So is absence. Not with the speed of light but at a gallop, the dead and absent disappear from view. Gradually Edwold put Day in an imaginary world where they were the best of friends. Day became a person composed of attractive faults, like a man who, though not handsome, is beautiful because of certain flaws and irregularities. The frictions of their time together he generously regarded as just a fusillade of farts at fate's rich banquet.

As he stands serving customers with their hunger for news of all the things they expect and for no news of what they really dread, I often wonder if he ever thinks of the day when a voice out of the cheerful, self-organising bustle of the Eureka Mall will yell, 'Hey, Oigle!' and Edwold will look down at the grubby desert in the palm of an offered hand and wish himself back to his hillside, unnoticeable among other bracken.

He thought O'Happy a great name. 'Why would he want to keep it quiet?' he said to Howie Gleet when Howie told him Granny was in hospital having her parameters altered.

Edwold still hasn't achieved a relationship with a woman, so boredom is something he doesn't associate with females. He has joined the Family History Association. Some of his forebears were interesting.

My companion was an empty church. I'd got tired of having people around, and kept my head down, putting in all the daylight hours at my loom, and since it was cool kept the potbelly stove alight.

A sturdy young rat came out sometimes into the middle of the floor and, if I kept still, footed up close to the stove and began to make gestures with paws and mouth. I called her Rona the rat after a ratlike woman I once knew. Would I buy some warfarin to give her a stroke. If so, at whom was this gesture aimed? What did I care if there was one rat more or less? Was it aimed at propitiating some household god of caution or cleanliness? Or would I eat Rona? It was unusual here to eat rat flesh, but it was unusual to eat lots of other flesh too, yet it was all edible. Some people were not stopped by the customs and rules of others.

Was it possible for a whole life to be a gesture? A substitute life? And if a substitute, a substitute for what? To be a lifetime of imitating others, fitting in, almost with an artist's perception, with appearances that just happened to be around you?

forty-five

hollywood hossan

Confident, and noisy as an egg-beater on take-off, he watched the caber-tossing at the Highland Gathering, and loomed at the Bride of the Year show at the RSL. The organisers relied on him for regular donations. Politically, he was for both incinerator and new jail. Let a hundred flowers bloom, he said in the *Bugle*.

I was invited to his house, a strapping, vigorous villa on the highest part of the Hill in Wiradhuri Circuit, the high side of the road. There was no sign in the big house that he was ever allergic to the law. Shed and garage held all the DIY equipment you could want.

The Hollywood Funerals boss regularly embarrassed his sons Michael and Peter by recalling in detail how they used to run round at funerals when they were younger, tripping over plaques in the lawn section, or shouting, 'Hey, this one's getting up!' Michael was the brightest boy in high school in his years there, and now away at university.

'Doing law. Be back here one day. Take his pick in this town,' his father asserted. 'Hear about his debate in the regional championships? Should have heard him talk. What was it? 'Those who fight for freedom and justice have as their chief enemy the state and its power.' A quotation from somewhere. Took the affirmative. Killed 'em. Stone dead. Maybe he'll go for politics. At all events, start off in a law firm. Peter makes things. Engineer, maybe. We'll see. Anyway, the best way to make a lot of bread is to start with some, and they will.'

In repose he has a mouth like the hairline scar a good surgeon leaves, but his grin is like a gummy shark's. He has a flattish face with a long heavy jaw; it reminded me of the large-jawed arm-dog bred for heavy guard duty and also attack. He grew up in the suburbs west of Sydney that cluster round the beginnings of the Eel River with a father whose constant saying was, Those who ask don't get and those who don't ask don't want. There was no evidence it made the slightest impression. His earliest memory was of deflowering the neighbours' agapanthus with a whippy stick and ignoring the storm that followed, since words without actions made little impression on him. His next was of standing over kids in the playground at scribble-school for their pocket money, or watching for kids sent to the shop and intercepting their cash, from which he graduated to lending deteriorating money with a bad grace to kids silly enough to pay one hundred percent interest. He was of the social class of those who do what they like, and by fourteen was as ingenuous as an insurance salesman, and crooked as a dog's hind leg, with an early appreciation of the fact that laws were like a shark-net: little fish could always swim through. He was the bright spark that put granulated paraffin in the resin tray of the boxer he bet against one night at Wenty Leagues Club.

Later he rose to become king of the district, in a kingdom that existed just outside the notice of the regular, law-abiding population. Well, they caught sight of that kingdom sometimes, but they should have been home in bed. A passing glimpse was safe enough, but a front-on meeting was as electrifying as watching the radio thrown into your bath with the music going. 'Reclaim the night' was utter rubbish to the ordinary folks: they'd never had it, it was carved up between crims and cops.

His aides and courtiers were knucklemen, wielders of iron bars and sawnoffs, all allergic to law, young men with scrotums full of social disaster, according to some. Though how they knew … Six of them could charge like a dozen riot police, and often did.

For sport he indulged his love of nature. He'd have been in his element if the vague Australian bush had contained unarmed lions and tigers, rhino and wildebeest, but he had to make do with unarmed pigs, kangaroos and foxes, and, on a few trips north, unarmed crocodiles; and once had the privilege of riding along in an egg-beater, potting wild cattle from the air. The cattle too were unarmed and left undisturbed to die in their own time. He travelled in four-wheel drives, didn't much like getting out of the vehicle, and communicated with wildlife over the sights of a Winchester. He was matter-of-fact about death, which perhaps was a vast and colourful painting in which each death was a brushstroke.

After dark, in his territory, he had lots of good and interesting times. Once he escaped pursuers in a coffin, another time in a borrowed ambulance, a 'wounds on wheels', as he called it. Once he and his crew gave concrete gumboots to a dealer who had strayed into their territory. The guy was dead of natural causes—and what more natural than to die after a blast from a sawnoff?—and they wanted him out of harm's way, so they'd be in the clear when the shit came back to shore. Hollywood said it wasn't his doing, they were tidying up. While the cement was wet they ran rods up from the overshoes inside the corpse's trousers to keep him upright in the river. Trouble was, no one missed him. Twice Hossan sent one of the boys down to take a look; both times there was the body, its legs still in the close and passionate embrace of concrete, standing in the mud, dressed and only a little chewed. Hossan expected to hear of fish swimming in the rib cage. 'Should have sat him on a chair. Funnier.' He gave dry axles to enemies who might pursue him and once purloined body parts from the cremmo and cooked a dish, Fricasee of Feet, for a joke.

He began to lose his taste for being king. Still had the nerve, but the resentments of old enemies and the speculative endeavours of a new crop of young cowboys each year, to see if they could beat him with their fists, wore him down. It was natural enough; they wanted to know where they fitted in the scheme of things. No one ever beat him. Like other lion men he was lazy. Let lesser men and ladies labour was his motto, but behind those two fists and two boots he was the best street-fighter of his day in Sydney's west.

The coffin he escaped in, still in the house they used as palace and fort, gave him the idea. He had money, which was a key to unlock faculties you didn't know you had. He also had a Sydney name for emergencies, a public servant in one of the minor state government departments, a man kept relatively free from ordinary duties, who was able for a price to smooth difficulties, and also able to help with advice on dealing with government in the matters of permits and licences. He paid his money and got his entry into the coffin business. He would up stakes, take the boys, farewell his faithful enemies, go to a country town and set up shop. Prudence was as strong a motive as any other.

He chose Lost River since he'd only ever passed through, and took to the undertaking business like chewing gum to a chair. A life of peace and order was a great thing now he was settled and had what he wanted. Hollywood Funerals. There was no danger of Hollywood allowing grey egalitarians to smear over him their universal paste, hiding his natural colours. He was a flamboyant undertaker, just what the town needed, though it didn't know that till he said so, with a cheerful, hearty attitude to death which went over well with the many who had no idea what to think or say when their companions eventually or suddenly ceased, and didn't want to dwell on the images of bodies turning black, green and purple under healed turf, or even to think the inevitable thought that we're all on the nose eventually. Hollywood knew, without needing instruction, that genuine mourners who required real reverence and not synthetic solemnity were a small minority. His own sympathy was as perfunctory as an ex-wife's kiss.

'Happens to all of us,' usually provoked the realisation in the dimmest, not only that it does, but that this time at least it had happened to someone else. With that clear, business could proceed with despatch. Even a joke didn't upset his clients. 'Life isn't all beer and skittles unless you've got the liquor licence at the bowling alley,' he would say to mourners uncomfortably dressed in their best, with that gummy shark smile like a grand final winner looking out over a crowd of supporters.

In spite of doctors' efforts to keep their sources of revenue alive, death was a steady earner. People insisted on dying and new sources of revenue for all business enterprises were slipping and sliding into the atmosphere constantly. His faithful aides fancied themselves at the wheels of long limos, but inside the funeral parlour, Hollywood was more intent on building up their gossamer skills. In effect it was a rehabilitation centre.

For good ideas and jobs well done he'd sling the odd century, nor was he above a little horsing around. 'Give 'em a skirl on the klaxon,' he'd say as they passed an older, staid and envious mortician, with that carefree laugh like a slighted Dobermann about to partake of flesh.

He got on well with a clergyman they called the Reverend Death. Something mucilaginous about his voice and the poured way he moved made a deep impression on clients who usually had only three contacts with a church: at baptism, marriage and death, and on none of those occasions were they aware of what was going on, unless they married sober.

The Reverend Death was a wonderful contrast with Hollywood himself. He gave the impression that each fresh death shook him, as if something terrible and unnatural had happened. The aura that hovers over strong emotion, no matter its motive, helped the theatre of the occasion. They made a good team, the Rev Death bringing a cartoon idea of reverence for and horror of death, and Hollywood's militant optimism and reasonable attitude that none of us has bought a ticket to life, we're all freeloaders, the house is completely papered, so we can't be too upset at the end of the show. His opinion was that trade was a substitute for conquest and pillage, and government a conqueror. Witness the tax office. The structures erected by government around us weren't laws of nature; he was confident he could find gaps when he needed gaps.

His first problem was to stand out from the other undertakers. He copied the birds and went for colour. I thought he might be the usual style-rustler from US magazines, but I was wrong. Black hearses became powder blue, the men wore matching suits, and carried blue coffins. He made departure a time of gloriously banal colour, cheerfulness, almost celebration. The demand for Hollywood-style funerals grew into a demand for special colours: pink, blue, white, gold. The next step was to keep equipment in all four colours, so you could order the gold hearse, blue pallbearers, white casket. Or any combination. Oddly, as with a flamboyant doctor of the past, pink had a great vogue. The all-pink funeral was a sight tourists came from far to behold. Hollywood often preserved bodies a little longer to make a good show on weekends for the tourists. A special for men was the slogan, 'Look broad in your box', an assurance their shoulders wouldn't be cramped to save timber.

He took me to the works to show me round. The preparation room with its strong smell of death, the casket showroom splashed with colour and shine. The uncouth hilarity of some of his unrestrained sportsmen left no space for any awkward squad of the emotions, if there'd been one. Some had equipment and bits and pieces all over the place, like a mad microbiologist's slides.

'Take a shoofty at this,' he advised—one of his helpers whiting himself to look like a drained corpse. Another was mixing ashes with a spoon. Yet another replacing a bean-bag of haemorrhoids bent on escaping. One saying 'snap out of it' to a corpse. A team of comfortable pariahs. He gave them a staff discount for 'eventual need'. I learned that most of them preferred cremation after they saw what happened to the body in the box. Colour changes. They didn't mind the unconsumed bits like ankles and knees being pounded to pieces with hammers. Won't notice it, they said.

For a joke he bought an abandoned operating table for the meal room. They loved it, ate from it, using the blood channels to hold their cutlery. The *Bugle* baulked at many of his advertising ideas, but one that worked well was a scene photographed at the coast: Hollywood and his staff in full rig, bearing a coffin and treading on oyster frames so it appeared they walked on water. The ad for 'Apple-cheeked corpses' ran for only one issue.

I saw workers struggling with disassembled accident victims, heard of corpses melting, and in one instance of two people decaying in a car and melting together; words like necrosis, putresce, mortify, gone bad and skin-slip. And of orange peel skin in the embalming room. There were stories of coffins set up with alarm clocks and snacks; notepads and pencils in case corpses came to later; noises in the box and cries of 'What idiot signed the death certificate?' And the fight over a body with Enterprise Funerals, in which the flesh slid off at both ends and the rival firms held skin instead of tendon and bone.

The next step is compressed cardboard and plastic, to help the environment, he said. And Pet Funerals could be big. The sign above his desk reads, 'Hollywood, for the mother of all funerals', just below a stainless steel Jesus.

'Can I interest you in our new conservative oak casket?' The humour gleamed in his eyes like the flash of a turning shoal of pilchards.

'Won't need it for a while, with any luck.'

'Suit yourself. Have a safe safari.'

'She'll be castor.'

I see him, or a descendant, on planet five of Alpha Centauri, advising the planetary police out of his considerable experience on payroll hijacks. In the meantime his earthly wife has developed a taste for opera and regularly travels to Sydney to enjoy what, to Hollywood, is a series of noises shrill and incomprehensible as the whistle used for piping visitors aboard naval ships. 'Going up in the world,' he sighed with regret.

I took away an image of Hollywood as a magic transformer. Ideas came to him at low power, were processed inside him, and emitted with far greater power. A reversal of the usual energy cycle. Sometimes I've wished I was weaving panels of Ming luxury, silk tapestry with gold thread, but was that a gesture too?

And were all the instances of my liking and admiring other people, or other anything, were they gestures, badges I thought it would be good to wear? Signals I was sending? How much of waking time was an effort to curry favour, to be approved, to be similar, to fit in? Were my passions pretence? Stances I took? Attitudes I could approve in myself, and felt would compare well with the attitudes of others I respected?

Yarrow, I could be a breeze, to touch your face, blow through your hair, surround you. A radio at your bedside, to watch you sleeping, hear you breathe. A book for you to hold.

forty-six

king khan

There's a job for him permanently on offer at the Pig. He tosses the caber at the Highland Gathering, his mother is an Anderson from Maitland, and he's one of two brothers who have nothing to do with each other. He has a mouth like two sides of a street containing only white houses. At the Show he's won the tomahawk-throwing five times and the dwarf-throwing once. Millie wouldn't let him do it again.

Even as a little boy he was tough as an Illawarra square dog, and so big for his age that Miss Powers, his first teacher, called him her Towerchap. Of all the kids she took on excursions he was the one who most enjoyed the zoo; he spoke to every animal, from the camels, deer and emu to the sad gorilla, bored monkeys, dusty elephants, lonely tiger.

Grandfather Khan lived in the Territory and worked with camels, as his father before him had done. The King's father was a wanderer and did labouring work town to town, settling in Newcastle long enough to have children with Scot-proud

Marie in a rented fibro cottage, and a fairly steady job with a council gang working on the roads. Mum described him as having 'a heart as big as the great outdoors, but he ain't got a brain in his poor old head.' She picked up the words from a movie, but picked up Dad from a dance. She used to say blood was thicker than water and that was why relatives seemed thicker than other people. Dad died at forty-eight, his life united with the larger universe, and had a great funeral, if only he'd known. Took ten men to carry the beer. After four hours steady drinking Grandfather Khan appeared, described an imaginary soak, and vanished. They all saw it.

The King did some wandering, then got married to Millie Murray of Penrith and moved to Lost River for a job with Dale, a mate of his from the same football team, who started a business in stone, slate and exposed aggregate. They both had a beer and played pool at the Shearers Arms, where the King was king. Deeper than that, he went there because it was there that he really amounted to something. He was proud of his Aboriginal descent, but reluctant to think much about it, at least in public. He was himself, rather than part of others. He was also a fighter and tough as that tool engineers used to shape mild steel. An atmosphere of hard-edged reality accompanied him, like the atmosphere of a bullfight, or a cement-gun in action.

In some miraculous way he managed to keep his pub exploits dark at home. He never came home drunk, and Millie appeared to accept that a man of his sort would go to a pub to be with his friends. The odd thing was that his two little boys would inspect his knuckles now and then. They knew. If there was a contusion anywhere on his brown skin he would merely say, 'Argument,' and leave it at that. He never raised his voice at home, at work, or in his kingdom. It was said that the only time he was big-headed was when he glanced into a distorting mirror at the Show.

Millie worried about him and money. He was a bad shopper and often paid too much. 'You're so guilty that you've got money in your pocket that you try to give them as much as you can,' she told him. It's because he was poor, as a child, she told herself, and smiled when she saw the enormous brown hands handling the fluffy yellow day-old chicks, which were his hobby. His domestication was essential to the little family's survival and progress, and he was happy with that.

He was an ordinary husband. When she tried occasionally to be too dominant, quietly insistent at first, then more strident, he defended by closing down, not responding. He was consciously not one of the bastards who would hit women.

As anywhere else, in the pub there were the strong and the weak, leaders and followers, builders and destroyers. The King was of the ruling elite, his natural level among men of strength and violence. He was always ready to fight, and because of that rarely had to, but sometimes when the night sky, as it gets in the tablelands, was a deep blue like a bruised eye in full colour, and it was the time of the crimson gambit, the words would be heard, 'Out of his way, give him a fair go,' and the King, with a look like the crack of a stockwhip, would take a second to weigh his opponent's height accurately, and his reach, and begin to fight lyrically, the onlookers fascinated by the sprung rhythm of the punches, usually straight as line of sight, and the reflexes, sharp as a wagtail's. But the episode would be more than a bit of a box-on, and end with the opponent, who had travelled to the pub for this very trial, in less than sparkling condition. As the old saying had it, it would be a case of the roof of his arse caving in, followed by a rush of cold shit to the brain, and the King would still be king. Lesser men like Forrester had gangs and followers: the King was splendid and solitary, out on his own like a country milestone.

The huge whisper that there was a fight on would bring a

rush of patrons, like seagulls after a returning fishing boat, out the back of any knuckly bar to watch. Alert eyes and painful smiles would follow each exchange, each onlooker living the fight, riding each punch, just as the football watcher in his lounge room sits on the edge of his sofa and now and then moves and gestures in tune with the action on the televised field. Often dozens shared the same fight in the carpark, just as millions boxed, played football or drove racing cars at a high standard from a safe distance.

'I have an old feeling,' he said, 'that I'd like to have been one of the first black farmers, but I haven't got what it takes. Like the town too much, being near people, being an employee, the grog and the pub. It'd be good to own land and rent it out; is that being a parasite, like Dad said whites were? Over the other side of the puddle in America, the Oonala, the Sioux nation, I read in the papers, are farmers now and go to school and look like everyone else. We will, eventually, when all this dies down. I'm not having my kids running round the bush with nulla-nullas. I know I've run away from spirit things, but the stories I know are all white stories. You have to be honest about what made you.

'No one can say I built nothing. Look at this shed I put up. Own design. Worked out the zincalume and Oregon and the bolts. Love bolts. Something complete about bolts. Did the concrete floor myself. Place for the tools, mower, Ryobi. Plus the chicks. Two days old, this lot. Pretty little buggers, aren't they?

'So. I'm me first, a voter second, part-Aboriginal third, plus Afghan and white. The stone and slate, I feel, is just a matter of rearranging the old rocks, not destroying. Even the aggregate from the gravel mine still contains fragments of the old spirits. I feel a kind of loyalty to the old culture; it was primitive and complicated at the same time, it fitted us and the land. No cities, no written records, no gardens to speak of, nothing permanent, only boundaries and ritual. And the sharing was compulsory. I reckon that part was invented so no one could get above the rest, and the old men hit any new ideas on the head so things'd stay the same. Yeah, a kind of loyalty, but these white ways are stronger. Neat little house, job at the stone and slate, kids well dressed, we sit on chairs, eat off plates, no elbows on the table. And a car to take us to the coast. You get some things together and you can better yourself. Staying equal means staying poor. Sharing everything sounds fine, but some are on the take all the time. I'll take these ways any time.

'I believe my people thought sex had nothing to do with kids. That means they had virgin births all the time, far as they knew.'

That fight today. One o'clock. Acker Borg.

'What's the time, love?' he called to Millie who was busy checking work she'd brought home from the finance company last night. Spreadsheets, she said.

'Too late for regrets.'

'Very funny, darl.'

'Half past eleven. You finished talking yet?'

'No. When do you pick up the kids?'

'Soccer finishes at twelve.'

As she left she commanded, 'Don't drink too much,' as she always did. 'I don't want some horrible person bashing you up in the street.'

'No, dear.'

'Don't just say No, dear, make sure you don't.'

'Yes, dear.'

'And don't keep saying Yes, dear.'

'No, darling.' He was wary of too many words, they were

handles for people to grab and pull apart the whole gist of what a man meant. Even a little wife could spin you in circles with words.

'Funny being able to think with the black and the white parts of me. Maybe I fight with the Afghan bit. We whites evolved ways to feed large numbers of people. I can't ever go back. I'm a sort of, what is it, exile from three lots of homes. I'm a stranger to the bush. This is the country that knows me, with shops and streets. I smoke tobacco, not pituri. I've never walked behind the wind, wasn't twice-born, raised to full knowledge in the tribe. I'd be a liar to say I believed in the Rainbow Snake, or Bula, or spirit children coming out of rocks and choosing their mothers. And if blacks were bosses I wouldn't take too kindly to being told as a white that I must retain my religion and observe sacred sites.

'Better put the old runners on, feel lighter on the feet. This work shirt'll do, might get a bit of claret on it, bung it in the wash when I get back.'

The roses are dog yellow and scar pink along the side entrance to the Shearers Arms. Regulars sit outside in the beer garden, a jukebox in the bar is going. The big fight is up on the dartboard notice. King v Acker Borg. The space where defeat will come has been left free of cars, the dusty bitumen is lavishly painted with cool June sunlight. The King feels the power of his arms as he walks. For some reason it makes him think of the enormous domestic power of his little Millie and how it seems to have such a good effect on the two boys

Acker Borg is unknown in Lost River. Campbelltown was his last stop, he won there. He travels round, challenging, trying to find who he is. He says he won't take no shit from no one, and has the scars to prove it. One long slash from right temple down the cheek to the spread nose, cuts above and below the lips, thick scarred lumps above his yellow–grey eyes, one of which will be badly damaged today.

The two men face each other in the square in the carpark. Both sincere and direct as attacking guard dogs. The King, as usual before a fight, feels all his veins are full of light, instead of the sagging darkness noticeable on days when nothing happens.

The fight lasts longer with abrasive bare knuckles, and there's more blood than with damaging and brain-deadening gloves, but then it's over and the shallow cuts make the damage look worse than it is. Both have experienced hands, and don't risk their bones.

As he put him down for the last time, flat out like a traffic accident, the King muttered, 'Take it you honky bastard,' surprising himself. His nostrils flaring like the dinomakera, the air pounding like a hard-worked heart. The words 'Black shit' came from the red mouth of the fallen challenger. He'd go on testing himself for a few more years yet. How much can I take? was the permanent question. Beaten, his tongue ran out like a shy furred animal, licked blood. Helpless as a stranded jellyfish, taut as wet toilet paper.

'Funny how, when the chips are down, the black in me comes out, and I feel this Gubba's shoulderblades are on the thin skin of bitumen that separates all of us from the sacred soil of my people, and I'm acting kind of in an official capacity.'

The deserted arena looks pathetic. Spatters and little red pools sinking into the bitumen. What was it for? Hierarchy and its resulting order? Are heroes monsters now? Losers wash the blood off at the back tap and breast the bar. He'll need to see about that eye, but it's back in its socket now. Once or twice he twitches like an agitated kangaroo spider, and he orders anothery, cautious and thoughtful as a car driver at the approach of police. Two soused hostiles make remarks, but he's too big to take notice of shit. He could wipe the floor with them, anytime.

The King picks up his beer, looks across at Borg. Just a Gubba. Garbage. Probably a few white ants up top. That book he read once, blokes burning the bastards, burning Alice and Darwin. Not the way to go, yet in the back of his mind lives the sadness of the black part of him, of his people who lost so much, so much blood sucked down into the earth, and are still so stunned by the loss that no amount of welfare, concessions, improvements or money has made them even slightly more happy or contented with their lives. Would it be better if, as in Ireland, the blacks insisted the strangers got out? Nothing's final.

Freedom, he thinks, is like an ocean. People paddle in the shallows.

To his mind's foreground comes again that sheepfarmer McNab from the southern ranges who beat him in the caber-tossing. Pity McNab didn't have a beer in the Arms. Good to have a man like him around. An equal. They'd got on well together. Not too many he could talk to on level terms. None, in fact. Dale was taken up with management now the business was expanding. Pat was getting involved with that Betty, and Tum Tums. A good feeling to be with someone like yourself. Those ginger-haired arms had power, though legs and lower back were the real engine. Getting a bit soft, I reckon. Being king'll have to do me.

Sometimes when he looked into himself he saw an older man, hair grey, one day going down gladly under a fair punch when he didn't need to, just to help some decent young bloke feel great. To signal the end of a reign. Retirement. Oh well. Time was like a winter wind that wore away the world. Maybe he'd do it one day when he heard pigs playing piccolos.

With his cartoon in front of me my thoughts returned to my own conflicts. Were all the promises I'd made, even to myself, also gestures? Were even such things synthetic? Images I wanted to stamp on myself? And the convictions? Yes, I had convictions once, there were things I passionately believed, political choices I made which, at the time, seemed to describe the me inside.

There were people populating my past who deserved more love than I could give. And now there was Yarrow. Were convictions, beliefs, choices, loves, all gestures? Postures? Was Yarrow? If so, whose gesture was she? Her own? Her parents'? Or a gesture made by some reality behind the commonplace we see and handle? I was putting actual things, people, actions, feelings, into words, then comparing the phenomena with the words that tagged them. No wonder everything seemed to be gesture, unreal, artificial: words rarely fit comfortably with things, as Duke saw with his white ball hitting the red.

Words follow lamely after happenings and processes, thoughts and feeling, trying desperately to keep up, but failing always. The verbal sphere and its logics is a different universe from the world where things take place.

But how could a weaver begin to understand such things? He couldn't understand a fellow human he dreamed about. To be under the one sheet with her. Thinking of her every chance I got and melting like butter into crumpet. Wouldn't she like to have been enjoyed? Was there still a chance I'd catch up with her and find her not as sure as she was about the desirable distance between us?

I wish we were a knot. To clasp and be together so long that I smelled of her and she of me.

forty-seven
treesha khalal

With bobbins charged and waiting, I took a last look over the cartoon for Treesha's section of tapestry. I'd had a superficial meeting with the family and a satisfactory talk with her alone, supplemented by a few quiet words from people who knew the husband.

Talking to Treesha alone was tasting a cup of poetry out of doors, and finding it fresh and sparkling as dew on roses. A sharing of the mind of summer while wintry July attacked. The way of her speaking put a shine on that ungraspable relic, the passing moment, whether she spoke of concrete surfaces with sandgrains showing, or her desire to have enough books in the house for her children to swim in. Within her family, her religion and her history, the world seemed a comfortable fit. From a secure base, her mind and efforts radiated outwards. Because she knew who she was, she put her whole self into all she did.

When she was pregnant the first time, and again when her first-born was in her arms, she was lifted above the town, became for a time part of the winds, higher than Explorer's Hill. She knew then what thoughts forests think, understood the speech of trees and joined in their song-murmurs. They told her of trees' night-feelings. She heard the prayer of the brown hawk on the fence wire before it flew. Treesha looked back on the pain of the birth as her own soul being born anew.

After telling me this, she added that still she was trying daily to learn the names of things her parents knew. She had sat me down in the lounge room and looked out briefly. Such beauty, from ignorant winter. The snow grew a thicker coat outside the house, the garden white, and the street, which was bordered by bare trees like maps of river systems. And inside, in the warmth, another joyful pregnancy, another fresh start in the sacred life of mankind, another time of a mother's pain, which is an honour under God, and to be nursing a child who will be guided to the right path. And a future voter with real teeth, as her breasts anticipate.

Other things don't seem so good when you've had them home a week, but babies got better for Treesha. Another baby! That will make three little bodies from hers. Moh would like a boy, she feels sure. She hopes it will be a boy. Again she will be the sucked one, femina. As her mother says, who lives with them, and her sister too, the one who felt the pain shows the love.

She will go along to Nursing Mothers, who made her so welcome the last two times. And when the girls go to school, she'll take her turn in the tuckshop and see them among their schoolfriends. By then yashmak, hijab and chador will be more common in the schoolyard.

I thought, watching her, that she had the self-possession that could see her translated without surprise or embarrassment to the lounge-cum-reception room of a large brothel adorned with the presence of unoccupied and not altogether dressed employees sitting around bored, waiting for business to pick up.

Treesha works part-time at Naughty Nighties; when the baby is older she will have five and a half days' work a week. God be praised for her sister and mother, both willing and happy to help. Rivers shall run at their feet in the Gardens of Delight. The girls at work are wrong, she won't be a restaurant for the new one and a chef for Moh. Her life isn't like that. She possesses a secret no one told her, that by loving service and by sacrificing to some degree her wants, she has attained a freedom that mystifies others. Many know the secret but none has been able to explain it.

Yet the one who adapts and obliges is not the underdog, but has the initiative, the whip hand, since all concessions can be withdrawn, all agreements cancelled: one of the reserve powers of the compliant.

She feels no rancour that she is the woman. A man can't be blamed for being a man. He works late a lot. Other men aren't as willing to work long hours as Moh is. She has spent time studying him. She's learned there's a lot he says that it's wise to ignore. She has gauged the daily rise and fall in his sexual readiness. Well, she had to, or be taken by surprise. The extra work makes him less ready, which is natural. Perhaps a man is the earth, a woman the moon. She isn't one of those women who measure how much the man loves them in order to judge whether it's worth loving back.

She wonders if it's possible to know things you have no direct evidence for. I tell her Einstein had not a scrap of evidence for his theory; evidence came when it was tested, though hints in the work of predecessors assisted his imagination.

She switched tracks and said that once she thought Moh was the strong one, who never deviated from what he intended, and she the weaker, a pale copy of the man, like the female guileless audience bird discovered on the far edge of Gubba Dam, apparently fascinated by the presence of humans, particularly when they spoke. Now, there were reasons to believe she was stronger than she thought. Apart from her private reasons, she overheard the manager say, 'A hard nut in a soft shell,' and knew it was of her. She hugged the sentence to herself.

I checked with her and, yes, she had discovered that her niceness had been taken for lack of confidence, her body language with its appearance of hesitation and tentativeness mistaken for ignorance of what was being dealt with, and her soft voice translated as both ignorance and uncertainty, by men whose ways had been formed in ruthless competition with other ruthless competitors, all of whom felt that firmness, or loudness, and the appearance of up-front confidence were signs of competence.

Yes, she said, getting back to her point, a woman is only half a woman if she's not strong. She had thought she'd need strength when she was a girl coming to a strange country, but the headscarf and long cloak protected her, giving a kind of prominent invisibility. If the boys couldn't see much of you, you weren't there. It was like the invisibility in a country where privacy was more valued.

Treesha appreciated the healthy flush of individualism that comes with greater freedom from government, secular or religious. She needed no philosopher to tell her to avoid blueprints for the future: she knew children rarely wanted what their parents chose.

Moh looked like being late tonight. Would he be thinking of sex? Probably not. So many things she had learned. Modesty has no place in bed, for instance: bed is for the hot animal, not the cool, white-skinned lady. Then, nakedness is more than naked, it's the real beneath the camouflage.

Why did he call her unpredictable? She didn't feel at all unpredictable. 'Unpredictable as a ball-bearing beetle.' Crazy things he says since we've become Australians. She had cooked the Turkish dish tonight, the Swooning Imam. Imam Bayildi. Two glossy eggplants can be seen in the kitchen on the white-topped bench, near a pile of tomatoes and several Meyer lemons. Steel pans and cooking tools shine like polished gems on the snow-white enamel of the stove.

She watched her two little daughters. What alarms, disappointments and pain were ahead for them? Treesha was in no doubt that existence was neither terrible nor absurd; it was the winning of the primary lottery. Nor did she consider individuals to be ends in themselves, rather conduits for other lives to get here, and once here, to receive. At the other end of life, death was a tide full of souls, advancing, retreating. Life entering a new phase without boundaries, like air.

The snow was still swishing down outside, swirling in all directions like small feathers in the light, compressed breeze. Before the snow began she'd been outside and seen the low clouds dropping. Coming to bring the world gifts.

It was good, looking back, that they hadn't leapt conjugally into debt, except for the house. For the rest, they waited till they could afford things, like the car. Life was short, debt long. Their first baby had for her cot an open suitcase on a chest of drawers. Now, with their little family well on the way, it all made radiant sense. Naturally they wanted there to be not too many differences between them and their neighbours; in the matter of possessions, most people like to feel fairly equal. Such a lot of life was other people, just as many of the simplest things were the most important. She wasn't unduly impressed by so-called needs; her native wit told her needs were elastic, could expand to the infinite and become insatiable.

There would be time for stories if the girls went to bed before he came home. Cinderella and her slippers, perhaps. Ali Baba and the forty thieves they liked too. They loved rituals; stories, dressing, washing. Rituals helped you feel clean and in order, kept the confusion and mystery of the world at a distance for a while.

She looked at the white outside, and him late again, on such a night; her two thumbs burrowing into her fists' cages of fingers. They didn't seem to be all that much better off for all his work. But they would be. She'd see to it. Her hands relaxed and she touched the silver coin medallion on her wrist, with its inscription, 'To Ardeshir, of divine race, be peace.' Only a copy, of course. But all coins were copies.

In the cant of the present day it is said that all people have all evils in them. I don't agree. Treesha was among others I've known who have little of any evil buried in them. She could be one of the angels fired to earth from heaven's cannon. When she loved, it was with the love that feels part of the other.

She knows of those, in a small minority in the world, who have banished guilt, thrown over responsibility for themselves; for whom self-control is an unnatural act and discipline a sexual innuendo, while she lives by them. The minority acts as if no God exists, which is foolish. How then can they have access to the invisible world, and how know the comfort of God growing more human every day, changing as we change? Even doubt has gone for them, so they support the unutterable burden of lives with not the slightest significance. Mere numbers in a population count. As if they live in a universe where no objects are made from other objects, but all is separate and repels all else.

Once God hadn't been specialised enough, then he was, and became quite single, even narrow. But now was a time of broadening, of diffusing, for Him.

Parallel to her official faith Treesha had another, older religion, in which she paid respect to the minor gods of cleaning, washing, ironing, folding and putting away neatly in sweet-smelling drawers. There were household gods of order, of having furniture in a pleasing pattern, of hanging washing outdoors to capture the perfume of sunlight. There were deities of respect for cleanliness, for cutlery that shone, for mirrors, for crockery shining white and clean. She intuited gods of place in the garden, gods in the timber of floors and furniture, in the metals of utensils, heaters, the car, even the electrical wiring. She was surrounded by objects, all of which contained their share of the sacred. And certainly there were special presences in Moh's heavy wrenches, spanners, drills and saws. Even in all those tins of bolts.

The official monotheism in which she grew up was a human tidiness in which the people were standardised; it wanted to be final for her, but she broke through. Something in her knew no standard humans existed: her sum of gods would be different from the gods of others. As would her martyrs, in daydreams, of imaginary religions.

In this weather Moh's tools must be cold to work with. She remembers the smell of work, of oil, of maleness about his toolkit, with its slightly greasy, slippery steel tools. Theirs was a dull, heavy shine; no care was spent on making them gleam like new. How they sparkled at first. But their daily use was sacred, too. So formidable they seemed, repository of many male secrets. He was not a spiritual man. She kept from him her secret religion, along with her efforts to fail her way closer to the god they partly shared.

Reaching from the white-blanketed world, the arms of trees slapped the windows. There was no traffic in Macquarie Street, no animals in sight. 'Yet there is not a creature on the earth whose sustenance is not provided by God. He knows its dwelling and its resting place.' The holy words comforted her. Thinking of them turned over her life's soil so that the drops from heaven got down to her roots.

It came into her head that death, all in all, was a good thing.

Where did that come from? Yes, somehow satisfying that all die and live together in paradise, reclining on soft couches, to feel neither scorching heat nor biting cold, instead of getting older and older, having to be tended like helpless babies.

She began to introduce the girls to the idea of bed. Outside, the hush of falling snow deadened the world. She let the girls play their last game with their woolly toys, wooden fruit and empty teacups, blank plates. Their carpet was littered with ducks, dogs, rag dolls, cloth books, plastic blocks and pyramid pieces, all colours, and a pink rabbit; all of them often persons, each deserving respect and consideration. There are no shadows in the children's warm room. When the last story is over, both are asleep. They will not see the darkness when the light goes out. The church bells have stopped ringing from their wooden belfry, the practice has finished. Perhaps new bell-ringers are being taught; some of the sequences were unusual.

On the mantelpiece the family copy of *The Recital* watches over the room. There is no dust on its cover. Treesha sets the table, white crockery on white cloth. Silver and glass shine. She puts his grape juice near his place. Mother and sister will be home shortly from their visit. Another family settled in Lost River, from a town not far from theirs in the old country. Her mother will call a cab. She anticipates the strength her mother will radiate when she is home, like a covering, getting into all her crevices, expanding her, lifting her up, taking all tiredness away. A mother's extra name is Endurance.

From the oven bread appears, and the silver bread knife from its drawer. A glow spreads from plates, glasses, silver, and the crisp and snowy tablecloth. She can almost hear the *zisk*! of knife against glazed china. She puts more wood on a happy fire. God is in the simplest things: laying the fire, putting on the kettle, hanging out the washing, watering the plants, eating together. God gives freedom: to love and to detest, to be obsessed or relaxed, to flow like water or be immovable in devotion, whether to people or to the invisible. And the greatest prayer can be silence, in the world's confusion.

She had her own thoughts about God, and perhaps this was a further branch of a religion personal to her, and thought that often God was an It, not a He: a space without dimensions, a depth without distance, and that this It was internal to her. Further, she felt that each new life, from bacterium to baby to star, was God opening Itself, a Whole exfoliating in a myriad individuals, events, annihilations, new beginnings. 'Extend the list as you like,' she said. 'Salvation is not the point. In this sense we're all saved: we're here. Existence is salvation, and the deepest mystery. Any further salvation is a matter of personal taste or need, an internal adjustment, how we apprehend the rest of God.'

So the explanation of the universe was in us. When the new baby comes she will point to him and say, 'This explains everything.'

'So,' I said. 'You have Allah within you.'

'The word God will do.'

'Why do you have this faith?'

'I was born into it. I came to believe it later. Let me put it to you as I think of it. Look at the world. Present atheistic science is the great absurdity; it thinks it's the whole story, when it's only a chapter. The more marvels are uncovered, on the tiny scale or the immense, the more wonderful the universe is. Daily more marvellous. Now if there's no It, or Person, or unimaginable form of consciousness to have charge of it or to have begun it, then we representatives of consciousness and of life—and life is surely the most marvellous thing of all—together with whatever life has arisen elsewhere, are the greatest and most advanced happenings in the whirling universe. Greater than the processes that produced us. Which is absurd. Especially absurd to a woman with two children and about to have her third baby.'

'Why do so many smart people reject this god?'

'Because this intellectual minority think they can contain in words things that overflow words. Also they forget we're not God's equals, but children.'

Last night she dozed off in bed, reading. Moh climbed into bed and was soon asleep. How he worked. She holds her breath in both hands while she goes to take another look at the girls. God is forgiving and merciful. Anyway, if Moh did play it would be as his father told him: only sheilas, my boy, never nice Muslim girls. Treesha looked at her arm. Is the soul inside the skin? How far inside? Is the skin part of the soul? Would his soul be less if his skin strayed?

In a way, I dangle from a cord. How to express it? The cord is part of me, and I spend my life dangling. The cord can be pulled, this way and that.

But to me she was far more: steady as a flow chart, enigmatic as a modem, complicated as a tapestry, powerful as a mouse manipulating many megabytes.

Moh climbs out of bed. He feels rather than hears the heavy, damped-down silence of snow, like the forced silence of a watching crowd in a sandy square on the other side of the planet waiting for the punishment to begin of one who has strayed from the Law.

This life is short, why not add some spice to it? Who knows if there really is a paradise to get your tripes twisted about?

Carmen pulls the bedclothes tightly around her nakedness. If he goes quickly she can attend to warming the house properly and getting her tea on. And rehearsal later. He checks that there's no lipstick on the dipstick.

They don't speak as he dresses, and it's just a 'see you' as he goes from a house that empties as he leaves, that he feels is without substance and, once out the door, almost without existence. He finds no reason to look back. The time has long gone when her kisses were the sort to suck out your brains, when she was kinky as a used rubber band.

His feet are heavy, they drag in the snow; the car, cold as a snowman's dick, starts reluctantly. God is compassionate.

On the short drive it occurs to him that where before, this woman used to demand more words from him than his feelings could support, now she had run out of steam, and found it hard to talk. When she did talk, she said nothing. Just animal stuff. Gossip. Lies about some Mrs F. A woman in blue.

Tapering off. Beginning to see her as all gristle. Then what? Then it will be part of the past, the long past that contains the moment when the Prophet ascended on his horse Al Borak. The past when white Marengo bore the Corsican monster on his back. Make it up to Treesha. Take her and the girls to the races, they love horses. The Winter Cup, yes. Snowflake has a chance, might even start at sixes.

God is compassionate. And merciful. If only the stairs to paradise stretched further than Macquarie Street.

Treesha was a lighthouse, a tower casting a light. I began to work.

If my choice of work, my tapestry-making, was a gesture in the form of a brand I'd decided to put on myself, a way of differentiating myself from others, was Treesha's faith also a gesture? Were some people real, with a reality beyond gesture?

In Yarrow's latest communication her voice was just strong

enough for me to hear a few sentences. 'What do I expect to achieve?' she asked. 'Very little. The achievement is in the effort. I still question everything. In my dreams I see nothing left standing …' Her voice had faded.

I was left remembering I'd never seen her with flowers, had never once lain with her, not one kiss, and certainly had never been a dolphin diving out of the water and down into her warm sea.

What made me so attached to her? Why had I become so woman-mad?

As I worked into the night the shadows in the church encouraged another shadow: that deeper transgression, worse than murders, that haunted me without giving me concrete images of its shape and face.

forty-eight

wayne door

'He's changed,' his mother said. Her face blended with the biscuity wallpaper. In texture too. Wayne, her youngest, so different from the other boys. He was related to nineteenth century bushranger Admiral Moonlight, the one who was always at sea.

If an anchovy wormfish had been genetically developed and was now swimming in Lake Eucumbene, it couldn't have been more of a surprise than when little bungle of joy, Wayne, that she didn't know she was carrying, poked his biggish head out into the peculiar light of the delivery room, and after the head, this funny little slippery body sliding out of her like meat out of a chute. April the first, the only birth where she laughed. Six pounds. And the other three so hefty.

His brothers imparted valuable knowledge, showing him an elephant beetle pulling a splinter, how to tell a scissors-grinder from a wagtail, how to skull-drag a fish, told him to get up straight away when he came a gutser, how to yell 'Pull ya head in!' and 'Carn the Rivers!' and how to pee up against the muzzlewood tree without being seen, then left him alone. He seemed to have few talents and even less assertiveness, but bearing in mind the noise, chaos and mischief precipitated by those with few talents and enormous assertiveness, perhaps it was no bad thing.

His brothers got him a Pulamalong satellite dog, which needs a leash even when asleep, but it was too strong for Wayne, so they gave it to the youngest cousin they could find, a Gleet.

Several times Mum threw him joyfully in the air, prepared to catch him again, but just as often he poured his most recent nourishment over her from a height, and also, due to the liquid slurry arriving first at hand and face level, he slipped from her arms and said hullo to the planet with unwelcome speed. The last time that happened, he ran for the safety of the backyard, where he kicked at one of his brothers' basketballs until he found an old cricket ball in the grass by the back fence. It became his friend, slept under his pillow, and was always willing to play when he wanted a game.

Greg, his eldest brother, on a brief visit home on his Yamaha, noticed the ball, and when April Fools' Day arrived Wayne was the possesser of a brand new cricket ball, lovely and red, with its six white rows of stitches fine for his fingers to go over and turn this way and that and generally love. It was too good to hit the ground, so he kept it for holding, and played with the old one.

Well on in primary he tried out for the cricket team. He had no gift for pushing himself forward, and selection seemed to rest as much on pushiness and self-evaluation as on any perceived talent or keenness of eye, but he made it to a kind of second team, where he mixed with the willing but unwieldy.

At home he bowled in the backyard, aiming for a white marker placed in the spot where Greg told him a good length ball would hit. The family were innocent of any theory to the effect that human worth is not commensurate with achievement but with uniqueness, but allowed him freedom to be different, to be unique, just as if they'd had the theory down pat. Eventually a teacher noticed he could run rings round his companions in the matter of bowling, and he joined the first team. The field was rarely set for his style of play, and many catches from his leg-breaks went to ground.

One Saturday afternoon he wandered, throwing his ball from hand to hand and spinning it up in the air from the back of his hand just like Shane Warne, and had gone past the Yoshilos' boomerang factory when he came too near boys doing something with a dead and eviscerated cow. They, like anyone else, would do whatever they thought they could get away with; they put him inside the cow. In he went, ball and all. He was inside for perhaps years and in that time a terrible fear concentrated itself in him, so great that all he could do was helplessly let it invade him. He was numb, his head felt runny like melted chocolate. They let him out when they'd got tired of waiting for him to yell, he recognised Big Bill Miller and his mates, and ran. It was a while before he mentioned the ordeal at home.

After four years of high school he stopped going there and went to Kimberly Konkrete like Mum said, and the man there, a friend of Mum's, gave him the job of looking after the grounds. He was sixteen and in a district junior team, but lacked something, perhaps the spitefulness and aggression that the very best bowlers have, the detestation, the hatred of that enemy protecting his wicket with a lump of wood. In the empty moments as he fielded at fine leg he imagined bowling sinkers, floaters, top spin, back spin and a nasty ball that curved in towards the batsman, hit the deck, then veered out again away from off stump. He'd seen it done in a game televised from Adelaide.

He didn't think in terms of 'hearts of willow' or of the murmur of light as it brushed the surface of the MCG, nor did he read cricket books such as *The Paceman Cometh* or *The Ethical Basis of Cricket*. He was just a boy for whom cricket was the universe. Helpful men tried to show him better ways to bowl, but Wayne felt his own way was best, not because it was, but because it was his own.

When he practised at home with a shoulder sore from a work accident, the constraint of a shortened arm action seemed to cause the ball to swing in the air, and when he did the same thing with his leg-break action, twice out of five times the ball curved in towards the stumps then, when it hit the pitch, broke outwards away from off stump. He could do it. It would be his special ball.

When he played with the district team in the new season, he found he could get his special ball to work sometimes. When it did, and the batsman went for the long handle and was beaten forty ways to Sunday, Wayne did a little Aztec two-step of delight.

The day came when, on an errand for Mr Welland-Smith, he saw Bill Miller again, bending over a vat of something up at the Pig. Wayne, although a stranger to cruelty, followed a law of revenge older than the afterthought called mercy, and darted forward quick as a Buckley's rushing cat and pushed Miller into the vat. He was out of there and completed the errand. On the way back, he glanced in at the killing shed and saw a red-drenched figure climbing awkwardly from the vat. With a shock he realised Bill Miller was no bigger than he was now.

On the way back to Kimberly something inside him that he hadn't known was knotted and tight until that moment relaxed its hold on him and let go. He felt great. Free and springy, as if he'd taken a step up and now was on a level with everyone. He got to Kimberly, marched into Mr Welland-Smith's office and asked to be trained as the next concrete driver.

'Got your driver's licence? Right. We'll get you a 3B licence, you can use the single axles for twelve months, the yard trucks, then we'll give you a go on the bogies.' Still surprised, Mr Welland-Smith rang Eileen Door and told her Wayne was perky as a wagtail on a bull's back, and the story of the request.

For the game against Burunguralong, Wayne got on to the captain to arrange for a fieldsman with a grab like an emu for a tourist's sandwich to field at silly point for the catches that came in an arc round there, and someone in the gully for his quicker ball. Next year he'd try out for first grade with the men. Hey, Jackie Miller was their scorer, Bill's youngest sister. Boy, was she pretty. Those white teeth and the smile. But not too much like that American girl on the box with fifty teeth and all showing. Bill was behind the door when looks were handed out in that family.

Wayne was brown as the Adaminaby stringworm. Tracing his cartoon onto the warps, I felt my day-to-day life was like pouring out something from inside me, endlessly. Something I ought to retain. I was a mess. Nothing added up. Too much didn't fit. The world and human life weren't a rational whole.

Nor was I a whole person. But how could I be? The words I used to understand the world, and understand myself, didn't fit together. The values I was taught to live by didn't fit together. Truth, happiness, honesty, kindness, tolerance, peace, freedom, the rights of others, intelligence, courage: mix them in any pairs you liked and at least half can't live together. I kept my head down, worked long hours.

And I was still stuck with gesture. The thought that when I

made a choice of companion, lover or friend, I would be gesturing in the direction of an image I wanted to project, and to see myself projecting, had a curious effect. It pushed me further towards Yarrow.

I saw the Bird infrequently. She paid no attention to my preoccupation, she was occupied with what she called the Birth of the Reader, saying the writer was ringmaster of the reader's imagination and talents. A new theory she'd got hold of, I think.

The tighter I shut my eyes in the church's darkness, the clearer Yarrow's face was to me; and the darker the night, the whiter her skin.

forty-nine

zuzz

Satch Sagamore, of Durras Circuit, bubble and froth researcher at the newly privatised section of the CSIRO, had no wish to figure in the tapestry, instead requesting to be represented by the family cat.

Her tail flicked, catching the eye. From an attitude of glamorous disarray, she settled herself comfortably into an image she was trying out. Her black coat was patterned, if you looked closely, with almost imperceptible vertical bars of tropical brown; viewed, that is, when she stood erect. As well, if you were to lift the ends of the fur and turn them against their natural flow, you would find she was black, with brown bars, only on the outer edge of her coat. Underneath, the thickly growing fine hairs were white.

From her position on the drystone wall fronting the house, Zuzz, in dreamy mood, reflected on the creation of the sun, moon and the little stars, and on the day she had observed what she concluded was a collision in the sky, after which the world darkened a little, then lightened again. She thought of the recent time of whiteness when the many-armed trees and the hills cupping the town were dressed in shawls of snow. And the rocking chair on the verandah rocking in the wind before the snow danced. And the sudden absence of high birdsong.

She thought of her four winters of residence in this hilltop house overlooking the town, and of the tall animals who lived here. Was it too much to say they exhibited catlike qualities? Except for their regrettable familiarity with, even partiality for, water. Or was she transferring cat wisdom to the maybe quite different world of tall animals? Perhaps there should be a way of thinking about not so much animal qualities as living–being qualities, like her own invention, the theoretical anthropoid bee. She put this in with other odds and ends she kept in a spare room of her mind.

They get angry like we do, they play, they form attachments, they hunger, they run, they hunt. They sleep and probably die, though I can't say I've ever seen one dead. I have heard from one of the local males, who travels a lot, that to the north there had been a female tall animal lying very still overnight on a wooden couch for many hours, but that was a long time ago. And when daylight interrupted the night, she didn't stir, even when others spoke to her.

I believe if all cats accepted the idea that tall thins do think, we might be more understanding and criticise them less. Cats need to understand that other animals don't comprehend our complicated social system, so they imagine we are mysterious. Let us recognise that all living things are our kin, even clumsy and effusive dogs.

Tall thins would have more time for contemplation if they opened their mouths only to yawn and eat. I think their barking voice—they have much in common with dogs—may have something to do with their constant going. They come back, they stay overnight, but they're off again when the sun's been up for several hours, just the time for napping. What do they do, where do they go? All one does, thinks, or says is worship, is sacred; perhaps for them, going is worship too. Or is the worship at the end of their journeys; that is, here in their houses?

If they do stay, I teach them play. Play together, stay together, and keep your cat interested. Play? With tail vertical I chase them like a lion. My sleek fur against their bare legs excites them. My head-butts bring a loyal stroking. When they see me suddenly begin to roll and pretend I've caught a little companionable toy—lizard, mouse, bird—it charms them. Or I pretend to be Angry Cat, and sting them with my fierceness. They begin to fight back, but can't go on with it, they're soft as a mouse's spirit. I like to roll over and lie on my back with legs up, forearms bent, hind paws bent at the wrists, the same as the front paws. They exclaim and call each other.

Suddenly I gallop room to room, pretending to be silly as a dog, unpredictable as a meteor. I bat the children's balls, Bolp and Bomp.

If they worry, I set the scene, get their attention, and let them hear my most powerful purr. It soothes them. While they watch me, time opens up, and they enter through the gap into a timeless space. I insist that I remain the focus of their attention. I stand on their desk papers, on their open magazines, and sometimes their books. Books held by hand are unsteady, they're not quick enough to balance my movements. Unsteadiness is uncomfortable.

I'm an indoor cat, but the freedom of the outdoors is essential to me. Free to come and go, indoors and out, all doors open: those are my needs. At dawn, I walk light as petals on the knuckles of the morning.

When they call me in the garden, I give them eyes: two pale green lamps that don't move. They call each other to look. I think about them a lot, which would surprise them if they knew. I wish they understood all my signals and indicators. They wish cats could talk, but we know the corruption that comes with words, and the complications, lies, betrayals that words make easy.

Down the long corridors of their extended time, memory brushes against them like a cat, but not always with soothing. I've heard them remembering, weeping alone or unhappy together. Sometimes they forget, and want me to show them happiness, but happiness is for small children and simple dogs. All I can show them is self-possession, and, when the time comes, dignity in death.

My corridor of time is shorter. They'll mourn me, I hope. When I die, it will be like the death of a lion. But while I live they are my servants under the Most High. My antics are enough to send them into a spin. My mind is innocent, they say, therefore my dignity is great. I condescend, I allow, I permit. I bend from the Himalayas of my intellectual ranges. The hierarchy in this house I adapt to, and mostly keep my claws sheathed for the smallest. The one at the summit of the hierarchy, who feeds me, has my special respect.

I am unique, therefore independent, like the spotted hopping cat. I will not be corrected. Nor interrupted while I'm concentrating. It is difficult to make an Eden of any circumstances, but I try. And invigorating humility is their gain if they perform little services for me, to train them to change places.

I want to tell them to let loose as much freedom as they can take, into the nervous chaos of their billions, and after a time of upset I foresee they will settle to a new, dissonant harmony, a healthier balance, further towards the freedom end of the scale. The return to them of their neglected souls will bring closer the raising of all the proletariats of this world.

I must sleep now. It amuses them to name me for my most puzzling ability, but they cannot know the depth of richness of my dreams and the thrilling visions that make up my life when I withdraw from their drab world.

Before I go, listen. There is no total: there are many totals, as there are many melodies, whether in the trees, on the ground, or riding on the air.

Zuzz was a bridge, and that's how she is in the tapestry.

When I got back to the church, the girl was there again. She'd carried the baby in a baby-holder on her back, and walked up Wiradhuri Hill.

'Here, mind the baby,' she directed, holding Jack out to me. She mounted the bike and headed for the steep descent. 'Take him inside!' she called over her shoulder.

'Where are you off to?' I shouted. 'It's about to rain.'

She stopped, turned. 'Shopping. I couldn't carry everything at once. Take him inside. I don't want him wet.'

I took him inside. Strings of warp-faced rain slanted in columns gliding quickly from the west. The fire was built in the potbelly stove. I put a match to it and soon the whole edifice was giving off heat, including the chimney pipe that ascended like solidified prayer straight through the roof. I put Jack's container near the stove on a rug and gave him a bobbin to play with, which he ignored, and when he started to grizzle, got his dummy unpinned from his woolly jump-suit, dipped it in the honey jar, and touched it to his lips. His jaws opened, then closed like a vice on the neck of the dummy.

I got on with Zuzz. Yarrow's face accompanied me in everything I did. I suppose it wasn't much, to say that all I had to offer her was a set of feelings, a kind of love without lies, but it was an advance, for me. Not that she wanted anything from me. I hadn't given up hope that I might see her, even now. It didn't matter that there was no heaven possible with her, and each day indeterminate. The things that lost their freshness when she left would revive immediately if I could see her.

Next time she spoke to me, her voice was faint. I strained to hear it.

'I don't understand your needs. I don't have anything like them. I want to be, to do. I don't want an anchor, don't need it.'

Same old message. But what could I do? I was locked onto her wavelength. She continued.

'I was conditioned early to think a relationship with a man was the thing to do. I did it. It wasn't. My life is work. I decided not to breed babies, but if I did, a syringe would suit me, the rest of it is so annoying. Dates, amusements, parties, travel, people, closeness: I've been there and it's a waste of time. The other half of a relationship needs too much humouring and attention. People break apart, anyway. My life is new ideas, concepts I can get my teeth into. I glue myself to them, they're my relationships until I've sucked out all they can give. You're the kind of man I get on with and if I was differently oriented I'd consider you. Men are convenient solutions to minor practical problems, just as for men women are handy solutions to urgent physical problems. Or psychological. One day those problems won't exist. I'm at a stage where all this body and hormonal fuss is as foreign as mudwrestling. Does that explain it?

I replied, 'I've discovered that the most ordinary-seeming people feel the presence of things they can't explain: hints, faint intimations, presences, the kinds of things that once led people to suppose the existence of gods and other realities behind, or embracing, the realities we see with casual eyes. I'm one of those people. Take your hands, one of the first things I noticed about you. There was a language they spoke, a song, a music of movement, as if they heard and responded to voices that hands hear. Just as some music, or forms of words, or forms of statuary or architecture, seem to have originated from a superior world, or to point towards such a world, so the way your hands move suggests to me a state beyond this one we see when we're not seeing, a state more marvellous, where such grace and eloquence are not the exception. Does that explain it?'

Obviously it didn't. She was gone. I wasn't even sure she heard me out. I felt as foolish as I did when in our arguments of the past she just broke off and said no more. As when she chided me for some estimate I made of a probability about something or other, that she termed a generalisation, which in her eyes was a misdemeanour. I remember I replied that if we didn't generalise we'd step in front of the next bus, never learn from experience, memory would be a waste of energy, and everything a new and unfamiliar experience. In addition, science would disappear, though I think she might have thought that desirable, the way her education had prepared her. At all events, I found she'd stopped listening.

fifty

old clampett

The Bijou had put on *Waiting for Godot*—the spot ad on 2LR called it Godotte—and at half-time I was introduced to Marilla and Old Clampett. His face had been assembled by an unkind committee, the parts obtained on mail order. He was given a lawyer's nose: long, dryish, inquisitive, and the charm of a bunch of parsnips.

I visited them in their austere brick veneer at the railway end of Afton Street. He showed me round the rather bare garden. Two old trees with sad boughs, a Trevatt apricot and a quince, dragged out the rear portions of their lives in the backyard. A cement-brick incinerator stood between them. A low man, with earlobes brushing his collar, and alarmed, spidery hands, he's old. He has a weak, phlegmish voice, off-white hair like jogger's breath on a frosty morning. The skin of his hand is soft and frail, you expect the sound of tissue paper when you pick it up to shake it. I counted five long, erratic, silver hairs on and round his Adam's apple. His manner is reassuring as the confidence of an eighteen-year-old brain surgeon.

He was a second child who spent his first years permanently aggrieved, naggingly jealous of his older brother. Even Grandpa looked sideways at him, watching him scuttle insignificantly away, and thought of a Sydney pocket beetle.

He was unable to do most sports, but a number of times got nearly naked—from childhood on he hated nakedness—and attempted swimming. In this operation he would dive wretchedly into Lost River Olympic pool and fludgel the water like a drowning spider. He never quite got the idea of staying afloat, so he kept to the shallow end. At least on land he had quick legs like the centipede terrier.

In the high school magazine Ron Clancy had written Old Clampett's description as 'A person with few uses. Soup, perhaps.' The teacher made him change it. 'A man of the future with concealed talents,' sounded better.

At seventeen, after school had done what it could, and his mother had died, Old Clampett found himself a home, a family, and a new mother from whose teat, if he was lucky and watched his rear, he could hang for life. He got a job. In those days it was for life if you wanted to stay, and did Old Clampett want to stay? Do barnacles chop and change like butterflies?

The timid, the untalented, go gladly into moulds, and these are generously provided in many kinds of employment. In droves the unimaginative make their minds subservient to what they think others lay down, choose what's on show, display no eccentricity, no flavour of personality. Lacking the remotest idea of initiative or enterprise, glad to sell what souls they have in exchange for the comfort of a place to go every working day, a job description and a pay packet. Never let it be said that true, natural-born employees give their lives and energies. They give nothing, they exchange labour and time for something worth far more to them: money to keep them alive and a status they could never hope to attain unaided.

Old Clampett took refuge in Lost River Engineering, a

branch of a statewide company of the kind which is a mandrel over which the individual is bent and moulded. He took its shape immediately. He wasn't without strong impulses, one of which was to shelter under the wing of a protector and snipe from cover at his protector's rivals. There was a certain combativeness in him. It showed in his eyes, which wriggled under their glasses like something shiny pierced by a pin. Like cancer, he fitted in, made his presence felt, and soon had everyone paying attention.

He was middle-aged at twenty-five, and his ducts, glands, waterways, arteries and organs were grizzled and full of complaint. Yet the whole held together into old age. Marvellous. Shy as a bunyip with women, he finally earned enough money to afford company, if not love, and insisted on rescuing Marilla Parsley from a good job and an uncomplicated life at Mitchell's Building Supplies and Hardware. Marilla translated things she'd heard about him as envy and lack of understanding of this small, thin, quiet man who seemed to want her.

The honeymoon overwhelmed him. Sex was a big threat, rather like the slow burn he experienced when he savoured the mild chilli he thought was an adventure at the Burning Log, the town's raftered and highly respectable restaurant.

Marilla knew as little about men as he did about women, and after that disturbing honeymoon went back to Mitchell's. She often sat thinking, her unimaginative hands caressing her cash register, wondering why she had married. Still, she had a new name. That was a change. And she wasn't exactly a spritzy sort of woman anyway. When Ebie appeared she wasn't sure she liked so much change. She had never hurt so much in her life, and was quite sure she was never going to again. So, even though she was colourless and ordinarily had nothing to say, she was capable of decision.

Ebie was a pretty girl. So cheerful, so eager to help Mummy make beds, or cakes. She got to lick out the mixing bowl. Old

Clampett remembered a saying of hers. Remembered? It was burned on his brain.

'Do people like me, Daddy?'

'Everyone likes you, Ebie. The whole world.'

'Does a billion jillion willion like me?'

'They sure do, love. Every last single one of them.'

And she would ask again later, the same question, of this strange object everyone said was her father.

Marilla began the long, close, enforced study of him that marriage entails. Even so, she liked him better than others did. She was convinced he'd had no childhood, and felt compassion. But what a family. Three people about as similar as hawk, herring and hippopotamus, and one as funny as a prize-winning carbuncle.

What was it? The sinister chumminess he exuded like an unfortunate sweat? The warlike wart on his narrow temple? The emunctory noises that seemed inseparable from his presence? The eternal rim of golden cerumen on the little fingernail of his right hand? Did all Lost River know he lived with an unreliable prostate and peed jerkily with a sound like pouring six cups of tea?

At fifteen Ebie left home. Full of unrequited dislike for both of them, she said to the woman next door, 'I don't like it here. I never get what I want. Everyone's as tight as a fish's arsehole.' And her father did spend as if something highly dangerous lived in his pockets. Ebie's leaving was one of the few times her two parents came close for a short while.

He had no idea why Ebie left. She didn't write. The thought that he might never see her again didn't scale the salients of his mind and come into view. He wished he could get a card from her saying 'Lots of love always', like other people got from daughters. Perhaps if he got rich. He began to buy lottery tickets.

He did his work, mainly clerical—facilitator, coordinator, whateverator—and was busy as a chef at peak time—no, make that a check-out at a sale—taking notes of others' mistakes, looking for figures that didn't scan, information that could be worth a fortune in changing times, for he was a born top-off merchant, a lion-tailed dingo. He was always on secret business, like a cat crossing a road late at night. He hardly needed company training courses with their sonorous objectives, he complied as soon as he could see his superiors wanted to fit him to new ways with a stretch here, a tuck there, and a bit snipped off all over. Head down at his desk, he could detect changes in the sound of the air as people passed, and knew who it was by the feel of the sound.

For forty-eight years he provided a one-man cheer squad to eight senior executives in turn, none of whom felt the slightest gratitude for or shame at accepting Old Clampett's inspired subservience. He attached himself to the one who seemed promising, till that star fell or burned out, when he quickly cut loose and waited for the next player. Like an enterprising flea waiting for the next healthy dog. The nattering jargon of the company, that grew more specialised over time, formed a large part of his world-view.

He loved being an employee, warm and hidden in the protective and kindly folds of the corporate body, along with the other secret people, the silent and private unknowns who peopled industry at the lowest levels, to whom secrecy and suspicion were more engrossing than certain knowledge, and rumours and conspiracy more satisfying than constructive effort. For them, hypocrisy was a virtue, the gripe vine and the secret ear the main channels of communication, and above whom was not a glass ceiling, but one of reinforced concrete, and rightly so.

Old Clampett had a passionate love of music. From the day when an older cousin gave him a cast-off set of chubby bongos, and later when he heard the lazy music practice of the girl next door, and responded to the smiles of rhythm radiated by the radio, he was in bondage to music. By the time he was ten he was bowing the dried intestines of sheep with horsehair, and that's how it sounded.

He told me he found a kind of morality in music. How had he formed the concept, with an acrylic conscience like his? Music was his only real love, apart from Ebie. And where was she? What was she like now? Would he find her among the squadrons of shoppers in Sydney, the city-lice infesting streets and buildings? But even he realised she wasn't lost to herself.

He began with Strauss, fell in love with sighed regrets overlaid by restrained and timid gaiety. He experienced from a sitting position, as that modern thing, a listener, the storms, calms, heroic good cheer and romantic flights of Beethoven. He detected tunes in speaking voices. He even constructed a tune generator consisting of a spindle on which were loosely assembled a dozen circlets that could be rotated. The circlets had the names of musical notes painted round their circumferences, so that if you read straight along the thing, you could read off a tune. It came to nothing, and lived its life in a drawer.

He listened to Dvořák, who wanted to shake the world. He certainly shook Clampett. Verdi, and his melodies. And to Berlioz, whose *Romeo and Juliet* entranced him without him ever having felt a comparable human love. He devoured Mozart, whose compositions appeared to emerge fully formed into sound. Often he wished the little bugger could be dug up, if only to be asked why no cello concerto, but there was that unmarked grave.

In Beethoven he travelled up to the last six theorems, as he thought of them, asking himself, What is he struggling with? He tried to follow, layer after layer, to the heart of it, but the heart was another layer. Each complication seemed to open out like petals into a bunch of impenetrable simplicities. Was he thinking the thoughts he had while synthesising and interweaving his simple tunes? Was it thought caught in the act of thinking? Or music thinking music thoughts? He couldn't understand how profundity arose from the simplest of ideas.

He was deaf to the music which had destroyed its contact with audiences, music only musicians could hear.

Marilla could only wonder at him as he sat and listened. His face was like an embezzlement; what was there in that head to respond to such music? Her face had grown more chins, like a soft concertina, though no complaint came from that patient sacrifice on the altar of family, as she suffered her lifelong ritual death.

The face of Ebie came and went between the harmonies, the way she played in the backyard, her little old wise sayings when she was four and five. He could still hear the way her voice sounded. In the meantime he had his music, his favourites, pieces that engulfed him: melodious, moving, memorable. To Old Clampett they were eternally new, as if the music were still wet on the page.

He feels old now, though his body still works, still propels him from one day to the next. His ear-fuzz is a field of antennae. Age is shrinking him, sucking out his inner parts, like a malevolent vacuum cleaner applied to a hole in his chair. His wrinkles, covering him like a mesh, are music's stretch marks, so much does he feel music part of him.

He can't explain what he experiences when he hears music that speaks to him. He struggles with words he understands well enough usually, but that seem evasive, empty, beside the point when he presses them to hold still and say clearly what he feels. His voice has turned white over the years.

'My favourites, the ones who speak in melodious phrases that seem almost like words, or maybe they're what words could become—I could hear them forever. Over time they've given me an appetite, not for an absence of melody, but for melody beyond those melodies: richer, even more satisfying. But no melodist has come yet, not for a long time. I wish I could be here when such a composer arrives. But music has opened a world to me that I had no idea existed; a world I can never explain. With music I'm not alone. Without music there's no solid ground under me.

'Then there's my dream-thing. Dream with open eyes. I went to hear chamber music at the Workers' Club auditorium. I felt pressing down over the world a sky, an atmosphere, a kind of space containing all possible music everywhere. As it pressed down, one strand of music, woven from the four voices of the instruments, rose up like a charmed snake, or smoke from a fire, and spread out fine strands that went to each person there, and they all seemed changed when the strands touched them. It was an enchantment, like when I was a kid in church and God came down to the altar and the bread and wine became more than bread and wine while I watched. It told me the world's alive with music and voices—everything's alive with them—if only I could hear them.'

He has begun to mourn his daughter. She'll never come. He understands her not liking him, he doesn't know anyone who does. He misses her. She is part of what his life means. Now she seems like a musical note which has escaped into the air that is the river of all music, a melodious sound that echoes in his head and tingles in the rest of his clumsy, unbeautiful body. At night he goes into the dark, looks up at distant stars, miserable that knowledge has robbed us of the old certainties. Once, we had souls, and souls went 'up there' when we died. Now we have nothing, no souls, no destination where we might see a loved daughter again, just an arithmetic of meaningless distances. And we did it ourselves, from a kind of instinct to diminish ourselves, to go down.

And Marilla, fast asleep in the house, a book on a shelf unread for forty years.

Old Clamps drives up to the top of Explorer's Hill and sits there perched on the blue basalt parapet like a floppy clock looking down over the town, so clear in Australia's dry light. Looking, looking, until thought is emptied out and only emptiness remains, and need. Death was next, the expression of souls in eternal conversation, and winter's cold grave, hard and certain. Yet he was wearing away without pain. Why didn't Ebie want to be found? Had her children left home? He coughed like an old fox on the hill in winter. Was she happy?

Each time he came there to go over his pain, which now was much of his life, he uncovered a new layer of questions, and when he lifted that, another layer was visible underneath. Only questions. And one immutable, toe-stubbing fact.

Just one visit before he died. A photograph. Anything would be something.

In his head there continually plays his version of the song of living, whose notes are sad moments, whose words hopeless thoughts.

Other words, shorter, more basic, soaked in the sorrow of a lifetime, extricate themselves from his tormented inner workings and mental pipework, and push their way out of his mouth, floating towards the town spread out below, but dying before they reach it.

'Ebie,' he says. 'Ebie.'

'Oh, Ebie.'

I see a small box on a dingy shelf and in that box is mostly dust, but in among the dust are the skeletal parts of a music mechanism. If you shake it the box gives out tinkly sounds, then subsides into silence and dust again.

At the Church of the Good Shepherd the girl was at the woodpile, chopping. She'd been back for several days. I'd offered her the old vestry as her quarters, it was the bedroom, and moved a camp stretcher for myself out into the body of the church, in the work space. Near the potbelly, in fact.

She'd prettied the place up. Began to cook. I like to eat in my own way, but she told me straight, 'I don't like the way you cook and I don't like what you cook. Eat this.' I ate it. Wasn't as good as mine, but she had to be allowed to do something around the place.

'Why here?' I asked once.

'I want him to live on a hill. I want him to start life high up. He can go down later if he wants.'

When the past ambushes me I'm tempted to write off the whole of human life as evil. Maybe that's what being human is, and no alteration of environs or inner self can cure it. Or are we innocent when alone and no laws apply? Are vile residues left only by contact with others?

The sense of rottenness, that there was no release, weighed me down so that a flight into work, though it gave some relief, was no real escape.

Maybe the person I was all those years ago couldn't have done differently. No way out there. It meant the evil I did was inescapable.

Was there a time when my choice of what to learn, what to take notice of, had been anything but a signal of something I wanted to convey to myself and the rest of the world?

fifty-one

edward cuttlebone

'Australians aren't as torpid as they seem, just haven't been pushed far enough.' He was tall, you might almost say elegant. There was that slight withdrawal that's easily taken for fastidiousness. The eyes have seen it all and liked none of it. There was a certain gentleness of appearance, like a soft-nosed bullet. His long car sounded like a humming-top gone to sleep.

An assegai hung on his wall.

'From semen to cemetery, nothing's worth living for, not success, friends, money, love: nothing. Perhaps hell is Lost River. You're thinking I'm a tragic old goat, I can see it in your face. *Tragos*. How can tragedy live in one bored to the bone? Bored as the patient ant-watcher. Life's geared to comfort now; we have so many choices in our lives that it's all much the same value. Boredom's the result. Sometimes boredom tastes of leather, sometimes of smoky air, usually of cardboard. I'd say plastic, if plastic had a taste.

'Am I old? Yes. Civilised? Possibly. Polished? To the point of slipperiness. Useful? No. Free? Not free to forget a useless life and the granite garden ahead. Where thought will be made conscious, with variable purposes in a place dark as the insides of skulls. Now I even go to church, though why I don't know. Perhaps to practise lowering my head, or to pray for the other planets and the health of the hairy sun. I drop my envelope with the agreed donation into the plate at St Matthew's. The Lord is my shearer. Must preserve the institutions and their shells. What it must be to be Christian, and believe, and never die. I'm not capable of it. Though having a little strength, a smear of genius, or knowing others with them, somehow prompts an intuition of a greater power, an absolute genius, a universal competence. And, to be frank, the animal which forms and entertains the idea of God is already more than animal.

'It's been a game. Nothing was as serious as they said: not poverty, not life, not death. All a breeze. Or was it a stomach-easing, amusing, ultimately boring dream? For some, survival is the sum of their desire. Not mine. Still not sure I wish I'd never come.

'I get visitors, absent friends returning from the dead. I say to them all, Preserve, preserve! The world would be poorer if hatred died or murder ceased, or love and kindliness spread their sickliness everywhere. Abolish no royals: laughter must not perish from the earth. At least the existence of royalty and inaccessible ermine helps us deal with envy.

'I married once, looking for order and help with loneliness, but in the end I was lonely with her. Now I'm at the end of my tether, but what's at the other end?

'I'm one who adopted an armory of habits to make choices easier, substituted obedience for ethics and a job description for a life, among that core in public service who despise the common folk and know who are the aristocrats. Yet that constant conflict in me, democrat versus bureaucrat.

'You know the greatest disappointment of my life? The day Bradman got out for a duck; he could have had that one hundred average.

'A retired spy. A pension for services rendered and the two poor devils I killed. The second one, with his wound that opened and grinned at me. Born between shit and urine, man, in a state of nature or an insect in ant-cities, is a beast and a monster. Funny how despicable it all seems now. And my one wound. A brief instant of looking down to see my own blood on my shirt. I was fumbling for more cartridges, clumsy hands. A feeling something bumped me hard. I lay down, shot people are usually prone. Looking up at the branches of the birch trees in that French farmyard. Pretty moss on the trunk, faint shadows on the undersides of the branches. Strange numb pains, head dizzy as if emptying. Then I heard the shot. Where was the universal grammar of fear? Why did I feel so little?

'Then in bed, in sheets white as a magpie's collar, my chest wondrous sore, the surgeon joking. 'Should have seen the round trip that bullet made. So interesting I had difficulty stopping the other surgeons from letting you proceed to post-mortem.' Made me feel strong and confident as an intruder trying to deflect a determined guard dog with a slice of bread and Marmite.

'I served under a chief who believed in strong arguments and soft voices, tender-hearted as an attacking surgeon. Wore evil like glasses he could take off. Some of his words had the painful thrust of a sudden suppository.

'Several wars, perhaps necessary blood-lettings, among nations who behaved worse than their citizens, worse than schoolkids in a playground. Always space in the parks for monuments to the poor wretches conscripted to have their lives taken at random. We must pray for arrogance to strike before we are struck. Then after the latest war, the real enemy, masked by the wartime alliance. Good old socialism–communism, successors to the alchemists, a pot of gold and humane living conditions for all, through government takeover, central planning. Imaginary solutions to eternal problems. Quick, forceful, crude, ruthless; rather than patient, gradual, careful and exact, like the pace of evolution.

'There's no way out of the human mess. Masters of almost everything except ourselves and the weather. Each worthless century we drag out this pantomime of lies in our world empire of lies. And every knucklehead has a vote. Democracy requires informed interest, and some wisdom, and unpopular decisions to be made, but knuckleheads feel their every wish should be acted on. Makes you wonder when the ship will hit the sand.

'I think the horrors the future holds are too dreadful to think of. People are even poorer specimens than I thought when I was young. All we can do is navigate accurately through this sea of shit. To whatever destination chance decides. One thing I know, egalitarianism is incoherent: it entails unequal treatment for some.

'It was a peculiar life, being trained to look at our fellow citizens without commitment. When I started back here again after the war with our lot I thought we automatically opened files on university graduates, the usual government suspicion of intellectual workers. Not so. But did we ever destroy those files on the ministers who came to office with Whitlam? I can't remember. Yet right up to the time I retired, any application to make freedom of information inquiries meant a file was started. Anyone who wants information is subversive. Some commitment to democracy, eh? We still have extensive domestic surveillance.

'Overall, our enemy was the totalitarian method in which no one person fails, only the whole system; where our pluralism could cope with individual failures while the system worked and remained intact. Peculiar, isn't it? The universe we have in our minds is a mental, imagined one. All hypothesis. Observation, testing, played a small role in building relativistic cosmology, just as it's played little part in the construction of that planner's dream state and citizen's nightmare that now has collapsed under the weight of its own inefficiencies.

'What kind of chimera are we? And we're getting ready to get out there in the universe and colonise it. Our psychologies try to explain and excuse us, but there are no excuses: time will expel us from this heaven. It must.

'A lifetime of endless paperwork and gossip, and the yawns of surveillance, adding up to what? Hints, deceptions, rumours. Nothing useful came of it. All the big things that happened—fall of the Shah, rise of the Ayatollah, collapse of the Soviets, fall of Gorbachev, Berlin Wall, end of the Cold War, Tienanmen Square, Iraq's hit on Kuwait, the Gorbachev coup—none of us foresaw. Not the Yanks, Brits or French, not Mossad. No one. Intelligence has had no decisive part in any significant historical event, ever.

'And back home, after the war, a spy in my own land. A life of carrying tales, like the most despised little shit in prep school. And what did it add up to, all those thick files on fellow Australians? Not one single spy. Get that? Not one single bloody spy. I'm ashamed of making a career of thinking there might be. I've examined my life: it wasn't worth living.

'Not only that, but after '89, when the opposition fell to bits, it seems there'd been a mole in our own organisation. Serves us right.

'Know what I look forward to? My father said dying was part of life, do it well. He did. Felt it coming and said, Goodbye old chap, and fell between the eighteenth green and the clubhouse. Great death. That's what I look forward to.

'I can't get over the idea that people like me, such soulless bodies, such patchily rational brains, are going to launch themselves into space, infest other planetary systems, and spread their kind through a universe which then will inherit the whole past of an elevated animal that doesn't know what it is or how it got here.'

I left him still shaking his head. I wove him into the tapestry as the site of an implosion.

Outside the church, fierce flechettes of rain attacked like an army. As I worked, I resumed my interior battle. No rationalisation had worked. What help was there? Remorse and guilt I could dismiss as useless or counter-productive, but I couldn't get rid of them. In the wider world I knew that no retreat from punishment as unhealthy or unnecessary had worked. Evil was real. Bad deeds were real. To put it as plainly as I can, this is how I feel. I'm back where humanity was at the time of its sudden ascent to the position of world butchers. Covered in blood, guilty in every cell. On my head, in my past, in the history of every gene, are deeds there is no undoing.

And for all my agonising to be gesture! Artificial. Something had emptied me of reality, even to myself. Was any part of me authentic? Was there any me underneath, even a tiny core?

The August vote on the proposed new jail and the high-temperature incinerator gave a clear go-ahead for their construction. Emma Mitchell had won. I was sure she had been involved in the campaign of rumour that directed attention from her projects onto Mrs F whose energy and ideas had made her jealous, and who, being a comparative stranger, was a natural target.

What had happened to Yarrow? What had prevented her getting in touch? If she could find me because she detected that I was thinking of her, why couldn't I find her? I was new to all this. Perhaps the ability would come.

fifty-two

uncle carbuncle

He takes his stance in my head as a big shareholder in the Pig, who has sold his other interests, mainly businesses on the new industrial estate. He started Jazz in the Bush, puts up two woodchopping prizes at the Show, gives money to local football and cricket clubs for kids who can't afford the gear. He dresses like a stack of old prayer books falling to pieces, his body loose on him as if he dressed in a hurry in someone else's. His face cheerful as a plate of empty oysters.

At the running of the Winter Cup his horse Bogeyman came third and he decided then and there to sell him. Old Uncle appeared to have the physical prowess of a damp mat. He edged round corners on windy days, in case a stiff wind blew him away. He was nimble enough, though, dodging dog cartridges as we headed for the bar.

'Some of my time, eh? Hope I remember. Hillsides of memory are steeper now, covered in a treacherous scree. Some streets of memory are the overpasses, with all the traffic.

You'll tread on some toes with this tapestry thing. People are happy to talk about themselves, but when they see their own words in print they're usually mad as cut snakes. Me, I'm too old for anger. Burn with a low flame and give off a thick black smoke.'

He opened his mouth, closed it when he'd finished. His face worn and wrinkled; I thought of a camel driver's boot.

Everything wears, it's the most enduring characteristic of things. Theories shrivel, one by one. The years are omnivorous. Time itself seems to be frictionless, shows no signs of wear, perhaps it's no thing. I was born into a language that helped shape me; it hasn't worn away, just dropped bits off, grown new bits.

Long ago I saw well from these eyes, now I feel a horror at coming blindness. Started in darkness in my mother, and will end in dark with no end. Of all things, to see is marvellous. My stomach was flat, muscles worked when I needed them, I knew everything. Carbuncles at twenty, and christened by derisive nephews. Now bald as a peeled garlic, dizzy when I stoop, stiff as a Talbingo walking horse, my left eye leaks, I have a mettlesome sphincter with little explodings as I walk, and talented teeth whose gums I can take out and clean. Life has squeezed me like a full beer can in its big fist, and popped the top.

Skin is thinner, splinters rush in easily, cracks appear on heels and fingers in winter. Where muscle was, pockets of loose skin sag. Skin crawls lizardlike on shanks, hands, arms. Painful pizzle, loquacious stomach, pee comes in dribbles since the prostate decided to grow. All else shrank. Go carefully down steps, shock absorbers gone.

Congratulate myself every morning: You're awake, you old sod. And used to act as if I'd live forever. Necessary delusion?

Funny how the whole body is more reliable than its parts, like the whole car.

My memory teems. More that I thought forgotten pours out every day. Freud's *Unbekannt* gradually opens in age. I remember the almost-passions, the hips that passed in the night, time wasted on people never seen again, the heat, enthusiasms, seedy finesse, stony weathers, failures, straw millionaires, companies floated and scuttled, loud socialites, strange beds, the money I made and lost and made again. A few slides in the mud down Mount Disappointment. And the borderless pillars of rain slanting across bare valleys of the mind. I haven't had a good life, and mostly haven't led one.

And now the cold eminence of years. The raised dirtheap of years. Looks grand from lower down, but not grand. The gifts of age, what do they amount to? Understanding? Some. Tolerance? Not much. Love? Very little, and certainly not of myself. What else? Bad temper, feeble joints, odd pains, no strength, syncopated systoles. I feel I look like one of those old guys who organise trivia nights for Junior League kids. And ever since sixteen I've never got used to shaving. Wonder why you don't go bald on the chops?

Worse, a tired mind no fire will ignite. Only the past. All the time the damned past. Live long and grow shorter, taste less. Life ought to be better than this. How zero was invented. By an old bastard like me. Each day try to scramble up to where last night's thoughts left me. And all the names that decades ago were so big, so full of meaning, importance, memorable deeds: politicians, sportsmen, prophets, murderers; names now empty, flapping like rags in the wind in streets no one visits. The present moment is the opium of the people, together with comfort and convenience. And now the Cold War is gone their greatest and most comforting worry is the new concern about, of all things, the weather, and the worry of warming.

I've been a fool and fools get worse with the years, but never fool enough to go for their paper utopias. You want a good life? Want respect? Get money. Forget politics; with all values under review, political action is meaningless gesture. In any case, representation has been killed off by a rigid party system, and parliament is two organised gangs. So look at us now. No better than a guided democracy. Not a real democracy. The people aren't trusted. Too many issues the government won't put to the people: capital punishment, education, whether our taxes are well spent, multiculturalism whatever it means, separation of legislature and executive, castration of parliament by the party system. Black and white issues. Lots more. No deliberation, all prepared attitudes brought readymade into the House, speaking to a prepared line. Result? Automatic exclusion of talent. The best people just won't be in that sort of shemozzle. If they were, they'd have to be paid a lot more than the pay now is. Still, I thank God for a federal system: blocked on one level, I can get redress in another.

Those I knew have leaked away out of the world, as the years dropped off the calendar. I'm left, friends gone, a stranger among strangers. At least businessmen look the same as when I was a boy. All slide their eyes off me, I'm unnoticeable as the bottom-dwelling footfish.

I've seen good and bad, down and out, honest women begging, lightning striking in the same place time after time. Discovered women need men like butterflies need parachutes. Discovered fear has become the addiction of the public; fear of everything: other people, food, air, water, weather, future.

No wisdom, merely seventy-seven years of blunders and stupidity, a late arrival at sad knowledge. At least I didn't lose everything in those few fraudulent years in the eighties. Kept enough to be safe. Safe? Good God.

Time's a fisherman, it hooks us, plays us a little, we feel the line slacken, then for years a steady pressure as we're hauled towards that bobbing marina on the far shore. Someone wants us at last, but it's death, that tarted-up obverse of life. Some live a lifetime in thirty-five years. I didn't. Didn't have the things classic youth is supposed to have, no seven devils, no discontent, no big hopes, wide horizons; just wanted to adapt, fit in, make some cash. Wasn't among the sixties people who loved protest and the feel of incipient revolution—and had no idea what revolution entailed. Actually it was the heady feel of rage they loved, no other outlets were respectable for them. I paid no attention to the failure that was the French Revolution, and only a little to the success that was the American.

Seen? I've seen dead bodies dried and light and stiff thrown up onto trucks. Epidemics of war veterans as we got used to history's rhythms of horror. Seen censorship taken to totalitarian extremes without censorship laws, arising from the people themselves. Seen street and house lighting change the nature of time. People of taste and sophistication selling Gethsemane olives, just as Dachau guards sang carols for Christmas and listened to Beethoven after a brisk day at the ovens. I've seen decades of compulsory X-rays for TB; now for political reasons there's no compulsion for testing for diseases just as deadly, and when TB returns, what then?

I've seen cities where folk have never known the taste of water; seen glaciers like rivers frozen in motion, broken off and sharp; seen moon shots, nuclear bombs, the hungry dancing on breadlines; the young treating their pop singers as priests and their priests as buskers; Australians employed as peons, waiters and flunkeys by those who have shown us that trade is war carried on by other means. I've seen the walls closing in on us when the intellectuals turned against freedom's uncertainties, finding equality a nice little earner and by nature a bottomless mine. And government continually increasing crime by making more laws. I've seen people forced together by mandated borders into unnatural community and their wars are endless.

I saw an old man stripped of money and family sitting in the gutter playing on a Jaws harp as if there wasn't a worry in the world; seen a prisoner tied and dowsed in petrol because a beacon was needed.

I've seen people look to government for security, to new Cromwells who will give them what's good for them. They paid in bitter subservience, gave up their freedom, and still government couldn't deliver. I've put my ears to the tallest buildings and heard the tremors deep in the concrete, right to the crustal foundations. I've seen a man look sidelong into a bank window and notice with disgust the big belly carried out in front of him and it was me. I've seen myself, old as I am, still trying to wring from my nature the cowardice I was ashamed of when I was young. Eyes remember.

What have I learned? The speed record for bad news increases each year. That the twentieth century wasn't the century of the common man, but the century of a science that forgets to say 'It may be' with every guess it makes, and of wars so ferocious they resemble world catastrophes, and of the surrender of power by the people to liars and maniacs who shed more blood than Napoleon. I've learned that the Holocaust put all humanity to shame, and has numbed us to such an extent that we pass over without recognition the far greater slaughter of millions more in Russia's collectivisation and China's tidying-up. That the common man and woman have lost faith in themselves and don't know what to do or what to believe. That nothing can do us good, nothing can save us, we have no meanings we can believe in.

I've learned that kidnap and terror need the headsman, but not while careers depend on convictions, that only adolescent minds can want to lay everything flat and start from scratch, that any ideal of imposed communality is looking backwards, that the road to uniformity is the road to inhumanity, that courage and perseverance in the face of opposition are great things, but not in fools.

I've learned that necessity is not the mother of invention: invention creates necessity. I've learned that what I don't know would make a fine and immense library, also that what I think and do are always wrong in the end.

I've learned that young men cause a great deal of the world's misery. Massacres, bloodbaths have a few things in common: direction from above, weapons, and young men, one of the worst plagues ever visited on the planet. And now young children are joining their ranks. No one else can be manipulated so easily to do the dirty work.

A rave? It's me. I'm old, sometimes go over the same things. Fitted into no decade, yet all of them. Waiting now for it to be over, to be time to crash, get the head down once and for all. Time for my lifelong grinning partner beneath the skin to make his appearance. All the images stored in this brain, preserved in liquid chemicals till death flips the switch, blood stops and is choked by predators already living in it, waiting, and memories dissolve in dead brain tissue. I'll have been one event in an endless series, but a series which had a beginning. Those of us who were born are the elect, inheriting life, light and death, fates avoided by those individuals who dodged fertilisation and birth.

This poor old body will find it wasn't the star after all. Its face, eyes, voice and limbs were servants of the blood and sensory equipment necessary for a brain's survival, which in turn obeyed genetic imperatives. And the end isn't sleep, sleep implies waking.

I came from my mother, but the end is gas and dust, so the whole thing, beginning and end, isn't symmetrical. Just as light and dark aren't symmetrical, white and black, heat and cold, past and future. Is there any symmetry at all? Interesting. But no more than the universal appetite for fiction.

Fiction, yes. And truths and realities. One lot cosmic, about which we can never know if we're right. Another lot domestic, we call it science, consisting of guesses and metaphors. And a third batch of personal truths and realities that people live by, some of them enough to make your hair stand on end. Cosmic, domestic, personal; and a fourth reality such as poets and visionaries see, a world behind our world that shows only bits of itself, and then only to the few able to see. I wasn't selected for that ability, or by it. The only reality I know is the personal, what has meaning for me. Still, reality is no less reality for our help in its construction.

We stumble on. The planet runs down. Everything wears.

'Do you have a dog?' he asked.

'A red dog adopted me when I came here. Why?'

'Never got along with dogs. One regret. Wouldn't mind a dog. Someone to talk to. They never took to me. Never understood I was yelling at them in a kindly manner. I'd like to have got on with dogs, feel more human somehow. A kind of test and I failed. Like the way I feel I'm finished, but not complete.'

At the church I gave No-name some cash to add to whatever she had, to buy warm things for Jack. She bought extra food and crockery, for some reason, though I considered my steel plates and cups as good as anything she bought, and made more remarks about my diet, though the fish she cooked had more bones than Rookwood. It was the first week in August, the westerlies strong enough to blow you off the hill.

I was equalising the distances between warp threads on the roller when the question fizzed up in me as to why we couldn't go back and undo what should never have been done. Why did time have to be in one direction? But the victims would already have suffered, wouldn't they? Were these conversations with myself gestures? Who was I trying to impress?

I heard No-name talking in her sleep. She rambled on about a large door in a big paddock below the hill, and a field of doors in the neighbour's piece of country. A cup and saucer tree, knife and fork plant, and cultivated patches where all necessities grew: tables, chairs, preserving jars, babies' bibs. Who was she?

fifty-three

gungible gumes

I imagined I'd seen him at Jazz in the Bush, and lurking at one of Boult's parties. He was so big, he stuck out like a horse in bed. A sandy face, complete with small round footprints. Several had spoken of him, such as Borry Blow and the Saint, who'd been at school at the same time. Borry told a story of some kid having conned Gumes into buying rare sand leghorns, supposedly a new breed but actually chooks supplied with a bucket of river sand. Borry remembered a set of puzzled remarks Gumes made in an English class when a teacher tried to get them to think about truth.

'No matter how differently we see things, we all see the same thing when we get our marks out of twenty, and we know that in the shop we handed across a twenty, not a ten. And if there's such a thing as a lie, truth must be somewhere around,' he said. 'It was a good try, but it didn't stop the discussion.' Saint Sal mentioned Gumesy's eyes and the holes he dug everywhere so he could put things away, safe.

It didn't matter what life threw at Gumes—'exticuated' was his word, meaning to stick it to you sharply—defeats, mistakes, misfortunes made no difference, hardly an impression. He bent before each blow of chance and circumstance and sprang upright again as if nothing had happened. Just as well.

When I reached the end of Tantawanglo Lane, following the directions in his letter, and got out of the pickup, Gumes was up to his gums in food and the air bristled unpleasantly with flies. He was immense, a behemoth. He sat slumped under his own weight, flogging those gums without mercy or regret, in blue singlet and massive jeans, on the adzed bench like a Mullen Gullen avalanche cow. His hair was drawn tight, half in a bun, half out. His big bare feet needed a dry clean, his big bare face needed a whole new expression; it was like a bread loaf, parts of which had escaped its tray. The rough plank table, cut from a whole tree, was spotted with shade and the splashed evidence of birds. Mist patches, light grey cobwebs of vapour, brushed the tall hills.

The harsh Australian light dimmed to tender shadow where it collided with the belt of trees beyond the house. He'd bought the bush block with money left by Grandfather Gumes, who made a fuss of him when he was little because he was roly-poly. Past the deeply scarred car-tracks, the yard was dotted with holes. Gumes suspected there were transgenic walking trees on the property, and that they were silently hated by other trees. His eyes took a bead on my face, eyes like depopulation.

'It's okay,' he said, watching me take it all in, 'Sammy's in the stew. Jumped in and I bottled him.' Sammy, tall as three fingers of scotch, had been sent by God to spy on him, but he'd fixed Sammy. A jar of superannuated stew sat smugly on the table.

'Mastigious.' Tasty, I think it meant. Developing his own language, as do people who spend a lot of time with themselves. He flicked at a fly with a green tea towel and got it, worse luck. He had hands like a pillory. What looked like a bucket of guts distributed in a row of jam jars watched me from a shelf by the wall of the shack. Clumps of hellfinder weed dotted the bare earth. Several glints of green tinsel, and some red, shone sordidly from the soil round the table. A party? Women?

At school—most of my tapestry subjects had vivid memories of school, but I hated school, so I've cut a lot of it—Gumes had taken up smoking to stop himself jogging, he said, and that was the nearest he came to sport, apart from being pip-spitting champion in primary and two brushes with football. Once, when the ball came to him and boys ran at him, he panicked, as if it were raining feathers, and threw it to the nearest and got out of the way. Next time he threw the ball away where it would do no harm. Once he climbed, not a tree, but the statue in Anzac Park, to shake hands with it, and could be heard spelling aloud what he saw round him. Then he discovered that nothing really had a name, but was itself, no names were needed. To him it mattered.

I drank a cup of his tea, which coated my tongue with an unpleasant heaviness. He didn't go on until the time had been ritually wasted. He'd told me in his acceptance letter of strange feelings, of colours melting, of coming out in painful lumps on the head because of actions he couldn't remember. 'Beltition', he called it. Perhaps he was set upon in the town. Feelings of splitting apart, head to foot, best relieved by tapping his fingers and blinking to a pattern. Visions of cultivated patches of glass and trees with leaves in the shape of cut-out figures. Thoughts came too fast, his mind couldn't keep up; something inside controlled him. Memories were fine one at a time, but they came in torrents. Impulses grabbed him, working his arms and legs, making him do 'dreadul ' things while he watched, helpless and afraid. I was familiar with the idea that our energy comes from strangers, the mitochondria and bacterial enzymes that colonise us, so that the lone self is a thing of the past, but not with anything Gumes described.

'There's pouring, molten stone beneath our feet. I see lines of trees in the distance melt and re-form. When trees here flop and buckle I blow them up again and they come upright. With the hose there.' He pointed to where the business end of a hose entered the ground. The skin of his fist was a light Cuban brown. Pores on his nose, like craters, gleamed in the August sun.

'Earthquakes, volcanoes, I have them all the time. See that slight unsteadiness? The continent moved a fraction north then. And the clouds breaking away from the atmosphere. Look at that; it's raining light! Hear it? And the ground, look, stamping and kicking! That light's hard as hail. Thank you, God, for the blue that protects our minds from dwelling on the dreadful heavenless lifeless universe. And thank you that nothing human is finally obselete.'

On a zoo excursion in year eight he talked to the chimps, capering and scratching as if he was one of them. A chimp came over, reached through the bars and patted the head of this strange animal.

'I still get that only-person-in-the-world feeling, in one-hour nights when everything is different,' he confessed awkwardly. He had an even voice, no dips and hollows, like an American salesman or politician. 'Or I'm the world and other worlds look over my shoulder.' He changed horses suddenly. 'But can people see me? Can they hear me? Is my survival a sin?' Again he changed tack. 'Will they find us, those people out there? I have doubts. Do you think saving us is something that ought to be done?'

His hand-painted corn-green Falcon pickup stood—asleep, he said—near the shed. A handful of chooks sheltered under it.

What looked like a Cann River knotted cat eyed them from behind a tree that might have sidled up a minute before.

He'd worked at a number of occupations: designed greeting cards, helped at a homeless persons' shelter, worked for the pets' cemetery, in a bookshop—which was a hopeless proposition since people couldn't get past him—at the Garden of Living Memories, and most recently at the In Touch pet shop. He once was bass drummer for the brass band, but tourists found him too comic. He tried the TV antenna business, but couldn't understand why, if there was poor reception out in the hills, people didn't take it as a fact of life and forget the whole thing.

His life was constant experiment, checking, and daily discovery. He laughed inappropriately—as professional carers say—at a word on the ground. Shouldn't have been there. I caught the shine of it just before it fizzed, wriggled and melted away. It was black shot through with green, like crows' feathers.

They say the individual has no one centre of identity, but many centres; Gumes was more aware of this than most. He could take nothing for granted.

'Others hear my thoggets.' His word for thoughts. 'The voices always at me: Shut up, don't sit there, go outside, stop everything. Till I feel I'll lose control and start hitting people. Get very beltremious at times.' Aggressive, I suppose. Though most people hide their aggression when more formidable people loom.

Storms raged and twisted round his head. When he spent some time in the house of screaming in tongues and rocking in silence he felt his legs were glass.

'It's a lottery, being here. We could all easily be other people. Millions of half-people trying to push into Mum's egg at the same time, and I won. Our happy comfortable days'—I couldn't help noticing the junked appearance of the place, bush and all—'are the eternity of death and darkness for those who never made it to the egg. To make up for the guilt of my aggression in being here, I often go out of existence. But always I find I need people eventually. And feeling that, I feel I exist. You see, Gumes needs people a lot.'

In his gunge theory, he was more gungible than most. His particular gunge, his chief taint, was need. He hated himself for it, despised himself, but couldn't escape the taint of need.

For much of the time Gumes, in a sense, knew nothing. Nothing was true, nothing existed. Then it would all reappear. It happened to me every morning. He was fascinated at the thought that the future was completely dark, the present ungraspable, and the constantly growing past was where we lived. 'That tiny moment just behind the cursor of the present,' was how he put it.

A wild-mannered dog ran into the clearing from the surrounding bush. A boy followed at a distance. There were no fences.

'This is Jason coming. Last time I saw him he couldn't see to stand. Get on the grog at an early age round here. Got his dad some cheap paint for the house from the DMR, main roads. Some red, some white. Red and white stripes, and glows in the dark. Pretty informal, the neighbours. Hoy their empty tins straight out the window. When there's a new baby the nappies go out the window too. Land in the tree outside. Tree full of white flying foxes. With khaki streaks. Yet they're the sort to pull the house down if the kitchen taps splash. They make mud bricks strengthened with pigs' blood. Previous house was up on stilts, it's still there, they had to get out of it. Kept a bull under the house, slept there at night in winter. Visitors one night didn't know about the bull, and when the bull kicked up a racket, they bored a hole in the floor—pissed, of course—and poured boiling water down the hole. The bull bellowed and ran like buggery, took the supporting posts, the house dropped on its side. Destroyed the water bed. They lived there for a while, till they got tired of climbing from room to room and sliding out of control into walls.'

Rawboned Jason arrived, Australian as a thong at twilight in midwinter.

'Dad skun a fox yes'dy. Brang the tail for you.' He fished it out of his shirt. The red dog, head under the green Falcon, was conducting the chook choir in an opera of barks, screams and murders. Gumes, thighs giraffing slowly, like a monument with hinges, lumbered heavily to the house, bringing back two bottles of home brew.

'Give this to your dad. And thanks.' Dad was a man silent as rust, with a nose of beefblood brown and country eyes like camera lenses.

'Is that trout still in the milk?' said Jason.

'No. Is Mum better?' Mum was someone to watch, like a wrecking ball. The gums of her false teeth had faded to a pearl grey, but she said she hated pink.

'She's cactus. Can't hold the chainsaw. She can swing the axe, but.' And left, with a happy dog.

Gumes held up the severed red tail. 'The entire planet is food, if we could digest it. Other organisms can.' He bent down. 'Oh, my foot's got out of hand.' And rubbed his shin. He often had trouble with the pins, the needles. 'I knew a man in psychiatric Sydney who laughed himself out of cancer. People who ate shit. Some with holes for three-pin plugs in them. People who wanted to be pets. And there was Jim, my only friend there.'

He would like to have got to know Jim better, and perhaps persuaded him that seeing each other more would be a good idea. Jim was very fair, and not a hairy man. Gumes found something satisfying in looking at Jim's grey–blue eyes, his long ineffectual fingers, his slimness. He found something gentle about Jim's neck, seen from behind. They lost touch after discharge.

'I'm still riddled with idiosyncrasy, which I sometimes mistake for common knowledge, even matters of principle. Or important decisions. Or is it just meaningless behaviour? Is there something in us that laughs at us? Replicating us for its own amusement? I hope I'm not being too expligious.' Over-explaining, was it? How did he hold himself together? Watching him, it seemed the recesses of his self yielded up other selves without limit, though maybe many were selves shared with others. I asked about dreams, and immediately Gumes was full of them, but I was disappointed to find Gumes contaminated with the superstition that dreams were susceptible to interpretation.

In the house he picked up a jointed cross of acacia wood. 'Feel the power in that!' he boomed. Why had his voice got so loud? I touched the cross. Nothing. 'Musclebound mind,' he concluded. If so, it's the only part of me that is. He showed me his lidded jar of eyes. Eyes? I didn't ask. He went on and on, wondering how to feed a world of the cashless, and how the purpose of life is to become God. His words kept leading me on, until I came to a stop against an horizon of darkness, but where he could clearly see. I asked about females, since several photos of women were nailed to the wooden wall. Large nails, too.

'There were some, but eventually I decided on total love. This one, Rosa, I listed all her parts and named them. Even interior organs. Made casts of her arms, legs, face, chest — though that didn't turn out well; in fact, it was a disaster—and her hands and feet. I intended to do that each year, to keep a record.'

'How did she react?'

His sentences ceased. She had noticed that, relying on supposition, he had surreptitiously unzipped. Rosa turned away, the edge of her smile became the beginning of that knowing grin. Never mind. He would go through with his kiss. And he had loved her, she knew. And he was certain of it. What the hell would she do with a Book of Parts?

He had the picture of the texture of her pubic hair so strongly in his head that as he bent over—quite a long way it was, not the best for the back—and lowered himself to kiss her head, he was convinced this coarse hair covering her skull was also pubic. The member for Down There began to stand, his head and collar protruding between the steel teeth of the zipper.

She was aware of how he had loved her. Oh yes, fully aware. All those carnations, till she got sick of the smell. He had assured, promised, dreamed of her, smothered her with passion; had investigated, exclaimed at, and kissed with intensity every surface, crevice and crack. Had possessed every word she spoke, rolled it round on some greedy tongue in that huge head of his, looked at it from every angle, drawn out its implications, its antecedents. How he looked at everything! Every loop, whorl and arch of her fingers, every line and angle, every shape and shadow. He knew the lines of her feet, the backs of her hands, more thoroughly than she did. Every scar. Till, Almighty God! She could gladly have pulled out his eyes and stuffed them down his throat, still on their strings.

'How did she react?'

'She cracked. When she saw Goliath at roughly eye-level, she whacked him with her jogging shoe and satirically threw several loops of red and green tinsel round his neck. She grabbed the casts, broke the lot, and threw the pieces at me, chasing me so she'd score a high percentage of hits. She burned the Book of Parts. A lot of violent swearing too. She said she wanted a little bit of sex, a lot of niceness, some fun, and mainly to be left alone to do her thing. It seemed unusual at first, almost fantastic, but like most things I gradually came to see some sense in it. Things I think often become different. A face, a word on a page.'

I decided not to ask about sex. His internal weather had changed, anyway. 'I'm not made for this world,' he groaned dispiritedly. 'It just isn't me. If the future doesn't need me, why not go now?' He sank into a heavy-set chair, which squeaked a treble of alarm. In the process knocking to the floor a colourful copy of *Rearguard Action*. He looked exhausted. Perhaps I shouldn't have pushed him to go over his troubles. I had the impression that inside him words, objects, meanings, seethed continually, fermenting, multiplying, expanding, till it was a wonder he didn't burst. And memories by the dipperful.

'Come on, Gumesy, you said in your letter life was a great workout and the best therapy.'

'Did I? Ooh,' he sighed down the scale. The walls rumbled slightly in sympathy. 'I feel an attack of the prones. Perhaps permanent. Going to a world of different light.'

'Not yet, you're just tired.'

'Light makes me tired. This is the closation of a particle of life,' he yawned sleepishly. Good God, I'm doing it.

'Don't go to sleep on me, show me your carnation.' His sculpture.

'On the bench.'

Near a carving in mountain ash of a foot shaped like a bird's wing, and another carving in honeysuckle wood of a bird with body, tail, feathers and feet but a clenched fist for a head—branded *Nerrigunyah Knucklebird*—stood a block of limestone. The petals of a carnation emerged from the stone like a Pieta.

I was a weaver. I didn't know about art, but I had a general idea of what was in. This wasn't. But as an achievement it was a marvel. Gumes, with no training, had mimicked a living delicate organism in a rigid intractable medium.

He was lying back in the suffering chair, eyes closed, still talking. Once he groaned explosively, like a hungry donkey sighting food. I heard 'Muh emdap enam mo.' He had found a place of limestone cliffs and had taken out a block of limestone. Clunchy, white and workable. He wanted to memorialise his time with Rosa. 'Out there, carvings of roses in the cliffs. A rose forest. Breed a rose that cannot wither.'

The stone carnation may not have been art as art is known in galleries, but Gumes was altogether an artist. Within the limitations of his material he had constructed, collected, carved out and patched together a life he could live in a world in which his deepest needs would never be known, and certainly not met. He was asleep. Splashes of green and red tinsel flashed from the floorboards.

I drove back towards other facets of daily civilised life: massacres muted by distance, leisurely executions, slow suicides, reluctant lives.

Gumes had told me three days before that the council scraped flat the corrugations in that end of Tantawanglo Lane and that they always rose again in three days. He was spot-on.

I gave Gumes the fresh colours of a Vida Lahey flower painting. He was a Proteus figure, his many shapes concealed. Whether he had a gift of prophecy I don't know. As for holding him down, you'd need a tranquillising dart with enough juice for a hippo.

Jack often needs something of the sort. He wakes around one in the morning. The sun's late up still in the third week of August, and I start work as soon as the light allows. I resent not getting a full night's sleep. Jack's a damn nuisance.

'Jack wake you?' the girl asks.

'Slept like a baby.'

If I'd been among the tender-hearted decades ago, who'd found it hard to imagine themselves in the shoes of the violent, but thrilled to it when they saw it represented on page or screen, what would my life be like now? Would I still have this taint on me?

Why does it trouble me so much? Even harmless-seeming desk-workers can mount takeover bids, destroy companies and lives, attack currencies and impoverish whole countries, then go home to sleep dreamlessly, consciences easy. Mine isn't. When Jack wakes I lie there for hours, awake too. I get up before the sun and try to move round without waking the little bastard. I don't really care if I wake him, yet I try not to wake him. I don't understand that, either. It's all gesture.

My whole life seemed to be a fiction. I had the strange feeling that already I was on that future astro-journey outside our sun's backyard. Gravity had been left behind. I was floating, out of touch with solid ground.

fifty-four

cornelia dogwood

Have you ever stopped what you were doing and found that the future, patterned or fabricated from you and your past intentions, was quite near you, had approached unseen and was watching you, quietly menacing as a glacier? You get on with your work, but now nervous as the Gurugu grasshopper fish that spends so much time jumping out of the water looking for a better place to swim. However much you'd like to be walking among friendly rocks that kneel by shaded bush pools, or discovering tiny river beaches where rocks have been mumbled to sand between the weather's gums, you're at your loom, and however fast you work those spiky seconds on the clock allow you no escape. The world is busy about its affairs, but your work will be unfinished when you cease. The future's eye is on you and you cannot be comfortable.

Then you talk to an artist who, you've heard, is never shaken. To whom the prison of existence is nonsense: for her, living is a privilege and the world an adventure, and it's perfectly normal to have more police than artists. She always seems to have the wind behind her. I'd glimpsed her at the midwinter party at Knudsen's, but now knitted up the airy and insubstantial contours of description with this red-cheeked, blue-eyed flower woman with the curling and humorous eyelashes and competent affectionate hands. Her little dog lay, a puddle of fur too comfortable to be bothered, but did open one eye.

I found Cornelia cheerful as a Crookwell potato hound. Wherever she looked she saw naked colours, dramatic shadows, joys, sweet sounds and invitations to share good things, and she painted them. Portraits when other commissions were slow, and paintings to hang in boardrooms and directors' suites.

Gravity oppressed her. On one painting she wrote, 'Not even universal pain can drown one small joy, or a universe of darkness smother a lighted candle.' She believed that nothing was non-representational. Her 35-year-old Beetle called Cratcheter would cratcheter up to the unpainted rear of the row of offices and shops in Cooma Street, where she had a first-floor rented space she'd turned into a studio. The rent was less than two slabs of beer. To be private she put 'Arezzo Ltd' on the directory. Inside the door was a large rubber dog.

She seemed a plain, direct, pepper-and-salt kind of person, without the aura of spice or friction that comes with vanity, or griping. She wasn't one of the Avon Guard of painting, nor was she the kind of eclectic pessimist who narrowed her range of permissible subjects. Her receptiveness to change was not the kind that comes of undervaluing what she had.

When she has a few drinks in, she walks like the high-stepping fire dog. She loves good red wine and being alive. Colour opens her mind's feelings, she says, and is grateful she had a mother, Marigold, who had the gift of being pleased. She woke pleased, could make herself pleased when she wanted to, and said, 'Being pleased puts good bugs in your blood.' Cornelia seemed to make the shadows near her brighter, perhaps she polished them.

Cornelia lives a freedom and isolation that spells peace, advantages easily obtained in a small country town. Her house is on ten hectares just below Toastrack Hill where, first thing in the morning and last thing in the afternoon, Gourgourgahgah is laughing.

Her work got under way with *Head of a Warrior*, and its burst of geranium red; *Murderer's Hand and Forearm*; then the religious series *Beautiful Lying Christs* with the one on the Jesus and John relationship; and the derivative set of three: *Christ's Baptism at Lost River Olympic Pool*, *Christ's Entry into Windang*, and *Crucifixion at Kialla*, with death shown as a complicated game in which circles are the key. She seemed a little smug about having kept away from popular history painting, and hadn't been guilty of showing a horse rider wearing on her, or his, shoulders, a computer silhouette with a diminished screen.

'I see myself as making honey for the human hive,' she offered expansively. 'And showing a little of what it means to be me. I see an artist as a maker, one who can't be content to live an abstract life, with nothing produced as a result of a life lived.

'Practise, learn to draw, learn to paint, use your pencil once a day, I was told. And every day practise how to look and you may eventually learn to see. After that, to respond. Start with faces, basic units of social life; faces in action, faces in use, when they take on meaning. My old teacher pointed me to the big window, the outdoors, so little of which is now acceptable as valid celebration for painting. Start from where you are, don't try to find a better place, he said.

'I found I began to feel the world. Part of me went out to it, mingled with it, and drew it back into me. I still remember at sixteen seeing the magic light in a breaking wave, and a light within that light. It affected my whole life.

'I stood looking at the waves a long time and twice again I saw that strange light. Maybe it wasn't even a light, but a pulsing. A cloud, a vapour, something intangible —a spirit— invaded me, penetrated all my crevices. I can feel the echo of it now, all these years later. What I saw, what I felt, changed forever the way I looked at the world. It changed me. I knew from that moment the world was alive in some way I couldn't understand. Ever since, I want to see in a painting a flash of that real world behind, and mostly separated from this one. Just a corner will do. A glimpse.

'I think that enjoying the world as it is, feeling the joy of looking at its features, as a baby looks into its mother's face, is a gift. I've found that there are people unable to see beauty in anything. Beauty in art? Go to animal or botanic illustration. Yet beauty is a gateway to the only transcendence many achieve. Throngs of people feel beauty is the thing that calls deeply to them when they're being their most serious and sincere. When they don't find it in the art of the day they suspect art is inferior, and they've been excluded, whether by fashion, or social or intellectual class. Sometimes they exclude themselves when it's plain as a pikestaff that the artist can't draw beyond kinder stage.

'Serious art is literary, you need the theory to understand it, but I think the more theory you cut out, the more of yourself can show in your work. To carve a career, you work out an extension of the current fashion, proclaim it in the jargon of the day, and the art public will find it in your work. Many can see anything in anything, if they're told what to look for. The main pressure is to paint for other painters and a network of teachers and gallery administrators who like to keep a firm hold on what's produced, and allow no change until all agree on the change.

'The arts are all round us in everyday culture: design of buildings, cars, appliances, tools, amusements, music, packaging; arts of our times. Many go to galleries hoping to find representations and celebrations of our day, done well, and better than photography can do them. No dice. What they get are half-digested psychologies that turn out to be fashions and are soon shed. No corner of another world lifted to show a glimpse of a further reality. Not long ago the primitive was discovered, but unbound from its religious and mystical purposes. If you look for the primitive in humans you'll find it. Just as modern humans do whatever can be done in technology and let the future clear up the mess, so, in their deep unwisdom, they forget that previous centuries knew their savage selves lurked under a thin veneer, that it was dangerous to dwell on and magnify the monster within. Old restraints were flimsy, but did in part work.'

She was really wound up, and gave critics a burst of rapid fire. So she wasn't all niceness, which can seem weak and sickly. She rattled off a list of works and responses to them.

'*Light in a Fragile Glass* was to show my interest in that frayed edge between light and darkness. *Christ's Tears over the Tasman Isle* got a great reception, because it was misunderstood. *The Knell of Parting Day in Collins Street* showed a big-city mirage in a summer haze. *My Surreal Dadda* wasn't one of my best pictures. *Children of the Fountain*, on drowned children who live in water and gaze up at the outside world, was intended to suggest hints of a life apart from the one you take for granted.'

'So you have stories, literary constructions, about what you paint?'

'Words can be connected up and given a certain sense, about anything,' she insisted. 'Yet words aren't enough. Stories can only suggest. Words aren't part of the natural world we find when we first open our eyes. They're not equal to objects or events. Definitions and descriptions stop short; we must experience, enter, feel and receive. So philosophy is endless. Stories, that is.'

She seemed happy with that account, but I'd have liked further explanation. Trouble is, I find I can't formulate the question I'd like to have asked.

'The boy in *Tied to the Bull's Horns*, where he's pinned to the sharp horntips of feral cattle, was my response to the plight of young males as I see it. Mind you, my dog doesn't understand my work and sometimes neither do I. It gets away, somehow. I like to think of how, past the descriptions, the shapes and colours, there is the thing itself, the It, with which we interact. And which is capable of prompting endless explanations.

'*Fighting Women of the Streets*, *The Quadrilateral Weaverbird*, *Tree of Knives*, were all exercises in the surreal, which for me is an analogue of God. To me, God is truth, the austere and supreme object to which we ought to aspire, no matter how we fail. I copy others in saying the god that can be known is not the real God. The real God is in the silent caves of air within the branches of a beloved tree living outside a kitchen window, in the wind, the sea's abysses, on stretches of bleak shore, in the cloud that approaches and passes, the thought that recurs, the new relation perceived, the wave that returns. In the memory of a colour of light within a wave treasured for a lifetime.

'I've made a dedication on this painting.' She showed me her *Blazing Hell full of Red Hot Phoenixes*. 'Here we are. "To the liberation of the soul in things." It's a liberation we have to do, singly. That liberation is a kind of worship. I try constantly to achieve it.'

As usual I didn't know what to say. I'm inadequate at times like that. So many things I don't understand. Next she went on about another theory she had of how people are sometimes projections of the landscape, and of things that surround them. 'So that when that woman was killed eighteen months ago it's possible someone was getting rid of a natural feature of their own landscape, their own life, that they'd come to feel was incompatible with their peace and the comfort of their continuing existence. So the hidden method. Poison injected into a crack at the edge of a coarse heel. Or a needle driven up the nose into the brain, the head held back so no blood appeared. The needle buried vertically in the lawn. Easy.'

I thought I'd better make an effort to converse, so I tackled her on her cheerfulness. She had an explanation for that too. I'd thought optimism and pessimism were two poles, with the norm between them. But she maintained pessimism was a pathological state, the other pole was a manic or hysteric state, and optimism the norm. She made it sound reasonable.

She did some painting while I caught up with my notes. Her concentration seemed a piety in itself. While she worked, she told me of a recurring image she had, of entering one of her pictures, finding it entrancing, travelling deeper and deeper into it, and living and painting there for the rest of her life.

She seemed to fit her life exactly. Most of the time I feel like something ordered but not called for. I patted the rubber dog on the way out. By way of response it farted noisily and Cornelia fell about.

In the pickup I remembered I hadn't mentioned Carmen Mummo. Word was they'd had a little thing going for a year or two, that Carmen told her lots of stories about a Lost River of her mind. Some of Cornelia's paintings were said to be based on Carmen's stories. Word also had it that Cornelia admired men of strength rather than of possessions, but there was nothing I could do with the information.

As I passed Anzac Park I noticed two side-by-side flags flying in opposite directions, as if the wind had got in between them and was blowing both north and south.

It was one of those suddenly warm days at the end of winter, though August was not yet done, when the light, on low beam in late afternoon, fades unnoticeably and you hear the Bogong moths hitting the windows and realise not only that it's getting dark, but that another spring, with its air soft and light and eloquent, is knocking at the door.

At the Church of the Good Shepherd the girl had invited her mother, several uncles, and some friends with their kids. There was a matter of apricot jam making Gumes more gungible, and some of the food in the fridge had been replaced by beer. A church service was in progress at the business end of the church, with kids duelling for the premier position at the old lectern, which someone had brought in from the shed. I got on with Cornelia's cartoon right away so details wouldn't be lost. The jovial visitors thought my addiction to work strange at first, then a great joke. Nothing would persuade them there was some work that didn't go better with beer.

Cornelia was a Pygmalion, in the way she loved her creations. If you'd seen the way she touched them, looked at them, you'd understand. I put it in the tapestry.

If I was right and all we do, feel, think or say is gesture, some trivial, some successful, to impress and support oneself and others—and just to be doing something, which is a large part of it—then I was mostly gesture. Posture. A fiction. The scraps of knowledge I'd acquired, the few good habits, the freedoms I shared, the guilt that plagued me: all gestures.

A child was giving a mock sermon, laying down the law at the lectern. Her head didn't reach the recipe book of mine that they were using as a bible. I had an image of myself against a background of nothing. I had no scale to measure myself by. Some tide had swept away any means of comparison. I couldn't tell if I was a mile high or a millimetre.

When I had finished the final section of the tapestry, I wove my weaver's mark, 'db', into the border, finished off, and wound the last of the continuous section on to the tapestry roller, freeing it from the loom. Next I unwound the roller, cut the work free, stitched up the gaps. There wasn't much warp shrinkage, and even less of the weft.

What the councillors would see as they deliberated, and the public as they watched, would be the lives of some of their citizens plus, at the end, the metaphor I designed to illustrate the next odyssey of humankind. A planetary seed-pod, an earth-shaped capsule filled to overflowing with the blind energy of the myriad gestures of human life and fecundity, bursting open under its internal pressure and scattering its human seed far into space, each seed carrying with it a selection of the evils and failings of its population's history. And perhaps a tiny hint of hope.

fifty-five

the blaze

August thirty-first, late afternoon, and the tapestry was fixed to the wall in the new council chamber. Was there a sincerity about it that was out of place? The room itself was as funky as a trade union meeting. The first viewers, council executives, trying to find something intelligent to say about it, looked silly as a bunch of cocker spaniels trying to talk. Ever seen dogs being trained to say hullo? They never get the 'l' right. It occurred to me the executives might have found my stories of their relatives and acquaintances offensive, or were jealous at not being portrayed, and were choking on official politeness.

My weaving year had ended. The white pickup floated me out of town. On the way to Wiradhuri I found it difficult to pick out details of the streets and houses fading in the rear vision mirror, though the road ahead was clear and distinct. No traffic was behind me. None at all, which seemed peculiar. It was now dark. Streetlights were on ahead of me, but behind me they hadn't come on. Then I was out of town, where no streetlights existed.

On a rise outside Lost River, I slowed and looked back. Patches of the town were in darkness, as if the town were tired, and couldn't sustain itself. I stopped the pickup. Something was bothering me. I wanted to clear my head of it before I went back to say goodbye to the church.

The attack on me by the word 'gesture' and its effect of leaving me feeling I'd been stripped to the bone, a living fiction, and that the world was all gesture, provoked a blind opposition in me. How had it managed to take me over, putting me and my life into its little box? It seemed plausible. It explained everything and diminished everything: it was a respectably modern theory. But maybe other words might do the same if I had the wit to think of them. Take 'dream'. If life was dream, yet contained the same joys, fears, deaths, pains, how could we tell it was dream? Life might be helpless gesture, but it was what we called life. It was all we had.

But there was something more. It was time to dig into myself for that deeper transgression. I think I knew all the time what it was, just didn't want to admit it. It wasn't mere peccadillo or youthful trespass or high spirits. I don't know much about evil, it doesn't come up a lot in a life of weaving, but there was something I hadn't done that was near as damn-it to evil. At crucial moments in the lives of others, I'd felt nothing. I refused to feel. I felt well enough for myself, I could do it when my wellbeing was the question, I enjoyed to the full every gratification, but for others, nothing.

When my father Jackson Blood died, I watched. I listened to the words at the grave, watched the faces, watched my mother, trying to feel what she felt, gauging the thoughts of the people at the service and graveside. When my mother died I tried to feel what Danielle, Randal, Preston and Orville felt; looked at the whole episode through the eyes of the nurses, doctor, funeral staff, relatives at the graveside, even casual passers-by, and traffic on the way to Rookwood. The magpie hunting in the grass, I tried to see what she saw. I was curiosity, but felt nothing.

The same when Orville died. I was a spectator. I did no harm, tried to do what was best at the end, when it came to deciding it was futile changing his blood for the nth time.

When I was a child one of my mother Lillian's kindly admonishments was 'Put yourself in their place.' She could have saved her breath. I felt their feelings, guessed their thoughts. I had their feelings. My own self was unoccupied. An outer part of me lived its life dressed in, and exploring, the selves of others. It was a kind of play, a game that came easily. Inside, I was barely warm. Put your finger into the soft maw of a sea-anemone in a rock pool, feel it gently suck, notice the very slight warmth: like that. I could hurt and feel nothing, give, leave, destroy and feel nothing; but I could feel what others felt, or said they felt, when they did those things. It was all at one remove.

Was I alive? Were others like this? Was it a protection? Had I lived once and was now dead in some way? Was I born to be an onlooker, uninvolved? There were a few times when I could have let go, relaxed my grip, but I wouldn't allow it. There was always a good reason. I would lose something of myself if I did. I would deprive myself of options. I wanted to feel nothing, just wanted to know what others' feelings were, to invade, to plunder, draw what I found back inside me to process it and use it as material for collection. It wasn't life. I neglected the life I was given, to live the lives of others.

Was this why I pointed toward Yarrow as soon as I met her? That quick mind, fizzing energy, sparkling strength. The muzzle velocity, the hitting power. Yet at the same time I was aware she was often completely heartless. She had little generosity of spirit, mostly competitiveness; no bigness of soul, only ambition. I was helplessly attached to her while at the same time she made sure I was completely detached and never joining. The two of us were travelling at our different speeds but had no destinations, only targets. Not so much living as aiming. There was no meaning in the life-contests we'd chosen apart from what we'd put into them, and since our meanings had no significance for anyone else, we were truly alone.

The lights that had come on in Lost River were going out, the town, with its streets, buildings, parks, traffic, shoppers, strollers in the mall, its pensioners, police and pets, all lapsing into the unclassified jumble of memory.

The usual evening glow arching over the town was gone, transferred to a hill north of Lost River. Its brightness increased as I approached Wiradhuri. In my elevated mood I played with the thought that this was an epiphany, a moment of transcendence, a god showing its face.

Ascending, I found a marvellous brightness illuminating Wiradhuri Hill, and when I looked back, the town was in darkness. The blanket of trees that were so thick in the forested regions of the Southern Tablelands had grown back over everything. On the flattened top of the hill the Church of the Good Shepherd blazed in one great flame higher than the yellow box trees and stringybarks. I remembered my premonition of twelve months before—that smell of burning—and raced towards the flame. The girl. Baby Jack.

There was no roar of burning, only a hoarse whispering silence. I stood in the open doorway. The loom was an arch of flame, the floor a lake of fire, the flame filling the interior of the church, yet nothing was blackened or burned away. I couldn't see the girl, or Jack, for in the way were my tapestry figures, from Chokeback through to Cornelia; all of them standing about in the red of the flame, not consumed.

I moved among them, looking for little Jack and his mother, for whom I felt a special responsibility. I found them, but not before the majority of my other tapestry figures had been transformed. Typically, they lost mass, shrank and became transparent, mobile and extremely plastic, so that, one by one, they gathered round me and, with sometimes fearful, sometimes regretful and dubious looks, melted wraithlike back into that seminal vessel in me where so many more waited in abbreviated and potential form.

I was left with a small band which had paired off in an order that surprised me. Jack and his mother stood alone. There was Gumes and Cornelia Dogwood, Big Betty with Saint Salivarius, Old Clampett with a revived Bubba Ylisaka, Fatstuff talking to Howie Gleet, Dando with Treesha Khalal—I understood that pairing—Sonya Ergot with Shoey Mortomore, Juniper Grey talking to Mac Black, and the yarn-spinners Morrie the Magsman and Carmen Mummo.

I thought at first they had begun a dance of some kind, but what looked like a dance turned out to be each one changing from youth to age and back again constantly. When they saw me approach they gathered round. With their individual kaleidoscopic changes they seemed like birds nervously revving their engines, about to take off on a long flight, responding to a call only they could hear. I was eager for tomorrow and had no doubt they were, too, though what form their tomorrows would take I didn't know.

I watched as they looked at each other with smiles on expectant faces, then walked quickly from the enveloping flame out into the night, each giving an enthusiastic kick at the hard ground as they made their separate take-offs, and disappeared over dark Wiradhuri Valley. Fire, church, pickup vanished. I was alone on a bare hill.

It was strange to see blackness where I'd seen the town's glow, the blue and orange lights, the few farmhouse lights, for the past year. In a few hours the blackness of the valley would be defeated, when its many colours would come to life again and be triumphant in a new dawn; and the age-old enchantment of the land would resume, and the ghosts of those for whom it was sacred would inhabit it as before.

A feeling of strangeness, of stillness in my head, stopped me. I felt a blank, a gap in hearing, a voiceless buzzer whirring in my head. Then, just as shapes, bodies, faces, words, rose lifelike under their own power from the well of the unknown inside me, the unsorted jumble of the forgotten, so, clear as headlights on a country road, I saw her.

Deep in a comfortable brown chair, legs tucked under her, she was reading in a spacious library. A woman, small like a wren, stood at one of the large, many-paned windows looking out at the washed light and amber colours of trees dressed for the fall. I recognised the bird-woman's hairstyle from the only picture of her I'd seen. If she would turn, I might see the sherry of her eyes.

'I've found you,' I said to Yarrow. The other woman didn't move. Yarrow looked up, then returned to the pleasure of words.

'Oh, it's you. So now you can do it too.'

'Why did you stop calling me?'

'Too uncomfortable. You want to be close. It turns me to stone, I can't deal with it. Back off and we can stay in touch. I'm busy, so much to learn.'

Everything I'd wanted to have and treasure had evaded me. What sort of fool was I to value all the things about her that she scorned?

'So now we're brother and sister? And after that, sexless minds?'

'Anything you like. At the moment I'm immersed in a new world.'

For me she was the world. Better for me if I could have cut out desire with a knife.

'Still questioning everything? Anything still standing?' I said, quoting her. 'Have you altered some annoying realities by altering your representations of them? And while objectivity and truth are impossible are you still applying the metaphors of theory as if they're objective truth?' Still nettled by her silence.

'I've moved on since then. The theory I lived in answered nothing for me, just tore down and made space for more theory. I lost myself in it. It had no passion, only a negative kind of hatred. There is a real world of feeling and sensibilities, with discoveries to be made. There may be no words for truth, but it may be experienced, I think.'

This was good. So she was floating, like the rest of us.

'I've found life itself is more important than its meaning.' I didn't see how that fitted, but she was smarter and better educated than I was, so I said nothing.

'I've exchanged the political for the personal, the group for the individual. And now you've joined our world—'

'Your world?'

'I escaped the cage of blood before you. You know I loved to ride my bike to the library, one less car and all that. I was run down at an intersection by a green sedan. I heard the woman screaming at me, "Get out of the way, you bastard!" before the impact. But that's not important. While I kept my distance from you I was beginning to experience an incompleteness. An emptiness had spread over my life. At that point I happened to open Emily's book, as I'd done in school years before, but this time, when I read "It was not death, for I stood up" the words spoke of a different world, and drew me into it. I wanted to know more, to see the reality behind our familiar world, its flashes, hints and shy revealings. So here I am.'

The great poet turned from the window. Like a schoolboy I checked for the freckles I expected to see. She began to speak, quickly and brightly. As I listened, I realised Yarrow would make many changes, her search would go on. She was right, she needed no one. Her life was within herself.

I don't know why, but I felt free. No longer a follower. I had lost myself in her, made myself transparent. Now I knew how to find her, and that was enough. Her face was locked on to Emily's. I withdrew from orbit. Perhaps in the time ahead I would achieve a new kind of love.

For the second time I opened that casket in me where experiences, desires, decisions and particular memories were kept, and fragments of life shoulder to shoulder with brief dreams.

There was a street map of Seattle, a petrol cap, an A tuning fork, a silver B-flat trumpet and a phrase of Rilke's, 'Dance the orange.' I settled down to practise the trumpet—my lip would return in time—remembering the master class when I heard that wonderful horn-player saying, 'Get the colours into the notes. Sing as you play each note, so the instrument sings and enjoys itself.'

fifty-six

Wednesday, September 3

'This is the hill I told you about,' she said. They put down the picnic things and sat on the rather attractive rocks, though the shale had sharp edges. The children, who had complained about the steep hill, were slumped on a patch of native grass tussocks, and began to pick at the tough stalks which had grown into corkscrew shapes.

'Did someone come and twist this grass?' the younger child asked.

'No one's been here for years, I'd say,' she replied to the child. And to her friend, 'Not since Monday, when I discovered it. Isn't it a fabulous view?'

'Incredible,' her friend said, to be compatible. 'But it's all bush. And such tiring hills. They go on forever, by the look of it. Hills beyond hills, like sea-billows. Nothing but trees as far as you can see.'

'What's a billow?' the other child said, lying on her back.

'A big wave in the sea.'

'Do you go to sleep on it?' and the children laughed, the laughter turning to giggles as one word led to another.

'I was hoping you could come to see it yesterday.'

'I had my hair yesterday. Tuesday's not a good day for me.'

'Well, I thought you'd see what I saw in it.'

'Are you thinking of buying land? Out here? You'd have to put in a road, get electricity on.'

'Just a shack. Weekender. Dirt road's fine. A place to come, let the quiet soak in. A small tank for rainwater. That's all we'd need.'

'Can we have the picnic now?'

'Not yet. Walk around a bit. Might be kangaroos down that slope. A creek, even. A wombat.'

The children struggled to their feet, not unwillingly, began to walk. The adults sat, pulling the quietness round them, tasting the peace they hoped they'd brought with them.

One of the children found a baby's sock in the shaly clearing on top of the hill. It was a clean sock. She scrunched it in her palm like a hanky and forgot about it. Down the hill they found a watercourse. They heard a muffled thumping and looking down the long sloping valley saw a family of kangaroos running somewhere they wanted to get to. But it was the picnic the girls wanted. They climbed back up the hill to where their respective mothers were talking of the chain of pools to the south, beneath the hill.

'You could almost imagine it as the place for a town,' said the first mother.

'I found a sock,' said her daughter. 'A little baby sock.'

'Throw it away, you don't know where it's been.'

'How did a sock get up here?' the second mother queried.

'Maybe there wasn't water enough to start a town,' the first mother resumed.

'Are you really going to buy this hill?'

'I might.'

'Let's have the picnic now,' said both daughters at once, in sensible voices, as if they too were adults.

It was a relief for the children to have something definite to do and to look at. And the familiar food. Mum made such good sandwiches, and both girls were looking forward to the funny things their mothers said, and their sudden laughter, after a glass of wine.

When they had cleaned up after them, they walked down the steep part to where the four-wheel drive was waiting. On the way down, the girl with the sock tired of holding it and stuck it in the fork of a black wattle. As she let go of the white cotton, a tiny electric shock of sadness, no more than a throb, travelled through her hand into her memory, where it would remain all her life, remembered intermittently, passed on to her daughter and finally to the granddaughter who held her hand and received it as she died.